# Maggie

## VIOLET HOWE

www.violethowe.com

Cover Design: Robin Ludwig Design, Inc.

www.gobookcoverdesign.com

Published by Charbar Productions, LLC

(p-v2)

ISBN: 0-9964968-8-2
ISBN-13: 978-0-9964968-8-9

*For Jenn*
*Through thick and thin, no matter how many changes we go through, or how many different roles we play in life, or how many times you flip that house around, one things remains constant…our love and support for one another. You are truly my forever friend, and I am so thankful for you. I love you.*

# BOOKS BY VIOLET HOWE

# ACKNOWLEDGMENTS

Jennifer – Thank you for your insight and your mad editing skills. This book would not be the same without your unique perspective and your input. Can't wait for our next cup of tea! (Or chicken.)

Alberto – I cannot thank you enough for sharing your knowledge and your time with me. I have thoroughly enjoyed our talks, and I'm sad that the book is done and we won't need to meet up anymore. Thank you for patience, your generosity, and your inspiration for an awesome character.

Bonnie – who is forever represented by Sandy, and to Sandy, who is also forever represented by Sandy. I can't thank the two of you enough for continuing on this journey with me. You know you're loved, and hopefully you know you're appreciated, too!

Teresa – You came through again with flying colors! I appreciate your input and your time. So happy that I inherited you when I joined this family!

Lisa, Donna, and Melissa – Thanks again for your time in making sure all my T's are crossed and all my I's are dotted. I appreciate you all!

Casey – Thanks for checking the language and helping me out with the horse stuff. I'm gonna keep you on speed dial for future novels!

Linda & Greg – Thank you for letting me tag along at the sale and thanks for answering so many random questions and out-of-the-blue texts.

Orlando Ballet – Thank you for connecting me with the amazing Alberto Blanco. Your generosity and kindness in helping a local author do research was much appreciated.

# 1 SILVER CREEK RANCH

The first time I made eye contact with Gerry Tucker, I broke my big toe..

I stared into his eyes, my vision blurred by the searing, white-hot pain surging up through my body. My teeth clamped together so hard my jaw hurt for days. Nothing compared to my toe, of course, but still.

Gerry liked to tell people it was the result of our immediate connection. *Electric. Powerful. Overwhelming.*

The reality was the toe had been broken twice before. A pretty common occupational hazard for a ballet dancer.

The toe was weak. Vulnerable.

So was my heart, back then. Thirty years ago.

A lifetime, it seems now. A lifetime rich and overflowing with love.

The love of family. Of friends. Of two beautiful children who have taught me that love is infinite and knows no bounds.

I'm grateful for having known such tremendous love.

But love does not always soar. It can take you to the depths of hell as well.

I've only *fallen* in love twice in my life.

The first time broke my toe and left my heart shattered in a million jagged pieces beyond repair.

Which is why there hadn't been a second time… until Dax.

I should have been immune. I had built a wall so impenetrable that I thought I was safe.

*Protected.* Unable to fall victim to love's intoxicating spells.

Boy, was I wrong.

My heart betrayed me.

I tried to brush it off at first. I tried to say it was simply a physical attraction.

After all, no one could dispute that Dax Pearson is easy on the eyes. I think he would quicken a pulse in a corpse.

And I'm certainly no corpse. I may have put a wall around my heart, but that didn't stop it beating. He did, though. No, really. As *clichéd* as it may sound, my heart literally skipped a beat when I saw him.

I had walked to the large windows that lined the back of the great room in the reception hall. The view outside was serene. Peaceful. The hall had been built on the east side of the ranch overlooking the large lake in the middle of the massive property.

A wide swath of clear heavy-duty glass meandered through the wooden floor, allowing guests to follow the path of the bubbling stream that flowed beneath the house and through the expansive lawn before feeding into the lake. The unique feature was highlighted in the brochure and proved even more impressive in person.

It surprised me that my daughter would be interested in such a rustic location for her wedding. Galen was a city girl born and bred, happiest in a high rise overlooking a concrete landscape or navigating the hectic throng of a Friday night downtown. Orlando and Miami had both proved too small to contain her big city dreams, but she and Tate had decided to have their wedding back home in Central Florida rather than ask both their families to travel to their new home in Manhattan.

I'm sure part of that reasoning was also to make it easier for her to pass off the bulk of wedding planning to me. Well, me and Tyler. While I'd coordinated plenty of large events in my role at the Performing Arts Center, I'd never organized a wedding before, so having a professional wedding planner for a daughter-in-law was a godsend. Tyler and Galen may have had their differences in the past, but luckily, they'd worked through them, and Tyler was all too happy to help me plan her sister-in-law's big day.

A blur of movement caught my eye as I gazed out the window, and it brought my attention back to the lawn. A horse and rider galloped full speed across the grass. The horse was headed straight toward the stream at its widest point right before it reached the lake, and it was obvious from the rider's stance and his grip on the reins that he was trying to halt the animal's progress to no avail.

The man was tall, broad-shouldered, and his long coat flew out behind him like a cape as he struggled to gain control of the animal. I was shocked to realize he sat astride the large beast bareback with no saddle in sight.

My heart beat faster and louder as they neared the water's edge, and then suddenly, the horse leapt. Its body stretched long and lean as it soared over the stream, and the rider bent low, molding his own body to the horse's as he held tight to its neck.

I gasped, and my heart skipped a beat.

It was an odd sensation, one I still find hard to describe. It was like

2

something moved in my chest. Something rolled or turned. It took my breath for the briefest of moments, and then suddenly there was a rush of pressure and the beat resumed, loudly and even more forcefully than before.

It might have frightened me if I hadn't been so fixated on the horse, who was still galloping toward the lake despite the rider leaning back and pulling the reins tight. The two plunged into the water, and the horse stopped abruptly.

The rider didn't. He flew over the animal's head and landed in the lake with a grand splash.

I flung open the French doors closest to me and gasped as the brisk cold of the February morning hit me, but I kept heading across the lawn toward the rider. I'm not sure what I thought I was going to do in terms of a rescue, but my instinct was to get to him quickly and make sure he was okay. The damp grass made it almost impossible to run in my stiletto-heeled boots, but luckily, there were three men charging toward the lake, easily outrunning me in their cowboy boots and heavy coats.

"Maggie! What are you doing?"

I slowed and looked back at Tyler, whose bewildered expression mirrored Bronwyn's, the ranch's wedding coordinator, as they stood in the open doorway. I pointed toward the water as I ran, and they both joined me when they saw the reason for my abrupt departure.

The cold, damp air rolling in off the lake seeped through my cashmere sweater, and I wished I had grabbed my coat from the rack in the foyer.

By the time I reached the sandy shore, one of the men had gathered the horse's reins and led it from the lake. He stood eyeing the animal with a wary expression, although it seemed to have calmed down once it was rid of its rider.

The other two men were waiting at the water's edge as the rider stood with his back to us and shrugged out of his wet coat.

"You alright, boss?"

"Yeah," the rider growled. "Damned beast would have to send me swimming on the coldest damned day of the year."

I shivered as another breeze rolled in, and I couldn't imagine how cold he must be in wet clothes.

No sooner had the thought crossed my mind than he tossed the coat to shore and pulled his shirt over his head as he waded out of the water.

My breath caught in my throat. He was much leaner than he had appeared in the heavy coat, but he was solid. As he peeled the wet fabric of his undershirt from his skin, I couldn't help but stare at the taut muscles rippling across his chest and abs. A rush of warmth surged forth from deep within me, and suddenly, the air around me didn't seem as cold as before.

Bronwyn's voice rang out behind me just as he tugged at his belt buckle to begin shedding his pants.

"Uncle Dax!" she yelled as she and Tyler joined me on the sand. "What happened? Are you alright?"

He looked up, and judging by his raised eyebrows and widened eyes, he hadn't expected an audience. Glancing down at his bare chest and stomach, he refastened his belt before meeting his niece's gaze.

"I'm fine, Bronwyn. Taking a little polar bear swim in the lake this morning. Sorry if I disturbed you, ladies."

His gaze shifted from Bronwyn to Tyler as he nodded to each in acknowledgment, and then he looked at me.

I'd never been a woman whose head was easily turned. That's not to say I didn't appreciate the masculine form. You can't be born a dancer and not admire the magnificent lines and sculpted curves of the human body. But I'd never been one to do a double-take on a sidewalk or go starry-eyed over a handsome face.

I'll be the first to admit it had been quite some time since I'd stood before any half-clothed man, much less one who seemed to be the epitome of perfection.

Maybe it was the cold air making me shiver. Maybe it was the beads of water dripping from the tips of his hair where it hung across his forehead and brushed the tops of his ears. Or it could have been seeing the gooseflesh prickling across his bare, muscular chest as his nipples stood taut against the cold.

I'm sure that was it.

It couldn't have been the square jawline that looked like it had been carved from stone. It couldn't have been the deep green velvet of his eyes or the laughter lines that crinkled at the corners. Surely, it wasn't the rugged masculinity or the confident stance that no man should be able to pull off standing there soaking wet after being thrown head first off a horse.

It certainly wasn't the way he smiled at me, one eyebrow raising ever so slightly as I held his gaze, the corners of his mouth lifting as his grin slowly spread, deepening the creases around his eyes.

No. It was the cold weather that made me shiver. Definitely.

## 2  THE COWBOY CLEANS UP WELL

"Pardon me for interrupting your visit," he said as he nodded in my direction. "You look chilled. Why don't you ladies head on back inside where it's warm? I think the show's over for now."

"What happened, Uncle Dax?" Bronwyn asked again.

"Kratos and I were trying to decide who was going to be boss. Evidently, it's still up for discussion."

The young woman's hand flew to her throat as she gasped. "You were riding Kratos? Are you nuts?"

"I would think you already know the answer to that one," said the older gentleman standing behind Dax, holding the still-dripping coat away from his side.

"I didn't buy him so he could ride me," Dax said, wringing out his shirts as he walked to the horse and took the reins.

The three men followed Dax and the horse as they made their way across the lawn. Tyler and I turned to follow Bronwyn back to the reception hall.

"I take it Kratos has never been ridden?" Tyler asked.

Bronwyn laughed. "Hardly. That horse is a demon from hell. They should have put him down, but my uncle insisted on rescuing him. Why, I do not know! He's gonna get himself killed."

"Does your uncle own this ranch?" I asked, assuring myself that it was only to make small talk and that I really didn't care who he was or what he owned. I stole a glance at his broad back as he walked in the other direction, but I quickly looked away when I realized he had turned as well.

"Yes, he does," said Bronwyn. "He doesn't really have anything to do with the events, though. He's more involved with the horses and the cattle. He stays away from weddings like they were the plague." She laughed as she held the door open for us.

I sighed as the warmth of the great hall settled over me, but then a shudder flitted across my skin again. Confirmation that it had simply been the cold before and had nothing to do with the half-naked cowboy who'd been dripping in front of me.

"Come over here to the fireplace. You'll be toasty warm in no time," Bronwyn said as she led us to an enormous stone hearth on the other side of the room. "We don't get to use it much, being in Florida and all, but it's sure nice to have it when we need it. It gives a nice ambience for a wedding, you know, if it's cold out. Now, when was your daughter planning, again?"

"August," I said, stretching my fingers wide in front of the fire. Tyler thrust hers out beside mine, and I couldn't help but notice the difference. They say the hands are one of the easiest ways to tell a woman's age. I rubbed mine together briskly, reminding myself to appreciate all those hands had done for me rather than concentrate on a few dark spots that had appeared in the last couple of years.

"Oh, well, you certainly won't need the fireplace then! That's a hot month for a Florida wedding. Was she planning on an outside ceremony?" Bronwyn said, her grimace clearly conveying her distaste for the idea, though she recovered quickly with a big smile.

"Believe me, I know August is hot for weddings," Tyler answered. "But we're working around the bride's schedule, and the dance company she belongs to runs their season from September to June. If she's going to have time down here before the wedding, we're looking at August. And yes, ideally, she'd like the ceremony on the lawn by the lake close to sunset, like the pictures you have there in the foyer. Then the reception here in the great hall. What's your maximum capacity?"

I tried to listen as they discussed guest counts, and round tables versus rectangular ones, but I was distracted. My mind kept replaying the horse and its rider leaping over the stream and then Dax flying through the air and into the lake. My thoughts lingered on the perfect curve of his bottom lip as he'd grinned and the sculpted perfection of his back as he'd flexed to reach for the horse's reins before they walked away. I could still see the thick bulge of a bicep as he raised his hand to lay it gently on the animal's neck, sharing a whisper that only he and Kratos could hear.

Bronwyn was thorough as we continued our tour of the house, and Tyler was dutifully attentive throughout, asking all the pertinent questions and securing the details needed for Galen and Tate to make their decision. I wandered along behind them in somewhat of a fog, genuinely interested in what they were discussing, but unable to keep my thoughts from drifting.

"Maggie?"

Tyler and Bronwyn were staring at me.

"I'm sorry, what?"

Tyler's mouth twitched with a grin as she cocked her head to one side. "Bronwyn asked if you think Galen and Tate will want to spend the night here in the bridal suite upstairs, or will they be leaving right away for a trip?"

"Oh, I'm not sure. We haven't really discussed their plans after the wedding."

Bronwyn nodded. "No problem! I'll go ahead and show you the bridal suite, and then you can always let me know later."

She unlocked a door and led us up the staircase behind it. Tyler let out a whistle of appreciation as we topped the stairs into a large open room with a vaulted ceiling criss-crossed with wooden beams. The back wall of sliding glass doors opened onto a deck overlooking the lake. There was a fireplace in one corner of the room, an overstuffed chaise lounge in another, and an enormous bed that looked even larger than king-sized, set against the front wall and facing the lake.

"This is gorgeous! I want to stay here," Tyler said. "Can I book this?"

Bronwyn laughed. "We only reserve it for our wedding couples, but we might be able to work something out." She winked at Tyler. "Now, there is an additional charge for couples to book the room, but it includes a breakfast downstairs as well as housekeeping. Come see the bathroom."

She led us into a room off the side of the bedroom that featured an oval Jacuzzi tub nestled into a large bay window setting and a walk-in shower big enough to hold at least three people.

"Holy cow," Tyler exclaimed. "Look at this closet, Maggie!"

I peeked inside the door she'd opened, surprised by the size of the closet with its elaborate system of built-in shelves and cabinets. In the corner were a washer and dryer with a folding counter and built-in ironing board and hanging rack.

"If you have the bride's dressing room downstairs, why would you need such a large closet up here for wedding couples to stay overnight?" I asked.

Bronwyn's smile seemed to falter for a moment, but then her lips lifted again. "This was originally constructed to be the main house for the ranch, so that would have been the master closet, but since it's been converted to a reception hall, it doesn't really get used. We have plenty of storage downstairs, and like you said, the bride and groom don't need a closet for their wedding night."

I surveyed the bathroom as Bronwyn shut the closet door. There were double sinks and a low vanity with a chair and lighted mirror.

"So, this was originally a house?" Tyler asked as we walked back down the stairs. "But the space down here is an open ballroom. Was it always that way?"

Bronwyn shook her head as we exited the stairwell onto the first floor. "It was planned to be a separate formal living area over there, and then a dining area back here with a family room that would be open to the kitchen. But when the plans…changed…the downstairs was never completed according to the original blueprint. We were able to really look at what the space needed to be for events and create it to meet those needs. One more thing I'd like to show you if you'll follow me."

I tagged along behind her and Tyler, but my mind was busy spinning the various scenarios that could make sense. I wanted to ask if Dax had built the house or bought it. I wanted to know why the plans had changed from it being the main house of the ranch to a rental event venue, especially if the owner had such a disdain for weddings. And as much as I hated to admit it even to myself, I was curious as to where he lived on the ranch and whether he lived alone.

The sound of the front door creaking open interrupted my thoughts, and I turned quickly to see if it was Dax.

*"Get a grip, old girl,"* I muttered to myself. *"You're being a little ridiculous here. Act your age."*

The heavy footsteps in the foyer grew closer, and I held my breath as I waited to see who it was.

I fought back a grin when he came into view, resisting the urge to take a step toward him as he walked in my direction.

He had changed into a dry pair of jeans and a pale blue chambray shirt. His hair was still damp, but it had been combed back off his forehead and away from his face. As he approached, the faint scent of a cologne tickled my nose with hints of spearmint, sage, lavender, and pure masculinity.

"I wanted to properly introduce myself," he said as he stopped before me and extended his hand. "I'm Dax Pearson, owner of Silver Creek Ranch. I was hoping to redeem your first impression of me."

I didn't tell him my first impression of him needed no redeeming. Instead, I smiled and shook his hand. "Maggie Shaw. Pleased to meet you."

His grip was firm, and his hand warm, despite just coming in from the cold. My hand felt small in his, and I withdrew it quickly, uncomfortable with the way my body was tingling in response to his touch.

"Maggie's daughter is getting married in *August*," Bronwyn said, "and this is her daughter-in-law, Tyler, who is a wedding planner."

"Ah." Dax turned to shake Tyler's hand. "An August wedding. This August?" He looked back at me, one eyebrow arched.

"Yes. My daughter is with a dance company in New York, and she has a break in her schedule then."

"New York. Do you live in New York as well?"

His eyes were an intense emerald, and it occurred to me they were very similar to my own.

"No. Tyler and I are local. We live in the Orlando area."

He nodded and crossed his arms. "I see. So, you'll be handling most of the planning for her then?"

"Actually, I will," Tyler said, stepping closer to my side. "Maggie has quite a lot of responsibility on her plate already, so I'll be the point of contact for my sister-in-law."

He smiled at her and then looked back to me.

"Well, allow me to personally welcome you to the ranch."

A rush of warm blood filled my cheeks, and I blushed like a freaking sixteen-year-old.

"Thank you," I mumbled, unable to find my normal voice. I couldn't believe the effect he was having on me, but I couldn't deny that it wasn't altogether unpleasant.

"I suppose I should get back to the barn," Dax said. "You are in excellent hands with Bronwyn, and since I know absolutely nothing about weddings, I will leave you ladies to your planning. Nice meeting you both." He was looking at Tyler as he talked, and then he turned to smile at me. "I hope to see you again soon."

With a quick nod, he left us, and despite the roaring fire, the room suddenly seemed a bit less warm.

"Okay, that was weird," Bronwyn said with a chuckle when the front door closed. "Uncle Dax usually won't come anywhere near here if we're discussing weddings. But then again, he usually doesn't embarrass himself by being thrown off a horse and into the lake, either. Let me get you a copy of the wedding packet to take with you. I'll give you each one, and would you like me to send one to the bride as well?"

"I don't think so," Tyler said. "Maggie?"

"What? Um, no. Galen doesn't need all the details. She likes to look at the pictures, but she wants me to do the finances and Tyler to figure out the logistics."

"She's lucky to have you," Bronwyn said. She gathered the packets for us and went through them in detail to make sure we understood the contract and deposit guidelines.

I only half-listened. My ears were still listening for the creak of the door and the return of his footsteps, but our meeting concluded without another appearance from the ranch's owner.

# 3 INQUISITION

We were barely out of the driveway and back on the road before Tyler mentioned my distraction.

"Well, he's quite a hottie, isn't he?"

"Who?" I asked, though I clearly knew who she meant.

"Kratos," she said, her voice thick with sarcasm. "He's one hot horse. You know very well who I'm talking about!"

"The owner?" I wasn't about to give up my ruse of disinterest. "He's okay, I guess. A little old for you, I think."

Her laughter filled the car. "For me? Oh. Wow. Okay. Am I supposed to pretend I didn't see what I saw?"

"What?" I glanced over at her and back at the road, my palms sweaty on the steering wheel. "What do you think you saw?"

"You guys couldn't take your eyes off each other! It was like electricity between you. I'm surprised your hair wasn't standing on end."

"Oh, please. I have no idea what you're talking about." I lifted my hand to smooth down my hair, but then returned it to the wheel when I realized how guilty it made me look.

"Maggie! Puh-leez! You might be able to fool an average citizen, but I am an expert at romance. It's what I do for a living. I know what I know, and I know what I saw."

I took a deep breath and searched my mind for something that would get her off the subject.

"Okay," she said, holding both hands up. "If you don't want to discuss it, I can respect that. But there is no way you're gonna convince me the two of you weren't totally digging each other."

When I didn't respond, she sighed.

"C'mon, Maggie. Admit it. You felt it. I know you did. The way you two were looking at each other down by the lake, and then the way he came in all spruced up and wearing cologne. You heard Bronwyn. He *never* comes in when she's with wedding clients."

"Yes, well, she also said he was probably embarrassed from taking a tumble. I'm sure he only wanted to reassure us that theirs is a professional operation."

She twisted in her seat to face me, adjusting the seatbelt across her arm to do so. "Oh, and I'm sure he makes a point to tell everyone he hopes to see them again soon."

I merged into the traffic on the turnpike. "Actually, I'm sure he does. Look, he wants us to book their venue and be a source of revenue. You're reading way too much into this, Ms. Wedding Planner."

"If you say so."

I smiled as she snickered and lay back against the seat, flipping through the brochure Bronwyn had given us.

"So, what did you think of the location?" I asked, eager to change the subject.

"Very nice facility. Ample parking. Plenty of restrooms. The kitchen's nice and large. I wonder if it was always planned as an industrial kitchen or if that's another change they made. They'll let us bring in our caterer, which is great, and they have plenty of A/V hook-ups for the DJ and any lighting we want to do. Seems to be a topnotch place. They've certainly invested quite a bit into making it ideal."

I nodded. "Kind of odd, don't you think? That it was supposed to be the main house and now it's an event venue? I wonder what changed their plans."

Tyler shrugged. "I don't know. We could ask Bronwyn."

"No. It's not important. Just curiosity."

She slapped the brochure against her legs. "Curious because you're interested!"

"I'm looking at locations for my daughter's wedding, and I'm curious as to the history of the building. Nothing more."

"So you say."

She was quiet for a while, making notes on her notepad as she thumbed through the brochure. We were almost back to Orlando when she closed the pamphlet and sat staring at me.

"What?" I asked with a glance in her direction.

"Can I ask you something?"

"Of course," I said, already dreading any question that would need to be prefaced with permission.

"Cabe says you haven't been in a serious relationship since his dad."

"Is that a question or a statement?" I asked, making a mental note to thank my son for discussing my personal life.

"I guess a statement that leads me to a question," Tyler said. "Why?"

"Why what?"

"Why haven't you dated anyone since Gerry? That was what—almost thirty years ago? That's an awfully long time not to have a boyfriend." Her voice was sad, wistful. Like she couldn't imagine how bleak my life alone had been.

I cast another glance over at her and brought my eyes back to the road. "You do know, don't you, that a woman can survive perfectly well on her own without a man?"

"Well, yeah," Tyler said. "But I think it's odd that you haven't dated anyone. You're gorgeous, Maggie, and you're so fun and outgoing. I would think you'd have guys all over you, that's all."

I navigated the exit and came to a stop at the traffic light before turning to look at her. "Thank you. I appreciate your kind words, and I assure you that you have no need to worry. It's not like I haven't been on any dates or haven't gotten any offers. I just happen to be fine with my life on my own. I go where I want to go, I do what I want to do, and I have never had a shortage of company for social occasions."

"No, I know that! I'm not saying...well, I didn't mean...I just thought it would be nice if you met a great guy and...."

"And what? Fell in love and lived happily ever after?" I laughed. "Tyler, honey, I realize this is what you do, but I'm not the fairy tale type. I don't need a prince to rescue me from my hum-drum life. My life is beautiful just the way it is."

Her face flushed red, and she looked out the window as the light turned green and the traffic started to flow again.

"I wasn't saying that you need a man," she said, her voice low and sheepish. "I just know how happy Cabe and I are together and how awesome it is to have him by my side. You know, to share stuff with. I was thinking how nice it would be if you had that." She cleared her throat. "I didn't mean to offend you."

I reached to take her hand in mine. "You didn't offend me! I'm not one to be easily offended. I'd think you would know that after all these years. Besides, we're family, aren't we? I would never want you to feel you couldn't ask me something or speak your mind. I think if there's anything we learned from the drama that occurred when you joined our family, it's that we all need to be open and communicate with each other. We may not always *agree*, but I would hope there's nothing we couldn't discuss." I squeezed her hand and let it go, and we rode in silence for a bit.

"Okay. I do have another question." She drew in a deep breath, and I could tell before she began to ask that I was probably wasn't going to like the question.

"What really happened between you and Gerry?"

My shoulders immediately tightened, and tension crept up the back of my neck.

*Way to go, Maggie. You gave her permission and rolled out the red carpet for that one. Now how you gonna get out of this discussion?*

I stared straight ahead at the traffic in front of me. "Oh, gosh. That was so long ago."

"Well, I know the two of you met while you were working on a show together. When you were a ballerina. I'm just curious how you got together and what happened, you know, when you broke up."

I tightened my grip on the steering wheel and let out a stream of curse words inside my head.

I couldn't fault Tyler for wanting to know about her husband's father, nor could I be upset that my son would discuss the man with his wife. It was only natural for them to talk about Gerry, of course. Especially since Cabe had recently connected with his half-brother for the first time.

But whatever communication Cabe chose to have regarding Gerry Tucker now had no bearing on the relationship I'd had with the man.

"It's hard to remember the details." I adjusted my hands on the wheel and tilted my head from side to side in an effort to ease the tension in my shoulders. "But yes. We worked on a show together. When I was young."

Young and naive. Passionate. Willing to mistake a man's lies for love.

The intensity of her gaze in my peripheral vision told me she didn't believe that I wouldn't remember what happened with the father of my children. And she was right. I remembered every detail. But it wasn't a topic I cared to discuss, even if I had just told her nothing was off-limits.

"Let's call Galen," I suggested in another blatant attempt to change the subject. "We can put her on speaker while we're in the car together and tell her about Silver Creek Ranch."

Tyler paused for a moment, and I silently prayed she would take the bait and switch topics. She didn't.

"Maggie, I can't imagine how bad it must have hurt you. You know, what happened with Gerry. I'm sure it's been hard for you to see Galen and Cabe be involved now. With the other kids. I'm sorry. I just...well, I just want you to know that Cabe would never do anything to hurt you. He feels like he's betraying you if he talks to them, but at the same time, he wants to—"

"Tyler," I interrupted. "Cabe is an adult. He can make his own decisions for what's best for him. I don't begrudge him wanting to know them. What happened between Gerry and me is water under the bridge. A bridge that collapsed and floated away so long ago that it's not even worth mentioning. So, let's continue with our pleasant day and call Galen to tell her about the ranch, shall we?"

To my surprise and my relief, she let it go. She called Galen and the two of us described the beautiful scenery of the ranch, the stream flowing beneath the floor, the magnificent suite upstairs, and the finer details like pricing and deposits.

Neither of us mentioned the tall, rugged cowboy and his unexpected dip in the lake. But I'm sure we were both thinking about him. At least, I know I was.

# 4 TYLER & CABE

"Have you ever wondered why your mom hasn't found anyone?" Tyler asked as Cabe refilled her coffee.

"What do you mean?" He filled his own cup and picked up Tyler's plate, scraping the bits of eggs she'd left into Deacon's dog bowl.

"I think it's sad, that's all. Your mom is a beautiful woman, and I think she deserves to find happiness."

"You think Mom is unhappy?"

"No. But she is alone. Don't you think it would be nice for her to find someone?"

Cabe washed the plate and rinsed it under the hot water to remove the suds.

"Where's this coming from? Did she say something while you were doing wedding stuff yesterday?"

"Not exactly." She shrugged and brought the salt and pepper to the kitchen. "I sensed an attraction between her and the ranch owner. Like, an unmistakable, electricity-in-the-air, kind of attraction. They couldn't stop staring at each other, and she seemed a bit, I don't know, preoccupied after they met." Tyler took a towel from the drawer and began to dry the dishes in the rack. "Then he got all cleaned up and came to formally introduce himself, which the wedding coordinator lady—his niece—said he *never* does, and Maggie's face lit up when she saw him again."

Cabe pulled the sink drain to let the water out and reached to take the towel from his wife to dry his hands. "Okay. So, knowing you, I'm assuming you asked her about this?"

"Well, of course! But the thing is, she denied it. She brushed it off like it was nothing."

Cabe shrugged and tossed the towel back to Tyler. "Maybe it was

15

nothing, then. Maybe your spidey-romance sense was in overdrive since you were shopping for wedding venues for my sister. Which I still can't believe you're doing, by the way."

She followed him down the hallway into the bathroom, grabbing her toothbrush as he put toothpaste on his own brush before handing the tube to her.

"I asked her why she'd never dated anyone since Gerry."

Cabe stopped brushing and stared at her in the mirror, white foam oozing from his mouth. "You what?"

"I asked Maggie why she'd never dated anyone since your dad. And I asked what happened between them."

He spit in the sink and turned to face her. "Ty, why would you do that? Don't bring him up to her. She doesn't want to talk about him."

Tyler bent and spit before looking up at her husband. "It's healthy to talk about things, Cabe. I know your family doesn't like to discuss stuff and y'all prefer sweeping it under the rug so nobody sees it, but you can't move past something unless you face it and get it out there."

"My mom is past Gerry Tucker, trust me. There's no reason to bring him up or to discuss him. God, you're as bad as my sister."

Tyler thumped his bicep as he started brushing again. "No, I'm not. But I think it's ridiculous that no one in your family can discuss the past. It shouldn't be taboo. Don't you have questions? Aren't there things you'd like to know? I mean, from what you've told me, all you know is the bare minimum about Gerry leaving. Don't you want to know what happened? Why it affected her the way it did?"

"I know enough to know Gerry Tucker is a lying asshole. I don't need to know anything else." He rinsed his mouth and dried his face and hands. "Leave it alone, Ty. Don't make Mom talk about it."

She rinsed her mouth and followed him into the bedroom, wiping her face with the back of her hand. "But don't you think it's strange that she's never had a serious boyfriend? I mean, Galen's what? Twenty-six? Almost twenty-seven? That's a long time to go without physical affection, don't you think?"

Cabe groaned. "Babe, I so don't want to discuss my mother having physical affection, okay? Besides, I need to get to work."

Tyler flopped across the bed on her stomach and watched him tie his shoes.

"But think about it. Why has she never dated anyone since Gerry? Is what happened so bad she wouldn't be caught dead in a relationship after him? That's sad, Cabe. She has to let it go. She has to give love another chance."

"She's gone out with people. She's had dates."

"But not boyfriends! Has she dated anyone for any length of time? Has she ever invited us over to have dinner with a guy or had some dude there when we go to her house for movie night? Do you think anyone's ever slept over?"

"Ugh. Ty, seriously. I don't want to think about my mom's sex life, okay? What she does is her business. I don't think she's gonna call me up and tell me when a guy sleeps over. At least, I hope she never does." He stood and grabbed his coat from the hook behind the door, putting it on as he walked down the hallway.

Tyler rolled off the bed and followed him, grabbing Deacon's collar as the dog started jumping on Cabe's leg, excited at the prospect of going outside for a walk.

"I can't, buddy." Cabe knelt in front of Deacon and scratched behind his ears. "We'll go for a run when I get home. Okay?" He stood and put his arm around Tyler, pulling her into him as his mouth closed over hers. "Mmm. Speaking of sex lives, how 'bout we discuss ours tonight? In detail?" He moved his hand down her body as his lips nibbled on her neck.

"I have a rehearsal dinner at six," she said, tossing her head back and running both hands through his hair as she pulled his mouth tighter against her neck. "But I'll meet you back here after."

He tucked his thumb under her chin and pressed his lips to hers, smiling as she licked his lips with her tongue and pushed it inside, making it harder for him to leave. He pulled away and then leaned back in for a quick peck. "Can't wait."

She stood in the doorway watching Cabe walk to his car as Deacon pulled against her fingers looped through his collar.

"I think you should ask her about this guy, Cabe," she called after him. "The ranch owner. You know, encourage her to pursue it. I think it would be good for her to put herself out there."

"Goodbye, Buttercup. Have a good day. And stay out of my mom's business. She can take care of herself, trust me."

Tyler closed the door and walked Deacon through the house to the backyard, sitting on the top step as he frolicked across the grass. She knew all too well what a broken heart could do to someone. After all, she'd almost lost Cabe forever because the scars on her heart had kept her from admitting she loved him.

She didn't want Maggie to be unhappy. Whatever had happened between Gerry and Maggie couldn't be undone, but at some point, even the most shattered of hearts deserves to beat again. What on earth could have been so bad that it had shut down Maggie's heart to any possibility of loving again?

# 5 THE BROKEN TOE

Once upon a time, I believed in those fairy tales that Tyler defends. I believed that Prince Charming would come along and sweep me off my feet and carry me into the sunset of Happily Ever After.

That was before I met Gerry Tucker.

And while he is most certainly the villain of my tale, I can't allow him to bear the blame alone.

There were other factors in play.

Nothing in my upbringing had led me to believe I'd ever have anything other than a charmed life.

My parents, thrilled to have adopted me after years of fruitless struggles to conceive, had indulged my every desire and whim.

When a dance instructor told my mother that her five-year-old showed extraordinary promise, I was whisked away from any sense of normalcy.

I'm not saying it's my mother's fault. I'd shown an interest and had a talent. She threw everything she had at pursuing my dreams, doing what she thought was best. What she believed any mother would do.

So, I don't blame her, but I can't ignore the part dance played in my downfall.

I never attended a school. Never sat in a class with my peers, whispering and giggling about boys. Never stared at the phone willing it to ring for a date.

My days and nights were spent inside a dance studio with private tutors cramming my education between practice sessions. My exposure to the outside world was limited, and my interactions with the opposite sex were based in friendship and performance.

Sure, some of the other dancers went out here and there. There were those who partied. Some who dated. They had the opportunity to have their heart scarred. To have it toughened up a bit. Get wiser.

But all I wanted to do was dance.

I missed out on developing the social skills necessary to navigate a cruel world. My bullshit detector was virtually non-existent.

As unbelievable as it sounds in today's world, I reached the ripe old age of nineteen without ever having a boyfriend. Never going out on an official date. Hell, I'd never even been kissed.

Looking back, I envy the girls with their high school crushes who had their hearts broken over the course of football games, dances, double-dates, and proms.

They had some idea of what to look for and what to avoid.

I stumbled into love blind. With a broken toe.

As a rule, I never made eye contact with any audience member during a performance, but that night was no ordinary performance, and it was no ordinary audience. We were performing for a small group of carefully selected patrons, featuring three extremely important guests — Gerry and two other financiers whose investments were crucial for our dance company's season.

As Alberto and I completed the steps leading into the finale, Gerry's gaze was so intense I couldn't resist a glance in his direction.

Our eyes had only locked for a moment when a searing jolt of pain coursed through me like lightning.

I held our eye contact and I held my position, just as I'd been taught. Never let them see you sweat, and never ever let them see you fall.

Gerry swore afterward he never knew anything was amiss.

"Sheer perfection," he would say when he told the story to others. "The epitome of a true professional, I tell you. She literally broke a bone and never stopped smiling. Stayed on her toes until the music ended. Can you imagine? No one knew."

That last part wasn't true. Alberto knew, of course. My flinch might have been imperceptible to our esteemed audience, but my partner knew the second it happened. His muscular arms tightened immediately, taking on more of my weight than usual so we could finish the performance and seal the deal at hand.

It was my first show as the principal lead. My introduction as the new face of the company after a heated argument between the artistic director and his prima ballerina had resulted in her abrupt departure. I was thrust from understudy to spotlight with less than two weeks to pull off the performance of a lifetime, and if it hadn't been for Alberto's patience with me, I don't know that we could have pulled it off.

But we did.

We earned their applause and their financial backing, and I was showered with praise and ushered across the threshold into what should have been a golden career.

The room had begun to sway by the time the heavy red velvet curtains finally came together to shield us from our audience, and I had immediately collapsed into Alberto's waiting arms.

"What happened? Maggie? Are you okay?"

"It's broken. I know it's broken," I whispered through tears as Alberto lifted me and carried me backstage to Lucas, our physical therapist.

I managed to stay calm while Lucas removed my shoe.

His skilled hands were gentle as he examined me, but when he turned my foot to get a better look at the toe, I clamped down on Alberto's hand and cried out in pain.

"Maybe it's not broken," Sandy said as Lucas tried to turn my foot again, more tentatively than before.

I glanced up at my best friend, whose face was creased with the same worry and apprehension wreaking havoc on my stomach. We both knew that while a broken toe was by no means a serious bodily injury, it could be lethal to a principal dancer's ability to carry a performance.

"Maybe it's just a sprain," she said, her voice much meeker than normal.

I winced as Lucas prodded.

"We'll see," said Lucas. "I'm going to send you for an X-ray so we know for sure."

I looked away from Lucas and toward what seemed like the entire ballet company crowded inside the tiny room. Their wide eyes and hushed whispers only added to my growing apprehension as the full implications of my injury began to sink in.

"Out of the way, out of the way. You all have some place to be. Let's get there," Ernesto said as he parted the crowd and watched them scatter. I groaned and Alberto gave my hand another quick squeeze.

"Maggie, my dahling, what has happened?" he asked me, but before I could answer he had turned his attention to Lucas and my foot. "How bad? Is it broken? Can she stand? Walk? Where is Benjamin? *Benjamin!*"

"I'm here," our artistic director said as he entered the room. "Maggie! What happened? Are you alright, love?" Benjamin knelt by my side and cupped my cheek in his hand.

I nodded, fighting back the tears. I couldn't break down. Not in front of Ernesto and the other dancers.

"I'm fine," I managed to get out, though my voice didn't sound like my own.

"Is she fine?" Ernesto asked Lucas.

"There you are!"

I turned to see who was speaking and gulped as I realized the handsome financier from the audience was standing in the doorway. He was even more handsome than he'd seemed from the stage. His dark blonde hair fell in easy curls, and his eyes were such a clear blue that they were almost translucent. He was tall, and his square jawline and high cheekbones could have easily been mistaken for a model's. I forgot to breathe, and I could hear my pulse pounding through my veins.

"Mr. Tucker." Ernesto quickly moved to stand between me and the gentleman who had stared at me so fiercely as I danced. "Everything is fine. Just a sprain, most likely. If you'd like to wait for us in the lobby, we'll all be along shortly."

Ernesto spread his arms wide in a feeble attempt to block Gerry Tucker from entering the room, but Gerry moved past him effortlessly. Alberto stood as the man approached me, and I was surprised to see that the financier was the taller of the two by a couple of inches.

"Ms. Shaw, Gerry Tucker. I couldn't wait any longer to tell you I was captivated by your performance. It was sheer perfection."

He took my hand in his and kissed it, executing a dramatic bow as his lips lingered on my skin. In that moment, the world disappeared. I was no longer aware of my throbbing pain, the curious stares of my best friends, or the stern frown of my producer. I knew only that Gerry Tucker was the most handsome man I'd ever seen, and he was smiling at me.

Something stirred inside me. Something animalistic woke up. For the first time, I became fully aware the male of our species existed, and that I was a female, meant to be by his side.

Before I could regain my composure and respond, Ernesto had taken Mr. Tucker by the elbow and tried to lead him away.

"Mr. Tucker, I'm sure Ms. Shaw and Mr. Abasolo appreciate your praise for their performance. They will both be joining us at the reception later, but for now, we need to handle a little housekeeping. If you could excuse us?"

Mr. Tucker's eyes never left mine. I thought he must be experiencing the same odd sensation I was, because I couldn't look away from him, and he didn't seem to want me to.

I took in his dimples, the stray curl that lay on his forehead, and the way his full lips parted to reveal perfect, white teeth. And those eyes. Oh God, his eyes held me in a trance, mesmerized and unable to speak.

"Mr. Tucker? If you could, please?" Ernesto asked again, his voice overly polite in deference to Gerry Tucker's wealth, but tinged with annoyance that his request was being ignored. Ernesto Campo was not accustomed to being ignored.

Alas, as I would soon discover, Gerry Tucker was not accustomed to being told what to do. He preferred doing whatever he wanted. And in that moment, he wanted me.

"Please tell me you'll join me at the reception, *bellissima*," he said, the wide smile broadening. "Honor me with your presence and allow me to bask in your beauty this evening."

If anyone said this to the older me as I spied the ripe old age of fifty on the not-so-distant horizon, I would have burst into laughter and asked if he was kidding.

But a hunger had stricken my younger self. I was suddenly starved for the attention of the opposite sex, having never known it tasted so sweet. I wanted nothing more than to be by Gerry Tucker's side, lapping up his praises and his flowery words.

Ernesto made his plea again, stepping almost between us as he tried to persuade his financier to listen to reason.

"She will be there! We will have plenty of time for you to talk with both our principal dancers and our director, but I must ask that you wait out front with the others while they get changed."

Ernesto's physical presence broke the trance, and Mr. Tucker's smile faded as he looked away from me, his eyes darting from Ernesto to Benjamin and Alberto almost as though he was realizing for the first time that we were not alone in the room. He released my hand and stepped back as he took in Lucas where he knelt holding my foot against his thigh.

"What is it? Is something wrong?" His blue eyes came back to mine, inquisitive and filled with concern. "Are you alright? Has something happened?"

"She is fine!" Ernesto broke in, taking Mr. Tucker's arm again. "Just a routine exam."

Mr. Tucker jerked his arm from the producer's, his eyes still on mine. "Are you all right?"

I nodded, wishing the others would just disappear so I could concentrate on memorizing his face and enjoying the tingle that tickled my loins every time he spoke.

"You're sure?" he asked, his deep voice reverberating throughout my body with tantalizing vibrations.

I had no idea what was happening to me. I'd never felt anything like it, and I desperately wanted to feel more of it.

"I'm fine," I managed to say, and immediately I felt the pain flooding my nervous system again, like my voice had somehow acknowledged reality.

"Then I'll leave you," he said to me alone, dismissing anyone else's presence. "But I'll be lost until I see you again."

A girlish giggle erupted from my lips, and I immediately covered my mouth and glanced up at Alberto, who was looking at me like I'd grown three heads.

Ernesto swept Mr. Tucker from the room, motioning for Benjamin to follow, and I looked back and forth from Alberto to Sandy once the men were gone.

"What? Why are you looking at me like that?"

22

"What the hell was that?" Sandy asked, her hands on her hips.

"Yeah, are you kidding me?" Alberto asked. *"I'll be lost until I see you again?* Who says that?"

"Evidently, Mr. Tucker does," I said, jutting my chin forward, indignant that they would mock such tender words.

"Oh my God! Tell me you did not fall for that," Sandy gasped.

I crossed my arms over my chest as Lucas placed my foot back on the floor and stood with a chuckle.

"You did! Look at her!" Sandy pointed to my face.

"What?" I asked, looking up at her and then to Alberto, who was grinning as he rubbed his chin with his hand.

The two of them never did understand what had transpired. I certainly couldn't explain it. I didn't understand it myself, at the time. I was too swept up in the passion of being in love with love.

If only I'd known then that catching Gerry Tucker's eye would not only destroy my dreams but also mark the end of the charmed existence I'd known.

# 6 FLAT FIFTY

Fifty sounds so old.

Especially since I don't feel as old as it sounds.

Since the age of thirty-two, I've always felt, somehow, like I was perpetually thirty-two.

My age wasn't something I gave much thought to on a daily basis, but when I did dwell on that big number looming on the horizon, I must admit it was a bit unsettling.

I had held up well, I suppose. Healthy eating habits, regular exercise, meditation. I always tried to get plenty of sleep. I'd done what I could. But despite my best efforts, I saw my age in the mirror the day after I met Dax Pearson.

I was going through my morning routine of stretches and movements at the *barre*, a holdover from my dance days that I had stayed committed to like it was a religion. It was as vital to starting my day as brushing my teeth or brewing my coffee.

I'd never devoted much attention to my appearance as I pushed my body through the motions it had first learned as a young girl over forty years ago.

Most mornings, I was lost in thought. Planning out the day ahead. Replaying a conversation with Galen or Cabe. Pondering what I would have for dinner.

But the morning after our visit to the Silver Creek Ranch was different.

The mirror held my focus as it shone a spotlight on the ravages of time.

My arms, still lean and toned, waved at me with an annoying jiggle as I raised and lowered them.

When I leaned toward the *barre*, I couldn't help but stare in the mirror at the way the skin on the top of my shoulder crinkled into a jigsaw pattern of fine lines. When had that begun?

I'd long ago noticed the loss of elasticity across my neck and chest, despite my Herculean devotion to daily sunscreen and the best anti-aging creams money could buy. But to see my shoulders betray me—shoulders once rounded and smooth, the pride of a strapless décolletage—was downright depressing.

I stood and turned to see my profile, fixated on the depths to which gravity had tugged my breasts. I lifted my arms high above my head to make my bosom rise to its former perch, but sure enough, as soon as I lowered my arms, my breasts fell back into disgrace.

I twisted my leg to the left and right and completed a series of *tendues*, *jetes*, and *fondue*, admiring the lean cut of my thigh muscle and the muscular curve of my calf. But when I glanced at the supporting leg, I could see the years overwhelming my kneecap as the excess skin pooled in tiny wrinkles.

Dreading what I would see, I shifted to look behind me in the mirror, flexing my arms in various positions to watch the muscles contract across my upper back.

Ah, there. I still had it. I could pull off a backless dress better than many women half my age. The sands of time had not taken that from me.

But then my eyes drifted downward.

When had my butt cheeks lost their pert roundness? Was that actually a sliver of shadow cast on the back of my upper thigh? I turned back to profile and flexed my glutes with all I had. They tightened as commanded, but it didn't change the overall shape much. There was a flatness there where there'd been none before. What the hell had happened to me? And why hadn't I noticed?

My scale hadn't budged in years. I'd worn the same pants size since Galen was born.

Things had shifted a bit, sure, but that's to be expected when a woman nears fifty. I stepped closer to the mirror and put my hands to my face, gingerly touching the lines at my eyes and pulling my eyelids up toward my brows.

How had I suddenly become so much older?

I didn't *feel* any different.

Certainly not like someone who was almost fifty. I mean, *fifty*. That's half a century. That's ancient.

How could that possibly be me?

I took a deep breath to dispel the cloud of dejection and abandoned the remainder of my workout to head downstairs for coffee.

I didn't have to question why I was suddenly so hyper-aware of my body's inevitable changes.

I knew why.

It was that stupid cowboy.

I'd been unable to stop thinking of him since Tyler and I left his ranch.

It was ridiculous, really.

We'd barely spoken beyond niceties, and yet, my thoughts kept returning to him.

The taut muscles of his abdomen. The impressive size of his biceps. The broad shoulders.

I swore as I realized I'd poured tomato juice in my coffee instead of creamer.

What kind of spell had he put me under?

Maybe it was hormonal. All part of that reaching fifty thing. Dealing with 'the change' and all.

I'd certainly never reacted so strongly to any male presence before.

Well, not as an adult. Not after everything that happened.

What was it about Dax Pearson that had completely flipped my insides and set them ablaze?

I wondered again if he had bought the property or built it. I wondered what had happened to the lady of the house to prevent her from getting that magnificent closet.

And despite my protests to my daughter-in-law, I wondered what had motivated him to stop what he was doing with the horse and come inside to personally greet us.

The piercing shriek of the fire alarm drew my attention to the smoking toast charred and blackened in my toaster oven.

I cursed again, which was very out of character for my normally calm and reserved mornings, and I resolved to push Dax and fifty out of my head before I burned the house down or left for work without wearing a shirt.

# 7  DEXTER J. PEARSON

A busy morning of meetings served me well in getting my mind focused, but any hopes of not thinking about the owner of Silver Creek Ranch were dashed when my phone rang as I was leaving the mayor's office.

"This is Maggie," I said as I walked faster to catch the light at the crosswalk before it changed.

"Maggie Shaw? Just the person I was looking for. This is Dax Pearson from Silver Creek Ranch."

I knew it was him before he said his name. There was no mistaking the deep voice on the other end of the line, richly tinged with masculinity and rippling across my skin like a current.

"Hi, Mr. Pearson. What can I do for you?"

A smile immediately tickled the corners of my mouth, and I couldn't believe how easily my body reacted to him.

"Actually, I was calling to see if there was anything I could do for you. That *we* could do for you. The ranch. I wanted to apologize for the commotion yesterday and assure you that nothing like that would happen on the night of your daughter's wedding."

"Really? Because Bronwyn promised us a repeat performance for the evening's entertainment. I believe she mentioned you'd be carrying sparklers for the dismount this time." The mental image made me smile as I spoke.

"Well, as entertaining as I'm sure that would be for your wedding guests, it was more of a one-time thing."

"Ah, a limited-run show. I guess we were fortunate to have caught it."

I realized the other pedestrians had already crossed the side street and the crosswalk countdown was nearing zero, so I rushed across with a glance toward the waiting traffic.

"Yes, fortunate indeed," he said. "I'm glad I could add to the value of your tour."

We both fell silent for an awkward pause, and I replayed Bronwyn's comment in my head about Dax having nothing to do with wedding events. Had she made him call to apologize or was this his own doing?

As though he could hear my thoughts, he cleared his throat and continued.

"I'm not normally involved with weddings—that's Bronwyn's area of expertise—but I thought it might be appropriate for me to—"

A car horn blasted through the air as I stepped into the next intersection, and I jumped back to the sidewalk in shock, embarrassed and a little frightened at the fact that I'd walked into oncoming traffic.

"Are you okay?" he asked.

"I'm fine. I didn't see the car, but he saw me, so all is good."

My heart was pounding from the potentially deadly mistake I'd made, but also in part because I didn't understand what was happening to me. What was it about this man that distracted me and made the world disappear? Whatever it was, I obviously needed to get as far away from him as possible, for the sake of my own life, it seemed.

"I need to go," I said, sounding much harsher than I'd intended.

"Okay, you have our number at the ranch, and now you have my number. So, if either Bronwyn or I could be of any assistance, just give us a call."

"Will do. Thank you." I hung up before any further disaster befell me.

I reached for the door to the Performing Arts Center just as my assistant, Karin, pushed it open and exited with a group of staff members.

"We're heading out for lunch," she said. "What are you doing here?"

"Um, I work here?"

Karin laughed. "Yeah, but you told Larry this morning you'd cover the hospital luncheon for him. You know, the dedication ceremony?"

The realization dawned in my brain like an explosion.

"Crap! I completely forgot. Damn. I even parked by the mayor's office so I could leave straight from there and not be late." I looked down at my watch and cursed again.

"So, your car's still there?"

"Yes. There's no way I'll make it by the time I get back to my car and drive to the hospital."

"Dana is parked right there by the curb. We'll give you a ride to the hospital, and then just call me when the luncheon is done and I'll come get you."

I looked at my watch again, willing it to miraculously turn back time.

"All right," I said with a sigh. "Maybe I can catch a ride from someone there or get a taxi so you don't have to make another trip."

Karin smiled. "I don't mind. I'm pretty sure *my boss* will be okay with me leaving the office." She winked as we walked toward Dana's car.

"*Your boss* is in some kind of fog today," I said. "She probably should just go back home and pull the covers over her head."

"I knew something was off. You put the coffee pot in the refrigerator this morning and set the creamer on the hot plate. Luckily, I came into the break room right as you were leaving and prevented the creamer from catching on fire."

My eyes widened as I realized I had no memory of the incident.

"I may need to see a doctor," I said. "I wonder if I should be on some type of supplement for memory or distraction."

Dana smiled as she unlocked her car and motioned for Karin and me to get in. "Happens to the best of us as we get older. I have to make notes for everything. Last week, I looked everywhere for my phone before I realized I was holding it up to my ear talking into it."

"You're not that old, Dana," Karin said. "How old are you?"

"I'm fifty-three."

"Oh wow," Karin gasped. "I didn't realize you were *that* old!"

I sat up and grabbed the side of her seat. "Excuse me, Miss Twenty-three. That's not *that* old. Show some respect for your elders, here."

Dana and I laughed as Karin stammered out an attempt at an apology.

"When I was your age, I felt like fifty was basically one foot in the grave," Dana said. "But the closer you get to it, the younger it seems. Am I right, Maggie?"

"I wouldn't know. I'm nowhere near fifty." I winked at Karin as she looked over her shoulder at me.

"Ha! Okay. Leave me hanging out here all alone," Dana said. "I still swear you dye that hair red. It's not natural for a woman to have no gray at all. C'mon. Tell the truth. Is that real or is it L'Oreal?"

"Eat your heart out, honey. L'Oreal has never touched this head of hair!"

We continued to chat about aging until we'd reached the hospital. I smiled and thanked them both as I gathered my briefcase and exited the car.

I was still smiling when I entered the lobby, but my smile faded when I reached the entrance of the banquet room and could hear the speaker from the other side of the doors. He'd already started the presentation, which meant I'd have to enter the room late. In front of everyone.

My hands immediately went clammy, and I briefly considered ditching the whole luncheon and catching a taxi back to my office. Unfortunately, I'd promised our community relations director that I would show up on behalf of the Performing Arts Center, so I had to make an appearance.

I took a deep breath and eased the door open, praying that everyone would be so focused on the speaker that my tardiness would go unnoticed. I scanned the tables to find an empty seat and was shocked to lock eyes with Dax Pearson.

He raised his eyebrows and grinned, and I tried to ignore the flutter in my chest. I was already smiling back at him before I could stop myself.

He lifted his head and scanned the room as well, pointing to an empty spot at a table near him.

A few heads turned here and there as I made my way to the empty seat Dax had indicated, careful not to make eye contact with him again in case I tripped and fell flat on my face.

The lights dimmed just as I took my seat, and I was grateful for the opportunity to disappear in the darkness. I only half paid attention to the video showcasing the hospital's new state-of-the-art trauma unit, but it was impossible to ignore the banner at the end of the video thanking the donors who made it possible.

The third name on the short list of six was Dexter J. Pearson.

I had wondered if Dax was a nickname.

The speaker droned on from the podium as the lights came back up, but I couldn't focus on his words. I ate my salad in silence, willing myself not to turn and look in Dax's direction.

When the banquet server cleared my plate, I took a long sip of unsweetened tea, casually looking toward Dax's table over the rim of my glass.

He was staring at me, a faint grin pulling at one side of his mouth, his eyes sparkling with some unknown mischief.

I looked back to the front of the room, quickly setting the glass of tea down, but miscalculating the move. The glass toppled, and tea and ice splashed across the table, drawing a chorus of gasps from those seated with me.

Heat flooded my cheeks, and my heart pounded so loud I was worried the whole room would hear it. I frantically dabbed at the wet mess with my napkin and apologized to those at my table as the server picked up the stray ice cubes.

I didn't dare look at Dax again for the rest of the meal, but I could feel his eyes on me, and my pulse continued to race.

When the presentation ended and the room stood to mingle, I went through the motions of shaking hands and exchanging pleasantries with those around me, but Dax was always in my peripheral. I stole glances as he greeted people and shook hands, and more than once I had to apologize for missing what was said to me while my attention was focused on him.

Eventually, I turned my back so I wouldn't get caught staring, but I could still feel his presence, the ache inside me pulling toward him like gravity.

"Well, this is fortuitous!" he said behind me, and a quiver tickled my skin as I turned to face him, catching my breath at the sight of his smile lighting up his face.

"What do you mean?" I asked.

"Fortuitous. It means—"

"I know what it means, Wyatt Earp," I said, returning his smile. "How is this lucky?"

"Well, we were just talking on the phone earlier, and now, here you are! I had no idea you'd be here."

"I had no idea you were one of the donors for the new unit. That's wonderful."

I thought I saw a faint red flush color his cheeks, but before he could respond, someone reached to shake his hand, and then another, and soon he was surrounded by a group of people. I stood there for a moment watching him interact, struck again by how handsome he was. He wore a pair of dark denim jeans with a pair of shiny black boots. His blue Oxford shirt was open at the collar, and the sleeves were rolled perfectly crisp on his forearms. It was the first time I'd seen him with dry hair, and I was surprised to see it was a lighter brown than I'd expected, almost blond in places where it caught the light.

The green of his eyes was a softer hue than I remembered, more like moss in the bright florescent light of the room. Less like mine than I had thought.

I waited a few minutes, but as his conversation got more involved, I felt like a groupie standing on the sidelines waiting for an autograph, so I gathered my briefcase and turned to go.

"Maggie, wait," Dax called out as I headed for the door. "Excuse me, gentlemen."

I stopped and waited for him to catch up with me.

"Where ya headed?" he asked.

"Back to the office. I was out all morning for meetings. Need to catch up on messages and emails."

I greeted a few people who spoke to me as they passed, and I waited as someone stopped to speak with Dax.

My body seemed to buzz in response to his presence. A wave of heat ran through me, and my heart beat so rapidly it almost made me dizzy. The sensation wasn't entirely unpleasant, but it wasn't something I felt comfortable with, either.

It was too much like the involuntary passion I'd felt before, and I had vowed long ago never to be that out of control again.

"Excuse me. I need to go," I said, interrupting his conversation with a banker I recognized.

"Let me walk you out," Dax said, and then he turned to shake the banker's hand. "Troy, we'll talk later. See if you can get all the parties in the same room, and I'll be there."

He held the door open for me as we exited the room, and I could feel the heat emanating from his body in the close proximity. The ache within me began to build in intensity, and I took a deep breath in my refusal to let it grow.

That turned out to be a big mistake, because the breath filled my nostrils with the scent of him.

Clean, fresh spearmint. A touch of lavender. A heady hint of sage. And that indescribable allure of masculinity.

I had to get away from the man. He was an unwelcome reminder that my hormones were likely raging in the metamorphosis of my body's aging process.

"Back to the office, huh?" he asked as we walked back toward the hospital entrance. "And where's that? Where do you work?"

"The Performing Arts Center."

"What do you do there?"

"I manage the Center's fundraising and social events."

"Ah. That sounds interesting."

"It can be. And what about you? What do you do other than build hospital wings and perform horse tricks?"

He laughed. "Hopefully something better than my horse tricks, right?"

I pulled my keys from my purse and stopped short as I remembered I didn't drive to the hospital.

"Something wrong?"

I frowned at him and looked down at the keys in my hand. "I completely forgot I have no car. I got dropped off. I need to call my assistant to come and get me."

"I can take you," he said.

I shook my head, perhaps a bit more vehemently than was called for.

"No, absolutely not. She can be here in a few minutes. Thanks, anyway."

"It's no trouble, really. It would be my pleasure to get you where you need to go."

I was certain he meant the comment innocently, but my body didn't take it that way, and I blushed as I considered where I needed to go and how many ways the strong cowboy could get me there.

Something was definitely wrong with me.

I hesitated, a battle waging within me between two equally powerful forces. My mind argued that any man able to produce that kind of effect was dangerous, and I needed to stay far away from him. But my body argued that it had been too damned long since those fires had been stoked, and if anything, a man able to produce that kind of effect needed to be held closer, not pushed away.

My mind had logic and reasoning on its side.

"Thank you for the offer, but I wouldn't want to impose. Nice seeing you again."

I pulled my phone from my briefcase and turned to walk away, but he sighed deeply and fell in stride beside me.

"Look," he said. "My only other appointment today is with Kratos, and having met the beast, I'm sure you can understand why I might want to delay getting back on him. You'd actually be doing me a favor if you helped me kill some more time."

Oh my God. His eyes. His smile. The slight cock of his head as he waited for my answer. Could he be any more enticing?

I hesitated a moment longer before throwing caution to the wind. "I guess it would be quicker than waiting for her to come get me."

"Dax! We need you in a picture. Pronto. Don't sneak off yet!"

I looked from Dax to the gentleman in the doorway of the banquet room calling for him.

"Be right there," Dax answered, his eyes never leaving mine. "I'll only be a minute, and we can be on our way. You want to wait here or come back inside with me?"

"I can just call—"

"Oh, c'mon. You just gave me a reprieve from Kratos. I'll be two minutes. Five, tops."

He tilted his head to the side again, his smile a little crooked as he raised one eyebrow, almost like he was nervous to see how I would respond to his plea.

His eyes were back to the deep emerald of the first time I saw him, but they held a spark I hadn't noticed before.

Another flush of warmth surged through me with a tickle between my thighs, and I shifted my weight to dispel it.

My mind flashed red warning lights and told me I was in dangerous territory, but something about his eyes held me. I didn't want to walk away just yet.

I nodded and moved toward the banquet room, and his smile grew.

"I'll make it quick," he said, holding the door for me.

Despite my mind's protests, I inhaled deeply as I passed him, breathing in the intoxicating scent again and marveling at the sensual reaction it caused.

What was it about this man that was bringing sensations to life that had long been dormant? I resolved to call my doctor as soon as possible to tell her my hormones were out of control.

I watched him as he joined the group photo, his laughter and his stance confident.

He was at ease in this room of movers and shakers, but I'd seen him just as confident standing in the sand dripping water after a horse tossed him.

For a brief moment, I allowed myself to consider what it would be like in his arms. To just stop fighting. To shut off the automatic resistance response and allow myself to be attracted to Dax.

After all, I was older than before. I was wiser. There's no way I would make the same mistakes as last time.

But then the old memories flooded my mind, and I turned and hurried from the room before I made eye contact with him again.

# 8 CHAMPAGNE BUBBLES

If only I'd had the same strength and resolve to walk away at nineteen.

Instead, I'd run straight into the viper's den.

Well, okay, maybe I didn't *run* since I was on crutches or in a therapeutic boot for the entire courtship, but I definitely didn't let anything or anyone stop me.

Sandy didn't like him from the start.

"Something about him gives me a bad vibe, Mags. Be careful, okay?"

I'd asked to borrow one of her little black dresses for the reception, hoping if I looked like a knockout from the knees up he might overlook the crutches and bandaged foot.

"I think he's nice," I told her as I surveyed the way the dress hugged my lean, muscular frame in the mirror. I may not have had the curvy hips or cinched waist of some of the other dancers, but the short hemline showcased my legs, and I had no doubt they looked good. "I wish I could wear heels," I said, staring at the bandage on my left foot and the boring, flat shoe on my right.

"You're lucky you're not at the hospital right now getting X-rays. I can't believe you talked Lucas into waiting until tomorrow."

I shrugged. "There's nothing they can do, even if it is broken. You know that. They'll put me in crutches and tell me to stay off it for a few weeks. No sense missing the reception to find out what I already know."

She bit her lip and met my eyes in the mirror. "What do you think Benjamin's gonna do with your position?"

A momentary panic gripped my heart, and I quickly pushed the thought from my mind. "I don't want to talk about that. Here, help me do my hair. Should I wear it up or down?"

The deep red waves hung almost to my waist, tousled and in disarray

35

from being twisted into a tight knot for the evening's performance.

"Definitely up," Sandy said with a frown at my reflection.

I pulled the mass of tangles up and tugged at loose tendrils to frame my face. "Why are you looking at me like that?"

"Because you look like a vixen with it down and flying all around your shoulders. I don't want to do anything to make you more attractive to this guy. I'm telling you, he's bad news."

I immediately released my hair and ran my fingers through it, liking the sound of *vixen*. "And you're basing this judgment on your vast experience with men?"

Her mouth fell open and immediately clamped shut. "Just because I date girls doesn't mean I can't spot a player when I see one. He was looking at you like you were dessert and he couldn't wait to devour you. I think he's a little out of your league, and you need to stay away from him."

Her words of caution only fanned the fire and made Gerry seem more attractive. Forbidden. Dangerous. Alluring.

Whatever he had awakened in me had no desire to play it safe.

My eyes found his the moment we entered the room. He was watching the doorway, as though he'd been waiting for me to arrive.

His jaw went slack for a moment, and then he smiled and made a beeline for me, leaving his conversation without a word of apology.

"I was beginning to think you might stand me up," he said, his grin wide.

His eyes went immediately to my hair, tumbling over my shoulders in a wild cascade, and then his gaze raked over my body in the tight-fitting dress. A little tremor of pride ran through me as he lingered over my legs, his expression clearly showing his appreciation, but then he saw the bandage on my foot, and he looked back up at me with eyes full of concern.

"You *were* injured!"

Alberto handed me the crutches I'd hastily given him when we came off the elevator, pleading that I wanted to make an entrance without them.

"I'm fine," I said to Gerry. "It's a broken toe. It happens."

He took my hand and did the same dramatic bow he'd done before, and my pulse raced at the anticipation of his lips touching my skin once more. He held them against my hand for only the briefest of moments, but the thrills it caused raced through me like a wildfire.

My hand was still in his when he stood upright to meet my eyes again, and I couldn't help but think we were like the classic scene of the movies where the two lovers meet and the electricity between them seems to come out of the screen. The only thing missing was the dramatic soundtrack. The string trio playing in the back of the room didn't quite cut it.

"There you are," Ernesto exclaimed as he joined us. His joy turned to a frown when he noticed the crutches. "Oh dear. Let's get you a seat and get you off your foot. Come this way. I see Mr. Tucker has already found you," he cast an irritated glance in Gerry's direction, "but I'd like you to meet our other special guests."

"I'm heading to the buffet," Sandy whispered as she disappeared through the throng of people beginning to surround us.

Everyone had noticed our arrival by then, and Alberto and I were both swarmed with well-wishers congratulating our performance and other members of the company inquiring about my foot.

Gerry stood smiling on the outskirts of the commotion for a moment after we were separated, but then I lost sight of him in the crowd as Ernesto led me over to introduce me to the other financiers. Just when I could no longer resist the urge to look over my shoulder and find Gerry, he appeared at my side to pull out my chair.

"Here, Ms. Shaw, your foot must be hurting. Sit."

I smiled. "Please, call me Maggie," I said, just as I'd rehearsed in Sandy's bathroom mirror before we left for the party.

He nodded as he sat in the chair beside mine. "Gerry, then. I've taken the liberty of getting you a glass of champagne."

I took the glass, but before I could thank him, the others at the table had started firing off questions about my background, the performance, and my injury. No matter how hard I tried to focus on what they were saying, my entire body tingled every time Gerry moved beside me. I wanted to sit and stare at him, to listen to him talk, and to feel the warmth in my core when he looked at me the way he did. But instead I forced myself to make eye contact with the others, only turning to face him when he spoke, and even then, making myself look away despite the desire to take in every detail of him.

I was turned away from him when I felt his breath against my cheek, and I jumped at the sound of his voice close to my ear.

"I'm going to get a drink," he whispered. "Would you like more champagne?"

I nodded, unable to find my words.

Perhaps I should have protested and asked for water instead. I'd reached the legal drinking age of nineteen earlier that year, but other than a couple of glasses of wine here and there, I'd never indulged in alcohol, especially not while under the influence of painkillers.

I'd felt the effects of the first glass right away, and by the bottom of the second, any awkwardness I felt with Gerry melted away as my inhibitions were numbed.

I'd never been a shy girl, but the excitement of the evening combined with the alcohol and pain pills brought out the life-of-the-party in me. I'd never laughed so unabashedly or been so witty and clever. I was the belle of the ball, holding court at the table as a steady stream of people stopped by to say hello or rave about the evening's performance.

In the weeks leading up to the show, I'd been so stressed with rehearsals that it hadn't really sunk in that I was the principal dancer. I had made it. I was the youngest to ever be named to such an honor at Miami City Ballet. All the hard work had paid off, and the attention went to my head right along with the champagne and painkillers.

My short-lived stint as a diva began that night, in a borrowed black dress with a bandage on one foot and a black satin ballet flat on the other.

Throughout the evening, I was always acutely aware of Gerry's eyes upon me. Of his admiration. Of his attention. His hand casually brushing against the back of my waist when he stood to help me with my chair so I could hug someone saying goodbye. His fingers lingering on mine as he exchanged my empty glass for another full one. The way he leaned in close when he was listening to me talk, so close that I thought at any moment he would surely kiss me, but just far enough away that the distance nearly drove me mad in my desire to be touched.

I think it was probably on my fourth glass of champagne that the room turned hot, and the lightheaded dizziness became unpleasant.

"Are you okay?" Gerry asked, as I looked around the room for an exit.

"I think I need fresh air."

"Okay," he said, his hand on my elbow to steady me as we stood. He gathered my crutches from where they were leaning against the wall, but they proved unwieldy and uncooperative in my altered state, and I handed them back to him in frustration.

"You want to just lean on me?" he asked, his arm outstretched.

I felt Alberto's hand on my shoulder before I saw him beside me. "You okay, Mags?" He bent to look into my eyes, and I nodded, still unsteady on my feet.

"I'm fine. Just need some air."

"There's a patio right over here. A balcony," Gerry said as he pointed. "I think maybe if you take the crutches—"

He handed them to Alberto, but Alberto ignored the gesture.

"I've got her," he told Gerry, putting his arm around my back and pulling my weight against him, just as he did every day during our routine.

He moved us through the crowd, and when we stepped outside, I took a deep breath of the night air, trying to dispel the hazy fog swirling in my mind.

"Why don't you sit here while I get you a soda," Alberto said. He set me down on a bench and turned to go, stopping as he saw Gerry entering the patio with a glass of water in his hand.

"I thought this might help," Gerry said. "I think the champagne may have gotten to her."

"She shouldn't have had champagne. She got a pretty good dose of meds earlier, and she hasn't eaten since breakfast."

"I'm right here," I called out, a bit more slurred than I would have wished. "I can hear you, you know."

"Why don't you get her something to eat, and I'll sit and keep her company?" Gerry asked.

Alberto frowned and crossed his arms over his chest.

"I would love something to eat," I said. He glanced down at me and back to Gerry, obviously not comfortable leaving me alone. "I'm fine, Alberto. I just need to eat. Will you get me something? Please?"

He glared at Gerry a moment longer before nodding slowly and leaving us.

"I don't think your friend likes me very much," Gerry said as he sat beside me on the bench.

I laughed. "He's just protective. He's my partner. It's kind of his job to look out for me."

"Your partner? Are the two of you an item?"

"Alberto?" I laughed harder. "No. Oh my gosh, no. Alberto is like my brother. Definitely nothing there."

Gerry relaxed against the back of the bench and gazed up at the stars above us. I tried to lean my head back and look up, but the stars were spinning and it made me nauseous, so I immediately looked back down at my hands in my lap.

"It's a beautiful night," he said, stretching his arms across the back of the bench.

I tensed for a moment, anticipating his touch, but it didn't come. I leaned back a little, searching for contact, but even when my back was flat against the bench, his arm simply rested along the top of it. I could feel the warmth of his closeness, but he didn't touch me.

"Here you go," Alberto said as he brought a plate of food outside. "I tried to get mostly protein, but I did bring a tiny piece of cheesecake since it's your favorite."

"Oh, cheesecake! Yes, thank you." I dug into the creamy goodness with my fork, moaning slightly as it melted in my mouth.

Alberto stood awkwardly at attention beside us, and I felt Gerry shift his weight and move his arm from the back of the bench. They were both silent as I ate, and if it hadn't been for the other partygoers mingling on the patio, the quiet would have been uncomfortable.

I was trying to figure out how to get Alberto to go back inside when Benjamin emerged from the party and called out to him.

"Alberto, there you are. I have someone you must meet."

Uncertainty flashed across my partner's face as his gaze shifted back and forth between Benjamin and Gerry.

"Go," I said, nudging his foot with my own. "I'm fine. I swear. I feel better already after having the cheesecake, and there's plenty of people out here so I don't need a chaperone." I grinned as I said it, but he frowned and rolled his eyes, glaring at Gerry once more before following Benjamin back inside.

"He seems like a barrel of fun," Gerry said, exhaling sharply.

"Aw, he is, really. He's just looking out for me. We've been friends since we were kids, and we've been through a lot together. That's all."

"Maybe someone should tell him you're not a kid anymore."

His voice was soft, and when I turned to face him, he looked so handsome it almost hurt. The moonlight highlighted the sharp angles of his cheekbones and made his eyes so light they nearly glowed. His curls framed the sides of his face, and his lips were full, slightly parted.

"Do you have any idea how beautiful you are, Maggie? How perfectly exquisite you are? The way you moved on that stage tonight, it was like my heart was pulled from my body and taken on the wind with you. Then when you walked in here and I saw you again, your hair like flames blazing around you...you have no idea what you do to me."

I had never wanted anything in my life like I wanted Gerry Tucker to kiss me in that moment.

It would have been the perfect first kiss. The stars above us, the moon lighting up the night, the faint strains of classical music in the background. And me, completely uninhibited and ready to take the next step toward womanhood.

I leaned toward him a little, uncertain of how the mechanics of a kiss played out having never done it, but certain that I wanted him to be the one.

He hesitated, and when his lips parted more with a flick of his tongue, I damned near moaned out loud. But then he leaned back before we made contact and swore softly under his breath.

"Maggie, I...."

Sensing the moment was slipping away, I moved closer, determined to make it happen.

He frowned, and turned his head just as Sandy joined us on the patio.

"Alberto said I'd find you out here," she said, coming to stand in front of us with her hands on her hips. "Mr. Tucker, nice to see you again."

"I don't believe we've met," Gerry said, rising as he offered her his hand to shake.

"This is my best friend, Sandy. Sandy, Gerry." I tossed my hair over my shoulder and crossed my arms, irritated with Alberto and Sandy for being such total killjoys, and feeling more than a little rejected by Gerry's refusal to kiss me.

"Maggie, you have a doctor's appointment pretty early in the morning, so I was thinking we should head out," she said, the terseness of her voice only irritating me more.

"What? What time is it?" I asked, looking at my wrist even though I wasn't wearing a watch.

"It's almost eleven-thirty. We need to go."

Gerry cleared his throat. "I'll get your crutches."

"No, I don't need to go," I said, wincing as I stood up and put more weight on my left foot than I'd intended.

His hand was underneath my arm immediately, and I gave him a half-smile, feeling awkward again after our botched encounter.

"I'll be right back," he said softly, nodding to me and to Sandy before he left.

She stepped forward as soon as he was out of earshot, talking low so no one else would hear her words. "Alberto said you're drunk. He said that man has been giving you champagne all night."

"I'm not drunk!"

"Shh! Hush. People are staring."

I glanced around us to see several sets of eyes upon me, but they all looked away quickly. "So, I had a couple of glasses of champagne. I'm an adult."

Sandy rolled her eyes. "Yes. An adult who doesn't normally drink. What did Lucas give you before you left the theater? What if you weren't supposed to mix that with alcohol?"

"He didn't say not to."

"Probably because he didn't think he had to. Who in their right mind would go get drunk in front of so many important people? After taking painkillers and having no idea — "

Her voice cut off when Gerry returned with the crutches.

He gingerly placed them under my arms and helped me get them situated.

"I'll see you inside," I said to Sandy. "Give me a minute?"

She stood still, and I thought for a moment she wasn't going to move, but then she turned with a huff and left us.

"Let me guess," Gerry said. "She's just looking out for you, too? Your friends are very vigilant. Either I look much scarier than I thought, or you must have a reputation for falling victim to shady characters. Is it me?"

"No, it's not you. I just...well, I normally don't drink."

Gerry chuckled. "I kind of guessed that, but it was too late. Why didn't you tell me? I would have gotten you whatever you wanted."

I prayed the moonlight would hide the embarrassment that crept into my cheeks and painted them red. "Was it that obvious?"

His smile was kind. "Not at all. You were absolutely adorable."

I rolled my eyes and groaned. Adorable was definitely not the look I'd been going for.

He stepped closer and put his hands on either side of my waist, touching his forehead to mine.

"Oh, Maggie. You make me wish we could escape time. That we could stop the clock and keep it from moving forward."

He moved to press his lips against my forehead and I leaned into him, wanting so much more. He pulled back and stared into my eyes, making me dizzy again.

"I don't have to go," I whispered.

"But I do," he said, his voice breaking as though he was in pain. "I would give anything to—"

"You coming?" Sandy asked from the doorway, and I waved her away without even looking at her.

Gerry took a step back, and I shivered at the cool air that rushed between us. He took my hand and brought it to his lips, bowing again without ever looking away from my eyes.

"Good night, Maggie," he said. "I know now why the willow weeps, for it senses there is one on the planet far more graceful and beautiful than it could ever be. Thank you for tonight."

He released my hand and walked away with my heart.

Sandy must have been watching because she stepped out on the patio the moment he was out of sight.

I hobbled past her without a word, waiting to unleash my frustration once we were in the elevator alone.

"God! Could you be any more annoying? I might as well have had my mother here," I growled.

"If your mother was here you wouldn't have been drinking all night and flirting with a total stranger."

"How is he a total stranger? Ernesto knows him! He introduced him to me."

"Ernesto knows he has money. He'd sell his left arm for a price. Besides, Ernesto didn't tell you to go make out with him on the patio."

My mouth dropped open. "I didn't make out with him on the patio. What are you talking about?"

"You two sure looked cozy when I came out there. Don't you think he's a little old for you?"

The thought had never really occurred to me. "Too old? Why? How old do you think he is? I'm nineteen, Sandy. Hello?"

"I don't know how old he is, but if he's flying all over the country providing financial backing for shows, then he must have been in business for a while. He looks old. He's probably, like, thirty or something."

"So now you're upset that he's wealthy? I can't believe you. For the first time, I'm actually interested in someone, and rather than be happy for me, you and Alberto both seem pissed off. You're totally overreacting. I've never been so embarrassed."

She held the elevator door while I maneuvered out with my crutches.

"You've also never been drunk. Or fawned all over somebody before."

"I wasn't fawning over anyone," I said as she gave the valet her address for the taxi.

She whirled back around so fast it made my head spin, though that might have been due to my state at the time.

"Everyone at the party was whispering, Maggie. Talking about how tipsy you were and how you seemed so smitten with Gerry Tucker. So, forgive Berto and me if we're a bit concerned to see our best friend acting totally out of character. I'm sorry if we cramped your night by not wanting anything to happen to you. I thought that was kind of what friends do."

The valet held the taxi door open and Sandy motioned for me to get in.

Humiliation, pain, and anger roiled with the nausea that had set in, and I wanted it all to go away.

"I'll get my own taxi," I said, lifting my chin in defiance. "I'm going back to my place."

"Don't be ridiculous," she said as she went to the other side of the car. "All your stuff's at my apartment already, and I'm supposed to get you to the doctor in the morning. Just get in."

She slammed the taxi door, and I hobbled over and got in to ride in silence.

# 9 AFTER ALL THESE YEARS

"Can you believe this lady has been my best friend since we were ten years old?" Sandy asked the waiter who was refilling our wine glasses. "I'm not about to tell you how many years that's been, but trust me. We've been together *a while.*"

We both laughed and clinked our wine glasses together as the waiter flashed us a disinterested smile and walked away, probably rolling his eyes as he went.

"Seems like a lifetime ago," I said before taking a big sip of wine.

"It *was* a lifetime ago. We were eight when we met, right? But we weren't friends until...what was that other girl's name? The one who pushed me down?"

"Natalie. How could you forget her name?"

Sandy set her wine glass down and slapped her hands on her thighs. "Natalie! That's right! I probably blocked her out of my mind somehow. She was vile, and I was terrified of her. I don't remember now what I'd done to provoke her that day—"

"She told you to put your bag on the floor so she could hang hers on your hook, and you told her no," I said.

Sandy opened her mouth in surprise. "You're right. How do you remember this? I remember now that you say it, but God. That was what? Almost forty years ago? How is that even possible? How is that *forty* years ago?"

I shook my head in disbelief and took another drink of wine to ease the pain of reality.

"I tell you what I do remember," Sandy said, pointing her finger at me. "I remember *you* marching across that dressing room with your hands on those narrow little hips, and you told her to back off. When you stretched your hand out to help me up, and you glared at her over your shoulder, I tell you what. You earned a friend for life right at that moment." She lifted her wine glass to me, and I raised mine to meet hers.

"The best friend a girl could ever have!" I winked at her. "I think I got the better end of the deal, to tell the truth."

Sandy laughed. "Natalie transferred to that other school in South Beach, remember? Oh, oh—and do you remember when we saw her the day of auditions for Miami? She kept glaring at us and talking behind her hand to the other girls from her school."

"I remember."

"I would have loved to have seen her face when she saw we both made it in and she didn't. To Miami City Ballet! And Natalie!"

She lifted her glass, and we toasted again.

"I'm so happy you're moving back to Orlando," I said, my heart filling my chest and the warmth of the wine coloring my cheeks. "Not that Atlanta's that far away, but we'll be able to see each other more often if we're in the same town."

Sandy finished off her wine and motioned the waiter over for another refill.

"I'm excited, too, I guess," she said as the waiter poured. "I mean, it's a no-brainer for Hannah's career. It's not like she could turn down such a big promotion. I don't know yet how this will work out for me. Orlando has several well-established floral designers. I've spent twelve years building a reputation and a clientele in Atlanta, and I'd be lying if I said it didn't make me nervous to uproot all that and start over."

I put my hand over my glass and shook my head at the waiter's offer for more.

"Nonsense. You'll do great here! There's year-round wedding activity and a ton of convention hotels. You already have some clients here, and I'm sure you'll be able to keep some of those from Atlanta, won't you?"

She shrugged. "Yeah, I will. I do feel better now that I found a great facility. I can't wait to show it to you."

"I can't wait to see it," I said as my phone vibrated on the table. I recognized Dax's number from his call earlier, and a flutter of excitement danced in my chest. "Do you mind if I take this?"

I didn't wait for her response, putting the phone up to one ear as I pressed my finger into the other to block out the background noise of the restaurant's dinner crowd.

"This is Maggie."

"Well, hello there. Dax here. I guess I owe you another apology. Sorry about this afternoon. I didn't realize it was gonna take so long for pictures."

"No, it's okay. I'm sorry for bolting without saying goodbye. I needed to get back to the office."

I turned my head to avoid Sandy's intense gaze.

"No problem. You mentioned you'd been out all morning, so I understand you couldn't wait. But I would like to take you to lunch to make it up to you."

My initial happy reaction was immediately drowned out by reservation. I dropped my head back and closed my eyes.

"That's so kind of you, but it isn't necessary. Really. I grabbed a taxi and made it back fine."

"All right, then can I take you to lunch just because I'd like to see you again?"

I smiled as I pinched the bridge of my nose with my fingers, my eyes still closed. "Oh. Um."

Sandy kicked me under the table, and my eyes popped open to look at her.

"Who is that?" she mouthed.

I waved her off, turning in my chair so I couldn't see her.

Dax cleared his throat. "Unless, of course, you don't—"

"No, no. It's not that. It's just a busy week at work. I've got a lot of meetings and going out to lunch pulls me away from the office. Everything gets backed up."

Sandy leaned around the table and snapped her fingers to get my attention. "Who is that?" she mouthed, audibly that time.

I frowned at her.

"Got it," Dax said, his voice quieter. "No problem. I just figured it couldn't hurt to ask."

"No, right. I mean, I'm glad you did. I just…it's busy, that's all."

My cheeks, already warm from the wine, flushed hot as I realized how badly I was botching the phone call.

"Okay, well I tell ya what," he said. "My calendar is usually pretty flexible, so when you see you have an opening, give me a call, and we'll grab lunch."

"Sounds good. Thanks for calling."

"Enjoy your evening," Dax said, and I could picture him smiling as he said it.

I smiled back.

"You, too. Thanks again."

I stared at the phone for a moment with the oddest sensation of missing his voice.

"Who. Was. That?" Sandy asked, sitting back in her chair with her arms crossed as she grinned at me.

"Oh," I said, tucking my hair behind my ear and avoiding eye contact. I still wasn't sure why Dax Pearson affected me the way he did, and the last thing I wanted was a million questions from the person who knew me better than anyone. "It was something to do with Galen's wedding."

"What? No," Sandy said. "There's something you're not telling me. C'mon, spit it out."

"What? It was the guy who owns the ranch where Galen is thinking of having her wedding. Why are you being so weird?" I put my silverware on my plate to signify I was done and folded my napkin on the table.

Sandy laughed. "Why am I being weird? Why are *you* being weird?"

"I don't know what you're talking about."

"Oh my gosh, Maggie! Just tell me already. Who is he?" She leaned forward and put her elbows on the table, playfully cupping her hands behind her ears. "I'm all ears."

I downed the remainder of the wine in my glass. "No one. I swear you're barking up the wrong tree. It's just the guy that owns the ranch."

"Why would he ask you to lunch? And where did you see him earlier today?"

I met her eyes for the first time since I'd ended the call. "Am I being interrogated? What, are you my mother?"

She laughed again and waved the waiter over for more wine.

I shook my head. "No, Sandy. No more wine. You only have to walk to the hotel elevator. I have to get in my car and drive home."

"So, stay here with me, and we can have a slumber party while you tell me who this guy is that makes your entire face light up when you take his call. And you took his call, by the way. That was the first clue. You never interrupt our dinners to take a call unless it's from one of the kids."

"It was about the kids! It was for Galen's wedding."

She watched the waiter pour the wine in our glasses and then motioned for him to leave the bottle on the table. "Not buying it, Mags. You forget who you're talking to? I know you, lady. I've never seen that look on your face when your phone rang. You were practically giddy. Which brings me to my next question, even though you haven't answered my others so far. Why did you turn him down for lunch?"

"How do you know he asked me out to lunch?"

She tapped her ears. "Did you forget what good ears I have, Little Red Riding Hood? It was tough to make out with the background noise, but I caught the gist of it."

"You're terrible."

"And you're holding out on me. You didn't tell me you met someone! Spill it. Who is this guy?"

"I already told you. He owns the ranch." I took another sip of wine, despite my protests before he poured it.

"You've said that. Where did you see him earlier today?"

"Well, *Mom*, if you must know, we both attended a luncheon at the hospital."

"Ah. So why don't you want to go to lunch with him?"

I sighed and waited as our waiter cleared the dishes from the table, politely refusing his offer for dessert.

"I don't think it's a good idea," I told her when he'd left.

"Why? Is he hideous?"

Dax's wet torso flashed through my mind with a brief glimpse of his grin, and I laughed.

"No. Definitely not hideous. Far from it."

She nodded, and I blushed under her scrutiny and the additional glass of wine.

"No personality?"

I recalled our brief conversations with a smile.

"Oh, he's got plenty of personality."

"How old is he?"

I rolled my eyes to the ceiling. "This is why I'm glad you never had children, Sandra. They would hate dating under you."

"You didn't answer. What? Is he a lot younger? Older?"

I looked to the ceiling and smiled. "No. I don't know. I don't think so. He looks to be our age."

"Well, hell, at our age, that could be a range of forty to sixty depending on how well he's held up."

My mind replayed him pulling his shirt over his head, and I grinned. "He's held up pretty damned well, but I'd say from the salt in his hair and the lines at his eyes that he's gotta be pretty close to us."

"And what is it about him that makes your face light up like this? I'm almost teary-eyed just seeing your reaction to this guy. What happened between the two of you?"

"Nothing! I swear. He's just nice. And attractive."

"Okay. So why no lunch?"

I covered my face with hands and grumbled. "Sandy, you know I don't like to go out with people."

She leaned across the table. "How do you know? You never go out with anybody."

I dropped my hands from my face and stuck my tongue out at her. "That's not true."

Sandy raised her eyebrows and held her hands up outstretched. "It's not? Really? Tell me the last person you went out with. And don't even say—"

"Bobby," we said in unison.

She rolled her eyes and crossed her arms again. "I knew you were going to say Bobby. Bobby does not count. You went to his restaurant a couple of times a week after work, and he'd have his chef make you a meal. That's not dating. That's him being lazy and writing off your dinner on his taxes."

"It's hard when you own a restaurant. He worked seven nights a week."

"Oh, give me a break. All right, let's say I let you count Bobby, which is such a stretch. Who before him? Name someone else you've dated in, oh, say, the last five years."

"What about Doug?"

"You went out, what, three times? And one of those was a company barbecue?"

"Okay, what about Preston? We went out several times. Dinner. The theater. Concerts. Movies."

"I told you when you introduced me to him. Preston's gay." She stabbed the slice of chocolate cake that had just been put in front of her.

"He is not!"

"He is. Trust me. I would know. We know these things."

"Preston is a very nice man."

"I'm sure he is. Did he ever try to get you in bed?"

My mouth dropped in fake shock, but I didn't have the heart to carry through with it so I laughed instead. "No, because he was a gentleman."

"Because he was gay. Which is probably why you were willing to keep seeing him for so long. I think it's time to admit that you have a problem."

I exhaled heavily and checked my watch.

"You do," she insisted. "You're afraid of relationships. You hid behind the kids for years and used them as an excuse—"

"I never used my kids as an excuse!" My indignation was genuine that time.

"Okay, maybe *use them* is the wrong terminology, but you always said you wouldn't date until they were out of the house."

"I was putting them first. And you of all people should understand why!"

"Oh, I know why. But you have no reason now! They're adults. Out of the house and on their own. One's married and one's engaged to be married."

I bit my lip and looked away from her, but she was unwavering.

"Maggie, you have not been in a serious relationship since Galen was born. That's twenty-six years. You can't tell me you don't realize that's a little bit abnormal."

"Why do I somehow keep ending up in this conversation with people?"

"Because you don't go out with anyone."

"All right, fine. I'll go to lunch with Dax. I'll call him right now and set up a lunch date. Will that make you happy?"

I picked up my phone and scrolled to his number in the call log, hitting dial before I could change my mind.

Sandy smiled triumphantly as she watched me.

The phone rang three times, and I was almost hoping he wouldn't answer when his voice suddenly filled my ear.

"Well, hello, Josephine Marcus."

"What?"

"You called me Wyatt Earp earlier, when I said seeing you was fortuitous, but it was actually Josephine Marcus who said it in the movie. *Tombstone*, right?"

I smiled. "Yes. You're right. It was Josephine Marcus."

"Did you find an empty slot on your calendar?"

My eyes met Sandy's and she nodded at me to go ahead, so I took a deep breath and asked if he was available on Thursday.

"Thursday works. Shall I pick you up at your office?"

Apprehension crept in, and I hesitated. "Oh. Um," I looked away from Sandy and rubbed my hand against my pants to try and dry its sudden moisture. "You don't have to pick me up. I can meet you downtown somewhere."

"All right. I had a place in mind for lunch, but it's over off Mills and Colonial. Is that too far?"

Sandy leaned across and whispered, "Just let him pick you up."

I waved her away and closed my eyes. "No, that's fine. Just text me the address and I'll meet you there. Wanna say one o'clock?"

"Perfect. I'll see you Thursday."

"See you Thursday."

Sandy poured me another glass of wine and I let her.

# 10 CUCUMBER WATER

My phone rang a few minutes after twelve, and when I saw his number, I thought he was calling to cancel. The level of disappointment I felt surprised me, and I forced my voice to sound nonchalant when I answered.

"This is Maggie."

"How fortuitous! That's exactly who I called!"

I smiled, still nervous to hear why he was calling. "Is that your favorite word?"

"Fortuitous? No, actually, I don't know that I've ever used it much before. It somehow seems appropriate this week, I guess."

His voice was wistful, and I resisted the urge to ask what was special about this week before he continued.

"I don't know if you've peeked out the window, but it looks like it's going to rain on our parade." He paused, and my smile faded as I realized he really was calling to cancel. "I'm sure you don't want to get soaked in the middle of your work day, so I was wondering if you wanted me to pick you up at the Arts Center valet or would you rather grab something to eat there?"

My relief at him not canceling was immediately replaced by a sense of panic at the thought of having lunch with him in the cafe downstairs. On a rainy day, everyone in the building ate there rather than braving the wet outdoors. I had no desire to answer a million questions about who I was dining with and why.

While my preference would certainly be to drive my own car, I couldn't ignore the logic in having Dax pick me up under the covered valet entrance.

"Valet is fine," I said, hoping he wouldn't hear the hesitation in my voice.

"Alright. I'll pick you up about a quarter 'til? Wear a red carnation so I know it's you."

I recognized the movie reference and smiled with a chuckle. "That might be hard to pull off with such short notice, but I'll be in a long black coat and black boots so you know what to look for."

"I have no doubt I'd recognize that red hair of yours anywhere."

I blushed, and my smile expanded. "Then I guess it's *fortuitous* for you that I'm not wearing a hat! I'll see you downstairs."

The hands on the clock dragged as I tried unsuccessfully to focus on the work at hand for the next hour. I'd been standing by the glass doors for several minutes already when I saw him pull under the *porte cochere* in a huge, black pick-up truck. I don't know what I expected him to drive, but the truck only solidified his cowboy image in my head.

I braced for the cold as I swung the door open, hugging the coat tightly around me as the wind whipped my hair across my face.

Dax got out and greeted me at the passenger door, waving away the valet to open it for me himself.

"I found you," he said, his grin wide and his green eyes bright.

"You found me," I said with a smile, thankful that I'd worn pants as I grabbed the door and climbed into the truck, which would have been nearly impossible to do gracefully in a tight skirt.

The warmth of the heated seat was a pleasant surprise, and I settled into it as I took in the luxury of the vehicle's interior.

It was remarkably clean for what I assumed was a ranch truck, and it smelled of the cinnamon air freshener that hung from the rearview mirror. An insulated coffee cup sat in the drink holder next to his cell phone, and the console tray beneath the stereo held a clear box of mint-flavored toothpicks.

A blast of cold air swept inside when he opened the driver's door and slid behind the wheel.

"Nice truck," I said, nervous at the thought of silence now that we were alone together.

"Thanks. It gets me where I need to go. Comfortably."

"I don't know that I've ever ridden in a truck before, but if I did, it wasn't like this."

I glanced behind me at the ample rear seat as he merged into the downtown traffic.

"Really? No one you know drives a truck?"

I shook my head. "Can't think of anyone. Of course, you're the only person I know who owns a ranch."

"Trucks are useful on a ranch. So have you seen *The Shop Around the Corner*, or had you just heard the red carnation line before?"

"Of course! I watch it every year at Christmas."

"Wow. Okay. And what about its modern remake?"

"*You've Got Mail?*" I tilted my head and looked at him, trying to picture the cowboy before me relaxing in front of the TV watching romantic comedies. I giggled at the mental image.

"What?" he asked, looking at me once he'd stopped at the traffic light.

"I don't know. I guess I'm just surprised that...I don't know." My voice trailed off as I tried to think of a way to explain the reason for my surprise without insulting him.

"That what? That I watch romance movies? Tough guys have feelings too, ya know." He smiled and directed his attention back to the road as the light turned green.

The casual mention of feelings stirred the anxiety lurking just beneath my calm facade, but I looked out the window at the rain, determined to keep it under control and enjoy the moment.

"I think the original was better," he said. "What was the book she was supposed to bring to the cafe with her?"

"*Anna Karenina.*"

"Yeah, that's right. Very good." He nodded in approval.

"I told you I watch it every year. Besides, when it comes to movie trivia, you'd be hard-pressed to stump me."

He raised his eyebrows and glanced at me. "Is that a challenge?"

"Do what you must," I said with a smile, feeling a bit emboldened and uncharacteristically flirtatious.

He slowed the truck and adeptly backed into a parallel spot along the busy street, and I'd be lying if I said I wasn't impressed by his ability to put the large truck in such a tight spot with the rain and heavy traffic.

"Let me grab the umbrella and I'll come around to get you," he said as he braced his arm against the driver's door.

"I have my own." I took my umbrella from my shoulder bag and unbuckled the strap to remove the cover.

"I can come get you," he said. "You'll be drenched by the time you get the umbrella open through the door."

"No more drenched than you'll be," I said. "I can open my own umbrella and my own door."

Dax shrugged with a smile. "Do what you must."

I was pleased that he didn't argue the point, but a little surprised. I'd half expected him to insist.

Even though I opened the door just wide enough to snake the umbrella up and out, the rain poured in, wetting my coat sleeve and pants leg before I could get the umbrella open. I could practically feel my hair frizzing as I hopped out onto the curb.

Dax stood at the rear of the truck underneath a wide black umbrella, clearly big enough for two. He waited for me to reach him and then looked both ways before crossing the street.

"So, this is Tako Cheena?" I asked, reading the name emblazoned across the restaurant's window. It was a small place, tucked in between a costume shop and a vintage clothing store. It had a total of seven tables and a long bar set up along the window for additional seating.

"You've never been here, then?" he asked as he closed his umbrella and reached to take mine, shaking it slightly before holding the door open for me to enter.

I shook my head, cautiously looking at the other diners to see if they seemed pleased with their meals.

"You're in for a real treat. It's one of my favorite places near downtown. Guarantee, after today, you'll be coming back."

Dax chose a table against the wall and held out a chair for me as I removed my coat and positioned it across the back of the chair so the sleeve could dry.

He handed me a laminated menu card from the bucket on the wall, but I noticed he didn't take one for himself.

"What do you recommend?" I asked.

"A little bit of everything. You won't know what you like until you try it."

I handed him back the menu. "Then surprise me."

His eyebrows raised a bit, but his smile grew wider. "Okay. I like it. How adventurous are you?"

"I'm here, aren't I?"

He chuckled. "Any allergies? Major dislikes?" I shook my head and he continued. "You want a drink? They have cucumber water."

The thought of him sipping cucumber water was too much for me, and my laughter bubbled up and out of me before I could contain it.

"What? What's funny about cucumber water?" he asked.

"Nothing," I replied, clearing my throat and trying not to laugh again. "I'm sure it's wonderful. Let's have cucumber water."

"It's good for you."

My laughter bubbled up and out again. "I'm sure it is. I would love to have some. I'm looking forward to it. I never knew cowboys drank cucumber water."

"Oh," he said with a smirk. "I reckon cowboys drink whatever they want to. I thought you didn't know many cowboys."

"I don't."

He leaned forward and grinned. "Then how do you know what cowboys drink?"

I laughed again, surprisingly relaxed and at ease with our banter.

"I don't. Obviously."

He signaled the waitress that we were ready and rattled off his order. "We'll have two cucumber waters," he said with a wink in my direction, "and give us a chicken panang burrito, a Korean beef taco, a panko-crusted cod taco, and a four-cheese arepa with slaw."

I noticed the way she watched him as he talked, and I felt an odd sensation of possessiveness, like he was mine for the hour.

It wasn't difficult to see why she might be attracted.

His ever-present smile was hard to resist, and his easygoing temperament was engaging.

He wore no coat, despite the cold, and the tan of his skin in mid-February indicated he probably spent most of his time outdoors year-round.

His gray button-down shirt was open at the collar and the sleeves were folded back neatly across his muscular forearms. His hair was slightly damp, and its waves covered the tops of his ears and rested along the edge of his collar.

He laughed at something the waitress said as she walked away, and when he looked at me, it was remarkably easy to smile back at him.

"Hopefully, you'll like something in all that," he said.

"I'm sure I will. How'd you find this place?"

"Oh, I'm always on the search for something off the beaten path. I try to stay away from the chain restaurants with the cookie cutter menus. Somebody recommended this place a couple years ago, when it first opened. Been coming ever since."

I smiled as the waitress set down two cups of cucumber water, and when she walked away, Dax raised his cup as though he were toasting.

"To cucumber water and new adventures."

I laughed and touched my cup to his. "And cowboys."

"Yes ma'am."

We both took a drink, and he looked at me expectantly. "Well? What do you think?"

I laughed again, sure that he must think I was like a giddy teenager with the number of times I was giggling.

"It's good. I've had cucumber water before, Dax. I was just surprised that you ordered it. I guess I thought you'd have, I don't know...."

"Something more manly?" he asked, one eyebrow arched.

"No, that's not, well, I guess. It sounds horrible when you say it that way, like I was stereotyping you or something."

He smiled. "So maybe I should have ordered a strong, foamy ale or a shot of whiskey?"

"Oh Lord. I've really stepped in it here, so could we change the subject?"

His laughter let me off the hook.

"Sure, what would you like to talk about?"

"How'd you get involved with the hospital trauma unit?"

His smile faded, and something dark passed across his eyes just as the waitress brought our lunch.

He didn't answer the question when she left, and I pretended not to notice.

"Are you ready for this?" he asked, cutting each taco and burrito in half and passing it across the table.

"So much food. I can't eat all this," I said, even as my stomach was growling at the delectable aromas assaulting my senses.

"You have to try a bite of each, so you'll know what to order when you come back."

It only took a couple of bites for me to determine that I would definitely be back, and I would never balk at any recommendation he made.

He stretched his back against the chair when we'd had our fill, and I thanked him again for introducing me to such a delicious find.

"So, you have the one daughter getting married? What's her name? Gail?"

"Galen."

"And I met your daughter-in-law, so I'm guessing you have a son?"

I nodded. "Cabe."

"Interesting names," he said.

"Coming from someone named Dax, I'm not sure how I should respond. But then, I saw the other day your name is actually Dexter, right?"

"Yes. Dexter James. My brother was two when I was born, and I guess he never could get Dex to come out correctly. His Southern accent drew it out and the name Dax kind of stuck. What about you? Any brothers or sisters?"

"No, I'm an only. And you? Just the one brother, or are there more Pearsons?"

Normally, I dreaded the standard getting-to-know-you drill of questions on a first date, but my curiosity about Dax had been building since the first time I saw him, and I wanted answers. Besides, it wasn't a date. It was simply lunch.

He nodded. "Mitchell. He and his wife live only a couple of miles from me, near my parents' place."

"Oh, your parents live near you?"

"You could say that. I live on one side of the ranch, and my parents live on the other side in the house I grew up in."

"That's convenient."

"Yeah, it is. It's just close enough to them to make it easy to visit and just far enough away to maintain my sanity."

I laughed. "My parents live in Delray Beach, and sometimes even that feels too close, so maybe my threshold for sanity has a little larger radius than yours."

"Are you close to your parents?"

"Yes. My mom and I are very close, always have been. My dad and I don't always see eye to eye, but there's a lot of love there. They don't visit as often as they did when my kids were young, but we talk all the time, and I head down to Delray whenever I can."

"Did you grow up there? In Delray?"

Inquiries into my past usually kicked up my defenses and made me want to end the conversation, but for some reason, it didn't bother me to share myself with Dax.

"No, not really. We lived in Miami when I was little. They moved to Delray when I was fourteen."

The waitress interrupted to ask if we were interested in dessert, and I put up my hands in protest.

"No way. You'd have to roll me out of here with a crane."

"I may have a wheelbarrow in the back of the truck," Dax said. "Want me to go see?"

The three of us laughed, and the waitress said she'd come back with the check.

"You say *they* moved when you were fourteen," he said when she'd gone. "So, you didn't move with them?"

"No, I was enrolled in a dance school. Kind of like a boarding school, I guess you'd say? So, I lived there full-time from the age of eight."

"Eight?" His eyebrows raised in surprise. "That's really young. What kind of dance?"

"Ballet."

"No shit? Really? I can see that. The way you move. The way you carry yourself. Very graceful. Do you still dance now? I mean, I know you said you worked for the Performing Arts Center, but do you dance?"

I shifted in my seat, uncomfortable for the first time since we sat down. "That ship sailed quite a while ago. You never did tell me what you do. You know, besides horse tricks and hospital wings."

His smile came easy, but my nerves were still tense, on alert for dangerous topics.

"We've got a pretty big cattle population, plus we've branched out into a couple of side businesses that fall under the ranch's umbrella," he said, scratching his chin. "One being the weddings and parties at the main house on my side, but Bronwyn handles all that."

"She does a wonderful job," I said. "It's such a beautiful event space."

He nodded. "That's all her. She put together a business proposal and laid out what she wanted to do and how she could make it happen. She's done quite well. I'm proud of her. The whole family is."

"Do you have any kids?"

The hint of darkness returned to his eyes, and he ran his hand through his hair before answering. "No. It wasn't in the cards for me, I suppose.

57

You just have the two?"

"The two I gave birth to, but I have Tyler, the one you met, and now I'm gaining Tate, my daughter's fiancé. So, I'll have four. Which is plenty."

"They're a blessing, I'm sure."

He smiled when he said it, but there was a sadness I hadn't seen before. Like the shadow of the darkness still lingered. I wanted to reach across the table and touch his hand, to offer some comfort for the unknown pain, but it seemed too strong a gesture for someone I barely knew.

"I guess I should get you back to the office. Looks like the rain has died down for the moment, so it might be a good time to make a break for it."

I glanced at my watch and was shocked to see it had been almost an hour and a half. The time seemed to have flown, and I couldn't help feeling a bit disappointed. There was so much more I wanted to know about Dax, and to end the lunch on what was obviously a sad note for him seemed unfair.

He picked up the check and pulled his wallet from his pocket, so I grabbed mine from my purse.

"How much is it?" I asked, taking out a twenty.

"I got it," he said as he handed it to the waitress with cash.

"No. I want to pay my part. How much was the total?"

"I asked you to lunch to make up for being delayed at the hospital. It was my treat."

I frowned. "That's not necessary. Let me pay my half. I insist."

He cocked his head to one side and peered at me, his eyes serious but with no trace of the sadness that was there before. "I tell you what. I'll make you a deal. I get this lunch because it was my idea. I called and asked you, and I picked the place and the menu. You want to be fair and square? You take me to lunch. You pick the place, and you pick the menu."

I hesitated, considering whether agreeing to a second meeting was too much. Too soon. But I couldn't ignore the way my heart soared at the prospect of another chance to talk to him, and before I could over think it, I extended my hand for him to shake.

"Deal," I said.

He grasped my hand in his and I inhaled sharply at the sensations the contact caused. We both drew back almost immediately, and I wondered if it was possible that it had the same effect on him.

He stood and took my coat from the back of my chair, holding it open for me to put on. Then he gathered our umbrellas by the door, and after he handed me mine, we stepped out into the light rain and walked to the truck.

"So, I'll wait to hear from you about where and when for lunch," he said as he pulled under the covered area at my office.

"Okay." I exhaled, still not sure it was a wise decision. I reached for the door, and he stopped me.

"Wait, I'll get the door for you."

"You don't have to," I said. "I'm perfectly capable of opening a door myself. But thanks."

The valet pulled my door open before Dax could respond, so he just smiled.

"Thanks for lunch," I said, tugging my coat tighter as I climbed out of the truck.

"It was my pleasure," he said, and it felt like he meant it.

# 11 NIGHT WAVES

I was flipping through the Silver Creek brochures again when Galen called.

"Hey, Mom. Did I wake you?"

"No, sweetheart," I said, yawning at the idea of sleep. "I'm sitting in bed, looking at the pictures of Silver Creek. It's a beautiful location."

"Thanks. I'm so happy you like it. Tyler said it seems to have everything we need. Tate wants you to look at a place over on the beach, but I don't really want to do the beach. What if it rains? I mean, at least at the ranch, we could be inside. It's pretty inside, right?"

"Oh, it's gorgeous." I wondered again who had designed the house and chosen its features. Dax didn't strike me as the type of man who would build a closet the size of a small bedroom for himself, although somehow I could see him incorporating the stream beneath the house into the flooring.

How could I find out who built the house? Would it be appropriate to ask him on our next lunch date? I winced when I realized I'd called it a date.

It would probably be a better idea to ask Bronwyn under the guise of curiosity for the event. That is, if Galen and Tate chose the ranch for the wedding.

"Are you there? Mom? Can you hear me?"

"Oh, yeah. I'm sorry, sweetie. I must have zoned out. What were you saying?"

"Nothing. It can wait. You sound tired. I'll call you tomorrow."

"Okay. Love you, G."

"Love you, too, Mom."

I laid the brochures on the bedside table and flipped the lamp off. I don't know how long I lay there staring at the ceiling before I drifted off, but I found myself in the midst of the weirdest dream.

We were on a yacht, out at sea, and the waves had gotten rough. I was below deck with Galen, and she was crying because the wedding was going to be ruined by the weather. I told her I'd go up and check the skies to see if it had gotten any better.

When I closed the bedroom door and headed for the stairs, Gerry stepped out into the hallway. Anger boiled up inside me, and I gritted my teeth together and clenched my fists.

"What are you doing here?" I asked. "You have no business here."

He smiled, and it turned my stomach. "Willow, what's wrong?"

"Don't call me that. I told you to never call me that again."

His hands reached for me, and in the dream they were long, superhuman, and able to cross the space between us in a second. I moved backward to avoid them, but I was against the door, and I didn't want to open it and let him see Galen.

"Stop!" I screamed as he walked toward me. "Stop! I want you to go away. You have no right to be here. You have no right! I don't want you here."

But then I blinked, and it wasn't Gerry. It was Dax. His eyes were filled with hurt and confusion, and he pulled his hands back and put them at his sides. They were normal hands, not scary at all.

"I'm sorry," he said. "I didn't mean to upset you." He turned and went up the stairs, and as the hatch opened, a huge wave pitched the boat and tossed him out of sight.

"No, wait!" I cried, moving toward the steps, but the boat rolled back the other direction and slammed me into the wall.

I woke then, my heart pounding and my pajamas soaked in sweat. I flipped the lamp back on and got out of bed, peeling off the pajamas and climbing into the shower.

I stood there with the water pouring over me until my heart rate returned to normal, but my mind wouldn't calm.

If only I had listened to Sandy. To Alberto. If only I hadn't been so headstrong and determined to prove myself. Determined to grow up overnight.

I turned the water off and closed my eyes. I wouldn't have the life I'd lived without the choices I'd made, whether good or bad, so it was hard to regret. But it would have been different if I'd known what choices I was making.

I didn't.

# 12 WILLOW

Maybe if I hadn't broken my toe, it would have all gone down differently. The X-rays showed it was a nasty break, close to the joint. I was thrilled when the doctor said no more crutches, but that was before he put me in the heavy, cumbersome boot and told me I wasn't to dance for four to six weeks.

The entire company was abuzz with the news that my injury had knocked me out of the lead role, but Benjamin reassured me that it wouldn't affect my standing the rest of the season.

I was sitting on the floor in the hallway outside the rehearsal room, literally bored to tears after only two days of not being allowed to rehearse with everyone else.

When I looked up and saw Gerry walking toward me, I couldn't help but smile. He'd been on my mind nonstop since we'd said goodbye at the reception, and I'd wondered if I would ever see him again.

"Well, if it isn't my beautiful Willow! Whoa. Weeping Willow. What's wrong? Who made you cry?"

I swiped at the tears and smiled up at him as he crouched beside me. "No one. It's silly. What are you doing here?"

He reached and wiped away a stray tear on my cheek with his thumb. "What's wrong?"

"It's stupid," I said, shaking my head. "I can't rehearse right now because of this dumb boot, and I have to be here, but I can't do anything, and watching everyone dance without me sucks."

"That's not stupid at all. That's torture. For someone who dances as beautifully as you do, I'd say that's like going without oxygen. How long before you can dance again?"

I shrugged. "I don't know. The doctor says four to six weeks, but I'm hoping I can be back in there before that. It all depends on how fast it heals."

"So, you're going to sit out here in the hallway for weeks? That can't be good."

"I can go in there, but I have to sit in a chair and watch. I'd rather be out here. Actually, that's not true. I'd rather be anywhere but out here."

He stood and rubbed the back of his neck. He was staring down the hallway, his brows furrowed like he was in deep thought or making a difficult decision.

"Screw it," he whispered, almost so low that I didn't hear it. "I tell you what, Willow, I've got a friend who's taking a group of us out on his yacht today. It should be a good time. Lots of food. Open bar. With non-alcoholic beverages for those who probably shouldn't drink." He winked at me, and I blushed. "Why don't you come with me? It's a big group, but it's a huge boat, so one more won't matter."

My heart raced with excitement at the prospect of spending the day with him, but logic shut it down. "I can't. I have to be here since I'm technically supposed to be, you know?"

He smiled, and warm vibes danced across my skin from head to toe. "You let me worry about that, okay? I'm heading in there to tell Ernesto how much money I'm willing to give him for the season. I think he'll be willing to do me a favor."

Sandy's voice in the back of my mind warned me that it wasn't a good idea. I barely knew the man, and I had no idea who else would be on the boat. Only that it was a large group, and there'd be drinking. I'd be out on the sea where no one could find me. Where no one even knew where I was. It was all in all a pretty bad idea.

Gerry crouched beside me again. "Whaddya say, Willow? Do you want to spend the day crying here on the floor, or do you want to spend the day on the deck of a yacht taking in the sun and the surf?"

His eyes got me. They locked on mine, and I was mesmerized. Breathless. Unable to refuse, though no part of me really wanted to.

An hour later, he had a limo pick me up at my apartment. He'd cleared it with Ernesto, and I'd snuck out without telling Sandy or Alberto because I didn't want to hear them tell me not to go.

The boot didn't look good no matter which sundress I put on, so I ended up choosing a red and white polka dot one that matched my red bikini. I braided my hair and left the braid hanging down my back, and then I grabbed a straw hat and tied a white ribbon around it.

"Wow," Gerry said when the limo pulled up at the dock. "I swear you get prettier every time I see you."

I grinned and held the hat tight against my head in the wind coming off the water.

"Ready for some fun?" he asked, offering his arm.

We made our way up the dock and onto the boat. I was limping in the boot and he was being patient with my progress. Gerry introduced me to a myriad of people as we boarded, and I smiled so much my cheeks hurt, ridiculously happy to be by his side.

He found two lounge chairs for us on the top deck and frowned as I fought to keep the hat on my head.

"I'm thinking we should put the hat down below. Here. Give it to me, and I'll store it somewhere and get us a drink. What would you like? I'm thinking something non-alcoholic?"

I nodded. "That would probably be best. If they have tonic water, I'd like tonic and lime."

"You got it. Relax, and enjoy the view. I'll be back in a minute."

The boat was underway by the time he returned, and I'd stood and limped to the rail to watch as we maneuvered our way through the marina.

"Here you go. Finally. Quite the line at the bar, as you can imagine. Here's to a day of nothing but fun," he said as he handed me my drink.

We toasted, and I laughed, so happy and looking forward to the day ahead that I could barely hold it in.

"That," Gerry said, pointing at me. "That right there."

"What?"

"That smile. I can't resist it. I think I'd do anything you asked to see that smile."

I laughed again.

"I don't ever want to see you cry again, Willow. It does something to me, in here." He gestured to his chest. "I know it sounds crazy, because we just met and all, but I see you smile, and it makes the whole world a little bit brighter."

I didn't stop smiling the rest of the day. I smiled as he introduced me to more of his friends; he raved about my performance when they asked about my foot. I smiled as we swam off the dive platform of the boat, thrilled to be rid of the boot for a while. I smiled as we ate a picnic lunch on the shores of an island where we'd anchored. I smiled as I sat between his knees in the crowded jacuzzi on the top deck, listening to the group share stories.

I was still smiling as we walked hand-in-hand along the railing that night, gazing at the never-ending blanket of stars above us.

"How long before we're back to shore?" I asked.

"Probably about a half hour. Maybe a little more. Why? You ready to go?"

I looked up at him. "Not at all. In fact, I was thinking about what you said the other night. That you wished you could stop the clock and keep it from moving forward."

Wisps of hair had escaped my braid, and Gerry reached to sweep them from my face, tucking them behind my ear.

I shivered at the contact, though I wasn't at all chilled. The tremors came from deep within me, starting like a vibration in my core, like energy building until it could no longer be contained.

I thought he was going to kiss me, and it crossed my mind that yet again, we had the perfect setting for a first kiss. The brilliant glow of the full moon, the light strains of a calypso band playing downstairs on the main deck, and the most handsome man I'd ever known gazing at me, his eyes filled of blatant desire.

His smile faded, and for a moment, it seemed maybe I'd misread the situation again and he'd changed his mind. But then he cupped my face in his hands, and he brought his lips so close to mine that I could feel his breath upon me. It took all my resolve not to reach up and kiss him. To take matters in my own hands and end the agony.

Finally, his lips brushed against mine so softly that I wasn't even sure they'd touched me.

"You're gonna be the death of me, Willow," he whispered against my mouth. "How can I say no to you?"

Our lips met fully, and the spark ignited. My back was against the rail, and my arms were wrapped around him as I clung to him, pulling him closer, though nothing seemed close enough.

He sank his fingers in my hair, loosening the braid until the entire mass of it blew free in the wind and surrounded us like an inferno of flames.

His hands were on my neck, down my back, along my arms, under my chin, and back in my hair.

I ran my fingers underneath the back of his shirt, digging my fingernails into the bare skin as he uttered a guttural sound deep in his throat. His lips left mine, pressing against my skin to leave kisses along my neck and across my shoulder.

His thumb grazed across my breast, and my nipple rose immediately beneath the thin, cotton dress. He returned his lips to my neck, and then his mouth covered mine, his thumb more aggressive as he rolled it back and forth, sending little shock waves of pleasure straight through me.

I could hear talking in the distance, and the reality of where we were and how public our display of affection was came creeping into my consciousness.

I pressed my hands against his chest and pulled my mouth from his long enough to whisper, "There's people. People are coming."

He claimed my mouth again, but then he pulled back far enough to look down at me between his lashes. His lips were swollen, and I lifted my fingers to touch my own bottom lip, surprised to find it completely numb despite the multitude of sensations I was feeling.

"You okay?" he asked, leaning his forehead against mine as he intertwined his fingers behind my back.

I nodded and grinned. "I'm wonderful."

His smile spread across his face. "Yes, you are, Willow. Yes, you are."

The group passed us, mumbling hellos as they went.

"I guess we should probably get our stuff together," Gerry said, pulling me in close and tucking my head beneath his chin. "From the lights of the harbor, we'll be docking soon."

"Do we have to?" I whispered. "Can't you just stop time? Stay here together?"

"Oh, God. You have no idea. You have no idea."

And he was right. I didn't have any idea.

Because he didn't tell me.

# 13 LIPSTICK STAIN

"Maggie, I hate to bother you, but I need your help." Tyler's voice on the other end of the line sounded panicked, and my thoughts immediately went to Cabe.

"Is everything okay? Are you alright? Is Cabe—"

"We're fine, everything's fine. I need to get the paperwork and the deposit out to Silver Creek Ranch before five today. There's another couple that wants Galen's date. I told Bronwyn I'd have our contract in by the end of the day, but the father of the bride for my morning wedding had a heart attack during pre-ceremony photos, and now we're at the hospital. They're going to try to do the vows in his hospital room, and then the bride and groom still want to have a reception back at the hotel. I've been on the phone for the last couple of hours trying to rearrange everything with all the vendors, and it just dawned on me that I have to get this out to the ranch. Is there any way you could take it for me?"

Her words ran together in her stressed state, and I was almost out of breath from listening to her. "Sure. Yes, no problem." I glanced at the clock and saw it was almost four. I'd be pushing it to reach the ranch before five, even if I left immediately. "What hospital? Do you have the paperwork with you, or do I need to go to your office to pick it up?"

"Um, I have it. I think it's in my briefcase. Let me make sure. It may be in the car."

I started packing up my things as I waited for her to answer, closing out of my email so I could shut the computer down.

"Yes, it's in my briefcase," she said. "I can meet you at the entrance of the hospital on Sand Lake."

"Okay," I grimaced. I'd have to face westbound traffic to get to the hospital, and then eastbound back to the turnpike entrance to head to Silver

Creek. "I don't think I'll be there before five."

Tyler sighed. "Let me call Bronwyn. I'll tell her what happened and see if I can take them tomorrow."

"No, don't do that. I'm already packed up and walking out of my office. I'll get them there, but does it have to be before five? Can it be a few minutes after?"

"Bronwyn has a meeting to go to so she won't be there after five. Let me call her and ask if there's some place you can leave the paperwork and the check. I'll see you in a few minutes."

My nerves were frazzled by the time I got to my car. The panic in Tyler's voice had started the process, and the abrupt interruption of my day and sudden departure from the office hadn't helped, but the realization that I was driving to Dax Pearson's ranch was what really put me on edge.

It had been over a week since our lunch at Tako Cheena, and though we'd left that day with the agreement that I would pick a place for our next lunch and let him know the date and time, I hadn't done either.

I'd made no effort to contact him, and he hadn't contacted me.

It wasn't that I hadn't enjoyed our lunch. I had. Too much, in fact.

Dax had consumed my thoughts for the rest of the day and evening, and he was the first thing I thought of when I awoke the next morning. He'd rarely left my mind for long since then.

That was dangerous. That was too close to being out of control.

Even though I would never admit it to her, Sandy was right when she'd told me that I choose to go out with people I have no intention of falling for. Without the intense attraction, it's easier to walk away. To cut ties and be out of the situation before I ever actually get in it.

But Dax was different. I could feel it. This was an attraction I had no control over. The connection was there, and it was strong. Immediate. Powerful.

I had no desire to pursue anything I couldn't walk away from, and I definitely wasn't willing to risk my heart. Not ever again.

No matter how handsome the cowboy was or how green his eyes may be or how many quivers his voice set off between my legs.

"I'm so sorry to dump this on you last minute," Tyler said as I pulled into the hospital entrance and reached out the window to take the file.

"It's no problem, really. I had no meetings this afternoon, and we're supposed to be tag-teaming this wedding planning, remember?"

I winked at her and squeezed her hand in mine. She looked tired, and the stress of the day had dulled the hazel of her eyes. I wanted to get out of the car and hug her, but time was of the essence.

"Hang in there, kid," I said. "I'm gonna call my son and tell him to have wine and a hot bath waiting for you when you get home."

"Oh, that sounds heavenly. Thanks, Maggie."

I pulled away from the hospital and dialed Cabe's number.

"Hey, Mom, what's up?"

"Hi, handsome. I just saw your wife, and she seems to be having quite the stressful day."

"Yeah, I talked to her earlier. Bummer about the father of the bride, but thankfully, they got him to the hospital in time. Ty said it looks like he'll make a full recovery."

"Yes. I told her I'd call you so you could have wine and a hot bath waiting for her."

He chuckled. "I'm a step ahead of you. I've got a bottle chilling, and I picked up her favorite sushi roll on the way home from work. I even bathed Deacon and vacuumed the whole house."

"That's my boy. Take care of your lady, and she'll take care of you."

"See, I listened to you!"

I smiled, and my heart warmed at the thought of Cabe being happy in his marriage.

Every bit of heartache I'd been through was worth it and then some if my kids could be happy, healthy adults who were able to love and be loved.

"So, I'm heading out to the Silver Creek Ranch to turn in your sister's paperwork and deposit. I guess we're going through with it. Can you believe she's getting married?"

"No. Poor Tate. I thought he was smarter than that."

"Cabe, be nice. Your sister is a great catch."

He laughed. "My sister is a high maintenance pain in the ass, and you know it. But Tate seems to love her, so I wish them all the best. You gonna see Mr. Pearson while you're there?"

I stiffened, tightening my hands on the wheel. "What do you mean?"

"I don't know," he said in a singsong voice. "A little bird told me there might be an attraction between the two of you when you met."

"Hardly," I lied. "He seems like a nice man, but he's not my type. Too outdoorsy."

"Opposites attract, Mom. Maybe you should give him a chance."

"I think your little bird's matchmaking aspirations have rubbed off on you."

"Just be open, okay? If there's something there, be willing to see what it is."

The phone beeped, and I looked at the radio display to see Tyler's name.

"Speak of the devil. Your little bird is calling me right now. Let me see what she needs."

"Okay, Mom. Love you."

"Love you, too, sweetheart!"

I pressed the button on the steering wheel to switch to Tyler's call. "I was just talking with your hubby on the other line, and somehow he got the idea that I have romance afoot at the ranch. Now why on earth would he think that?"

"Oh. I may have mentioned it."

"*Nooo*. Really?"

She laughed at my sarcastic tone.

"I'm sorry. I couldn't help it. You two seemed so cute together, and there was obviously an attraction there. Aren't you the least bit curious to find out more about him?"

I was quite a deal more than the least bit curious, and she didn't even know Dax and I had seen each other at the hospital or shared lunch together. Of course, she didn't need to know that.

"How's the bride's father?" I asked, blatantly changing the subject.

"Better. He's still stable, and the doctor has given permission for the bride, the groom and the officiant to be in the room with him and his wife for the vows. Everyone else will have to wait back at the hotel, but the officiant has agreed to do a second ceremony at the reception so all the guests can watch them exchange vows."

"Good. I'm glad it worked out. I know that must have been frightening for the bride. Well, for the entire family."

"Yes. Just when I think everything that could happen at a wedding has happened, something always surprises me."

"Life is like that."

"Hold on," she said, and I could hear her talking in muffled tones. "Be right there. I'm on the phone. Give me a second." Her voice came back on the line. "Okay, I'm back, but I need to go. I spoke with Bronwyn a few minutes ago, and she said you can leave the paperwork and the check underneath the black mat in front of the door. She'll swing back by after her meeting to pick it up so it's not out there all night."

"Okay. Got it. Best wishes to the bride and groom for me. Hope the rest of the event goes smoothly for you."

"Me too!"

We ended the call, and my thoughts turned to my destination.

Would Dax be there? Evidently not, if Bronwyn had left instructions to leave the papers under the mat.

Where on the property did he live? The driveway we'd taken had been long and narrow, winding quite a ways off the main road to reach the reception hall. I didn't remember seeing any other drives shooting off that one, but I didn't know where the road continued after we turned into the parking area for the hall. The barn was visible from where we'd parked, and I'd assumed the drive went there, but was his house perhaps beyond that?

In the few times we'd talked, we hadn't gotten into the particulars of his day-to-day work. Would he be in the barn when I arrived, or was there an office somewhere else on the property?

What would his reaction be if he was there? Would he be happy to see me or irritated that I didn't call? Maybe he hadn't even given it a second thought. After all, he hadn't called me to inquire about where and when our next encounter would be, so maybe he was relieved that I didn't call again.

I turned up the radio to drown out the chatter in my brain, cursing my thoughts for being so utterly consumed with someone I barely knew.

By the time I'd reached the iron gates of the ranch, I'd gone through every channel preset and two cycles of scanning in an attempt to find something to distract me. My thoughts kept returning to Dax no matter what song I landed on.

I paid closer attention than I had when Tyler and I navigated the drive the first time, noticing the length of the wooden fence that lined either side of the road and wondering if Dax had been the one to paint it black. There was a second fence behind the first, made of wire, and I couldn't help but question why anyone would go to the trouble of erecting two fences when the drive was easily over a half a mile long.

The house came into view as I rounded the last curve, and my breath caught at the sight of it framed against the lake with the sun setting in the background. The water glowed behind it in vivid shades of orange, pink, and yellow, and the leaves of the large oak tree to the right of the house were a brilliant green in the waning golden rays. It was a beautiful estate, and my mind drifted again to the master suite upstairs and the change in plans Bronwyn had mentioned.

Whoever had built the house had obviously chosen its placement carefully. It was underneath the only large tree anywhere nearby, and I wondered if the creek flowing beneath the floor was a planned feature from the get-go or if it had been a means to an end in having the house under the tree with that view of the lake and the setting sun.

I pulled my car into the circle drive and reached to grab the folder from my passenger seat, pausing to check my makeup in the rearview mirror and telling myself my concern with my appearance had nothing to do with the ranch's owner.

A few fluffs from my fingers and my hair looked good as new, but my makeup seemed a bit pale in the fading light. I pinched my cheeks to bring some color and dug through my purse for lipstick.

I had just leaned forward toward the mirror with my mouth open, lipstick in hand to reapply, when a loud tap on the window startled me. I screamed and dropped the open tube, immediately letting loose a swear word as it hit my pants leg and deflected onto the console and into the floorboard, leaving a trail of deep burgundy splotches as it went.

Dax stood patiently as I retrieved the lipstick and then turned the key to power the window down.

"I didn't mean to startle you," he said. "Sorry about that."

"It's okay. I wasn't expecting anyone to be here."

His eyebrows lifted as though to question why I would be applying makeup for no one, but to his credit, he didn't say anything.

"Here," I said, handing him the folder. "I was supposed to leave this under the mat for Bronwyn. Could you make sure she gets it?"

He took it and opened it, perusing the contract for the briefest of moments before closing the folder and looking back down at me with a grin.

"Well, darn. Here I thought you had decided we were doing dinner instead of lunch."

Warmth flooded my cheeks and dispelled any paleness that might have been there before.

"Oh. About that…."

Dax tapped the folder against his leg and chuckled. "It's alright. I understand. You were blown away by how great my choice was for lunch, and now the pressure's on. You've been feeling intimidated by having to follow up my success, and that's why you haven't scheduled our lunch yet."

The warmth of his eyes and the openness of his smile were contagious, and I felt any nervousness begin to melt away.

"You guessed it. You figured me out," I said, returning the smile as he leaned forward and braced his hands on the car door.

"I tell you what. I'll give you a few hints. You know. Help you out a bit. The only things I don't eat are liver and raisins. I mean, not together. Separately. Although, come to think of it, I definitely wouldn't want them together, either."

"Okay. Noted. No liver. No raisins. No liver and raisin combo."

"And I'm not too crazy about fondue."

I laughed, more from the feeling of happiness that had overtaken me than from the humor in anything he'd said. As impossible as it seemed, I had missed him. This man I barely knew, whose presence I'd only been in less than a handful of times. Yet, that was the feeling. As I listened to him talk and my eyes took in the features of his face, I realized how much I'd wanted to see him again.

"What on earth is wrong with fondue?" I asked as I tilted my head to one side and peered at him. "It's dipping in cheese and chocolate. What's not to like?"

He stood up straight and stretched his back, moving his arms out to the side and twisting back and forth as he spoke. "Nothing's wrong with it if you aren't hungry, I suppose. Going to a restaurant where you have to cook your own food is bad enough, but when you can only cook it one bite at a time? That's torture. If I'm gonna do that much work preparing a meal, I want to be standing over a grill and be able to eat the whole thing once I sit down."

"Okay. Another point noted. No fondue."

"I mean, other than that, I'm easy. You ought to be able to find some place to take me that fits outside those parameters."

I couldn't stop smiling as he stood there talking, looking so damned irresistible that I had to force my eyes to maintain eye contact. I'd caught myself staring at his bicep as he crooked his arm to adjust his hat, and my mind immediately took me back to the image of him pulling his shirt over his head as he walked from the water. I bit my lip and shifted slightly in my seat.

He'd obviously been working in some capacity when I arrived. His jeans were dusty and marred with dirt. His T-shirt was snug against his chest and damp with sweat, and he smelled more of horses and barns than his usual spearmint, lavender, and sage, but somehow it was still alluring.

"I'll let you know what I find," I managed to say.

"I look forward to it. So, we're having a wedding, huh?"

"Excuse me?"

He held the folder up and waved it. "Your daughter? You're dropping off a contract and a check?"

"Oh. Yes. A wedding. Yes."

His grin broadened, and I hoped he couldn't see the effect he had on me. I was certain he hadn't reached his age in life without realizing he was a good-looking man. He was probably quite accustomed to female admiration, but I had no interest in playing the part of fawning older woman. If I was the older woman. Without asking his age, I had no way of knowing for sure.

I studied the stubble on his chin and noted a bit of salt and pepper interspersed. It was hard to gauge from the lines on his face with him tanned the way he was, but surely he had to be at least forty-five. Maybe even a couple of years older.

Not that it mattered. It wasn't like I was auditioning him for a romantic interest. Still, curiosity made me wonder.

The pause in conversation grew longer as we both stared at each other, and the thought occurred to me that I might not be the only one sizing things up and being curious.

A dog barked in the distance, and Dax turned in the direction of the barn, the movement snapping me out of my daze and returning me to reality.

"I should go," I said, putting my hand on the key in the ignition. "I'm sure you have things to do, and I've got a long drive back."

He looked down at me, but then the dog howled, and he turned toward the barn again before meeting my eyes once more.

"Hey. Before you go, would you be willing to help me with something?"

The momentary sadness I'd felt at my impending departure lifted, and I answered with a bit more enthusiasm than I'd meant to.

"Sure!"

"Come with me. You can leave your car there." He opened my door and held it as I stepped out.

# 14 PUPPY LOVE

"Should I grab my coat?" I asked as I stepped from the car.

"Sure, if you think you'll be cold."

"This coming from the man wearing a short-sleeved shirt in February."

"Today wasn't cold. It was a beautiful day. Good day to be working outdoors."

Another howl pierced the air, and Dax whistled loudly in the direction of the sound.

"Is that your dog?" I asked.

"One of them. He's the loudest, for sure."

I grabbed my coat from the back seat and shook my head as Dax offered to help me put it on.

"I got it," I said, smiling as he held both hands up and took a step back.

"Just offering."

"I appreciate the kindness behind the offer."

"Let me put this folder inside before I end up leaving it in the barn and it getting lost. Bronwyn would kill me, and I'm sure you'd be none too pleased yourself."

I waited by the car as he walked to the front door and unlocked it, stepping inside only long enough to drop the folder on the small table by the door before locking it again and walking toward me.

A shiver ran up my spine and across my limbs at the sight of him approaching. All muscle. All cowboy. All man. Damn.

"You're shivering. You cold already?" he asked. "I've got a coat in the barn if you need it. Might be heavier than that one you're wearing, but it probably smells like horses."

"I'm not that cold. Yet."

The dog barked again, and farther out in the woods beyond the barn, another dog answered him.

"Is he okay?"

"He's fine. He's just sounding the alarm that I'm not moving quick enough for him. That other one you heard just now, she's the one we need to help. I found her about an hour ago, and she'd given birth to a litter. Nine puppies in all, and all of them breathing when I left. I want to get them in the barn for the night. It'll be too cold for them out there. I'd come up here to get a blanket to move them when I saw your car in the drive."

As we got closer to the barn, I saw his truck parked beneath an overhang. A large black and white dog was pacing in the back. He let out another howl when he saw us getting near.

"I'm coming, Cody. Calm down."

"Why doesn't he jump out of the truck?"

"Because I told him to stay," Dax said in a matter-of-fact tone.

"Oh. Okay."

"Let me grab the blanket. You want to stay here so you don't get your shoes dirty?" he asked, looking down at the Manolo pumps I wore.

"Sure."

"Although, I guess that's going to limit how far you can go into the woods. I didn't think about that. Would you be horribly opposed to sliding your feet down in a pair of rubber boots?"

I chuckled at the mental image of me wearing a pair of rubber boots with my tan slacks. "No, I'm not opposed to it, but how far out in the woods are we going?"

"Oh, it's not far, and we haven't had any rain to speak of recently, so there's not any mud, but I'd hate for you to mess up your shoes on my account."

The distant bark rang out again, and Cody danced back and forth in the bed of the truck, grumbling and groaning.

"I hear her, buddy," Dax said, ruffling the dog's fur and patting its head. "We're headed that way. Give me a minute."

Dax disappeared inside the barn and returned moments later with a large wool blanket, dotted here and there with bits of hay. He tossed it in the back of the truck and handed me the ugliest black rubber boots I'd ever seen in my life.

I put up my hands in refusal. "I'm sorry. Do you have anything in a different color?"

His eyes widened, and I burst out laughing. "I'm kidding! They're fine. Give them to me."

He grinned, but a bit of uncertainty lingered in his eyes.

I kicked off my shoes and braced my hand on the side of the truck to balance as I slid my feet inside the cold boots.

My toes curled in rebellion against the damp feel of the rubber, but as I tucked my pants into the tops of the boots and stamped my feet into place, they were actually much more comfortable than the heels I'd been wearing all day.

I laughed at the sight of my slacks shoved into the barn boots, and when I looked up at Dax he was shaking his head with a grin.

"This is certainly a fashion statement I've never made before," I said, taking a few exaggerated steps in the boots. "What do you think?" I asked as I pointed my toes on the left foot and then the right, doing a little twirl as best I could in the clumsy shoes. "Is this a look I should wear more often?"

"No, the coat's all wrong. You need a black coat if you're gonna wear black boots," he said, his grin growing as he held the truck door open and waited for me to climb inside. I made it in with a little more ease than the first two times I'd ridden with him, and I was thankful yet again that I wasn't wearing a skirt.

Cody barked as Dax went around to the driver's side to get in and start the truck, and he didn't stop barking as we followed the paved drive down to a gate, which Dax got out to open and then got out again to close behind us.

"What are you keeping in with the gate?" I asked when we were on our way again.

"Cattle. There shouldn't be any in this pasture, but it's a habit ingrained to always close the gate behind me. Life on the ranch."

"You said you had a big cattle operation. How big is your ranch?"

He shrugged. "This side, the Silver Creek side, has three separate pastures, but the bulk of the ranch is beyond that tree line. It's twenty-five thousand acres total.

I may have let out an audible gasp.

"Twenty-five thousand acres? Are you kidding me?"

"Why would I kid you about that?"

We left the dirt path we'd been on since the gate and ventured across the grass. I could see faint tracks where he'd come this way earlier.

"That's a lot of acres."

He nodded. "Yep. It is. Most of it's been in my family since somewhere around 1872."

"Wow. I had no idea. I didn't see anything about this on the wedding website."

"No. You wouldn't. Silver Creek Ranch is a separate entity. Separate business. It's on family land, but my father deeded it to me when...well, when I started it. To find the big ranch, you'd have to be looking for Pearson Cattle and Citrus."

He stopped the truck and got out, reaching to grab the blanket from the back.

"Cody, out."

The dog sailed out the back of the truck and danced around Dax's legs like the happiest creature on the planet.

"You coming?" Dax asked, his hand on his door.

"Oh. I thought—oh—never mind." I hastened to open my door, surprised and a bit embarrassed that I'd been sitting there waiting for him to open it.

"Sorry," he mumbled. "I noticed you don't seem to care for me doing things like opening the door, so I'm trying to be more respectful of your wishes." His cheeks held the faintest hint of color, and he looked away as he said it, snapping his fingers for Cody to fall in line beside him. "She's right this way."

I followed close behind him, trying to put my feet wherever he stepped lest there be some snake or other creature underfoot. The light was fading fast now that the sun had broken the horizon, and the woods ahead of us looked dark and uninviting.

If anyone had told me earlier in the day that by nightfall I would be embarking on a hike in the woods with Dax Pearson, I would have said they were nuts. But there I was, tromping into the unknown in a pair of borrowed rubber boots.

Cody ran ahead of us, but his white patches were easy to spot in the distance. He had stopped barking, and when we reached him, he was sitting near the mama dog, watching as Dax knelt beside her with the blanket.

Her puppies squirmed as they fought to get closer to their mother's warmth and her milk, their eyes not yet open but their mouths eager and seeking.

"Oh, my goodness. Look at them! They're so tiny," I said, squatting beside Dax. The mama dog looked up at me with wide, weary eyes, and I couldn't tell if they held fear or gratitude. Maybe both. "What's her name?"

Dax shrugged. "I have no idea."

My head turned quickly in surprise. "What? You don't have a name for her?"

"She's not my dog."

"Whose dog is she?"

He shrugged again. "I don't know."

"Well, how'd she get here?"

His eyebrows scrunched together as he surveyed the puppies and laid the blanket out beside the mother. "She walked here."

I frowned at Dax, but he was too focused on the task at hand to notice. "I assumed she *walked*. From where? Does she live on the big ranch?"

He shook his head. "She's not one of ours. She's a stray. Happened to make it this far before she went into labor. I'm going to wrap the puppies up in the blanket and have you carry them, and I'll pick her up and carry her. She hasn't been moving much, so I'm worried she may be injured. I didn't want to distress her by taking them to the truck without her, or moving her without them. With you here to help me, we can move them at the same time so she knows they're coming with her."

I nodded, touched by the compassion and care he was showing the stray.

The puppies grunted and squealed as he pulled them from her, and she raised up on her side to watch him. I worried she may nip at him or at me, but she seemed to understand that we were trying to help.

The darkness was advancing faster beneath the trees, and a cold breeze swept across us. I shivered against it and tucked my coat tighter around me before stretching my arms toward Dax. He handed the squirming bundle to me, and I stood, careful not to let any of the puppies fall out of the blanket.

The mother's yelp as they left her sight tore at my heart, and I crouched back down beside her.

"They're right here," I cooed, pulling back the blanket from their heads so she could see them. "We're not taking them from you. Your babies are safe and warm."

Dax moved his hands carefully over her abdomen, and then he gingerly pressed his fingers along her spine and both back legs. She didn't move as he examined her, but her eyes darted back and forth from Dax's prodding fingers to the squiggly bundle in my arms.

He frowned and sat back on his heels, scratching his chin.

"Is she okay?" I asked.

"I think she's just exhausted. I don't feel any breaks or obvious injuries. There's no puncture wounds from an animal and no road rash from a car. Who knows how far she walked before she had them. She may just be tired. Hungry, I bet. Thirsty, too."

"Maybe she belongs to one of your neighbors."

He chuckled as he bent to slide his hands beneath her, slow and gentle. "That's the thing about having so much land. You don't have many neighbors."

The dog protested with a whimper as he lifted her from the ground, and he whispered to her, his voice so low and soft that I couldn't make out his words. Whatever he said must have worked, because she relaxed against him.

We walked side by side so she could smell her puppies and know they were near.

For the most part, the puppies settled into the blanket and lay still. A couple of adventurers tried to go under my arm or push against the blanket above them until their little noses were visible.

It was dark by the time we got back to the truck, and Dax paused for a minute as he reached the tailgate.

"What's wrong?" I asked, my eyes immediately going to the sweet dog in his arms.

"Nothing. Just trying to decide if it would be better for her in the back of the truck or if I should try to get her on the floorboard. I'm afraid she's gonna get jostled either way, but she'd probably rather be near her pups."

"Put her back here," I said, indicating the truck bed. "I'll ride back here with the puppies so she can be with them."

I could see the surprise in his eyes as he turned to look at me.

"You sure?"

"Yes. Why not? You can't get her in and out of the floorboard easily. I don't want her worried about her babies. So, we'll all ride back here. With Cody."

The confidence in my voice was purposeful, because my mind was freaking out over the prospect of riding in the back of a truck, across a field, in the dark, with one possibly injured dog and one extremely hyper one.

"Cody. Up. Lay down."

The big dog leapt in the back of the truck and immediately lay on his stomach, head on his paws.

"Wow. He really minds you. I wish my kids would have minded me that well."

"Yeah, well, you've seen the extent of his commands. He can't herd cows, he can't run hogs, and he's never met a stranger. So, he's pretty worthless as far as a ranch dog goes. Goofball!"

His warm smile as he looked at Cody left no doubt as to the affection he felt for the dog.

I stepped aside so he could ease the mama into the back of the truck, once again whispering to her in low, hushed tones as he pulled his arms from beneath her, patting her head as she licked his hand.

"Wanna hand me the blanket?"

I nodded and shifted the puppies in my arms to give him the bundle. He laid them next to their mother and opened the blanket just enough for her to be able to nuzzle and reassure them.

He turned to me, lifting his hand, then dropping it, and then lifting it again. "Do you want me to help you get up?"

I smiled at his uncertainty, and then looked at the distance between the ground and the truck bed. "Oh, I'm definitely going to need your help. How do I do this?"

He smiled. "Oh, that's right. If you don't remember ever riding in the front of a truck, I'm thinking it's a sure bet you've never been in the back of one."

"Definitely a sure bet. Is there a graceful way to do this?"

Dax laughed, and I laughed back, not accustomed to being nervous about how to move my body.

"I can't say I've ever seen anyone climb in the back of a truck gracefully, but I promise no matter how awful you look doing it, me and Cody and the little mama won't tell anybody, and the puppies' eyes aren't even open yet. So, your secret's safe with us."

"Then let's do this before I lose my nerve and put you back here while I drive the truck."

"We can do that if you'd rather."

"No. I can do this. If she can walk across the wilderness and give birth to nine babies, I can climb up in the back of the truck and keep her company."

Dax's smile beamed. "Would it completely offend you if I picked you up and set you in the truck so you don't have to climb up? That might be more graceful, if that's what you're worried about."

The thought of his arms around me made my knees weak, and the anticipation of his touch set my skin on fire.

"Okay," I said, my voice more of a whisper than I'd intended.

He put his hands on my waist and lifted me as though I were a feather, setting me on the tailgate without the least sign of effort.

He pulled away quickly, almost like he'd been burned, and I could feel the heat where his hands had been, despite the layers of clothes between his skin and mine.

"I think you can take it from here," he said, adjusting his hat.

"I think so." I spun my legs around onto the truck bed and scooted backwards on my coat until I was next to the puppies.

"Hold onto the side of the truck if you need to. I'll go slow."

"I appreciate that."

# 15 WITHOUT CRACKERS

True to his word, Dax took his time getting us back to the barn, and by the time he parked the truck, a couple of the puppies had found their way out of the blanket and nestled themselves against their mother to nurse again.

Cody lay in his place, watching me and the puppies with wide eyes, his tail wagging each time I made eye contact with him.

"Y'all okay back here?" Dax asked as he exited the truck. "Everybody survive the ride? Gracefully?"

I laughed. "That is the most graceful ride I've ever taken in the back of a truck."

"I'm glad the bar wasn't set too high."

He held out his hand and I grabbed it, bracing for the current I knew I'd feel when we touched. Despite the cold chill of the night air, warmth flowed through me as he tightened his hand around mine.

He pulled me forward to the edge of the tailgate and before I could jump down, he placed his hands on my waist to pick me up.

When he'd lifted me from standing to sitting, it was a swift motion that held no contact other than his hands on my coat. But from a seated position, Dax needed to edge forward between my knees to have leverage to pick me up.

His eyes caught mine and held there, and for a moment, time stopped. His breathing slowed, and the heat generated in the space between the two of us almost made me envy him for not having the heavy layer of a coat.

The pressure of his touch tightened, and he slid my weight forward as he stepped back, standing me on the ground with my back against the tailgate.

His hands lingered at my waist, nothing at all like the fast retreat they'd made before, and I didn't dare look up at him because I feared the desire raging inside me would be mirrored in his eyes.

Cody wasn't nearly as enamored of the moment as Dax and I were. He grumbled and shifted his weight, sending a clear signal to his owner that he was ready to leave the truck no matter how long we wanted to stand there.

The moment was gone, and Dax took another step back, taking his hands away from me even as I longed for them to stay.

"Cody, down."

The dog complied immediately, and I watched Dax as he covered the puppies back up in the blanket. When he'd gathered them and wrapped them up, he placed them in my arms, his eyes on mine as his hands brushed against my skin on his way out from under the bundle.

"Okay, old girl," he said, and I blinked, startled. "Let's get you out of this truck and settled into some warm hay."

I was relieved when he turned to face the mama dog as he talked, and I chuckled at my original thought that he meant me.

He lifted her into his arms and moved past me toward the barn, flipping the light switch with his elbow as we entered with me as close behind him as possible so the little family wouldn't think they'd been separated.

He led us past several stalls, and I nodded at the horses we passed along the way, each of them standing with noses out toward us, curious to see who was moving in.

I eyed Kratos with a more wary glance, but he turned away from us, perhaps deciding we weren't worth his interest.

Dax stopped in a stall at the rear of the barn, laying the mama dog in the nest of hay on the floor.

"There you go," he said. "Rest now with your babies."

I knelt beside her and laid the blanket on the ground, opening it so the pups could make their way home.

"I'll be right back," he said. "I need to get her some food and water."

Cody followed him as he walked away, and I glanced around me at the horses' inquisitive stares before tucking the blanket under the mama and babies to ensure their warmth.

"Dinner is served!" Dax returned, bending to place a bowl of dog food on the hay and then kneeling to put a bowl of water beside it. "You hungry? Thirsty?"

He ran the back of his hand along the top of her head, and she nuzzled him. He scooped up a handful of water and drizzled it over her mouth, and she responded.

It didn't take her long at all to rouse herself enough to get to the water bowl. She drank long and hard, and I wondered how long it had been since she'd had water.

She rubbed her wet muzzle against Dax's jeans and then took a hesitant bite of the food he held as the puppies clamored around her, trying to nurse even as she was attempting to feed herself.

"She seems to be standing fine," Dax said. "I'd like to see her walk a few steps so I can tell if she's limping, but I'll leave her alone for now. Let her eat."

"Maybe it was because she was hungry and tired. Dehydrated." I reached to pat her back, and she looked over her shoulder at me before continuing her meal.

"Speaking of hungry," Dax said as he stood, "I'm starving. I know it's technically your turn and all, but I've got a pot of chili that's been simmering all day. Would you like a bowl?"

He offered his hand to help me stand, and I ignored the offer and stood on my own.

"No, thank you. I should head back."

I brushed the hay off my pants as I walked to the barn entrance and realized I was still wearing the black boots.

"Oh. My shoes. I was about to wear these home!"

He gave a little chuckle and retrieved my heels from the shelf by the door.

"You sure you don't want to stay and eat?" He leaned against the door of a stall and watched me struggle to remove the boots. "I make a mean bowl of chili. Beats driving the hour or so back to Orlando to eat. Trust me, there's nothing between here and there."

I wanted to stay. I wanted to ask questions and get answers and spend more time listening to him talk. But fear had reared its ugly head and reminded me not to get too close.

"I'll be fine until I get home. But thanks."

He stood up straight and stretched again, covering a yawn with his hand.

"Besides," I added, "it looks like you need to get some sleep."

"Not before I eat! At least let me make you a bowl to take with you. You can eat it when you get home. I guarantee you'll say it's the best chili you've ever tasted."

I hadn't even thought about dinner before he mentioned it, but once he brought up chili, hunger pangs gripped my stomach. I reasoned that it couldn't hurt to take a bowl to go.

"Okay, that would be nice. Thank you."

He led me through a hallway and into a larger section of more stalls, but there were only a couple of horses there.

We continued to the back of the barn, and I had begun to think maybe he had a loft apartment upstairs. Instead, he pulled open a wide sliding door to reveal a fifth-wheel travel trailer parked behind the building. There was a hammock tied from the camper to a small tree near the barn, and a long, wooden picnic table at the rear of the camper where a grill and wet bar extended from its exterior. A large screen television hung beneath the awning on the side of the camper, and there were two canvas lounge chairs in front of it.

"This is where you live?" I asked, trying not to register shock on my face as I took in the unexpected setting.

"Home sweet home," Dax said as he swung open the door and climbed the steps to go inside.

The interior was more spacious than I'd expected, with slide-outs on the other side of the camper to expand the living room seating area and dining table. A full kitchen with granite countertops and a center island dominated the space to the left, and I could see a staircase at the end of a short hallway leading to parts unknown. An electric fireplace glowed beneath the large television on the wall where we'd entered.

"Wait. You have twenty-five thousand acres, a barn bigger than most apartment buildings, and a house next door with a master bedroom to die for, but you live here? Behind your barn? In a camper?"

Dax shrugged as he removed the lid from the Crockpot and stirred the chili.

The rich, spicy aroma filled my nostrils, and my stomach growled in response.

"It's got everything I need, and if I get ready to go somewhere else, I can hitch it to the truck and take it with me."

He tasted the chili and closed his eyes with a moan before looking at me with that irresistible grin. "You don't know how lucky you are. This might just be the best batch I've ever made."

I joined him at the kitchen counter and gazed over into the pot, nearly salivating at the smell.

"Maybe I could stay for a quick bite."

He laughed and reached in the cabinet above us to pull out two bowls.

I turned to survey the room more closely as he busied himself scooping out the chili and gathering the condiments from the refrigerator.

A keyboard sat alongside the sofa, and a guitar was propped against the recliner. Sheet music and notebook paper littered the sofa cushions, and I couldn't resist the urge to walk over and take a peek at what he'd been playing.

The notes were handwritten, and it appeared from the markings and obvious erasures that he was in the middle of composing a song.

"Do you write music?" I asked, turning to face him.

"I try. Sour cream? Cheese? Green onions?"

"All of the above. What kind of music do you write?"

"Evidently the kind that's difficult to get right. I write songs all the time, but I never seem to get them exactly like I want them. You want a glass of tea? It's sweet."

I laid the paper back on the sofa where I'd found it. "I'll have water."

He set the bowls on the dining table, and I debated whether it would be inappropriate to ask him to play.

My mind was reeling from the revelation that the perfectly chiseled, philanthropic, animal-loving cowboy in front of me was also a musician and a writer.

The universe was either being very cruel to me or very kind. It was hard to know which.

"Ice or room temperature?"

"Ice, please. So, you play the keyboard and the guitar?"

He nodded as he held my glass beneath the dispenser in the refrigerator door and filled it with ice.

"You like music? I can turn on the stereo. Have some ambience while we eat?"

I pictured him turning on some cheesy mood music, and suddenly the casual bowl of chili seemed layered with ulterior motives. I wavered for a moment, uncertain if I should stay.

He picked up a remote and aimed it at the shelves in front of him, and I cringed as I waited for the romantic playlist to start. Instead, the familiar strains of AC/DC's *Back in Black* filled the room around me.

"Whoa! Too loud. Sorry about that," he said as he lowered the volume. "Ready to eat?"

I smiled and relaxed once more. I never thought I'd be happy to hear someone play AC/DC as dinner music.

He'd mentioned before that he was starving, and his eagerness to be seated and eat was apparent as he motioned for me to come to the table and pulled the chair out for me. We both pushed it in once I was seated.

"It looks amazing." I took the paper towel he offered and laid it across my lap, staring at the presentation of chili with a dollop of sour cream, a sprinkling of cheese, and a spattering of green onions.

"We're using the fancy napkins tonight," he joked as he tore off a paper towel for himself and then took his seat.

"Well, it is chili."

"Not just any chili, though. Take a bite. Go ahead. You'll see."

I plunged the spoon in and blew at the steam that rose from the bite I gathered, making eye contact with Dax as I put it in my mouth. His eyes were bright with anticipation, and he leaned forward with his elbows on the table as he waited to hear my verdict.

An explosion of flavors hit my taste buds as I savored it on my tongue. The pungency of cumin, the bite of cayenne, and the bitter tang of sour cream, with a blend of more spices that mixed perfectly with the tomatoes and beans.

"Well? What do you think?" His smile lit up his whole face, and even had it not been the best chili I'd ever eaten, I wouldn't have said anything to disappoint him and diminish that smile.

I nodded and wiped my mouth with the paper towel. "I think…that's probably the best damned chili I've ever had."

He slapped the table and laughed. "I knew it! I told you. I've been first runner-up for the past three years at the ranch's chili cook-off. But this recipe—" he pointed to the bowl with his spoon before digging in "—this recipe is the winner. Mark my words, I'm taking home the trophy this year."

I swallowed the second bite and nodded again. "I think you're right. Of course, I haven't tried the competition, but they'd have to be pretty good to beat this."

"Oh, crackers. I forgot crackers. You want some? I don't do crackers in my chili, so I forget other people like it. I have them."

He pushed back his chair, but I waved my hand at him, covering my mouth while I chewed and swallowed.

"No, thank you. I'm enjoying it just the way it is."

We ate in silence for a few more bites, and then there was a knock at his door.

"Come on in," he shouted, not even bothering to get up to see who it was first.

I was surprised to see Bronwyn enter, and she appeared equally surprised to see me.

"Ms. Shaw, Tyler has been calling you. She's awful worried that she hasn't heard from you. She left me several messages but I was in my night class and he doesn't allow us to have our phones out. I saw your car in the drive when I came to pick up the contract."

My hand went to my throat as I stood. "I'm so sorry. My phone! I left it in the car. I didn't realize…I didn't… I have to call her. I need to go."

I moved toward the door, and Dax stood.

"Wait, I'll put your chili in a plastic bowl. You can take it with you."

"It's okay. I need to get on the road. I'm sure Tyler's worried sick. I'm surprised she and my son aren't out searching for me." I turned back to Bronwyn. "They're not, are they?"

She shook her head. "I called her when I got out of class and told her I'd let her know if the contract was here. And then I called her when I got here and told her your car was parked out front and that I'd call her back when I found you."

Great. The last thing I needed was for my matchmaking daughter-in-law to find out I'd had dinner with Dax. She'd have our wedding planned before the weekend.

"Where's your phone, Uncle Dax? I tried to call you, too."

He had dumped the contents of my bowl into a plastic container and was pressing the lid into place as he walked toward me.

His hand went to his pocket, and he frowned as he handed me the chili.

"Must be in the barn. Maybe the truck. I'll walk Maggie back to her car and see if I can find it."

Bronwyn nodded, looking back and forth between the two of us, curiosity dancing in her eyes.

I opened my mouth to explain about the puppies so she would know why the two of us were having dinner together, but Dax spoke before I could get the words out.

"Your coat. Don't forget your coat." He lifted it from the sofa and held it open for me to put my arms inside. I was so distracted in the moment that I didn't even think to protest about his help, but when he made to go out the door with Bronwyn and me, I stopped him.

"You don't have to walk me to my car. I'm sure Bronwyn can show me the way, and your chili's getting cold. Go eat."

He smiled, and my body reacted despite the stress.

"Don't be ridiculous," he said. "It's the least I can do after you stayed and helped me. It's my fault you've got the APB out on you now."

Bronwyn's eyes narrowed, and I knew she was dying to ask, but she refrained.

The three of us walked through the barn and along the drive back up to my car where it was parked in front of the main house. Bronwyn thanked me for bringing the contract and excused herself to go inside and retrieve it, shooting a questioning glance at her uncle as she walked away.

Dax held open my car door and I bent to get my phone from the cup holder.

"Seven missed calls. Five from Tyler and two from Cabe. Oh boy. I'm in trouble."

He chuckled. "Well, I hope you don't get grounded, because I'm looking forward to see where you take me for lunch."

I looked up at him, his eyes sparkling in the light coming from the lamppost by the garage. My heart was racing, and I felt like a teenager, waiting to see if she might get kissed. My mind scorned the thought, and I turned away from him and sat down in the car, reaching to pull the door shut.

I'd left the window down not realizing how long I'd be gone, and the car was damp and cold with the night air.

Dax leaned forward and braced his hands against the car's door frame as I turned the key in the ignition and switched the heat on, rubbing my hands together against the chill.

"Thank you," he said, his voice solemn and thick.

I met his eyes and swallowed hard at the emotion I saw there.

"I had a nice time tonight." He smiled as he said it, and though his voice had returned to normal, his eyes still held a tinge of sadness.

"Me too," I admitted. "It was an adventure."

"Life should always be an adventure." His grin widened, and he tapped the windowsill with his hand as he stood.

My phone rang in my lap. It was Tyler, and I took a deep breath, not eager to have the inevitable conversation.

"No liver, no raisins, and no fondue," he said as he backed away from the car. "Drive carefully."

I nodded and pressed the button on the steering wheel to answer the call, refusing to look at him again as I drove away.

# 16 MAKING CHOICES

It didn't take long to assure Tyler I was alive and well, and when she found out I'd been unreachable due to dinner with Dax Pearson, she was nearly beside herself. Her enthusiasm only added to my apprehension.

I called Sandy as soon as I hung up with Tyler, knowing my old friend would understand the panic I was feeling.

"I don't see the problem," she said when I'd explained the evening's activities. "You enjoy his company. You're attracted to him. He's obviously attracted to you, but he seems to be taking it slowly and respecting your distance. How is this not the best thing ever?"

So much for understanding.

"Sandy! C'mon. You know I don't like this dating thing, and you know why I don't. I need to stay away from this guy, but it's like the more I see him, the more I want to see him."

"That's generally how attraction works, Mags."

"I don't want to be attracted to him!"

"Sounds like it might be too late for that. Why not explore it? See where it takes you. What's the worst thing that could happen?"

I sighed and lay back against the headrest as I stared at the dotted line in the beam of my headlights.

"You have to ask?"

"Look, I know you had a rough break. No one deserves what happened to you, and no one can fault you for being gun shy. But I say twenty-six years is long enough. You're not getting any younger. Maybe it's time to take a chance, and if this guy's as special as you describe him, you might not want to pass him up."

"Gee, thanks. Nothing says reassurance like telling me I'm getting old and this may be my last prospect."

She laughed. "That's not what I said. Hell, I haven't even met the guy. But the way you talk about him, I hear something in your voice that tells me this one's different."

"He *is* different. That's what worries me. I don't want to give up my independence."

"Who said you have to? It's only lunch."

"Yeah, and only lunch leads to only dinner which leads to only more than I want to deal with. I like my life. I like being able to do whatever I want whenever I want."

"I think you're getting ahead of yourself. Why does going to lunch with the cowboy mean you can't do what you want to do? Don't over think it."

I groaned and wished matters of the heart weren't so complicated.

"Look, Maggie, if you enjoy being around him, then be around him. If you get to a point where you don't enjoy it, then don't. Part of being independent and being able to choose what you want to do with your time is that if you want to share it with someone, you can. It doesn't make you less independent if you get pleasure from being with someone else."

"Oh, really? Look at your life," I said. "You're uprooting your business that you've spent years building to follow Hannah to Orlando."

"Yes, because I *choose* to. She's my partner, and I want what's best for her. I believe this opportunity will not only enhance Hannah's career but also improve both our lives in the long run. Besides, it gets me closer to you!"

"Don't get me wrong—I'm thrilled that you're moving closer, and I'm happy for Hannah. But you're making your decisions based on her life. I don't think I want to be in that position again. Where I'm giving up my own dreams and my own security for someone else. I think I'm better off on my own."

"First of all, I'm not giving up my dreams. I'm still going to do the job I love, but in a different city. Plus, she and I made these decisions together. It was a mutual decision for the life we've built together. But hey, if you don't want to date, don't date. Call the guy up, tell him you're not interested, and you don't ever have to see him again."

Disappointment washed over me at the thought of never seeing Dax Pearson again. Of never looking in his eyes, or seeing his mouth break into that grin that melts my insides, or hearing the deep, rich rumble of his voice. I couldn't deny that I wanted to know what it was like to be held in his arms. To have his mouth on mine and feel the touch of his hands on my skin.

I took a deep breath and let it out slow, fighting my body's immediate response to my train of thoughts.

It had to be hormones out of control. It couldn't be normal to react so strongly to the mere thought of intimacy.

"You still there?" Sandy asked.

"Yes."

"You okay?"

"Yes."

She paused, and I struggled to find the words to express everything I was feeling.

"It's okay to be scared, Mags." Her voice was quiet, somber and soothing. "It's okay to be cautious. But it's also okay to feel. To want to be with someone. To be attracted."

I nodded even though she had no way of seeing me. I didn't trust my voice to speak without betraying the depth of my emotions.

"I tell you what," she said, "Alberto will be back stateside in two weeks. I'll come down to O-town, and the three of us will go out. We'll come up with pros and cons and decide what you should do. Okay? We can even invite this cowboy along. We'll grill him if you want."

"No! Absolutely not." I laughed.

"C'mon! We know what you need, and we can ask him all the tough questions and let you know if he passes. Then you have nothing to worry about."

"Thanks, but no. If I do decide to go out with him again, I don't need the two of you making him run the other way."

"I think you already decided. You just have to be okay with the decision."

I turned on my blinker as I approached the exit and thanked my lifelong friend for always being there. If only love could be as steadfast in romance as it is in friendship.

# 17 CLOSET RAID

Her words continued to replay in my head as I navigated the busy streets of Orlando to make my way home. My thoughts drifted back to another time I'd been caught up in attraction, and unfortunately, I'd completely ignored Sandy's advice then.

I   After the day we spent on the yacht, Gerry and I were inseparable. Every waking moment, he was at the forefront of my mind. It was the first time I ever knew what it was like not to be consumed by thoughts of dance.

"What are you doing?" Sandy asked as I raided her closet for the third time that week. "How can you just keep missing rehearsals like this?"

I shrugged. "Gerry talked to Ernesto and told him it doesn't make any sense for me to sit there while you guys rehearse. I mean, obviously, when my foot heals a little, I can probably do more, so I'll come back then. Right now, I'm having fun. For the first time since I was eight years old, I don't have to be at rehearsal every day. I don't have to spend every waking hour practicing dance. I'm enjoying my life. What's so wrong with that?"

"But you love dance." She picked at a loose thread on her comforter as she lay on her stomach and watched me try on her clothes.

"Yes, but I've discovered there's also a lot of other things in life that I love."

"Like my clothes?"

I turned to the side in the mirror so I could see her reflection. "Your clothes are much cooler than mine. My clothes are all boring. You know that. Does this make my waist look fat?"

Sandy groaned. "You don't have an ounce of fat on your body. But you will, if you keep eating out every night without exercising."

I stuck my tongue out at her and twisted to see the back of the dress, pleased at the way it hugged my sculpted rear end.

"Maybe I'll go shopping. You want to go shopping with me?"

"When? I have rehearsals. Daily. I have a performance coming up. Remember that life?"

"Yeah. I remember. Oh! I gotta go. I didn't realize what time it was. Gerry has a car picking me up downstairs."

"How does he afford all this when he never works?"

"He works. He works every morning, and he sometimes has meetings or phone conferences in the afternoons. His work is with theaters all over the world, so he can call them from any hotel room and conduct his meetings. It's not like he needs an office for that."

"Okay, but where does he live? You said he came to town to meet with Ernesto and he's been staying in a hotel. How long is he here? Doesn't he have a house to get back to?"

I gathered my makeup off her counter and checked my lipstick in the mirror one more time. "He has an apartment in New York, which I told you the last time you and Alberto grilled me about this. He's only staying here to make sure the show gets up and running. And to spend more time with me!" I laughed as I said it, my joy bubbling over despite Sandy's dark outlook. "Thanks so much for loaning me the dress. I'll go shopping and get my own clothes soon, and then you can borrow them any time you want, okay?"

I kissed her on the top of the head and clopped my way to the front door with the boot on one foot and a white sandal on the other.

"Be careful, Mags. Don't lose yourself over this guy, okay?" Sandy called from the bedroom as I opened the front door.

"You worry too much!" I yelled back. "I'm happy. Let me be happy! Love ya. Bye."

# 18 MONEY TALKS

Gerry was all too happy to go shopping with me the next day, picking out clothes and bringing them to the dressing room for me to try on and model for him. I could tell immediately which ones were hits by the desire in his eyes and the sly grin he wore.

"You're trying to push me over the limits of what a man can endure, Willow," he said when I emerged from the dressing room in a see-through black lace number that dipped almost to my tail bone in the back.

He stood and came to me, walking like a lion toward his prey. I shuddered with a grin and took a step back into the dressing room, giggling as he walked inside with me and closed the door behind him.

We'd moved past the ceremonial first kiss that day on the yacht, and each day after that, our passion had continued to grow and become more physical. I knew I would have to make a decision soon, and I think I had already made it, despite my assurances to Sandy that I was not going there.

Gerry slid the black lace over my shoulder, bending his head and sinking his teeth lightly into my bared skin. I squealed loudly, and the dressing room attendant knocked on the door.

"Excuse me? Um, we only allow one person in the dressing room. Sir, you're not allowed in here. Sir?"

I covered my mouth with my hand to keep from laughing out loud, but when he dipped his teeth lower to playfully bite my nipple through the lace, I cried out in pleasure, no longer interested in laughing.

She walked away, and I raked my fingernails through his long curls as he unfastened my bra and freed both breasts for the taking.

He knelt before me, sliding the black lace dress down over my hips as his mouth followed his fingers. By the time the attendant returned with the store manager to knock on the door again, I had learned the power of the human tongue and what depths of madness it can take you to.

I dressed quickly and we left the store in laughter, neither of us caring that they asked us never to return.

If I'd had my regular routine—if I'd been surrounded by my tight circle of friends instead of being removed from everything my life had been— then who knows? Maybe I wouldn't have fallen so hard so fast. Maybe things wouldn't have progressed at such an insane rate of speed.

But I'd lived my entire life in such a sheltered bubble. I knew nothing about the real world, and my days with Gerry were like living in a fantasy existence. He made his calls and took meetings in the morning, but by late morning or sometimes early afternoon, he'd send the car to pick me up and we'd set off for the day, often not returning until the wee hours of the night.

My life became a whirlwind of social activity, often accompanied by Gerry's myriad of elite friends who treated Miami like their own personal playground. We brunched in South Beach, we spent the day poolside in the sun or out on a yacht, and we dined by candlelight at one of Miami's most exclusive eateries or sat in reserved booths at the most popular nightclubs.

It's embarrassing to think of how naive I was and how caught up in my own ego I became. So easily wooed with empty words and too easily impressed by his attentiveness.

The sudden lifestyle change was intoxicating, but it was his touch that did me in.

Gerry awakened something primal within me, both physically and emotionally, and I was like an addict, always wanting more. He could leave me breathless with just a smoldering gaze, and as much as I enjoyed the party atmosphere of his friends, I began to crave the stolen moments alone.

It was all uncharted territory for me, but I was emboldened by the desire I saw in his eyes to push the limits of my newfound sex appeal. It was fiery and intense, and he never failed to whip me into a frenzy with kisses so intimate and hands so adept they left my heart bared for the taking.

I was certain it was love. Head-over-heels, out-of-control, throw-all-caution-to-the-wind love.

It would have seemed almost perfect, had it not been for the ever-present pain in my foot made worse by ignoring doctor's orders and the often almost paralyzing fear about what my absence and injury would mean for my role with the dance company.

Gerry refused to let me give in to either pain or worry, bolstering me at the least sign of distress from either.

"What do you need? Are you hurting? Here, sit, sit," he'd say, snapping his fingers for someone to bring me a stool for my foot. Water, food, ice— whatever I needed appeared within seconds.

"Don't you worry your pretty little head at all, Willow," he'd croon. "They cannot get rid of you. I won't allow it. Do you have any idea how much they need my money? I'm bankrolling everyone's paychecks. They know you're with me, and they can't touch you."

I cringe at the memory of his words now, but at the time, they elevated my sense of importance and comforted my fears. It's frightening how much I allowed him to change me in such a short amount of time.

I became more confident and more self-assured, and any doubts I may have harbored about deserving my prime position opposite Alberto vanished.

Under Gerry's nourishing care of my ego, I quickly came to believe that I was the most deserving dancer in the company, and the season certainly would not go on if I wasn't allowed to return.

"Nina?" I sneered when Alberto told me over lunch who had replaced me in the upcoming performance. "Ha. She's not ready. She doesn't bring the chemistry that you and I have. That's ridiculous. Gerry says Benjamin shouldn't even be rehearsing the next show until the doctor releases me and I'm able to perform."

"Not rehearsing?" Alberto drew his eyebrows together and frowned. "Maggie, we can't stop rehearsals because you're not there. You know that. We're rehearsing multiple shows based on the stager's schedules. The entire company has to keep working."

"Gerry says it shouldn't."

"Well, *Gerry* isn't a director. Or a dancer. He may have money, but *Gerry* knows nothing about ballet."

I flinched at the venom he used when he said Gerry's name. I knew Alberto wasn't fond of my new love, though I didn't have a clue why. In my eyes, Gerry had been nothing but wonderful to me, and I couldn't fathom why my best friend would speak of him with such disdain.

"Maybe not, but his money is bankrolling the show. So that pretty much makes him the boss, doesn't it? If Gerry says the season can't go on without me, then it won't. I thought you'd be on my side. I'm a little hurt."

I stuck my bottom lip out in a pout, which I had quickly learned would bring Gerry to his knees begging to set my world right.

Alberto's reaction was less than concerned. Thank God he'd known me long enough to forgive me for that period of time in our relationship. It's a true testament to our friendship that he even still speaks to me after the way I acted back then. The decisions I made.

"For the love, Maggie, it's not that I'm not on your side. But you're being a bit unrealistic, don't you think? You're going out partying or off to dinner every night, and you think we're going to sit around doing drills? Waiting for you to grace us with your presence?"

I leaned across the table and sneered at him. "I. Am. Injured. Why does no one other than Gerry seem to care about that?"

"We care! But it's a broken toe. It happens. Christ, it's happened to you, what, three times now? You certainly didn't stop working before."

My mouth dropped open in indignant shock. "You heard the doctor say this break is worse than the first two. You heard him say I had to stay off my foot or risk permanent injury. How dare you!"

"Yes, but you're not staying off your foot. You're traipsing all over Miami and going out on yachts for Christ's sake. You haven't even showed up at the studio for the past three weeks."

"Ernesto excused me—"

"Ernesto excused you, but Benjamin didn't. He hasn't complained about you not showing up at all because he's under pressure from Ernesto to keep Gerry happy, but you could still be there. You could be going through stretches. Through notes. You could still be immersing yourself in the work and hearing stage directions and guidance from our director. You're not on vacation."

I slapped my hands on the table, unable to believe I was being treated so unfairly by my so-called best friend. "You're dancing with Nina! What do you care whether or not I'm there, sitting in a chair taking notes?"

Alberto ran his fingers through his blond hair in a motion of frustration so incredibly familiar to me but not usually caused *by* me.

"What happened to you, Maggie? What has he done to you? I don't even know who you are. It's like these last few weeks, you've just disappeared. I don't know who this is in front of me," he gestured toward me with both hands, "but it's not the same girl I knew."

At the time, I brushed off his words, gathering my purse and storming out of the restaurant as best as someone can storm in a hobble.

I called Gerry in tears as soon as I got home, and he was by my side within the hour, wrapping me in his arms and assuring me that Alberto was out of line. That Alberto was jealous of my talent and of my budding career that seemed likely to surpass his own.

It was all nonsense, of course. Alberto had been one of my most faithful friends for years, and I could always rely on him to give it to me straight and to look out for my best interests, then and now.

But that night, I didn't listen to the right voice in my ear.

"My sweet Willow, your friend is right," Gerry whispered as he held me and covered my face in soft kisses. "You are not the same girl he knew. You have blossomed into a beautiful woman, and he is unable to see you for who you've become. He's still limited by who you were." He stroked my cheek with the back of his hand and gently tucked my hair behind my ear. "He doesn't see what I see. He doesn't appreciate how incredible you are. He can't help that he's held back by his own shortcomings. You really should be with someone more talented to showcase your abilities." He sat up and gathered my hand in his, bringing it to his lips. "Do you want me to have him fired? I can, you know."

Despite my hurt, my entire system reacted in shock to the suggestion that anything would happen to Alberto.

"No! No, absolutely not. Alberto is an incredible dancer, and he's my best friend."

Gerry tucked his knuckle under my chin and lifted my face to his. "Then I shall make sure nothing happens to him. Your wish is my command, Willow."

Then his lips were on mine again, and as usual, any fears or concerns dissipated as a tide of sensations overtook me with the touch of his hands and the feel of his mouth on my skin.

I was nineteen. I was young and beautiful. I was full of myself, and I had no idea how far in over my head I was.

After weeks of rising passion and waning attempts to hold off, I gave my virginity to Gerry Tucker that night and sealed my fate.

# 19 COWBOYS WEAR LOTS OF HATS

I'd picked up the phone at least a dozen times throughout the week to call Dax and invite him to lunch, but every time I talked myself out of it before I dialed his number.

My normal Saturday routine was to visit the farmer's market after I finished my morning workout, but it was a drizzly, dreary, cold day, and I decided I'd rather be bundled under a blanket on the couch.

It seemed every channel either had a western or a romantic comedy on, and nothing could tear my thoughts away from him.

What did he like to do on Saturdays? Was he busy on the ranch, doing whatever cowboys do on the weekend? Was he writing music and strumming his guitar? Was he rescuing puppies or trying not to break his neck on Kratos?

Finally, I gave in and dialed, holding my breath as it rang.

"Well, hello there."

The rich timbre of his voice resonated through me, and it was like my body woke up and came to attention.

"Hello."

"What are you doing on this blustery day?" he asked.

I smiled and closed my eyes, picturing his face and the grin I could hear when he spoke.

"I'm curled up under a blanket trying to find a decent movie on TV."

"Hmm. That sounds much better than what I'm doing, which is shoveling hay."

"Yeah. I'd pick this over that."

He chuckled, and my body reacted with a rush of heat strong enough that I had to fling the blanket to the side for relief.

"I was wondering if you're free for lunch," I said, my voice tentative.

He hesitated, and I wished I could pull the words back.

"I could probably make that happen," he answered after the pause. "What time were you thinking? And where did you come with up?"

"There's a little Thai place that's closer to you, so you wouldn't have to come into Orlando."

"I don't mind driving to Orlando. You tell me where I need to be and what time, and I'll be there."

I gave him directions to the Thai place, and we agreed to meet at one.

It changed my entire outlook for the day. I switched off the television and cranked up the stereo before nestling into the tub for a long soak, eagerly anticipating the afternoon ahead.

The wintry chill was perfect late-season sweater weather, so I opted for a pair of dark denim jeans tucked into knee-high boots, topping it off with an olive-green sweater that I knew would highlight my eyes and a dark brown open-front poncho with a scarf in shades of brown, green, and blue.

His truck was already there when I pulled into the restaurant parking lot. I'd been hyper with excitement knowing I'd see him, and I couldn't hold back the smile that spread across my face when he stepped out of the truck and walked toward my car.

He was wearing his ever-present jeans and boots but no hat. His wavy hair was damp, and I could tell from the scented mixture of cologne and shampoo as he approached that he'd showered right before coming to meet me.

"Hello," he said, and his smile was so wide that I thought the excitement must be mutual.

"Hi," I said as he turned and motioned toward the restaurant.

"After you."

He moved to open the restaurant door as we reached it, but then he hesitated and stepped aside without opening it, indicating I could go first. I wasn't sure what he was doing, and I paused, which made him reach and grab the door at the same time I did. Then we both dropped our hands simultaneously, laughing in our awkwardness before he opened the door and held it.

"Sorry about that," he said as we took our seats. "I'm still getting used to all this."

"All what?"

"What to do, what not to do. I was brought up with all the traditional manners. A man holds a door open for a lady, he walks on the traffic side of the sidewalk, he pays the check, holds her coat. My mama would have tanned my hide if I'd done any differently. Now, it's not...well, I guess times have changed."

He paused as the waitress brought us menus and took our drink orders, and then he continued.

"So, I apologize if I offend you by doing all that."

"Um, it doesn't *offend* me. I just…." I paused, unsure of how to explain my feelings when I'd never examined the reason for them. "I suppose I don't like feeling confined by the roles. I've been on my own a long time, so I take care of myself. It makes no sense to me to wait for you to open a door when I could do it."

He nodded. "I can understand that. I see it as more of a courtesy than anything else. I certainly don't intend it to be confining."

"No, I know. I didn't mean *you*, specifically."

"I'm trying to be aware of it, but it's second nature to me. Habit. Not something I consciously think about, so I slip up."

His sheepish expression was endearing.

"It's okay," I said. "It shouldn't be a big deal. If you're standing there, and you want to open the door, you open it. I'll walk through it. But if you're on the other side of the car or somewhere it doesn't make sense in the natural flow of things, then I'll open it. I mean, I appreciate you trying to respect my feelings, and I'll do the same and respect that it's part of who you are to do it."

He smiled, and he seemed to relax a bit, his shoulders releasing some of the tension that had charged the air since the door debacle. "Sounds good. You know, when you get married as a young man, you kind of figure you're done with worrying about all this. Then life throws a curveball, and you find yourself back in the deep end, trying to figure it all out again."

His smile faded and he looked toward the windows, taking a deep drink from the glass of water the waitress had brought.

"So, you were married? How long?"

"Twelve years." He didn't meet my eyes when he answered, and his shoulders and face were tight again with tension. "What about you? How long were you married?"

It was my turn to tense up, and I hesitated answering, caught off guard by the question even though it was inevitable.

I hated those questions, and I hated the answer. I'd faced it too many times over the years as the kids were growing up from well-meaning soccer moms, teachers, and play-date parents engaging in what should have been normal conversation.

*How long have you been divorced? Where does their dad live? How often do they see him?*

They were questions that hinted at normal life, yet my story and my children's story wasn't normal.

Dax looked up when I didn't answer, and I was surprised to see pain clouding the normally joyful green eyes. It struck me again that they were similar to my own.

I took a deep breath and rushed out the words on the exhale. "I was never married."

Dax's face reacted much the same way everyone else did—momentary shock almost immediately replaced by embarrassment that the question had been asked, followed soon after by a peering curiosity.

"The kids' dad…well, he…we never married."

I'd never found out a handy, catch-all answer to the question, which usually didn't matter, because whatever awkward response I mumbled always put off all but the most inquisitive people.

In today's more modern thinking society, there were plenty of people who didn't marry, but when the kids were younger, we were the exception in the community around us.

Many times I considered making up a story that I liked better than the truth, but it was dishonesty that had created the mess, and I refused to perpetuate it with more dishonesty.

Luckily, once Cabe and Galen had graduated and moved on with their lives, the question rarely if ever came up, and it had been a long time since I'd had to deal with the heat of shame that was radiating from my body.

"Oh. Okay." His voice was solemn, and he gave a brief nod and looked down at the menu. If he wanted to know more, he wasn't going to ask right then. "So, have you ever eaten here?"

"Yes," I said, thrilled that I didn't have to explain my background. "My son, Cabe, attended the University of Central Florida, so we'd meet here as somewhat of a halfway point."

"Ah, UCF. I taught a couple of classes there a few years back."

I nearly choked on my water. "You taught classes? At UCF?"

"Yeah. You okay?" he asked as I coughed and covered my mouth with the napkin.

"Yes, just surprised. I wasn't aware you were a teacher. Or professor."

"Oh, I'm not. It was for a specific study I had conducted at the ranch and the implications of the results. My master's is in animal sciences, but I also have an extensive background in environmental science, and with the scope of landscape at the ranch, we're able to partner with the university for quite a few studies."

He said it all so matter-of-factly that I thought perhaps he was going to ignore that my mouth was hanging open while he talked, but then he chuckled and leaned across the table to speak in a softer voice. "Should I be offended at how shocked you look right now?"

I closed my mouth and tried to formulate words that weren't insulting.

"No. I didn't…well, I…I guess I…well—"

"You didn't know they gave cowboys degrees?"

"No, it's not that," I said, but in all truth, it had never occurred to me. I had assumed one didn't need a degree to work on a ranch. Certainly, not a master's degree.

"It's okay," he said with a grin, almost as though he could read my thoughts. "I'm sure lots of people don't think of cowboys needing degrees. But I'd say other than three I can think of off the top of my head, every employee we have at the ranch has at least a bachelor's. Mostly in the sciences that might pertain to raising cattle, maintaining grasslands and water, conservation, and so on. A few have more business-related backgrounds, but those are usually the ones seeking to move into ranch management."

I decided honesty was the best policy, especially since my reaction had been too obvious to play off. "We've never actually discussed what it is you do on the ranch, so I suppose it did surprise me."

"I partner with our geneticists and nutritionists to make sure we're producing the healthiest, heartiest beef cattle possible. I oversee our foremen and ensure they are staying on top of records and necessary care for the cattle and work with the state's veterinarians in conjunction with our property. I'm in charge of the day-to-day operations of the breeding program. I also work hand-in-hand with the state of Florida's conservation efforts to use the ranch for the benefit of learning about our environment. And I've been known to wrestle with a gator or two to relocate them when necessary."

My mouth was open again. "Wow. And here I thought you just rode horses into the lake and rescued puppies."

"Oh, I do that, too."

"Okay. So, you basically run the ranch?"

He shook his head with a low whistle. "Oh, no, ma'am. Not at all. That would be my brother, Mitchell, and my daddy. They handle the business end—the sales, the contracts, anything to do with numbers and profits. There's a few side businesses—sand pits, shell excavations, and others—and they take care of all that as well. I handle the animals and the land the animals are on. I'm not as important as it sounds. I happen to be in charge of some extremely capable people who make me look good, so I get to wear a lot of hats and have several titles."

The magnitude of the ranch's operations stunned me, and I realized as the waitress approached that I hadn't even looked at the menu.

"Can you give us a minute longer?" I asked, and she smiled and left.

"So, what do you recommend?" Dax asked without bothering to open the menu.

"They have a great liver and raisins platter with fried rice."

"Well, I won't be having that, I can assure you."

I laughed, and he picked up the menu.

"I don't know what you'd like," I said. "Do you even eat Thai food? I guess I should have asked that before."

"Sure. I'm more interested in your recommendation than getting something I'd pick for myself, though."

After a brief discussion on the appropriate level of curry and whether or not he preferred rice or noodles, I ordered a platter of chicken panang and a Pad Thai plate with steamed dumplings and crab rangoons for starters.

"That's probably too much food, but those are my favorites, so worst case scenario I'll have leftovers tomorrow," I told him as the waitress took our menus and walked away.

He asked how Galen's wedding plans were coming, and I asked how the puppies were doing, surprised to find he'd taken pictures to show me with his phone.

"Wow, they've really grown. It's only been a week, right? Look how big they are. And how's our mama dog doing?"

He scrolled through and found a picture of her standing with Cody. "She's good. Up and moving around fine now, so I think it was just exhaustion. If you're not busy when we're done here, you should ride out and see them. Say goodbye."

"What do you mean? They're moving?"

"Yeah, to the housing community on the big ranch. One of the cowboys is going to take them."

"What about the mom?" My heart hurt as I thought of her sad eyes.

"Her, too. Once they're weaned and a little older, he'll start training them for herding."

"Did you try to find out who the mama belonged to? Did you ask your neighbors?"

"I did put out a call to those who live in the area, but no one claimed her. Do you have any pets? You're welcome to take one if you'd like."

"No, no, no. I babysit my son's dog, Deacon, from time to time, but I'm not home enough to keep a dog company, and I'd hate for one to sit home alone without me."

"Well, if you'd like to come see them, you're welcome to, and if you change your mind and decide to take one home, that's fine, too."

We talked as we ate, and by the time I paid the check and we walked back to our vehicles, two hours had passed.

"Thanks for lunch," Dax said. "I'll definitely come back here. Nice find."

"Thanks for joining me." I had the oddest sensation of longing. I didn't want to leave his company, and even though we'd spent the better part of the afternoon together, it didn't seem long enough.

"Alright, well, I guess I'll be on my way," he said, pulling his keys from his pocket. "Can I open your car door for you? Technically, where I'm standing I'm closer to it than you are, so that puts it in my territory, right?"

His eyes held a bit of a competitive gleam, and I laughed as I judged the distance and conceded with a nod that he was indeed closer.

I pressed the unlock button on my keys and waited for him to open the door before walking over and leaning against the car, not quite ready to get in and say goodbye.

He stood with his hand on the door, and even in the cool, brisk breeze, I could feel the heat between us.

"I enjoy spending time with you, Maggie," he said, his voice just above a husky whisper.

The air was charged with desire, and I wanted him to lean in and kiss me more than I wanted to pull away.

"Me too," was all I could manage as I looked up at him, searching the green eyes clouded with emotions I couldn't decipher. He sighed, and I braced for his touch, but it didn't come.

"You gonna come to the house? See the pups? Or do you have somewhere else you need to be?"

His voice was thick and deep, and the rumble of it drove me wild. I considered making the first move, standing on my toes to reach his lips with my own, but my mind talked me out of it.

It tried to talk me out of going to the ranch, but when I thought about driving back to Orlando alone and sitting on my couch watching movies, even with the prospect of calling up a friend and heading out to dinner, it was no contest. I knew I'd rather be at the ranch.

He spoke up when I didn't. "I'm not taking them for another couple of weeks. You've got time if you want to see them."

"Actually, today works for me if it works for you," I said before I could change my mind. "I'd love to see them."

His smile spread across his face, and the light in his eyes stoked the fire that had been burning inside me since he stepped out of the truck hours earlier.

I'd spent the last twenty-six years convincing myself that I didn't need a man in my life, but I sure as hell wanted this one.

# 20 TAKE A RIDE WITH ME

I dialed Sandy as soon as I pulled onto the highway behind his truck.

"I thought you were going to call me when you left the restaurant," she said without a hello. "I've been on pins and needles checking my phone while I was setting the flowers for this wedding. Where've you been?"

"Lunch just ended."

She gasped. "Really? It's after three. Must have gone well."

"I'm following him back to the ranch."

"Holy cow! It must have gone real well!"

I laughed. "No, it's not like that. I'm going to see the puppies."

"Okay, is that some euphemism for him seeing your puppies?"

"No! The puppies from the other night. In the woods. He invited me over to see them."

"Oh. Okay. And you're going?"

"Yeah, why? Do you think that's a bad idea? Should I not go?" I almost put on the brakes.

"No, no, go! Go! I'm just surprised. Pleasantly surprised, but surprised. So, lunch went well?"

I bit my lip, replaying portions of conversations in my head. "Yeah, it did. He's such an interesting guy. So many layers. There's a lot more to him than meets the eye."

"Well, from the way you described him, what meets the eye is good, so anything beyond that is cake, right? Speaking of cake, I have to go put the topper on the cake because they're rolling it into the reception soon. Call me as soon as you leave there, okay?"

"I will."

"And if that's not going to be until tomorrow morning, at least text me and let me know you're spending the night."

"Oh, good Lord, Sandy! I'm not spending the night. I'm just going to see the puppies."

"Hmm. Okay. If you say so."

I wasn't sure if I needed to park in the circle drive of the house or follow him to the barn, but he stuck his hand out the window and motioned for me to stay behind him, indicating a spot near the barn where I should park.

Cody greeted Dax heartily as he got out of the truck, and I braced for impact when I stepped out of my car, accustomed to Deacon's habit of planting both front feet on my stomach and nearly knocking me down. But as Cody came toward me, Dax whistled, and the dog immediately sat, his tail wagging in full exuberance as I approached him and patted his head.

"Hello, Cody, and how are you today?"

His entire body wiggled with excitement, but he held the sitting position until Dax called for him.

I followed Dax into the barn to the stall where we'd left the puppies the night he found them, and I couldn't help exclaiming in joy when I saw the cuddly little balls of fur rolling all around the hay and tousling with each other.

"Oh my gosh! They are so adorable! I can't believe how much they've grown!"

Dax swung open the stall door and I stepped inside, kneeling in the hay to reach forward and pick up one of the warm, snuggly cuties.

"Watch where you kneel. I changed out the hay this morning, but no telling what all they've added to it since then."

The mama dog nuzzled at my elbow, and I turned to pet her, astonished to see how much healthier she appeared after a week of food, warmth, and rest.

"Wow! You look like you feel better," I said, ruffling the fur on the back of her neck before looking up at Dax. "Did you give her a name yet?"

"I've been calling her Little Mama."

"Gee, that's original," I said with a grunt and an eye roll.

"Feel free to bestow a moniker upon her if you'd like. The task is yours for the taking."

I held her face in my hand and examined her eyes. She was taller than I'd realized the night we'd met, likely because she had been laying down pretty much the entire time and was in distress.

"She's a pretty big dog, huh?"

Dax nodded. "I think she's probably a lab mix. The pups definitely have some Australian shepherd in them based on their coloring and the blue eyes a few have. But I'd say she's more lab."

"I think I'll name her Debra."

He scoffed as he leaned against the stall door. "Debra? That's not a dog name."

"Why not? You named a dog Cody. Why can't I name a dog Debra? It's sweet."

"You can, I guess. It's just not a dog name."

I smoothed my hand over the top of her head and rubbed her ear. "I think it's a wonderful dog name. What do you think, Debra?"

She gave me a wag of her tail and then turned her attention to the puppies seeking sustenance beneath her belly.

Kratos let out a loud snort behind us, and I stood and turned to face the huge stallion in his stall across the corridor.

"Is he telling me he likes the name, or he doesn't?"

"Who knows with that beast!"

I chuckled at the look that transpired between the two of them.

"I take it you and Kratos are still at odds over who's boss?"

"*I'm* clear on who's boss, but he's holding out on acknowledging it. He'll come around, though."

"What if he never lets you ride him?"

Dax smiled. "He will. In his own time. I'm in no hurry. It's not like he's ever gonna be a herding horse. He's too fiery for that."

"So, what will you use him for?" I asked as I watched the horse paw at the hay and stamp his foot.

"I won't use him for anything."

"So why did you buy him?"

Dax walked over to Kratos and held his hand up, moving it almost in slow motion as he watched the horse's reaction. He was silent until his palm rested on the horse's neck, and then he turned to speak to me as he stroked the muscles beneath the mane.

"He actually wasn't for sale. A young rancher had him at the sale barn—the son of a rancher, I should say. He'll inherit the title, but he hasn't done much in the way of earning it. Anyway, Kratos was having none of it that day. I watched the young man try to whip the horse into submission, and when I'd been silent as long as I could—which wasn't very long—I stepped forward and took the reins. For reasons even I don't understand, Kratos calmed at once and let me lead him from the yard into a stall. As you can imagine, the man was quite pissed to have been shown up with his own horse, but in the end, we came to agree on a price that soothed his pride and got Kratos out from under any future whippings. Isn't that right, boy?"

The horse let out a loud whinny and bucked his head up just as Dax pulled his hand back.

"He seems to be nodding."

"One of the few things we agree on, I suppose."

The horse in the stall next to the puppies answered Kratos's neigh, and Dax made his way over to him.

"Alright, Dallas. We'll pay attention to you, too."

He walked right up to Dallas and patted his shoulder with no hesitation, smiling as the horse nudged his arm. Their relationship seemed much more relaxed than the one he had with Kratos.

Dax turned and looked at me, his head tilted and his eyes bright with the spark of an idea.

"I'm willing to bet that if you had never ridden in a truck, then you've probably never ridden a horse."

"You would be correct. I sat on a camel once. Not sure if that counts. But no. I've never been on a horse."

"Would you like to?"

I looked up at Dallas and glanced back to Kratos, excitement and apprehension rousing a flurry of butterflies in my stomach.

"Um, sure?"

Dax laughed. "Was that a question or a statement? Because you didn't sound sure."

"It's something I would like to be able to say I've done, but not necessarily something I've been dying to do."

"We've got a couple of hours before the sun sets. I'd love to show you some of the ranch, and horseback is hands-down the best way to see it."

My insides tingled with the prospect of doing something so intimidating, and I glanced around the stables to see if there was a smaller horse. I spotted one a few stalls down that seemed smaller, and I pointed to her.

"What about that one? Can I ride her?"

His eyebrows rose and the shock was obvious on his face. "You want your own horse? Okay. I'd figured you could ride with me, but hey, if you're up for it."

"Go big, or go home, right? Is it hard to do?"

He shrugged. "It's not hard, but she might be a bit more skittish if you're nervous. Are you nervous?"

"No," I lied, and then I laughed and said, "Yes."

"Okay, well, come and meet Fallon."

I followed him to the smaller horse and smiled as my internal butterflies swarmed. It felt like they were dive-bombing my insides.

"Can I pet her?"

"Sure," Dax said as he laughed and ran his hand up the broad space between her eyes.

I laid my hand against the side of her neck, amazed at the warmth that radiated from the contact. She shifted her weight, and a ripple ran across her skin, making her ears twitch. I buried my fingers into the thick black hair of her mane, surprised at the coarseness of it when it appeared to be like silk.

"Hello, Fallon."

Dax grabbed a lead from the hook on a nearby wall and slipped it over her head. I stepped back as he pulled the stall door open and led her out into the open area in the center of the barn.

I kept a cautious distance as I followed them, heeding the warnings I'd always heard about horses kicking. I flattened my back against the wall and gave them a wide berth as he examined her feet.

When he'd finished, he stood upright and placed his hands on his hips, staring at me with a grin.

"You sure you want to do this?"

I nodded and swallowed hard at the lump of fear that had risen in my throat, but the tingle of excitement was coursing through my veins. How long had it been since I'd actually been physically afraid? How long had it been since I'd pushed myself past something so intimidating that my mouth went dry and my feet felt glued to the ground?

"You don't look sure."

I forced a smile and licked my lips, trying to get moisture to return to my mouth. "I want to do this."

"Alright," he said, with a slight shake of his head.

I watched him dress Fallon in her blanket and saddle, my body teetering between nausea and exhilaration. I stayed plastered against the wall while he led Dallas from his stall to take his place by Fallon, and I tried to distract myself by focusing on the bulge of Dax's biceps and the sculpted muscles across his back outlined beneath the fabric of his white shirt.

To my surprise, he grabbed a heavy coat from the hook by the door, but then he turned and offered it to me. "You want something heavier? We'll be back before sundown, but it's gonna be chilly this late in the afternoon."

I nodded, and he held the coat out for me to slide my arms inside the sleeves. The weight of it was comforting, and the smell of him lingered on it even though I'd never seen him wear it.

He took another coat from the same rack and tossed it over Dallas's saddle and then turned to me with a grin.

"You ready?"

A nervous giggle escaped me and my hand went to my throat. "Oh, God. Yeah. I'm ready. Let's do this!"

I took a step toward him, and my stomach lurched. I moved my hand to cover it and whispered, "Just breathe."

He turned and raised an eyebrow. "*Ever After*? Drew Barrymore?"

I smiled and exhaled. "No, I really was just telling myself to breathe, but good call. Good movie."

"Well, come on, Cinderella. Your noble steed awaits."

# 21 INTO THE WOODS

"Put your left foot here," Dax said, indicating the stirrup.

I took a deep breath and lifted my foot, and he helped wedge it securely in place.

"Okay, now grab the horn and swing the right foot up and over."

I giggled again. "Up and over. You make it sound so easy."

"It is. I'm right here, and I won't let you fall."

His voice was calming, a little above a whisper. I had seen him speak quietly to Kratos on the lake shore that day, and again with the mama dog the night we led her out of the woods. His tone was reassuring, and his confidence was bolstering.

I grabbed hold of the saddle horn and pushed my weight into the stirrup, lifting my right leg up and over as instructed. My rump landed firmly in the saddle, and Fallon shifted her weight beneath the addition of mine, a movement which was quite unsettling from the dizzying height atop her back.

"Whoa," I said, instinctively tightening my grasp on the saddle horn to steady myself.

"You're okay. She's only adjusting," Dax said. "Here, cup your hand like you're making the letter C with your palm down."

I did as he instructed, and he placed the reins in my hand.

"Now, close your hand over it, but you want to have some slack. Don't pull it tight unless you want her to stop. If you want her to go left, lay the reins on the right side of her neck like this to gently guide her to turn that way. To go right, that way." He placed his hand over mine and moved them together as he talked, and the combination of the moving, living creature beneath me and the sparks that flew from the contact with Dax almost overwhelmed my senses. "You have your feet firmly in the stirrups? You're

112

going to want to ride with your weight on your feet. Go ahead and try. Stand up in the saddle, and let me see if the stirrups need to be adjusted up or down for you."

I leaned forward to shift my weight in the stirrups and stand. It was odd to feel off kilter. I'd done all manner of leaps and jumps in ballet, and I'd been held high above my partner's head and even tossed. None of that was as intimidating as standing astride Fallon's back completely out of my element.

I sat back down when he finished with the stirrups, and my stomach flipped as Fallon swished her tail and turned her head toward Dax. Even though her movements were small, it felt as though the ground itself was shifting, and I had to force my mouth to smile when Dax looked up at me.

"Now, if you keep your butt in the saddle, it's gonna bounce you to hell and back, and that will make your feet hit her sides and she'll think you want to go faster. Which, of course, leads to more bouncing and more kicks and the cycle intensifies. So remember, keep your weight on your feet."

"Got it," I said, lifting myself to set the weight onto my feet again.

Fallon danced to the right a little in response to the movement, and I jerked my hands onto the saddle horn, forgetting that I held the reins.

"Okay, now remember, you don't want to pull that tight. Give her some slack. She's gonna follow Dallas, so you don't have to do a whole lot. She won't go off on her own as long as he's leading her. You sure you're okay?"

I nodded, trying to hold my position so she wouldn't shift again. I was having a hard time acclimating to her moving beneath me without my control. Actually, the whole experience felt like I had no control, but unlike emotional situations where the feeling would make me shut down, the physical fear fired me up and motivated me to overcome it.

A splash of red on the wall behind Dax caught my eye as he worked with the straps on Dallas's saddle. It was a weathered insignia painted on the wood. "Double D Ranch" was scrawled in a fancy script in red letters, with two D's intertwined in the center in black. As I studied it, I realized the faded D's were supposed to be horseshoes. There a year of establishment beneath the design, but before I could determine what it was, Dax and Dallas had started walking.

Fallon immediately fell in line beside them, and I lurched forward at the uneven rocking from side to side as she placed her weight on each leg, one at a time.

Dax looked up at me and grinned, his eyebrows raised in question. "You okay?"

I nodded and grinned back, still unsure of my balance as my body tried to match the rhythm of her gait.

"You look like a natural," he said, his smile widening as he flashed me a quick wink.

"Ha! I don't feel like one," I said, looking back down at Fallon as a warm blush flooded my cheeks.

He paused to open the gate at the edge of the barnyard, and Fallon stood patiently beside Dallas while we waited.

Cody's barks behind us drew my attention, and I tried to turn in the saddle but stopped immediately when I felt Fallon move.

"Where's Cody?" I asked as Dax led Dallas through the open gate and waited for Fallon and me to follow.

"He has to stay in the barn. If you remember when you were telling me how impressed you were with his skills, I mentioned that they were limited. Running alongside a horse is not one he's mastered. He gets so excited that he loses all sense and doesn't follow any commands at all. He's the biggest pain in the ass to ride with."

Dax closed the gate behind us and swung into Dallas's saddle with so little effort it seemed an extension of his body. His movement was so fluid it was almost like I was watching it in slow motion and soft focus.

He was at least six inches taller than me on the ground, and with the added height of Dallas above Fallon, Dax seemed to tower over me when we were side by side.

He talked as we rode, pointing out land features and telling me the history of the ranch. After a while, the flat, green pasture lands gave way to woods, and he led us into them without a moment's hesitation despite the lack of any visible trail or markings.

"I assume you know where we're going? And how to get us back home?"

He glanced over his shoulder at me and his lips curled into a sly grin. "I wouldn't be much of a cowboy if I couldn't find my way home on my own ranch, now would I?"

"Guess not," I said.

Fallon and I had settled into a somewhat comfortable pace, and I began to relax a little. In the beginning, I was so paranoid about keeping my weight on my feet that I didn't dare actually sit in the saddle. It didn't take long for the perpetual hover to start a fire in my upper thighs, though, so I had to figure out a balance that worked where I could sit but maintain the majority of my weight in the stirrups. I made sure I held my feet out away from her ribs to ensure I didn't accidentally give her the wrong signal with a bump.

The terrain had gotten rougher the deeper in the woods we went, and I realized we were climbing.

"Are we going up?"

Dax nodded. "There's a great vantage point at the top of this hill where you can see a good deal of the ranch. Probably the most you can see from one spot without being in the helicopter."

"Do you have a helicopter?"

"Yeah. I'll get you up in that some time."

"I might actually do better with that. With machinery, we have some measure of control. With animals, not so much."

He looked over at Fallon and then grinned at me. "She's not out of control. She's following Dallas, and she's ready to listen to you. Send her to the right."

I moved the reins as he had instructed me to, and Fallon veered to the right, maintaining her steady pace. I moved them the opposite direction, and she fell back in step beside Dallas.

"See? You have control."

"Ha! I have the illusion of control. She could break free and do whatever she wanted at any time."

He looked up toward the tree tops and sighed. "That's all we ever have in life, isn't it? The illusion of control? We don't actually control anything. Despite our best efforts."

The melancholy tone had returned to his voice, and I stared at him, wondering what caused it.

His profile was carved perfection—the jaw line straight and squared off, the lips full, and the chin jutting slightly. The waves of his hair caught the streams of sunlight that broke through the tree cover here and there, bathing his rich, brown locks in hues of gold.

His shoulders were broad, and his back straight, and even though his stance in the saddle was relaxed, he seemed alert and ready to react to any situation that might arise.

He was every bit the cowboy, and though I'd never realized what a turn-on that could be, I couldn't deny that the heat generated between my thighs wasn't only due to the friction of the saddle and the constant movement of the horse.

He looked my direction, and I averted my eyes, embarrassed to have been caught staring in case he could somehow read my thoughts.

My gaze settled on Dallas's right back flank, which held a faint brand of the same intertwined Ds I'd seen painted on the wall in the ranch.

I turned in the saddle as much as I dared so I could see Fallon's rear end, and the same double Ds graced her right side.

"So, what's the Double D Ranch if your ranch is Silver Creek and your dad's is Pearson?"

He seemed startled by the question, and he gave me an intense stare before an expression of recognition came over him.

"Oh, you saw that in the barn?"

"Yes, and the brand on Dallas and Fallon."

He looked away from me, pausing so long that I thought he might not answer the question.

"When I started this ranch—when I got the land from my dad—it was called the Double D Ranch. But when Bronwyn decided to use the property for weddings, she thought brides might not like having to put Double D Ranch on their invitations. I guess it could have a different connotation under the right circumstances."

He didn't look at me as he talked, and I couldn't gauge from his voice whether it was a subject best left unexplored, so I plunged ahead with my curiosity.

"Why Double D? Where did that name come from?"

His shoulders lifted as he took in a deep breath and held it, and when he exhaled they seemed to droop lower than they had been before.

"My wife, Deanna, came up with it. It was my name and hers intertwined. Dexter and Deanna."

The catch in his voice made me hesitate, but I still wanted to know more. The mystery of the main house and the impressive bedroom closet upstairs had intrigued me since the day we met, and I was too close to getting an answer to give up so quickly.

"How long have you been divorced?"

He looked at me, and I flinched at the pain in his eyes, immediately wishing I'd left it alone.

"We didn't divorce. She died of injuries from a car crash. Eight years ago."

"I'm sorry," I said, trying to think of a way to take it all back and go a different direction with our conversation.

"Me too," he said, flashing a tepid grin that didn't make it to his eyes. "It was a dark time."

I felt certain they'd built the house together, but I didn't know if they'd ever occupied it. Bronwyn had mentioned they remodeled to accommodate having events once the plans changed, and the accident must have been the change she'd referenced.

"For a long while, I wished I could follow her. I woke up every day blissfully not knowing for the first few seconds, but then it would hit me like a Mack truck, and the pain would cut me to the core all over again every single morning. She was everywhere I looked, and everything I saw. The horses, the stables, that damned house. I couldn't bear to be in that house—*her* house—without her, so I stopped the construction. I probably would have torn it down if Bronwyn hadn't wanted it so desperately."

I finally had the answer to my question, but it sat like a rock in my stomach. I would have rather not known if it meant I could have spared him the pain of discussing it.

"I'm sorry, Dax. I didn't know. We don't have to talk about it."

"It's okay," he said with a bit more of a grin, though it still didn't reach his eyes. "It feels good to talk about her sometimes. To tell someone she

116

was real. No one in my family brings it up. I think it's either too painful for them, or they think it's too painful for me, so it's like she never existed sometimes. Our relationship with my parents wasn't always on the best of terms, so I think that factors into their feelings as well. Feeling guilty, perhaps. My father had no patience for the pursuit of horses."

"Why?"

"Too much of an investment with too little of a return. Too much risk. He's a cattleman. Horses are a necessity for work, not for hobby. Deanna was brought up with thoroughbreds, and she and her sister, Revae, were completely immersed in that world. I thought we could bridge the two. I could work my family's ranch and maintain my roles there, and she could have horses on our portion of the ranch and follow her dreams. My father would only agree if we annexed a part of the ranch so we could set it up as a separate business entity. He wanted no part of it, and after she died…well, I didn't pursue it any further."

He grew quiet, and we rode in silence except for the crunching beneath the horse's feet and an occasional scurry of a lizard or squirrel darting through the woods.

The heaviness of his words hung in the air, and the sun's rays had sunk too low to stream light through the tree branches.

## 22 KEEP ROLLING

We were approaching what seemed to be a clearing, but once we came out from under the trees, it was actually a small bluff that dropped a few feet before the tree line continued. From the top of the bluff, the view opened up and there was beauty as far as the eye could see.

"So, this is Pearson Ranch," Dax said. "Not all of it, of course, but a good chunk is visible from here. If you look over there, see that second tree line at the edge of those pastures?"

I followed the direction he indicated and nodded.

"You can make out my parents' house there. See it? It's white. There's a large barn to the right of it. The trees might block your view, but if you look closely, it's there."

I raised up in the saddle, pushing more weight into the stirrups and straining to see what he described.

"Oh, yeah, I see it. Wow. I bet it's beautiful up close."

He nodded. "It is. Too late in the day to reach it, but we can take an earlier ride again sometime if you'd like."

I nodded, thinking that while I wouldn't mind taking another ride by his side, I wasn't sure I was into meeting the parents. That reeked of relationship far beyond the casual encounters I was already struggling to accept for what they were.

"Hey," Dax said as he turned to face me. "I'm sorry I went off on all that back there. I didn't mean to put such a damper on the day or pour out my life's tragedies."

"It's fine. I was happy to listen. Well, I mean, not *happy*, obviously, because, well, it wasn't happy, but...you know what I mean."

"I think so. I feel very comfortable with you, Maggie. I find myself wanting to talk to you. Wanting to tell you about my life and learn more about yours. It's like—"

Suddenly, his words were cut off by a loud rustling charge through the woods behind us. I shifted to turn in the saddle right as Dax turned his horse to face whatever was coming. His hand went instinctively to his hip, but if he was accustomed to having a weapon there, he came up empty.

Fallon had begun to dance beneath me, and I wasn't sure how much of that was her being nervous from the unknown intruder or her reacting to my fear. Maybe both.

"Get behind me!" Dax said, motioning to me as he nudged Dallas forward.

I pushed my toe gently into Fallon's side and scooted forward as I laid the rein against her neck, trying to coax her to move behind Dallas.

At that moment, Cody burst through the brush on my right and charged toward me and Fallon. He started barking the moment he saw us, and Fallon bolted beneath me, surging forward past Dallas as Cody nipped at her tail.

Dax whistled and yelled, but the dog was in hot pursuit of us, his teeth chomping at her tail and her back legs, which made her run faster.

"Maggie, pull back on her reins and put your weight on your feet!"

The reins had fallen from my hand in my panic to grip the saddle with both hands. I couldn't shift my weight to my feet without lifting myself up, and I was too scared to do it.

Dax and Dallas caught up with us quickly, and he continued to yell at Cody and whistle, but to no avail. The faster Fallon ran, the more Cody barked and nipped at her.

She stumbled as his teeth hit her flesh, then she turned without warning to head down the uneven terrain of the bluff.

I lurched forward in the saddle, holding on for dear life as Fallon took us downward with Cody still matching every stride.

Dax was riding as close beside us as he could with the challenges of the landscape, and though he tried multiple times to grab the loose reins that flew free around her front legs, it was useless.

"You need to get the reins," he shouted. "Can you reach them?"

I leaned my right hand as far forward as I dared, unwilling to let go of the saddle horn with the left, but I couldn't grasp them, and the movement had pitched me off balance.

Cody's teeth closed on Fallon's tail again, and when she darted to the left to escape him, my weight was too far to the right to hold on.

It seemed like slow motion and at the same time, it was so fast I couldn't comprehend what was happening. One minute, I was on the back of the horse, reaching for the reins and holding on as though my life depended on it, and the next minute the ground was rushing up to greet me as I flew from her back.

My shoulder took the brunt of the initial impact, but thankfully, the steep grade of the bluff sent me rolling as soon as I made contact with the ground, helping to minimize the damage. When I came to a stop, I was flat on my back with the breath knocked out of me, stunned too much to inhale or exhale.

Cody was the first to reach me, and his hassling, dripping tongue in my face was an assurance that I was indeed alive despite my lack of oxygen.

I heard Dax's feet hit the ground almost immediately after I landed, and within seconds he was on his knees beside me.

"Maggie! Maggie! Oh my God, are you okay? Are you all right? Can you hear me? Is anything broken?"

My lungs burned and my heart pounded from the inability to take a breath, but then a sharp pain shot through me and I inhaled the largest gulp of air I'd ever taken. I coughed and sucked in another breath as I tried to move to a seated position.

"Whoa, go slow. We need to make sure nothing is broken," Dax said, putting his arm behind my back to support me.

"I'm fine. At least, I think I'm fine," I croaked out, trying to catch my breath and coughing again with the effort.

"Can you move your arms? Your legs? Did you hit your head?"

My shoulder had begun to throb, and I pulled the coat sleeve down for a closer inspection.

"There's no blood," I said. "It hurts, but I don't think it's broken."

He ran his hands across my shoulder and down my arm, bending it at the elbow and asking me to move my fingers. When he was satisfied that it wasn't broken, his eyes met mine and before I even knew it was coming, he took my face in his hands and laid on me what might have been the most passionate kiss of my lifetime.

I was already lightheaded from the wild ride, the fall, and the lack of oxygen, and as his tongue plundered and explored, a whole new level of dizziness swirled inside my brain. Every nerve ending was on high alert already, and the sensations he was causing were heightened by the adrenaline pumping through my veins.

I lifted my arms to bury my fingers in his hair, but my shoulder protested and I winced in pain.

He pulled back immediately, looking down at me with eyes dark with desire and lips swollen and wet.

"I'm sorry," he whispered as he started to pull away. "I shouldn't have—"

"Oh, good grief, Dax! Shut up and kiss me!"

I placed my hands on either side of his face and brought him back to me, taking my turn as the aggressor as I moved my tongue between his lips and dug my fingernails into the back of his head.

He shifted so that he could put both arms around me, and I moved tighter against him until I could feel his heart pounding with mine.

I wrapped my good arm around his neck, nestling in even closer and pushing the kiss deeper until his tongue twisted with mine and he tilted his head to take back control.

He laid me back against the hard earth, and I pulled him with me, parting my legs as his knee wedged between them.

I tugged at the back of his shirt until I could get my hands underneath to make contact with his skin, which was surprisingly warm despite his lack of a coat. I raked my fingernails up and down his back as his mouth continued to ravage mine.

He burrowed his hands inside the heavy coat I wore until he had them beneath me, his arms encircling me. He held me tight as he rolled over onto his back, positioning me on top of him as I broke free from his kiss.

My hair fell forward to shield us as I stared into the deep green velvet of his eyes, my own desire reflected in the heat I saw there.

I touched my lips to his, more tentatively than before, and he reached to brush my hair back, grazing his knuckles across my cheek.

The frenzied passion had passed, leaving in its place a gentle exploration that was tender and inquisitive.

We touched each other's faces, traced each other's brows, and took turns sharing the softest of kisses.

Just as the sense of urgency began to take hold again, Cody lay down beside us, reeking of dirt and the sweetly sour smell of a dog who's exerted energy and gotten hot.

It was quite distracting, and I laughed as I sat up, still straddling Dax.

"I don't know whether to thank that damned dog or kill him," Dax whispered, pressing my fingertips to his lips.

"You can't kill him. But how did he get out?"

"Beats me. He's a freaking Houdini sometimes. I'm positive I latched the stall door, so unless he climbed it, I'm at a loss."

"Maybe Mama Dog Debra let him out. Or Kratos."

Dax rolled his eyes and grunted. "Yeah. Wouldn't surprise me if it was Kratos. I swear he's out to get me."

"You? It was me who got injured!"

Worry creased his forehead, and he reached up to touch my shoulder. "I'm so sorry. Are you sure you're okay?"

I nodded and lifted my shoulder in a slow rotation. "It's probably going to hurt like hell tomorrow, but I'll be fine. I have an insanely high tolerance for pain. Ballet does that to you."

I got up and extended my hand to Dax, who grinned as he took it and stood, bending to knock the dirt off his jeans as I wiped my hands across the back of my own. "Your white shirt is ruined," I said as I looked at the dark reddish-brown blotches of dirt that covered his back.

He glanced over his shoulder to look at the shirt and shrugged. "It was worth it."

I smiled as I brushed it off as best I could and waited as he did the same for the back of the coat I wore.

"Here, I'll take it off," I said. "I think there's less areas without dirt than there are with."

He helped me shrug out of his coat and held it out to the side, beating his palm against it as puffs of dust rose up around him.

"This might be a lost cause," he said, walking over to Dallas and taking the coat that was thrown across the saddle and replacing it with the dirty one. "You can wear this one instead. It may not be as warm, but at least it's clean."

"Where's Fallon?" I asked as he slid the coat over my arms, taking care not to jostle my shoulder.

"Probably back at the barn by now," Dax said, scowling at Cody, who was lying beside us with his head on his front paws, calm as could be.

"Can Dallas carry both of us?" I asked as I brushed more dirt from my jeans.

"Yeah. He'll be fine."

He held the stirrup for me, then he gave me a little shove up as I heaved to get my leg over Dallas's back without the use of my right shoulder and arm.

Being on Dallas's back was even higher than on Fallon's, and after taking such a hard tumble, I was even more uneasy. Fortunately, Dallas stood perfectly still as Dax swung up into the saddle behind me, even as I scooted forward to give him more room.

His thighs were snug against mine, and his chest was firm against my back, which made me feel secure but oddly aroused at the same time.

"You can lean back if it's more comfortable," he said, reaching around my waist to switch the reins to his other hand.

I politely refused at first, not wanting to overload Dax, but as the gentle sway of Dallas's footsteps rocked me back and forth, I gave in and relaxed against the comfort of his solid strength.

By the time we could see the barn, the sun had dipped just below the trees beyond the lake, and the hazy gray of twilight had descended. We'd ridden in silence the whole way back, and I couldn't help but wonder if his thoughts were as jumbled and conflicted as mine.

On the one hand, I had thoroughly enjoyed the time we'd spent together, especially the part where we rolled around on the ground like teenagers. But another part of me was frantic about the sudden leap we'd taken into the realm of the physical.

Was it too soon? Was it too much? Was it too late to back out? Was it wrong to feel so good when I wasn't sure if I wanted to feel it?

What had made him kiss me like that? He'd just brought up the painful experience of losing his wife. Had that made him vulnerable or put him in an emotional state?

Was it seeing me thrown from the horse and being grateful I wasn't injured?

I reached up and rubbed my shoulder, thankful it wasn't broken and that I hadn't lost my tolerance for physical pain. I had no desire to test my tolerance for emotional pain again, and I stiffened at the very thought.

"You okay?" His voice rumbled in my ear.

I nodded, sitting up to take my weight from him.

"You were fine where you were," he said. "In fact, I was rather enjoying it."

So was I, but the tendrils of fear had arisen from the residue left behind by my past, and I couldn't relax again.

Fallon was standing at the gate, just as he had predicted she would be. Cody had tried unsuccessfully to spook Dallas through most of our trip, but since the older horse was much calmer and not intimidated, the dog would give up for a while and trot alongside us. When he saw Fallon, he broke into a run, stopping to look back at us when Dax bellowed his name, nearly deafening in its proximity to my ear.

Dax insisted on examining my shoulder again once we'd reached the barn and dismounted, removing the coat and my poncho as he picked bits of nature from my hair.

"I told you I'm fine," I said as he pressed his fingers up and down my arm and across my shoulder, sending a little rush down my spine that had nothing to do with injury. "I'm sure I'll be stiff tomorrow and probably bruised, but I think your coat cushioned the landing."

I shivered as the increasing cold of night swept in on a breeze, lifting my hair and carrying it across my face. He reached to brush it back, tucking the strands behind my ear, and I had an eerie flashback to a night on a boat so many years ago.

I bristled and stepped back, and though I could see confusion in Dax's eyes, I couldn't explain what had changed.

"It's getting late," I said. "I need to get on the road. Thanks for the adventure."

He tilted his head to one side, his eyes questioning and filled with concern.

"You all right?"

I grabbed my poncho with a quick nod and turned to walk toward my car, caught off guard by the sudden hot rush of tears that threatened to spill from my eyes.

"Good night," I called over my shoulder, praying he wouldn't follow me. I was blinking rapidly, but the moisture was still coming, and I didn't know if I could hold it back much longer. I certainly didn't want him to see me crying, and I had no desire to try and explain why I was. I didn't even understand it myself.

I closed the car door and started the engine before I dared to look back toward him. He was still standing where I left him, under the eave of the barn with his hands in his pockets and pain etched across his face.

I managed a wave before I pulled away, and then the tears broke free and flowed.

# 23 THE THREE MUSKETEERS

Dax called at nine the next morning.

I let it go to voice mail as I stared at the phone in my hand and fought the wave of nausea that swept over me.

Despite my best efforts to focus on work, after reading the same email three times and having no idea what I'd read, I grabbed the phone to listen to his message.

*"Hey Maggie. I was calling to check on your shoulder and make sure you're feeling okay after your tumble. I'll be in the saddle the next couple of days so I might not have a great signal. Talk to you soon."*

I deleted it and swallowed hard to push down the lump in my throat.

"You didn't call him back?" Sandy asked as we talked later that night.

"No. I need some distance."

"You need a swift kick in the ass. Luckily, I know just the person to give it to you. What time are you picking up Alberto on Friday?"

"He lands a little before five, so by the time he goes through customs and gets his bags, I'm thinking we should be back here by six, six-thirty at the latest. Depending on traffic, course. What time are you here?"

"I should be to your place by five, so if you leave me something prepped, I could have dinner ready when you guys get there."

"He wants Cuban food. He says they don't have good Cuban food in Rome. Then he wants us to take him out dancing."

"Dancing? Seriously?"

"I know. I've told him before the clubs in Orlando aren't like the clubs in Rome, but he says the three of us haven't danced together in ages. He wants to go out dancing."

"Do clubs let people our age dance?" Sandy asked. "What if they card us at the door and tell us we're too old?"

I laughed, though she had raised a valid point.

"I don't know, but the trio hasn't been together in years. If he wants to dance, we'll find a place."

We did find a place, and when Alberto broke out his hip-hop and break dancing moves, we were quickly welcomed into the fold. By the time we left around midnight, the entire club had circled around us on the dance floor like Alberto was the featured entertainment. They even demanded an encore song when we tried to leave the first time.

"My feet are killing me," Sandy moaned as she slid off her shoes just inside my front door. "I haven't worn heels in ages. Now I remember why!"

"I want to go back tomorrow night," Alberto said. "That place was jumping!"

"I think I only recognized one song the entire night," I said, uncorking a bottle of wine.

"It was a great crowd though, wasn't it?" Alberto's face was still flushed with excitement.

"Yeah, it was," Sandy said as she grabbed three wine glasses from the cabinet. "But you! I can't believe you can still move like that. Can you believe him, Maggie? I'd be laid up for days if I did half of what he did tonight."

We settled into the sofa and chairs outside on the patio, and I yawned as I poured the wine.

"Don't do that!" Sandy admonished. "You start yawning, and I'm done for. It's way past my bedtime."

"I'm surprised you made it this late," Alberto teased. "I remember when we lived in the little blue house, you used to go to bed at like, eight o'clock. We lived with a toddler, but you were always in bed before Cabe."

"I can't help it," she said. "I need more sleep than the average person."

I smiled at the thought of the little blue house in Miami where the three of us had lived for the later months of my pregnancy with Cabe and the first two years of his life. Despite my circumstances then, they were some of my fondest memories.

"I swear you're part vampire," Sandy said, glaring at Alberto. "You never sleep, and you don't age. Look at him!" She turned to me as she pointed to Alberto. "He looks the same as he did the last time we saw him. How is this fair? How is this not sorcery?"

She was right; he did look the same. His blond hair held no streaks of gray. The faint lines at the corners of his eyes were all but imperceptible. His dancer's body was still every bit as taut and tight as it had ever been.

He grinned at her and shrugged. "Italian food. Italian wine. The Mediterranean sun."

"Sign me up for that fitness plan, am I right?" Sandy teased as she rolled her eyes in my direction.

"You're just jealous because you're an old married woman now," I said.

Sandy frowned. "I might as well be single with all the hours Hannah's been working lately. She's at the office 'round the clock trying to tie up loose ends at the firm before she transfers."

"I can't believe the two of you will be in the same city without me," Alberto said with a pout. "Maybe I should see if Orlando Ballet has any openings. I could move into your pool house, and we could go dancing every weekend."

"Yeah, because when your resume has Vienna, Paris, and Rome on it, moving to Orlando is the next obvious career choice," Sandy said, pouring herself more wine. "Besides, this pool house might not be available to rent. Maggie might be living on a ranch soon."

"Oh, stop." I closed my eyes and shook my head. "Don't even go there, Sandra."

"So, has she told you about him? The cowboy?"

"Oh, Lord. Here we go," I said, reaching for the bottle and refilling my glass.

Alberto looked at me and grinned. "She mentioned on the phone that she'd met someone."

"Did she mention they were rolling around lip-locked in the dirt?"

His eyes opened wide. "No, she failed to disclose those details. Last I heard, they'd had lunch and shared a bowl of chili. Are you holding out on me?"

"Oh, please," I protested. "Like I get a phone call every time you get a piece of action. Not that I want one, mind you!"

He laughed, but Sandy was determined to make her point.

"You need to talk to her, Berto. She's gonna screw this up if you don't."

I scrunched my face in confusion. "Screw what up? So, we've had lunch. Big deal. We took a horseback ride, the end of which resulted in the right side of my body being black and blue and me not being able to move my arm this week. You haven't even met him, so how can you say I'd be screwing up?"

"Because he seems to make you happy, and I want you to be happy."

"I'm happy being alone! Very happy, thank you!"

Sandy uncrossed her legs and leaned forward, resting her elbows on her knees. "Well, would it hurt you to share that happiness with someone else? If this guy intrigues you, interests you, *and* turns you on—why not pursue it?"

"I'm not going to discuss this."

"Oh my God! It was a lifetime ago. Let. It. Go!"

"Ladies, ladies, ladies," Alberto said, raising his hand. "While it thrills me to no end to see that some things never change, it's been a long day, and I'm too tired to play referee."

Sandy turned to face him, her hands outstretched. "I just want you to talk some sense into her. Would it kill her to have a little love in her life?"

"What about him?" I asked, pointing to Alberto. "Why aren't you on him? He's not in a relationship!"

Alberto cleared his throat and grinned. "That depends on what you define as a relationship, but that's another conversation for another time. Sandy, the decision isn't up to you."

"That's right. It's not," I said, my chin raised in defiance.

"Maggie's heart was dealt a crippling blow when it was young and formative," he continued. "She had to close it off to survive. It was self-defense."

"Yes! Exactly!" I nodded, crossing my arms in smug confidence that he was going to hand it to her.

"I understand that," Sandy said with a groan. "Hello? I was there. I just think at some point, she has to take a chance. She's played it safe long enough with the boring ones. This guy is different, and she knows it."

I looked to Alberto, eager to hear him shut her down.

"Maybe he is, maybe he isn't." He shrugged. "That's not for you or me to say. It's Maggie's choice."

"Yes! That's right," I said, thrilled to have someone else take her on for a change.

"So, you're telling me you're okay with her never falling in love again? How is that healthy?" Sandy was sitting on the edge of her chair, her eyes flashing anger and her cheeks red with emotion and wine.

Alberto closed his eyes and pinched the bridge of his nose. "How many times can we have the same conversation? When it comes down to it, it doesn't matter what you say or what I say. You should know that by now. It's not up to us. She has made her decision, and even if we don't agree with it—even if we think it's the wrong choice—we have to live with it and accept that it's hers to make."

"That's right," I said, nodding furiously until his words sunk in. "Wait. What? What decision? I've already made what decision?"

He took a sip of his wine and sighed. "That Gerry Tucker is the love of your life."

"What?" I slammed my glass down on the end table, nearly spilling its contents. "That's not true. Gerry Tucker is most certainly *not* the love of my life. *Please.*"

Alberto shrugged again. "He must be. If you don't allow anyone else the chance to be loved by you, then by default, he's the only candidate." He looked at Sandy and back at me. "By you closing yourself off to even the remotest possibility of falling in love again, then Gerry Tucker remains the great love affair of your life. Sad, disgusting even, but true."

Sandy stifled a giggle and I threw a look at her that silenced it immediately.

His words stunned me, and I had no response ready. I'd never considered it in those terms.

Alberto leaned forward and held my hand. "Mags, I know you had your heart broken. Shattered. You were betrayed, and you paid a high cost for it. But if you continue to shut yourself off, then you're still paying for a debt that's been satisfied. The kids are grown. They're happy. They're healthy. They have lives of their own. It's time to move on."

Sandy came and sat on the sofa next to me as a light breeze stirred the air.

"Sweetie, at some point, you have to stop blaming yourself."

"Don't even say that, because she immediately discounts it in her mind," Alberto said.

I jerked my head up and stared at him, nervous at what his insight would reveal next. "She knew on some level, but she didn't go with her gut. That's why she can't forgive herself. Never mind that we've all done it— gone into something knowing we shouldn't have and regretting it later. Maggie's just happened to be a far-reaching, long-lasting mistake. She can't let it go because she thinks she's gonna screw up again. Don't ya, Mags?"

He stood and stretched, his lean dancer's frame bending backward with an arc before he walked over to plant a kiss on the top of my head and pat Sandy's shoulder.

"Good night, ladies."

"What?" Sandy and I both said in unison.

"You're going to bed first?" she said. "Since when?"

"Since my body is still on Rome time. I've had a hellacious travel day and a fun evening of fellowship, wine, and dancing, which I've truly enjoyed. But believe it or not, this vampire has to get some sleep. Besides, we've had this conversation with Maggie a hundred times before. The outcome never changes. Good night. Love you both."

Sandy was silent as he left, and when he'd pulled the French door of the pool house shut, she reached up to swipe the lone tear that had escaped to roll down my cheek.

"I don't want Gerry Tucker to be the love of my life," I whispered.

"He doesn't deserve to be. And maybe this cowboy doesn't either, but you won't know unless you give it a try. Just because you screwed up once—"

"Twice," I interjected.

"Okay, twice. But it was the same person, so I don't think that counts as twice, but anyway. Just because you screwed up *twice* doesn't mean you're going to screw up again. You're not the same girl you were then. You're a woman, now. A smart, fierce, successful, independent woman."

I swiped angrily at the stubborn tears that refused to disappear as I reached forward to grab my napkin from the tray on the low table.

"I don't know what's wrong with me. I can count on one hand the number of times I've cried in the last ten years, but I seem to be in tears every night this week. Do you think it's hormones?"

"Honey, do you like this man?" she asked. "Are you attracted to him?"

I nodded, holding the napkin against my eyes and willing the tears to stop.

"Do you want to saddle him up and ride him like a cowgirl in the hay?"

I dropped the napkin and stared at her. "You're insane."

"Yeah. Hay would be all itchy, but you're missing the point. If you're interested, you need to take a chance."

I shook my head. "I don't ever want anyone to have that kind of power over me again."

"Love is powerful, no lie. But you can't think this guy would be anything like Gerry. Let's face it. No one would be like Gerry. *Snake.* What's your instinct tell you about this man?"

"We're gonna trust *my* instinct? 'Big mistake. Big. Huge!'"

"Did you not hear what Alberto said? It wasn't that your instinct was off, it was that you didn't follow it. If you had, then you would have let us be around Gerry more instead of pulling away. You would have insisted that he meet your parents. You would have called him out on anything that seemed fishy. You knew we didn't trust him, and you ignored that. But you wouldn't do that again, would you? I think if anything, you're hyper-vigilant the other direction. You need to find a balance in the middle. Give the cowboy the benefit of the doubt, but listen to the little voice if things aren't adding up."

"So, what...I should invite you along for our next lunch date? Insist he meet my parents right away? How will that keep me from getting hurt again?"

She smoothed my hair back and rested her head against mine. "Oh, Mags. Nothing can guarantee you won't get hurt again. But you can't have love without risk. It has no value if it can be easily given and just as easily lost. Look, I'm more than happy to meet this guy and tell you my opinion, but the truth is you don't need my approval or your mother's. You need to trust the woman you've become." She sat back and twisted a lock of my hair around her finger. "And I caught that *Pretty Woman* reference, by the way. Don't think you slipped that past me."

I smiled and she stood, reaching to take my hand and pull me up with her.

"Let's get some sleep, so we have enough energy to keep up with him tomorrow," she said. "The three musketeers, together again!"

## 24  I HAVE A SECRET

I lay awake long after I said good night to Sandy at the guest room door. It was comforting to have the trio under the same roof again. Well, technically the pool house was a different roof, but still. Having them with me made me feel whole, even if the questions they'd raised had taken me back to memories best left buried.

They were right.

I did know something was wrong.

On some level, I must have.

Why else would I have kept the relationship secret from my mother?

It was one thing to pull away from my friends and the other dancers. After all, I was injured. I couldn't dance. I was resentful and hurt to be excluded from my normal routine, so it was only natural that a new interest would take their place with my time.

But my mother and I were close. Despite having lived most of my life away from her house, I shared every aspect of it with her. There was nothing I hid. Until Gerry.

She and my father were in Europe when Gerry and I met the night I was injured. Another piece of the puzzle in creating the perfect storm, I'm sure. If she'd been around, if we'd been having our near daily chats, then I know she would have stepped in earlier.

As it was, by the time they returned to the States for Thanksgiving, I was already deeply ensnared in his web. Yet, I didn't mention him. I spent the entire holiday weekend with my parents and never mentioned that for the first time in my life, I was dating someone.

When they noticed my melancholy mood, they chalked it up to disappointment over the time missed dancing and the loss of the principal role due to my injury. They had no way of knowing I was pining away for

Gerry, who had flown home to New York to be with his family for the holiday.

I couldn't wait for us to be reunited, and when I met him at the airport for his return flight after the weekend, he promised me we'd never be separated again.

So needless to say, I reacted with strong emotions when he told me a week later he'd be flying home for Christmas as well.

"But I thought we'd spend it together," I said, stunned. "It's our first Christmas."

"So come to New York," he said, taking both my hands in his and kissing them.

"I can't go to New York. It's Christmas. I have to go to my parents'. They would be devastated if I didn't come home. Christmas is a very big deal in my house. I told you that."

"It's a big deal for my family, as well, Willow. Look, we'll have countless Christmases together. The rest of our lives! We can make it through this one apart. Next year, maybe we'll spend Christmas Eve in New York and then fly to Miami and be with your parents Christmas Day."

"Why can't we do that this year?" I asked, my shoulders fallen as I realized he wasn't going to give in to my demands.

"It's simply not possible this year. Believe me, I wish it was."

"So, make it happen. You said my wish was your command."

He wrapped his arms around me and kissed my forehead. "Oh, sweetheart, don't twist my words to stab me with them. Your wish *is* my command. But you owe it to your family to give them Christmas, and I owe the same to mine. I'll only be gone two weeks, and then I tell you what. When I come back, I won't even get a hotel. I'll come unpack my suitcase at your place, and you'll be sick of seeing me in no time."

"This ruins Christmas."

"No, no, it doesn't." He squeezed me against him, and then leaned back to look at me. "Wait a minute. I've got an idea. Let's go away. The two of us. We'll take a trip the week before Christmas, and we'll celebrate it early. Just you and me. What do you say?"

My spirits lifted at the thought of going away with Gerry. "Where would we go?"

"Aruba. I want to take you to Aruba. Have you been?"

"No!" A smile broke through my pouting frown.

"Oh, God, you'll love it. The sand glitters. The water is like nothing you've ever seen."

"Better than South Beach?"

"Oh, Willow. It puts South Beach to shame. I can't wait to see you lounging on the beach in a tiny, little bikini." He moved in closer with his hips, taking my face in his hands as his eyes darkened. "Or diving into the cool waters of a secluded pool surrounded by tropical flowers." His tongue darted across my lips, and I opened them with a moan. "But my favorite part will be taking that bikini from your body with my teeth and making you cry out my name." His mouth closed over mine and there was no further discussion.

We were going to Aruba.

However, I knew I couldn't leave the country without telling my parents.

I put it off as long as I could, waiting until the night before our flight to tell them.

"So, I've met someone," I said casually as my mom chattered on about the deal she'd found on a handbag. I twisted the phone cord around my finger, staring at the skin as it turned white from the lack of circulation.

"Oh? Really? That's wonderful! Tell me about him, dear. What's his name? Where'd you meet him?"

"Gerry. Gerry Tucker. I met him at the dance studio."

"Oh? He's a dancer?"

I hesitated, unsure of how much to tell my mother. The desire to keep things from her was one of the warning signs I ignored.

"No, he's a financier. He's backing our season."

"Oh." Her tone changed. "How old is he?"

"He's a bit older, but you'd love him, Mom. I know you would. He's traveled, like, the whole world, and he does business everywhere, like Dad. He loves the arts. He's so supportive of my dancing. He tells everyone that I'm a superb dancer."

The silence in response was out of character for my mother.

"Mom?"

"I'm here. So how long have you known him?"

"Um, a while. Ernesto introduced us. He knew Gerry, and he's just a great guy. I can't wait for you to meet him."

"I see. So, the two of you have been out? On dates?"

"Yes, and he's so charming, Mom. He has a friend who has a yacht, and he carries me so I don't have to walk on the dock with my foot in this stupid boot. I mean, it's real chivalrous of him. And his friend, Maryann, says that she knows someone in the Paris ballet. She said she might be able to talk to them. Put in a good word for me."

"Paris, huh? Why didn't you mention this gentleman when you were home for Thanksgiving? Were you seeing him then?"

"Um, yeah. I mean, it wasn't serious then or anything." It was the first time I'd ever outright lied to my mother.

"And now? It's gotten serious now?"

I was pacing the floor of my apartment, questioning my decision to bring it up and knowing already from her reaction that she'd never be on board with me going to Aruba with Gerry. What was I thinking? Why did I think she'd be okay with it?

"Well, yes. It has. We're in love."

"Really? In love. Exactly how long have you been seeing this man? And how old did you say he was?"

"I don't see what his age really matters."

Her silence sucked the air from the room.

"Mom, I think you'd really like him. Just wait until you meet him. You'll see."

"How old is he?"

"He's older."

"How old?"

I bit my lip and pressed my forehead against the window as I stared at the drops of rain sliding down the pane. "Thirty-two. But please don't rush to judge him for that. He's so good to me."

"Thirty-two? He's a grown man, Margaret. For heaven's sake."

"And I'm a grown woman. I'm nineteen. I'm an adult." I plopped down on my couch and squeezed my eyes shut, wishing I'd never told her a thing.

She exhaled loudly. "Barely an adult. And a rather sheltered adult, at that, though I guess I'm to blame in that regard. How long has this been going on? And why did you not tell me sooner?"

Guilt fueled my defensiveness. "I don't know. Maybe because I didn't want to get the third degree like you're giving me now."

"I beg your pardon? Young lady, I'll ask that you remember who you're speaking to. I am most certainly in a position to ask questions when my daughter casually tells me she's in love with someone who's almost twice her age when I've never once heard her mention a boyfriend before. How long have you been seeing this man?"

"*This man?* His name is Gerry. And he's not twice my age."

"I want to know how long you've been seeing this man and why this is the first I'm hearing of this."

"You were out of the country!"

She sighed, and I could see the exasperation on her face from memory. "And yet we've talked how many times since I was back in the country? You were with us for Thanksgiving the entire weekend. Why not have him come over and introduce us then?"

"He was in New York with his family."

"Okay, then have him come over tonight. Your father and I would love to meet him."

The tone of her voice didn't sound at all like that was true.

"Tonight won't work. I'll bring him over soon, I promise."

"How about this weekend?"

I hesitated, unwilling to press forward with my confession about Aruba.

"Friday night?" she said when I didn't answer. "Or would Saturday work best? I can cancel our tennis plans on Sunday."

Her voice held an edge to it, and I knew she wasn't being accommodating. She was being determined.

I swallowed hard and tried to decide what would be worse—telling her I was leaving for Aruba and having her blow up and possibly forbid me to go, or having her somehow find out I went without her knowledge.

Neither seemed like good options.

"Margaret? When will you bring this man, this Gerry, to meet us?"

"Well, we're actually going out of town this weekend, and then—"

"Going out of town? Where? Alone?"

I swallowed again, my mouth completely devoid of saliva. "Aruba."

"What?" she shrieked in the phone so loud that I had to pull it away from my ear. "The hell you will. Oh, no, ma'am. You are not going to some island country with a man your father and I have never even met. And after a month of dating? Have you lost your mind? Oh my God, Margaret. Are you sleeping with this man? Oh, God. Oh, God help me."

Embarrassment and frustration colored my cheeks and sparked my anger.

"I am an adult! I don't need your permission to go out of town with my boyfriend. I have my own apartment and my own job and my own life. I can do what I want."

"An apartment I pay for and a life I've financed, so you might want to be careful how high and mighty you get, young lady."

"I have to go. I should have known better than to try and talk to you. You don't understand anything. I'll call you when we get back."

I hung up before she could say anything else.

My father's phone call was inevitable, and sweat covered my palms as I considered not answering it. Knowing he would probably just drive to my apartment if I didn't, I went ahead and picked up the phone.

"Hello?"

"Sweetheart, your mother says you're flying off to Bermuda with some man. Tell me she misunderstood, please."

"Aruba."

"What?"

"Aruba. We're flying to Aruba, and his name is Gerry."

"Maggie, what are you talking about? Who is this man? How long have you known him? Why on earth would you fly out of town with someone you've barely met? Sweetheart, what's gotten into you?"

I was packing my clothes when he called, but somehow cutting the tags off brand-new lacy underthings didn't seem right while on the phone with my father, so I left the suitcase in the bedroom and sat on the edge of my tub.

"Dad, I love him. He's the most wonderful man I've ever met, and I want to go away with him."

"He can't be that wonderful if he'd take you out of town without even meeting your parents first. What kind of man would do that? Has he asked to meet us? Why has he not insisted on meeting us? Why would you not insist on that? How long have you been seeing this man?"

The hurt in my father's voice cut me like a knife, and my eyes filled with tears.

"He wants to meet you, I swear. It's just that you were out of the country, and then he was in New York for Thanksgiving, and then he'll be gone again for Christmas. This is our only chance to get away, but as soon as—"

"Your mother says he's over thirty. Why, Maggie? Ask yourself why a man over thirty would be interested in a nineteen-year-old."

The hurt in his voice had become tinged with anger, but his challenge as to Gerry's interest in me put me on the defensive again.

"Why can't you and Mom see that I'm an adult? That I have plenty to offer someone to be interested in? Why are you both hung up on Gerry's age?"

"Because I have a pretty good idea of what he's after, and I'm not sure you realize what that is."

I grunted in protest. "He's not *after* anything, Dad. We're in love. We're gonna spend the rest of our lives together."

"Oh, Maggie. Don't do this. Slow this down, sweetheart. Don't rush into it. You have all the time in the world. And what does the studio say about you going out of town? What about rehearsals?"

"I'm still on the injured list for a few more days, and Gerry has agreed to back the entire season, so he talked to Ernesto. It's fine. They've cleared me to be gone for the week."

"A week?" His voice rose in his growing frustration. "No. I forbid this. There's no way in hell I'm letting you make this mistake. You're not thinking clearly. Bring this man to the house this weekend. Let your mother and me meet him, get to know him. Let this thing take its natural course. You're rushing it."

"I'm not! You don't understand. If you knew him—"

"But I don't know him, and neither do you! You've lost your mind!"

I drew back in shock. My father had never spoken to me with so much volume and anger. "How much do you know about him? What could you know in such a short time? About his background? His past? His family? What do you really know?"

"I know all I need to know. I love Gerry, and he loves me. We're going to Aruba, and you can't stop me."

"We'll see about that." My father hung up on me for the first time in my life, although it wouldn't be the last, nor would it be the last time Gerry caused it.

It didn't matter at the time, though. I packed my bags and took a taxi to Gerry's hotel, and the next morning, I flew to Aruba with a man I barely knew.

## 25 SOCIETY PAGES

It was surprisingly easy to push my parents to the back of my mind while Gerry and I were in Aruba. In fact, it was easy to pretend the rest of the world didn't exist.

We stayed up late every night after watching the sun set over the water. We slept in every morning and had breakfast delivered to our own private patio. We swam and lounged in the sun, feeding each other luscious fruits and consuming colorful adult beverages adorned with fancy umbrellas.

My favorite times were those we spent in the privacy of our bungalow, exploring the many ways two people can give each other pleasure.

I learned everything I thought I needed to know to be a woman.

Gerry had the limousine drop me off outside my building when we returned, promising to join me for dinner after he'd made calls and caught up with work.

I was tired but lighthearted as I exited the elevator in my straw hat and colorful sun-dress, dragging my suitcase behind me.

When I put the key in the deadbolt of my door, I was shocked to find it unlocked, but nothing compared to my reaction at seeing my parents seated on the sofa. They looked haggard and pale. Older than when I'd seen them weeks before.

My mother rushed to greet me and threw her arms around my shoulders, knocking my hat from my head in her exuberance.

"Oh, thank God. Thank you, Lord. You're home. You're safe. Oh, thank you, God."

"What are you guys doing here?" I asked, my voice hesitant.

My father rose and went to stand by the window, his hands on his hips and his face set in a stern expression I didn't recall ever seeing him wear.

I pulled away from my mother's arms. "Mom, what's wrong? Why are you guys here?"

She was crying, and she wiped her eyes with the back of her hand before reaching up to stroke my cheek.

I avoided her touch and dropped my keys on the table by the door. "Tell me what's going on."

My first thought had been that they were angry with me for going to Aruba, and for some reason, they'd come to my apartment to chastise me for it. But the level of her emotion and the silence from my father was unsettling, and I wondered briefly if a family member had died while I was gone or if some other tragedy had befallen us.

"Why will neither of you tell me what's going on? What are you doing here?"

"We've come to take you home," my father said without ever looking in my direction.

The blissful high I'd been sailing on for the past week plummeted, and anger surged up within me. I wasn't the pliable teenager they thought they knew. In my mind, I'd become a full-fledged woman of independence, and it was time for me to take a stand against their authority.

"This *is* my home, and I'm not going anywhere with you."

My father turned to face me, and the sheer look of rage on his face struck fear in my heart.

"Do you have any idea what you've gotten yourself into?"

My own anger flared in response.

"If this is about Gerry, you're wasting your breath. You can leave right now because I'm not going to put up with it. If that's why you're here, you can get out of my apartment." My efforts to keep my voice from breaking failed.

"I paid for this damned apartment and everything in it, and you may be grown, but there's a lot you don't know. So, I suggest you lose that damned attitude!"

I shrank back from the venom in his voice.

"Bill, calm down. You're not helping anything," my mother said, her hand outstretched toward him. She turned back to me, and her expression confused me with its odd mixture of fear, anger, and pity.

"We've talked to Benjamin, dear. He says you haven't been to rehearsals in over a month. He says they're considering disciplinary action. They may remove you from the company."

Panic surged up inside me. "No, that's not true. Gerry talked to Ernesto, and—"

"It's not Gerry's decision," my mother said, her voice steely.

"But, no, Gerry is paying for the season. He gets to say—"

"You signed a contract, Margaret. You had an obligation."

"But Gerry talked to him—"

"Did *you*? Did *you* talk to Ernesto personally? Did you talk to Benjamin? Because they both say they've heard nothing from you for weeks! You are in danger of losing everything we've worked for your whole life!"

"Wait, this can't be true."

"Enough!" My father yelled and crossed the floor between us. "This is ridiculous. Tell her, Peggy. You tell her or I will."

My mind whirled in its effort to understand what was happening. My mother's words replayed in my head, jumbled and incoherent. Her tears and the pain on her face as it contorted in response to my father's voice stabbed at my heart.

I'd never heard him speak to her that way, never seen the veins in his neck bulging and his face redder than if he'd been in the sun all day.

"Tell me what?" I heard myself ask, although I was certain I didn't want to know. Anything that had caused my parents to morph into these unrecognizable versions of themselves couldn't be good.

"Honey," my mother said, her tears flowing anew. "He's married."

I didn't understand. Nothing made sense. Of course, Ernesto was married. We all knew that. I'd met his wife, Angeline, and so had my parents.

"What are you talking about? Who's married?"

My father's hands shook and his face turned even redder. He spoke through gritted teeth, and I was shocked to see tears fill his angry eyes.

"This man you've been traipsing off with. While you were destroying your career and your reputation, his wife was at his home getting ready for their annual Christmas ball."

He grabbed a newspaper from my coffee table and thrust it in my hands.

It was a social publication from a paper in New York, and there on the front page was a picture of Gerry with his arm around a dark-haired woman with harsh features and bright red lips. My hands trembled as my eyes scanned the headline.

"*Mr. & Mrs. Gerald Tucker to Host their Ninth Annual Holiday Charity Gala.*"

My knees buckled and hit the ground as the air rushed from my lungs. The entire room seemed to tilt and everything in my peripheral vision went black as I blinked against the tears that blurred the words on the page.

"*I can't thank my beautiful wife enough for her hard work this year. I've been out of town through most of the planning these past few weeks, so she's made me promise to take her away to our favorite bungalow in Aruba as soon as this party's over. She's outdone herself, though. This will be our best event yet.*"

There were more pictures—one of their mansion in the Hamptons, one of last year's famous guests with the happy couple, another of the hand-engraved invitations that had been sent months ago—and there were many more painful words, but I didn't get to read them. I'd collapsed in a heap on the floor, my sobs overwhelming my nervous system to the point of hyperventilation.

My mother knelt on the floor beside me, her arms around my shoulders as they heaved, her own tears flowing with mine.

She chanted, "I'm so sorry," over and over again, but her words were distant background noise to the fevered chaos in my mind.

How could this be? There had to be some mistake. They were wrong. It couldn't be him. He couldn't be married.

Pain racked my body as though tiny needles were piercing my skin from head to toe, and my stomach jerked in spasms as I retched and tried to crawl to the bathroom. I didn't make it, and as I emptied what was left of my tropical breakfast on the carpet of my living room, my mother held my hair back and cried with me.

I had been right in one regard. Tragedy had befallen our family, and someone had died. I just hadn't known yet it was the girl inside of me.

## 26 FATHER KNOWS BEST

"I don't understand," I whispered as I lay with my cheek on the cold tile of the bathroom floor.

My mother stroked a wet cloth over my forehead and smoothed my hair back with it.

"I don't either, sweetheart."

"How can this be? How can this be true?" Tears pooled on the tile and my voice cracked and trailed off at the end.

My father's footsteps echoed on the wood floor outside the bathroom, and he spoke for the first time since he'd thrown my world in my face with a newspaper.

"He's a liar. A con man. He took advantage of you. This is what happens when you trust someone you don't know. Someone who doesn't have the decency to even meet your parents."

"Bill, please," my mother whispered.

"Someone who sabotages your career and everything you've worked for."

"Bill, enough."

"God only knows what could have happened to you in Aruba. What were you thinking?"

"Bill, I said, enough! She's white as a sheet. Can't you see the pain she's in?"

"Your mother has been sick with worry. She hasn't slept in days. Up all night pacing the floor."

She rose up on her knees and waved him out the door. "Go! I have never raised my voice to you, William Shaw, not in twenty-eight years of marriage, but so help me God if you don't leave this girl alone, I can't be responsible for my actions. She's been through enough, and she's in shock.

142

She doesn't need your condemnation right now."

"Condemnation?" His voice was incredulous, but he heeded her plea, and I closed my eyes against the vibrations of his footsteps as he walked away and slammed the front door.

My mother wet the cloth again and dragged it across my forehead, but I pushed it from me, twisting my face away from the water as it dripped down my cheek.

"I don't understand," I cried. "I don't understand. This can't be happening."

I covered my face with my hands and drew my knees up under my chin, descending into uncontrollable sobs once more.

I have no idea how much time passed with my mother sitting by my side on the bathroom floor, but when my stomach was emptied and my eyes held no more tears, I found the space confining. I was desperate to get up and out of there.

"Where are you going?" she asked as I pushed myself up and ran from the room.

My entire apartment looked different. Everything was tainted, overlaid with a hue of betrayal and reminders that my love was a lie. Ticket stubs. A shriveled bouquet. Snapshots of the two of us in a carnival booth. A magnet on the fridge holding a love note left on my pillow one morning.

No matter where I looked, I was stabbed with pain, a physical reaction to an emotional overload that at times would double me over or take my breath away.

I stumbled over the suitcase by the door, and the sight of my straw hat crushed beneath it was too much to bear. How could my heart have been so filled with utter happiness that morning, only to be stripped and left barely beating in tattered ruins by late afternoon?

My eyes caught sight of the newspaper where I'd dropped it, not too far from the large stained area of the carpet that still held tiny remnants of paper towels from my father's feeble attempts to clean up after me.

I closed my eyes against the picture of Gerry smiling with his wife, the very word ripping through my brain like a jagged saw.

"How did you know?" I asked. "How did you find out?"

My eyes were still closed, but I heard her cross the living room floor and pick up the paper.

"Your father called Ernesto when you wouldn't answer your phone or come to the door. He couldn't believe you'd actually flown away. Ernesto gave him Gerry's contact information, and your father hired an investigator to find out who he was."

I whirled around and glared at her, my anger and pain in dire need of a target. "An investigator? He hired *an investigator?*"

"He was out of his mind with worry, sweetheart. We both were. This came out of nowhere. You leaving town with this man. No warning that you were even seeing him until the day before you left. Then when he talked to Benjamin and found out you'd sacrificed your career. It was so out of character for you."

I closed my eyes again and shook my head, immediately placing my fingers on my temples to block the pain it caused.

"I didn't sacrifice my career. I told you, Gerry talked to Ernesto."

"Margaret Ellen, that man has been lying to you. Wake up! He's a con artist. A liar. Nothing he has said to you has been true."

I shook my head again, vehemently this time, ignoring the pain. "No. No. There has to be some mistake. Some reason. You have it wrong. You have it all wrong. I need to talk to Gerry. He'll explain. He'll be able to explain."

Tears poured down my face as I struggled to convince my brain to ignore what I knew and focus on what I thought I'd known.

"I have to get out of here," I said, suddenly panicked and filled with anxiety. "I have to go. I need air."

"Okay. Let's get your things together and when your father comes back, we'll go home. We'll get you to a doctor and—"

"What? Why? I'm not going to a doctor. This is my home. What are you talking about?"

"Maggie, you have no idea who this man is, and I don't need any detailed explanations, but I'll assume you've been intimate with him."

"Mom!"

"You need an examination. Who knows how many other women he's done this to? Or what he might have?"

The words stung and the reality behind them was like a dagger piercing what was left of my heart.

"No. No doctor. I can't do this. I need air. I need to be alone."

I ran for the door, but right as my hand touched the knob, the phone rang.

My body froze. I knew it was him. He was either calling to say he was about to leave the hotel or calling to say he'd been delayed.

Suddenly, the haze at the edge of my vision cleared, and puzzle pieces clicked into place.

He had to be at his hotel for regular phone calls. We'd only spent the night there once or twice, and always with the condition that I needed to wake early and leave so he wouldn't be distracted in doing his business calls. Even when he stayed over at my place, he'd leave at an ungodly early hour in the morning to head back to his room and conduct business.

It was *her*.

The wife.

He'd been keeping his scheduled conversations with her.

But he'd introduced me to all his friends. We'd spent countless hours with them. Wouldn't someone have mentioned his wife? Wouldn't he have been worried that he'd be betrayed? Or did no one in Miami know about her?

Not only that, but we'd just spent a week together in Aruba, the memories so fresh in my mind that I still smelled like suntan oil, and I could feel the tenderness between my legs from the time spent engaged in intimacy.

My stomach roiled at the thought of Gerry in bed with that dark-haired woman. The newspaper had mentioned Aruba. Was it the same resort? The same bungalow? The same bed?

I turned and sprinted to grab the cordless phone before it stopped ringing, slamming the bedroom door in my mother's face before she could protest.

"Hello, sexy," he said. "I was getting worried when you didn't answer. Were you in the bath? Without me?"

His voice invoked another wave of nausea, and I swallowed down the bile that rose.

"Change of plans, love," he continued without waiting for a response. "I'm going to send the car for you and I'll meet you in the lobby here. I've been waiting for a call that hasn't come, and unfortunately, I can't break away for dinner until it does."

I closed my eyes and dug my fingernails so deeply into my palm that they broke the skin.

"Is it your wife?"

Gerry paused for a moment. "What?"

"The call you're expecting. Is it your wife? Margot, right?"

He cleared his throat and I could hear him shift the phone receiver to the other ear.

"What are you talking about? Willow—"

"Don't call me that!" I screamed. "Don't ever call me that again."

"Who have you been talking to?"

I slid off the bed and onto the floor, my hand gripping my abdomen but unable to stop the pains that ripped through me.

"I think the better question is who have *you* been talking to, Gerry? You son-of-a-bitch."

"Willow, wait—"

"I told you not to call me that. In fact, don't call me anything. Don't call me at all. I never want to hear your voice again."

I slammed the cordless phone against my nightstand over and over again until it busted into tiny shards and pieces all over the floor, leaving a jagged scar in the wood.

My mother opened the door cautiously as I wailed, not even caring that snot flowed from my nose and mixed with my tears and the saliva dripping from my open mouth.

I cried until there was nothing left in me. No emotion left to feel. No feelings left to process. No tears left unshed.

"Sweetheart," my mother whispered when I'd grown quiet, staring at the wall as I absentmindedly pulled at a strand of carpet on my bedroom floor. I didn't remember her leaving my side, but I'd heard the two of them whispering in the other room. My dad seemed to have calmed down considerably. I guess you can only function at the highest level of frenzied emotion for just so long.

I turned to look at her as she knelt beside me, her warm brown eyes red-rimmed and swollen from her own tears.

"We should go," I said, pushing myself up to standing and flinging my closet doors open. Every outfit carried a memory. The dress I'd worn the first day on the yacht. The jeans he loved because of the way they molded to my butt and thighs. The little black dress that he'd taken off of me in the back of the limousine.

I closed the closet door and turned to face my mother. "I need new clothes."

"Yes, of course." She stood silent as I walked past her into my bathroom, pausing when I realized the most essential of my toiletries were still packed in the suitcase.

Could it really have just been hours ago that I'd packed that suitcase? Laughing as Gerry had pulled me down on the bed and threatened to make us miss our flight? If we'd missed that flight, I still wouldn't know. I'd still think I was the luckiest girl in the world to love and be loved.

I closed my eyes and flipped off the light in the bathroom.

"Let's just go. I don't need anything from here."

I stopped when I came out of my bedroom and saw my father sitting on the sofa. For the first time, I noticed the dark circles under his eyes and the disheveled state of his normally rigid hair. His eyes lifted to meet mine, and I squared my shoulders and lifted my chin, dreading another round of hearing him say I told you so.

He stood and came to me, placing his hands on my shoulders.

"I am so sorry, baby girl. It kills me to see you in this pain, and I would give everything I have, everything I own, to take it from you. But I promise you this, Gerry Tucker will never hurt you again. He'll never get that chance, because I will do everything in my power to make sure of that."

He closed his arms around me, and I longed for easier days when my father's arms could make me feel safe and secure. Somehow, I knew then, even in my emotional shock and numbness, that I would never again feel that way.

# 27 COUNTING BACK

In everything that happened in the immediate aftermath of Aruba, it never occurred to me that I might not dance again.

The ramifications at the dance company were crowded out of my mind by betrayal and love lost.

The thought that my career might be over—that my life of dance, my world as I knew it, might be gone forever—wasn't even in my realm of possibilities.

But the universe had not revealed all its cards yet.

Christmas went by in a nauseating blur. From the day my parents brought me home from the apartment, I did little more than sleep, leaving my room only for necessary bathroom trips or to put out the untouched plates of food my mother insisted on bringing me.

They canceled their annual New Year's Eve soiree, concerned that the festivities and the people in the house would be too much for me.

I doubt I would have known that a party was happening. I was too self-absorbed to even realize the date until it had passed and my mother mentioned it in her daily coax for me to get up and take a shower.

"It's a new year, sweetheart. Don't you think you'd feel better if you showered? Look at it as a fresh start."

I pulled the covers over my head and told her to go away. Again.

Sandy and Alberto both came to visit more than once, but I refused to see them, despite my mother's threats to let them in my room if I didn't shower and come downstairs.

I knew she wouldn't go through with it. She was too mortified for anyone to see me in that condition.

I didn't care how I looked, but there was no way in hell I was ready to face my best friends. I didn't want to live out the humiliation of my choices.

Especially after they'd tried to warn me, and I'd treated them so badly.

It was ten days into the new year when I finally decided I needed a shower and clean sheets. I opened the window blinds and squinted at the unwelcome rays of sun, furious that the day would dare be bright when my world was still cloaked in darkness.

I was standing in front of the shower waiting for the water to get warm when I glanced over my shoulder at my reflection in the mirror.

The change in my appearance caught me off guard. My skin was pale, and my eyes were sunken and surrounded by dark circles that spoke of days on end with no sunlight, a bare minimum of food, no exercise, and too much sorrow to contain. My cheeks seemed hollow, and I could see my ribs.

I turned to look at my back, and drew in a sharp breath at the clearly visible knobs of my spine. I'd always been lean, thin even. But I'd never looked so emaciated. I had twisted back to a profile view, ready to step into the water when I noticed my stomach.

It was rounded, not like a ball, but definitely more curved than I remembered.

I'd often had problems shopping for a swimsuit because my hip bones protruded higher than my abdomen, and if a bikini bottom wasn't snug against my skin, it would stretch across my pelvic valley from bone to bone and leave my pubic mound exposed.

That problem no longer existed. The valley was gone. I laid my hand across it in disbelief, turning to face the mirror.

The loss of weight was obvious in my face, my waist, and my arms.

Why on earth would my abdomen have gained?

A sick feeling washed over me as I frantically tried to count back to the last time I remembered cramping.

I'd hit puberty later than most at seventeen, and even once it began, I'd never had a regular menstrual cycle. The doctor had assured my mother and me that it was no cause for alarm, and that many athletes with vigorous workout schedules and low body weights did not experience regular periods.

I'd never bled for more than a day or two at a time, and I sometimes went two or three months without a period, but I did usually have cramping with or without the outward signs of menstruation.

I didn't remember having any cramps at all since I'd met Gerry, and certainly none since we'd first been intimate.

I turned off the water and wrapped a towel around me to sprint across the hallway to my bedroom, desperate to find a calendar.

My mother's voice called out from downstairs when my bedroom door closed. "Maggie, are you out of the shower? You want a sandwich?"

I didn't even bother to answer her as I shuffled through my nightstand

and my desk in search of a calendar, knowing the entire time how unlikely it would be to find one in a room that had been largely unoccupied for several years.

When my search proved fruitless, I headed back across the hallway to the bathroom, whipping off the towel and examining my belly from every possible angle. By my mental calculations, it had only been eight weeks since Gerry and I had sex the first time. Was it possible that I would already be showing? I might not have seen it if I'd been at my normal weight, and it wasn't a change that anyone else would have noticed, but I couldn't deny the difference.

I stared at my breasts, wondering if it was my imagination that my nipples seemed darker. Larger.

My bust had never been ample, which was a blessing for dance, but the dwindling that had affected all of my body except my stomach had somehow also missed my breasts. They seemed to have the same fullness as before.

I'd been in a constant state of nausea and lethargy for weeks, but I'd assumed it was my body's natural response to overwhelming emotional pain, disappointment, and depression.

Surely, that had been part of it, but something much bigger had been set into motion. It seemed the bad choices I'd made were going to be far more consequential than a painful break-up and the loss of my standing in the dance company.

# 28 LAKESIDE LUNCH

"Did you get in touch with Galen about Saturday?" I asked Alberto as we scanned the lunch menu at an outdoor cafe overlooking Lake Eola.

"Yes, the little minx finally called me back. I have a two-hour layover at JFK, so she's going to drive out to the airport and meet me for a late lunch."

"Excellent. I'm glad you two will get to visit."

"She sounds happy," he said as he closed the menu.

"I think she is. She definitely likes Manhattan. She's excited about the wedding, and I know she's thrilled that you're gonna make it. Thanks for that, by the way."

"Are you kidding me? I wouldn't have missed Cabe's if it hadn't been right in the middle of opening weekend. I take my duties as godfather quite seriously, even if I haven't been in the country to help out as much as I would have liked."

"I wish you had been! I needed all the help I could get with Galen. I thought that girl was going to be the death of me for a while. She may still be. I think she got the worst of my character flaws and Gerry's."

"She's certainly fiery."

"That's an understatement. I feel like I didn't give her enough boundaries growing up. I allowed her to be a bit too headstrong, I suppose. Parenting based on guilt rarely produces the best in children."

Alberto handed our waiter the menus as we placed our orders.

"She said her career is going well," he said when the waiter had gone.

"Seems to be. I can't thank you enough for getting her that audition."

He shook his head and brushed away my thanks with his hand. "All I did was make a phone call. She nailed the audition and danced her way into the troupe. That was all her." He paused a moment before continuing. "Is

150

she still talking to Gerry? His kids?"

I nodded, ignoring the punched-in-the-gut feeling I got whenever that topic came up.

"She doesn't tell me when she talks to him, but I assume she still does. I think she knows it upsets me, even though I told her it was fine. But she mentions the girl often. Julie. They've become close, it seems. Evidently, Julie has an apartment on the Upper East Side, so they've hung out quite a bit since Galen moved to New York."

Alberto frowned. "I know that has to be hard for you, but it *is* her half-sister. It may be good for her, you know, to help her feel like she has connections. With him."

I sucked down half my glass of water, trying to ease the knot in my stomach.

"You're right," I said, and I paused as the waiter brought our appetizer. "That's why I encouraged it to begin with, but it doesn't make it any easier. Maybe I should have let him be involved all along. I don't know."

I scooped up a piece of roasted artichoke and scraped it clean between my teeth.

"Do you think he would have been?" Alberto asked, his blue eyes steely. "Beyond an occasional phone call or perhaps a hasty dinner while he was in town for business? I know he promised and pleaded, but you know as well as I do that Gerry Tucker didn't make promises he intended to keep. Don't forget that. I was there. I know you did the right thing."

I wanted to think so. But had I? Had I been right to keep the kids from knowing their father?

At the time, I told myself—and Gerry—that I was doing it to protect them. He couldn't be trusted. We couldn't depend on him. Couldn't believe what he said. So I convinced him—and me—that the best thing for the kids was if they never saw him. Never knew him.

"Who can say for sure if it was the right thing?" I asked. "I have my doubts. Seeing the way it's all affected them. Cabe's anger. Galen's angst. Her starvation for affection and attention. Perhaps it would have been better if they'd had at least some contact with him."

"I think they've both turned out well. They're both successful in their careers, and they both seem to be happy in their relationships. Cabe and Tyler spoke very highly of Tate. They think he's been good for Galen."

I asked the waiter to bring more water and nodded to Alberto. "He has been. He's a saint. Tate is well-balanced, even-keeled. I only hope he can continue to put up with her once they're married. How did your dinner at Cabe and Tyler's go? I'm still bummed I had a work event the only night they were both available."

"It was great," Alberto said as he munched on his salad. "I loved watching the two of them interact. Cabe is certainly smitten with her."

I smiled, and the tension in my body eased with the thought of Cabe and Tyler's happiness. "He is! And he has been, for years. I'm just glad they both finally got past their hang-ups and found their way together. I swear I've never seen two people more well-suited for each other."

Alberto wiped his mouth with the napkin and folded his hands under his chin. "Speaking of getting over past hang-ups and finding someone, have you called the cowboy back?"

I sighed and poked at my salad with my fork. "He has a name, you know. Dax."

"You haven't called him, have you?"

"I've been a little busy being your tour guide," I said.

Alberto nodded. "Hmmm. Too busy to pick up a phone? Really?"

"You've had me out pretty much every single night, except last night when I was working an event."

"You've found time to call me from work every day. You can't call him from work?"

"And say what? I stormed out of there with no explanation and I haven't returned his call. It's been over a week. He's probably either pissed or thinks I'm nuts."

"So, all that talk about being ready to move forward, maybe it's time to take a chance, he's a great guy…all that was just blah, blah, blah to get me and Sandy to shut up?"

"No, but I…."

My phone vibrated on the table, and I reached to look at it.

"Speak of the devil." I held the phone up for Alberto to see Dax's name on the screen. "How's that for timing?"

"Well, what are you waiting for? Answer it. You said you're ready, right? There's no time like the present. Ask him out. Invite him over for dinner. Make a move."

I stood and walked toward the balcony railing, taking a deep breath as I accepted the call.

"Hello there," I said, trying to sound casual, as though I hadn't walked away without a word after our first kiss and then ignored his call for over a week.

"Hello there, yourself! How are you this fine Wednesday?"

His voice moved over me like the cool water of a pool on a hot, sweltering day, and immediately I felt more awake and alive.

"I'm good," I said, my smile spreading more by the minute. "Somehow I had forgotten how good it felt to hear him talk. "And you?"

"Tired, but a good tired. We've come into the busy spring season on the ranch. A lot to be done, pretty much nonstop hours. But I love it. I love the work, and I love the adrenaline. So, it's good. Tell you what, though, when I finally get to lay down at night, I'm out like a light."

I chuckled and pictured him stumbling into his camper, tired and sweaty at the end of a hard day's work. I had to halt my train of thoughts before they had him completely undressed.

"I could use a good night's sleep myself," I said. "I've had some friends staying at the house with me this past week, and we've been pulling long nights around the pool with wine and memories, so I'm starting to drag a bit."

I wondered if I should say that was why I hadn't called. Pass it off on being busy or preoccupied with visitors. Anything other than the truth—that I'd been terrified of what I felt for him. He didn't seem to need an explanation, though.

"That's too bad. It turns out I need to be in Orlando on Saturday afternoon to meet a plane and oversee the transfer of some equipment. I was hoping I might get to take you out to dinner afterward. But if you've got company...."

I glanced over my shoulder at Alberto, who flashed me an encouraging smile.

"Actually, my friend is flying out Saturday morning, so I happen to be free that night."

Alberto's smile spread, and he gave me a thumbs-up.

"Excellent," Dax said.

"Don't you mean *fortuitous*?"

He laughed, and I laughed with him.

"Can I pick you up," he said. "Or would you rather meet somewhere?"

Alberto was watching me with a look of anticipation one might see on someone whose team is about to score the winning point.

He'd been right, though. I didn't want to remain crippled by the past. I wanted to pursue my interest in Dax.

"You know what, Mr. Pearson? I'd like to prepare dinner for you," I said.

"Uh-oh. You're not going to try and outdo my chili, are you?"

I laughed again, reveling in how easy it was to feel joy with Dax. "No. No chili. That's your specialty, and I wouldn't dare encroach upon it."

"Alright. I should be done at the airport by five. What time do you want me? And where?"

"I'll text you the address. Wanna say five-thirty?"

"Sounds great. I'll call you if anything changes, or I'll see you then."

"I look forward to it," I said, surprised to realize how much it was true.

Based on Alberto's smile as I returned to our table, it was hard to tell which of us was happier about the call.

"So, what did he say? What did you say?"

"He's coming over for dinner Saturday night. Thank you for the suggestion. I did what you told me to. Are you happy?"

"Yes," he said, rolling his eyes. "Finally. Good Lord."

"He didn't say anything about me not calling back. Here I was all worried he'd be upset, but he said he's been working a lot at the ranch."

"Maggie, the man is busy cowboying. He has no time to be sitting around waiting for his phone to ring."

"You're right. You're always right."

"Ha! If only you'd remember that more often. I paid the check so we can get out of here and get you back to work. Are you ready to go?"

"Yes! I feel like this release of nervous energy. Like I've got a buzz. God! I'd been dreading calling him after putting it off, but I really wanted to talk to him, and now it's done. He called me."

"Yes, he did. He's obviously interested, that's for sure. But he's not overbearing, and he seems to be secure enough in his own life not to need your constant attention. I'm liking him."

"You haven't even met him," I said, pushing against Alberto's arm as we walked toward the door.

"Well, I'll be back for the wedding in August. If he still makes you happy by then, I'll get to meet him."

"You should move back. It would be so awesome to have the trio in the same city again."

"How long has it been?"

I clicked the key fob to unlock my car doors. "Well, let's see. I left Miami with the kids when Galen was what? One? But you moved to New York before that, right? When did you transfer?"

He cut his eyes to me over the roof of the car and glared. "I stayed in Miami to be in the delivery room with you for my goddaughter's birth, and you don't remember this?"

"No, of course I remember you being there. But when did you actually leave? I remember moving Cabe into your bedroom once you'd gone, but it's kind of a blur as to what the timing was. I was a little busy with two kids and a downward spiral."

We both got in the car, and I immediately cranked up the A/C to combat the warm March sun.

"The way I remember it, Little Guy pretty much took over my room as soon as you moved back in, but I wasn't officially gone until Galen was like three months old."

"Right."

My mind drifted back to that dark, crazy time. Me, seven months pregnant, showing up on their doorstep with a three-year-old in tow and begging for a place to stay. I forced the memory from my thoughts and turned my attention back to the future. Alberto was right. It was time to leave the past behind.

# 29 AN EVENING POOLSIDE

The rest of my week with Alberto flew by much too quickly. Our airport goodbyes always put me in a funk for the rest of the day, but knowing I would see Dax in a few hours kept me from descending into sadness.

Since we'd already done Latin-Asian fusion, Thai, and chili, I decided to branch in a more Italian direction with a pancetta *Amatriciana* sauce over penne pasta with my signature *Tiramisu* cheesecake for dessert.

When Dax rang the bell promptly at five-thirty, I had everything prepared with the bread in the oven, the outdoor patio table set, and music playing softly in the background.

I almost forgot to take off my apron in my excitement to answer the door and see him again.

Alberto's last words when I dropped him at the airport echoed in my head as I slid the deadbolt open.

*"Live your life in the present, not the past and not the future. Enjoy it for what it is."*

He'd also added *"and get laid tonight!"*, but I was choosing to focus on the more proverbial wisdom he'd offered.

Dax's face was covered by a vivid bouquet of daisies in a rainbow of colors when I opened the door, and I laughed as he lowered it just beneath his brilliant green eyes to say hello.

"I couldn't show up empty-handed," he said, "so I stopped to get a bottle of wine at the Publix down the street and they had these there. I don't know; they're probably dyed with food coloring or something, but they were bright and cheerful, so they reminded me of you."

I took the flowers and the bottle of wine, inviting him to follow me to the kitchen.

"It smells delicious, whatever it is," he said as he watched me cut the flower stems and put them in a vase of water.

"I went with Italian, since we hadn't done that yet."

"Can't go wrong with Italian," he said, walking to the bay window to look out onto the pool and its lanai. "Nice pool house. Do you get much use out of it?"

"Not as much these days. When the kids were younger, my parents liked to stay out there. Have some privacy and a modicum of quiet. Then when the kids were teens, they always enjoyed it for having their friends over. I kept the fridge stocked with all their favorites and made sure I popped in often enough with a plate of cookies or a tray of pizzas so I could keep an eye on what was going on. It sits empty most of the time now, although Alberto's been out there the past week."

"Alberto?" he asked, turning with one eyebrow raised.

"Yeah. He's a life-long best friend. Like my brother, basically. He lives in Rome. For now."

"Rome. Again, can't go wrong with Italian. What does he do there?"

I poured the pasta into a strainer and leaned back to keep the steam from frizzing my hair. "He's the artistic director of the ballet. He's been there going on four years, so his contract will be up soon, and I hope he moves back closer. He was in town to stage a show with the Orlando Ballet."

"You need any help with anything? I'm standing here watching. I could be more useful."

"No, I'm all set. I figured we'd eat outside, if that's all right. It's so nice out. Oh, I'm sorry. Do you want some wine? I don't know where my manners are."

"Actually, I'd love some ice water, but I can get it if you'll direct me to the glasses."

I grabbed a glass from the cabinet and handed it to him. "There's ice in the door of the fridge, and there's filtered water in that spout on the island sink."

He filled his glass and promptly drained it before filling it again.

"You must have been thirsty," I said.

"Yep. It's been a long day. I'm ready to relax and slow the pace down for the evening. You have a beautiful home, by the way."

"It's a little bit bigger than the camper." I grinned over my shoulder at him as I pulled the bread from the oven.

"Yes, it is. The pool house might even be bigger than the camper. Do you mind if I use your restroom? I'd like to wash up before we eat."

"Sure, it's the first door on the right in the hallway."

When he returned, I was placing the food on the outside table.

The window gave me a clear view of him as he walked into the kitchen, and I watched him through the glass like a voyeur. His broad shoulders filled out the navy blue shirt that he wore, with the curve of his biceps just visible beneath the shirt's short sleeves. I leaned over to get a better view of his hips in the faded blue jeans. The movement caught his eye, and I waved to him to come out, embarrassed to have been caught checking out his backside.

As I watched him cross the threshold and walk toward me, part of me wished he'd just throw caution to the wind and take me in his arms, picking up where we'd left off after Fallon tossed me in the dirt. The look in his eyes as he grinned seemed to mirror my own thoughts, and a slight tremor ran through me as I remembered the feel of his mouth on mine.

"Doesn't get any better than this," he said as he pulled out my chair. "Beautiful weather. Beautiful setting. Beautiful lady. And a dinner that smells and looks damned delicious."

I caught a whiff of his familiar spearmint-lavender-sage scent as he pushed my chair in and took his seat next to me, and I resisted the urge to sniff him and fill my lungs with the intoxicating aroma.

"Bronwyn seems real impressed with your daughter-in-law," he said as I filled his plate. "Says she certainly knows what she's doing."

I smiled and passed the bread to him. "She's hot stuff, that one. I love Tyler to pieces. She makes my son happy, so that makes me happy, of course."

"A mama's dream, right? To see her children happy?"

I searched his face to see if his question held any bitterness toward his parents for the disapproval he'd mentioned before, but he seemed relaxed.

Our dinner passed with small talk as he answered my questions about the equipment that had brought him to Orlando, and he listened to a rundown of my upcoming events at the Performing Arts Center.

"Man," he said with a huge smile when his plate was empty. "You outdid yourself. We're done with finding restaurants. I can just eat this whenever you want to make it."

I smiled, pleased that he had enjoyed my efforts.

"So now, that huge painting at the end of your hallway," he said as he sat back in his chair. "The ballet dancer. That's you?"

I nodded and took a sip of my wine.

"It was. A lifetime ago."

"It's stunning, Maggie. So is the subject, obviously," he said, sweeping his hand toward me. "But that painting. It's almost like she's going to step out of the canvas and dance."

"My parents had that commissioned when I first joined Miami City Ballet. I should probably get rid of it, but it's so massive, and I know they spent a fortune on it."

"I'm sure it holds sentimental values, too. Memories."

"You could say that."

"So, you were actually a dancer, then? I mean, you didn't just take ballet lessons. You were the real deal?"

I took a deep breath and looked up at the darkening blue of the sky as evening fell. "Yes, I guess you could say I was the real deal. The youngest dancer to ever make principal in the history of Miami City Ballet."

"Well, all right! That's impressive. How long did you dance?"

"Not long enough," I said, draining my wine and standing to clear the dishes. "I'm gonna get another drink. Are you sure I can't pour you a glass?"

"No, thank you." He stood and helped me stack the dishes, following me into the kitchen to place them in the sink.

"There might be some beer in the pool house fridge, if you'd rather have that."

"No, I'll stick with water. I was up before dawn this morning, and I think if I drank anything, I'd be too sleepy to drive home."

"There's a bed in the pool house, too. I mean, if you need it."

He chuckled as he handed me the remaining dishes to put in the dishwasher. "Is that a proposition?"

I met his gaze and grinned at the mischief I saw there. "No. Just an offer for a place to sleep. If I ever give you a proposition, you won't have any doubt what's being offered, and it won't be for the foldout sofa bed in the pool house."

He tossed his head back and laughed, and I bent to get soap from beneath the sink for the dishwasher.

"You know what? I'd love to dance with you some day," he said.

I looked up in surprise, expecting him to be joking, but his eyes seemed serious despite his impish grin.

"Do you dance?" I asked.

He shook his head. "Not with any formal training like you've had. But I enjoy a dance floor. Take this song, for instance."

I tilted my head and listened to the beginning strains of Ed Sheeran.

Dax was leaning against the island in my kitchen, his arms crossed and one ankle slung casually over the other. He looked so damned irresistible that I wanted to close the distance between us and unleash the fire that had been smoldering since the first time I'd laid eyes on the man.

How bad could it be to simply let go? Would it be terrible to say to hell with it and let passion take its course?

As though he could read my mind, he pushed off the counter and slowly walked toward me, his eyes locked on mine as he spoke.

"If we were someplace that had a dance floor, and I saw you across the crowded room, and this song came on, I'd make my way over to you and ask you to dance."

A rush of warmth flooded through me, sending the most delightful vibrations to regions of my body that had been neglected far too long.

"I'd say yes," I whispered.

He took another step toward me and a slight tremor ran across my skin.

"There's an open area out on the patio," I said, nodding my head in that direction.

He extended his hand, palm up, and I placed mine in it, drawing a sharp intake of breath at the tiny shock waves the contact caused.

He led me outside, bringing my fingers to his lips and then turning to place his hand on my lower back, pulling me close as he raised our joined hands to his shoulder.

In my short-lived career, I danced with several professional partners, my body held against theirs, hot and sweaty, while I was turned and flipped and touched from head to toe.

In each of those instances, my mind was focused on the dance. The next step. The next turn. The execution. The rhythm.

Thank God my dance with Dax wasn't a choreographed event, because I couldn't focus on anything other than the proximity of his body to mine. The burning presence of his hand on my back. The obvious desire in his eyes. The heat building between us as we moved together.

It was one of the most sensual experiences of my life, and by far, the sexiest dance I'd ever participated in.

He had rhythm; there was no doubt about that. For a man his size, he moved with more grace and ease than I would have predicted.

And though I had expected a traditional schoolboy shuffle, he surprised me with his finesse and his skills.

The music carried us as he led me in twists and turns. My short black skirt twirled out around me every time he sent me spinning away from him, and I held my breath each time in anticipation of coming back together.

At one point, it seemed he was leaning down to kiss me, and my lips parted for him, but then he spun me around to put his chest against my back, his warm breath in my hair as he tilted my head, trailing his mouth down the side of my neck while his arms encircled my waist. My knees went weak as his fingers lightly caressed the outside of my thigh, his thumb teasing its way beneath the hem of my skirt. I leaned back against him, reaching up behind me to run my hand along the back of his neck, pulling him toward me as I pushed my chest forward in a plea for his touch.

He denied the request, turning me to face him instead, his eyes staring into mine as the burning need inside me raged out of control.

I was lightheaded, dizzy with desire, and I clung to his arms, sliding my hands underneath his shirt sleeves to grab hold of his rounded biceps and marvel at their unflinching strength. I wanted to tear the shirt from him. I wanted to explore the sculpted abdominal terrain I'd seen that day at the lake. I wanted to be beneath him—covered by his strength with his skin pressed against mine, wet with sweat and exertion.

As the song came to a close, he dipped me, leaning over me with one hand beneath my back and the other on my throat, until I was nearly begging for him to take me then and there.

He brought me slowly back up, and I clutched at his arms again, fearing that if he let go, my legs would buckle beneath me and I'd hit the ground.

I gazed up at him, and there was no doubt that the fire threatening to consume me had overtaken us both.

His mouth crushed mine, and I couldn't get my hands on his shirt buttons fast enough, eager to touch him unhindered by even one layer.

Our lips didn't part as he shrugged out of the shirt, and the moan in his throat as I ran my hands over his bare chest spurred me on. I spread my palms across his ribs and around to his back, raking my fingernails across the flesh as goose bumps rippled over his skin.

He slid his hands deeper down my back to press me tight against his hips, and I stretched onto my toes to reach him better as our tongues tangled and twisted in a battle for dominance.

The shift in his weight as he leaned forward took me off my toes and dropped my height back down beneath him, despite the heels I wore. He smoothed his hands over the back of my skirt with a slight squeeze, and then he ventured underneath. His touch on the backs of my thighs was so light at first that it almost tickled, but then his grip tightened as he cupped my cheeks in his hands and lifted me, setting me on the counter of the outdoor kitchen and bringing us eye to eye.

I could feel his heartbeat beneath my hand on his chest, pounding in rhythm with my own as he tore his mouth from mine and pulled back to look at me.

"What are you waiting for?" I asked, breathless.

"I was told I would get a proposition," he said with a sexy grin.

"Hey Goose, you big stud," I whispered, intertwining my fingers behind his head to pull his lips back to mine. "Take me to bed or lose me forever."

A chuckle rumbled deep in his chest.

"Show me the way home, honey," he growled against my lips. He lifted me again, and I wrapped my legs around his hips as he carried me to the patio doors.

## 30 IMPORTED SILK

He navigated the door with ease, carrying me wrapped around him like I weighed nothing at all. We made it halfway down the hall before he paused, pulling back from our kiss long enough to ask "Where am I going?"

"Last door on the left," I answered, and his mouth took mine again.

He walked us to my bed and laid me on it, bending over me to bury his head in my stomach, my breasts, and my neck as his hands gripped my hips.

I pushed against his chest and tried to sit up.

"Oh, wait, I need to pull the duvet off and put it on the chair in the corner."

He raised up and looked down at me with a grin. "Are you serious right now?"

I propped my elbows under me and smiled back at him. "Yes. This is imported silk."

He stood with his hands on his hips, grinning at me like a shirtless vision of magnificence carved in stone.

"You proposition me with a line from *Top Gun*, and then shut me down for a silk bedspread?"

"It's not a bedspread," I said, pulling off the throw pillows and placing them in the trunk at the foot of the bed. "It's a duvet cover."

He laughed. "Well, excuse me. The camper didn't come with one of those."

When I had the duvet stripped from the bed and folded on the chair, I turned to face Dax, who was still standing on the other side of the bed.

Suddenly, the foggy haze of arousal cleared enough for the reality of what we were about to do to sink in. I hugged my arms across my body, fighting to keep the fears at bay.

"You all right?" he asked.

I nodded and lifted my chin in defiance against my own mind. "I'm fine. You?"

He smiled. "We don't have to do this, you know. We can just hold each other."

My hands trembled as I reached to loosen the top button of my white silk blouse. His gaze followed my fingers as I unfastened each button, and I could hear him exhale when I let the shirt fall to the floor.

It had been quite some time since I'd undressed in front of someone, and even longer since I'd given myself to one whose opinion mattered so much.

I had hoped the muted light streaming through the window blinds from the patio would cover any imperfections of age, and judging by the look of approval on Dax's face, he was pleased with what he saw.

I hooked my thumbs into the waistband of my skirt, sliding it over my hips and letting it drop.

I'd left my heels on purposely, knowing that if I still had a figure asset that the years hadn't touched, it was my legs. And they showcased better in heels.

I took a step past the discarded clothes and placed my hands on my hips, my head held high as I tried to ignore the tremors of excitement that were causing my limbs to shake.

"Your turn," I said with a smile.

Dax let out a low whistle and came around the bed to stand in front of me, reaching for my hips.

I stepped back and shook my head, wagging my finger at him. "Your turn," I said again.

He grinned and pulled his boots off, then unfastened his jeans, his eyes never leaving mine as he tugged them down.

His thighs and calves were just as ripped as the rest of him, and I couldn't believe how well the denim had camouflaged his bulk.

"I'm guessing you lift weights. A lot," I said.

"Not as much as you'd think. A lot of it is hay bales, lugging equipment around, day-to-day stuff. But yeah. I've been known to throw around some free weights and do some presses."

"Nice."

"Glad you think so." He arched an eyebrow and gave me a crooked grin that intensified the throbbing in my nether regions. "Your turn."

I looked down at my body and held my hands out. "What? I'm already undressed."

"Well, if we're taking turns," he said, stepping closer to me, "technically I'm wearing one piece of clothing. By my count, you're wearing two."

He lifted his fingers to trace the lace pattern of my white bra, lingering over the nipple as it hardened and strained against the thin fabric. I bit down on my lip as he bent his head forward and closed his mouth over the raised mound, his tongue darting against the material.

He slid his hand to my back and released the fastener with a quick flick of his thumb. I inhaled sharply as he pulled the garment away, exposing me to the cool air and his hungry gaze.

He cupped both breasts in his hands, bending to take each one in his mouth. I twisted my fingers into his hair, moaning as he gently tugged my nipple between his teeth.

His progress continued with a touch as light as a feather, running his fingers and his tongue over my ribs and around my bellybutton before dipping his thumb into the front of my panties.

His name fell from my lips, and he looked up at me, watching me as I watched him, his hands firmly gripping my hips as he knelt and teased his tongue across my abdomen just inside the lacy waistband.

I grabbed hold of his shoulders to brace my weight as he eased the lace down over my thighs and carefully lifted each foot up and out.

He slid his hands up my legs, curving his palms over the back of my calves as his mouth burned kisses onto my skin like a brand.

By the time his fingers reached my inner thighs, my legs were trembling, and he guided me to the edge of the bed, laying me back as he knelt between my legs and lifted my knees over his shoulders.

In my state of heightened sensitivity, every touch sent shock waves through me, and the multitude of sensations was so overwhelming that it was hard to pinpoint where the pleasure was originating as he explored the most intimate parts of me with his fingers and with his tongue.

I pulled at his hair and dug my nails into his shoulders as he drove me to the brink of madness, but then everything in me exploded in euphoria, and I collapsed back against the bed, my limbs heavy and momentarily paralyzed in a state of bliss.

I felt his weight on the bed as he joined me, and I reached for him, pulling him to me as he buried his face in my hair and his body in mine.

"Oh, God, Maggie," he whispered as I clung to him, both of us moaning with ragged breaths as he moved inside me.

I wrapped my legs tightly around him, the stiletto heels digging into the backs of his thighs as I arched up to take him deeper.

He called my name again at the end, and my eyes filled with tears of release as we rocked back and forth, holding each other in the slow subsiding aftermath.

"Wow," he said when our heartbeats had slowed. He rolled to lay on his side and reached his arm across my stomach to pull me snug against him. "I was worried I may have forgotten how to do that, but I guess it's like riding a bike."

I laughed and looked up at him, resting my hand on his forearm as his thumb stroked my ribs. "I don't know how long it's been since you rode a bike—and I don't want to know—but your bike riding skills are intact as far as I'm concerned."

He smiled as he kissed me and then rested his head against mine. "I feel like I just ran a marathon. I'm exhilarated and exhausted all at the same time."

"Well, you were already tired before."

He raised up his head and looked down at me with a grin. "Sweetheart, I will *never* be too tired to do that. At my age, I might be slow rounding second, but I'll always be ready to step up to bat."

I laughed, and he laid his head back down, nestling into my hair on the pillow we shared.

"How old *are* you, by the way?" I asked, a bit embarrassed that I didn't know under the current circumstances.

"Forty-five. And you?"

I cringed a little. "Forty-nine."

Dax shrugged. "Four years. I don't think that will earn you cougar status."

"Well, darn. There goes my plan. You gotta go."

"I can't move," he said.

I bent my leg to prop my ankle on the opposite knee so I could reach the strap to take off my shoe.

"What are you doing?" he asked.

"I'm taking my shoes off."

"No, don't. That was about the sexiest damned thing I've ever seen. I think I'm gonna have scars on the backs of my thighs. Battle wounds from taking on a cougar."

I slipped the stiletto from my foot, turning onto my side to reach the other one as Dax shifted his weight and propped himself up on his elbow.

"Hey, did you say you made cheesecake?"

"So, you're exhilarated, exhausted, *and* hungry?"

His lips brushed against mine, and an aftershock ripped through me. "I guess that's what you do to me, Maggie Mae. You make me feel everything all at once."

I smiled, not even flinching at his mention of feelings. I was at peace—my heart content, my body blissful, and my head free of conflict or fear. "If I get up and go get you cheesecake, are you going to be awake when I get back?"

"Yes, ma'am. I promise. Scout's honor."

"Were you a boy scout?" I asked as I grabbed my robe from the closet.

"No. Do you have to be a scout to say scout's honor?"

"I think it has more validity that way." I wrapped the robe around me and tied it, pulling my hair from beneath the neckline and letting it fall around my shoulders.

"All right. Then I promise with a cowboy's honor. How's that?"

I shrugged as I walked toward the door. "I don't know that cowboys are known for their honor."

He called out his response as I made my way down the hall toward the kitchen.

"Yeah, well, they're not known for their bike riding skills, either, but you said I did that pretty damned well."

When I returned to the bedroom with a slice of cheesecake and a glass of ice water, he was lying on his stomach across the bed. The sheet was twisted around his hips, leaving the top half of one buttock exposed in a milky white contrast to the deep tan above it.

The contours of his back and shoulders were impressive even in the dim light, and a little flicker of desire fluttered deep within me, despite being so recently satiated. Something told me it would take quite a lot to fully quench my desire for Dax Pearson.

"Are you asleep?" I whispered when he didn't move.

"No ma'am," he responded, muffled by the pillow. "I don't break my promises."

A little warning bell sounded in my head, reminding me never to trust a man who tells me he won't break his promises.

I sat the cheesecake on the nightstand and went to the bathroom sink, flipping on the light once I'd closed the door.

A wild woman stared back at me in the mirror—her skin flushed, her eyes nearly glowing they were such a vivid green, and her blazing red hair wild around her like a mane.

I leaned forward to stare more closely at my reflection. At the tiny lines and the deeper ones. I combed through my hair with my fingers and pressed my hands just in front of my ears, pulling the skin of my face back to lift it and smooth it, transforming me into a younger version of myself.

I released it immediately, letting the skin return to its current state.

I wasn't that young girl anymore.

She might have had tighter skin and a tighter body, but I had wisdom and the advantage of hindsight. I wouldn't make the same mistakes again.

I closed my eyes, inhaling deeply, trying to talk down the fear before it got a foothold.

"Hey," Dax called out. "Are we sharing this cheesecake? Because it's almost gone, and it's so good I may not be able to stop myself."

My eyes opened, and I smiled at the Maggie in the mirror. She smiled back at me.

I opened the door and took in the sight of a naked cowboy eating cheesecake as he sat on the side of my bed, twisted up in my sheets. A renewed resolve to live in the moment came over me, and I released the breath I'd been holding.

"It's all yours," I said. "And there's more where that came from."

"Don't tempt me."

I stood at the edge of the bed and watched him enjoy the last morsels of the cheesecake before taking the empty plate from him and turning to go. He reached out to grab my robe, guiding me back to stand between his knees.

"Where are you goin'?"

"Taking this back to the kitchen."

He took the plate and set it on the nightstand, and then he untied the belt of my robe, sliding his hands around my waist and pulling me to him.

"What are you doing?" I asked, laughing as he nuzzled his face between my breasts. "I thought you were tired."

"I was, but then you fed me cheesecake. Now I'm ready for round two."

# 31 DETECTIVE DEACON

I woke up with a colossal pain in my neck. Despite being enticing to touch and sexy as hell, Dax's bicep was not a good pillow. I lifted my head off his arm and reached up to knead the back of my neck, wincing in pain.

The clock on the bedside table said six, which didn't surprise me since my body's internal alarm had been set on six for years.

My normal routine would have been to get up and brush my teeth, tidy up any strays that had escaped my hair bun in the night, and head across the hall to my dance studio for my morning warm-up. But the sleeping cowboy with his knee thrown over my thigh, one arm under my pillow, and the other arm across my stomach was not part of that normal routine.

I tried to ease myself out from under his leg, but he stirred with a bit of a moan, so I froze, resigning myself to being pinned to the bed a while longer.

It wasn't like it was a bad place to be.

I lay awake, staring at the ceiling as I listened to Dax's steady breathing beside me. With nothing to do but think, I replayed every moment of the night before with a mixture of elation and trepidation.

On the one hand, it had been a pretty incredible night. It was some time after one when round two ended and we finally fell asleep in a tangle of limbs and sheets. I hadn't been a nun since my relationship with Gerry ended, but none of the lackluster encounters I'd had here and there had even come close to the night I'd spent with Dax. Our physical chemistry was off the charts, and just the memory of his touch was arousing.

Beyond that obvious attraction, I simply enjoyed his company. He had a laid-back manner that made him easy to be around. He was smart, funny, independent, compassionate, and downright sexy. The more I got to know him, the more I wanted to know. He was full of surprises, and I suspected

I'd only begun to peel back the layers of Dax Pearson.

On the other hand, I was terrified for all the same reasons.

I'd never known an attraction like the one we had.

Even though my time with Gerry was passionate, it was also reckless, and on many levels, scary. In hindsight, I realized I never really knew Gerry, and he never truly cared to know me. We were two people attracted to the idea of each other, and even that was based on lies.

What I had with Dax was different, which should have been a good thing, but I couldn't help being scared that there was a shoe about to drop.

Was there some secret about him I didn't know? Was there some shift in his personality I hadn't seen yet? Were there things in his past he was hiding, or character flaws I hadn't discovered?

Besides, what if I determined I could allow myself to fall and he decided differently? I didn't want to give my heart to someone after all these years only to be rejected or find out he didn't feel the same.

The chatter in my brain was too much to deal with lying down. I had to get up. To move. To lose myself in the motions of exercise and center my body and mind.

I pushed gently against Dax's knee, sliding my leg away from his. Then I braced my foot on the floor and used the leverage to pull myself out from under his arm and off the bed.

A trail of discarded clothing littered my bedroom floor, and I blushed as I tiptoed past it on my way to the dresser. I pulled out a tank top and tights, pausing to make sure Dax's breathing was still steady before heading across the hall to the studio room.

My reflection in the mirror startled me. I hadn't confined my unruly curls as I normally did at night, and my hair was in utter disarray as a result.

I twisted it up and tucked it in as best I could without a hair band, and then I tugged the tights on and pulled the tank top over my head.

By the time I'd finished warming up all the big muscle groups and doing my stretches and splits, I was already feeling better.

I was focused on the mirror at the *barre* as I moved through a series of *ronds de jambe en l'air* when a movement in the doorway caught my eye. I looked up to see Dax lounging against the doorframe in just his jeans.

Would there ever be a time I could look at him and not feel my heart beat faster? Would I want there to be?

"Good morning," he said.

"Good morning. I'm sorry if I woke you."

He shook his head. "Not at all. I'm normally up early. I woke up and didn't know where I was for a minute, and then I figured it out but you were gone. So, I came looking for you. Whatcha doing?"

"Um, I guess you could call it my meditation. When I was a dancer, we always started each morning with a warm-up and a technique class. It was such a habit engrained in my daily life that I never abandoned it. I suppose it's been my way of staying connected to that world. It helps me retain some of the skills and knowledge I had, but it's beneficial in other ways, of course. It stretches my whole body, works through the joints, and gets the blood flowing."

He sat on the floor with his back against the wall and his legs stretched out in front of him.

"What are you doing?" I asked.

"I want to watch you."

"Watch me? Why? It's just stretching and drills. It's not like a dance or anything."

"I enjoy the way your body moves. I want to watch you."

A memory flashed in my mind of him watching my body move the night before, and throbbing ache pulsed in my pelvic region as I remembered what he'd been doing to make me move.

I cleared my throat and started again at first position, explaining each move to him as I executed it.

I went through *pliés*, *battements*, and *frappés*—telling him their French names and their English translations as I demonstrated each.

Then I stepped away from the *barre* and performed a few combinations in the center of the room, my eyes focused on the mirror though I could feel his on me.

"You move with such grace, Maggie."

"Thank you. Did you know they say only two percent of the population has a ballet body?"

"I did not. You certainly get my vote, but I don't know what constitutes a ballet body."

"Several things. A long neck," I said, tilting my head to the side to bare my neck to him. "A relatively short torso but long legs." I lifted my foot by my ankle, bringing my leg to my ear as I arched slightly to form a straight vertical line with my legs, my foot high above my head. "But what most people don't realize is how crucial the hips are." I lowered my leg and brought my ankles together with my toes turned out. "To stand with your feet at one-hundred-eighty degrees, your hip rotators must have a ninety-degree turnout." I dipped in a demi *plié* and rose, dipping lower into a grand *plié* with my knees over my middle toes.

"Holy hell, that looks like it hurts," Dax said.

"Not at all. It's an amazing stretch."

I came back to first position, and then bent to place my palms on the floor stretching my back and hamstrings.

"Mesmerizing. I would love to see you dance across a stage."

"Hmmm. Not likely at this point, but thank you. Speaking of dance, where'd that come from last night? I had no idea you could do that."

"Are you talking about out on the patio or in the bedroom?" he asked with a grin.

I laughed and walked over to him, extending my hand to pull him up. "Both."

He wrapped his arms around my waist and pressed his lips gently to mine.

"Please tell me that's coffee I smell," he whispered.

"It's set on a timer and should already be in the pot and ready to pour by now. C'mon. I'll fix you a cup and make you breakfast. But first you have to tell me where you learned to dance."

"Oh, I've always loved to dance," he said as he followed me down the hall to the kitchen. "Nothing fancy with names and positions like what you do, but I can't sit still when there's music playing. I feel like I hear the music with my body. I know that might sound weird."

I stopped and turned to face him. "To a dancer? No. It makes perfect sense to me."

He reached and took my hand in his, squeezing it and bringing it to his lips. "I enjoyed dancing with you last night."

"Out on the patio or in the bedroom?"

He grinned and pulled me into his arms. "Both."

The loud peal of the doorbell startled me, and I jumped, turning to stare at the door.

"You expecting someone?" Dax asked.

"At seven o'clock on a Sunday morning? No."

I went to the peephole and cursed beneath my breath when I saw Cabe standing outside my door with Deacon.

"Oh crap!" I whispered, scurrying over to Dax and turning him back toward the bedroom. "Go, go, go."

The bell rang again as I shoved him inside and closed the bedroom door. "Stay here."

I turned and ran back toward the foyer, reaching the end of the hallway just as I heard the key turn in the door.

"Mom? You up?" Cabe called out as he stepped inside, led by Deacon who jumped on me and nearly knocked me down.

"Deacon, get down. Mom, tell him no. Don't just let him jump on you like that. Hey, whose truck is in the driveway?"

I pushed Deacon off me, and he immediately bolted down the hallway to sniff at the bottom of my bedroom door. I ran after him and grabbed his collar just as he started scratching and clawing at the door.

"C'mon, Deacon," I said, pulling him along with me. "Let's get a treat. You want a treat, boy?"

He fought me the entire way back down the hall, twisting around to look back at the bedroom door and barking with all he had. He broke free and ran back to the door, slamming against it as he barked and clawed at the wood.

I was right behind him and looped my hand through his collar just as Cabe headed down the hall toward us.

"What's up with him?" Cabe said. "Deacon, get over here."

Cabe took the dog from me and knelt in front of him. "What's wrong with you? You're acting like there's somebody in…."

He looked up at me, and I could see the logical progression of his thoughts as it registered on his face.

"Oh. Okay," he said.

I moved past Cabe and went to the pantry to get Deacon's treat box, shaking it loudly as I called the dog in my most excited voice. He came running, and I made him sit before giving him the treat.

Cabe followed me into kitchen, and I didn't dare meet his eyes. My entire body was hot with embarrassment, and I opened the fridge as much to get cool air as to hide my face from my son.

"Mom," he whispered. "Psst. Mom!"

I closed the refrigerator door and turned to face him, my cheeks burning up.

"Who's here?" he whispered.

"Dax Pearson." I looked down at my hands, feeling like a teenager who'd been caught sneaking around.

"The ranch guy?"

I nodded, my eyes still on my hands.

"Well, alright." He chuckled, and I looked at him in surprise. "Tyler was right, then. She's going to love this."

"No, honey! Don't say anything! Let's just keep this between us. I don't want to make a big deal out of this, please?"

He laughed. "I can't believe I just busted my mother."

"Oh, please. You didn't bust anything. I'm fully dressed and for all you know he slept in the pool house."

"Did he? You know what, don't answer that. I don't want to know," he said, grinning as he shook his head with his hand covering his eyes.

I realized in that moment that Deacon had left the kitchen.

"Where's Deacon?"

I was concerned that he'd gone back to investigate my bedroom, but I didn't hear him barking or scratching.

Cabe and I both left the kitchen looking for him, and I was shocked to see him lying on the floor outside my bedroom door, calm as could be. I noticed the door was slightly ajar, and I wondered if Dax had been doing some impromptu dog training.

"Um, I'm gonna go before this gets even weirder," Cabe said, stopping abruptly in the hall. "You sure you're still okay with Deacon being here?"

"Yes, of course. What time will you be back? Or is Tyler picking him up?"

"Ty should be done between four and five, so she'll swing by and get him then."

He called Deacon to him and knelt to pet the dog and tell him goodbye. Then he stood and shot me a sideways glance with a grin as he walked to the door.

"Have fun fishing," I said. "Catch us some dinner!" I tried to make my voice cheerful and nonchalant, but it sounded more like I was doing a fake commercial.

Cabe stopped at the front door and turned back to hug me. "It's okay, you know? You deserve to be happy, Mom."

A knot formed in my throat as I patted his back. "Thanks, sweetheart. I love you."

"Love you, too. Be good, Deacon."

As soon as he was gone, I sprinted for the bedroom and flung open the door. Dax was sitting on the edge of my bed, completely dressed with his boots on. Deacon sat calmly in front of him, enjoying a nice ear scratch.

"I let him in to keep him from barking," Dax said.

"I'm so sorry. I completely forgot I told my son I'd dog sit today."

"Dog sit?"

"Yeah. Tyler has a wedding, and Cabe is going deep sea fishing with a buddy, so Deacon would have been home alone all day. I offered to take him. I'm so sorry I shoved you in the bedroom and shut the door. I just didn't know what to do or what to say. It was awkward as hell."

"No problem," he said, grinning. "I'm just relieved it was your son. From the look on your face when you heard the bell, I was worried I might need to take off running and climb the fence. I thought there might be an angry love interest on the other side of that door."

I shook my head. "No. Nothing like that."

"Then when the beast here came clawing, I wondered if I might still need to be worried."

I smiled at his teasing.

"Karma, I suppose," I said. "I walked in on Cabe and Tyler in the pool house one morning when he was living out there. This was before they were married. Now, granted, she was fully dressed when I came in, but they were in bed together and she'd obviously stayed the night. Still, I think it was worse being on this end of it. Figures that the one time I have a man sleep over, I happen to get caught!"

"Are you going to get grounded?" he asked with one eyebrow raised, his grin wide.

"No, I'm not going to get grounded," I mimicked as I returned his smile.

"Good," he said, standing to wrap his arms around me and put his forehead against mine. "because I have an idea of what we can do the next time we get together. Now, are we still having breakfast, or do I need to sneak out the back door in case he comes back?"

# 32  EMERGENCY DOVES

Cabe called Tyler as soon as he got in his car. "I probably shouldn't even tell you this, but I know you have a bride from hell today and I figured this would make you smile."

"I need a smile. She just told me they have nine unexpected guests coming. Nine! That's a whole damned table. How am I supposed to come up with extra linens, Chiavari chairs, and a centerpiece out of nowhere on a Sunday morning? Not to mention food to feed these people. I need to call the caterer, so give me this good news and let me go."

"I just left my mom's to drop off Deacon, and I noticed when I pulled in the driveway there was a black pick-up truck parked there."

"What? Get out! Dax Pearson has a black pick-up truck."

Cabe chuckled. "I also noticed that it was covered in dew, so it must have been there overnight."

"What? Oh my God! I knew it! What did I tell you?"

"So, I ring the bell. *Twice.* And no answer."

"You're kidding! Oh, please tell me you did not walk in on Maggie and Dax. That would *not* make me smile."

Cabe frowned at the thought as he exited his mother's neighborhood and merged into traffic. "No. That's disgusting. I mean, I did use my key and open the door because I was a little concerned that my mom wasn't answering. You know she's up at the crack of dawn no matter what. So, she comes down the hall, looking completely flustered—"

"Was she dressed? Like, clothes for the day dressed?"

"She was wearing her dance get-up, you know, like she was doing her exercise thing."

"Hold on, the photographer's assistant has a question."

Cabe listened as Tyler explained that the bride could not add three extra boutonnieres since the florist had already left for the ceremony site.

"Okay, I'm back," she said. "Oh, so she was in her workout clothes? Maybe it wasn't him. Isn't Alberto staying in the pool house? Maybe he rented a truck."

"No, Alberto flew out yesterday morning. Besides, she confirmed it when I asked her. It was Dax Pearson."

"Get out!" Tyler said again. "If Dax Pearson spent the night, why on earth would your mother get up and work out?"

Cabe sighed. "My mother works out every morning. Even when she's on vacation. That woman can't start her day without it."

"Hmm," Tyler mused. "Maybe they were getting together for breakfast."

"I don't think so. I didn't ask for details, nor do I want any, but I definitely got the impression he'd been there all night."

"What did he say to you?"

Cabe laughed. "I never saw him. Deacon was going nuts at her bedroom door, so evidently he was in there. Again, I didn't ask."

"Wow. I can't wait to tell Bronwyn."

"No, Ty, don't do that! Mom asked me not to say anything, but I knew you've been chomping at the bit for them to get together, so I wanted to tell you. Don't go telling everybody else, okay?"

"It's not everybody else. It's his niece! And she's been chomping at the bit, too. She said her uncle hasn't been out on a date since his wife died, like eight years ago, but since he's been talking to Maggie, he's been in a really good mood. She wants him to be happy, and I want your mom to be happy. So if they can be happy together, this is awesome. I have to tell Bronwyn."

Cabe shook his head in exasperation. "Babe, c'mon. Let's just let things take their course. Oh, and I told Mom you'd pick up Deacon between four and five."

"Alright. Did you tell her you're fishing with Jeffrey?"

"No. I just said I was going with a friend, and she didn't ask who, so I didn't say. I'm not going to lie to her if she asks, but I know it upsets her. She says it's fine, but I can tell it bothers her. Not that I don't understand why, so I just won't bring it up unless I have to."

"Galen mentioned that she's thinking about inviting Jeffrey and Julie to the wedding."

"Oh, that's not cool. That would definitely upset Mom. You need to talk her out of that."

"Me? I'm just the wedding planner. She's your sister. You talk her out of it. Hold on."

He listened as someone on the bride's side of the family explained to Tyler that they wanted to surprise the bride with a dove release and wondered if it was too late to get some doves for the ceremony.

"Did you hear that?" she asked once they'd walked away.

"Yeah. You have emergency doves in your car, right? Just in case someone needs a dove release within the hour?" He laughed and shook his head, which he did often in response to what his wife dealt with at work.

"Yeah. I'll pull those out of my butt along with nine chairs and a centerpiece."

Someone yelled Tyler's name in the background, and Cabe chuckled. "Sounds like you need to go. Have fun. Love you."

"Then kill me now!" she whispered and ended the call.

## 33 RED CRINOLINE

I spent the rest of the day after Dax left in a blissful daze, lounging around the house with Deacon.

My body was still tender and tingling from the intimacy of the night. Vivid images of erotic memories flashed in my head throughout the day, quickening my pulse and sending a rush of warm sensations straight through me.

It took a day or two for panic to set in, and by mid-week I'd convinced myself I needed to tell him it was a bad idea and we should part ways.

But the next time he called, just hearing his voice calmed my fears and reminded me how much I enjoyed him before I could tell him otherwise.

"What are you doing next Thursday night?" he asked.

"No plans that I know of. Why? What are *you* doing next Thursday night?"

"I told you before that I had an idea of something I'd like for us to do together. I did a little research, and it turns out next Thursday is a perfect night for it."

"For what?" I asked, intrigued to know what the activity was and impressed that he was putting so much thought and time into it.

"I think I'd rather surprise you."

"Oh, no. I don't think so. Go ahead and tell me."

He refused. Even after I asked multiple times. He turned a deaf ear to my pleas and seemed to find much joy in doing so.

"I'm going to go out on a limb and guess that you don't do well with being surprised, Maggie Mae."

"I like to know what to expect. I don't feel comfortable when I don't know what's going on."

"You know, a little unpredictability can be a good thing."

"Easy for you to say. You don't have to figure out what to wear without knowing what's going to be appropriate."

"Just wear a dress and some heels."

I rolled my eyes and shifted the phone to my other ear. "A dress and heels doesn't tell me anything. How formal?"

"What do you mean?"

"That's not like a universal outfit dress code. Do you mean a strapless sun dress with some sandal wedges, or do you mean a sequined cocktail dress with strappy stilettos?"

"Well, as much as I'm enjoying the memory of you in stilettos and the faint bruises that I'm sure are still on the back of my thighs, I'd say go with comfortable heels."

"There is no such thing," I scoffed. "It's an oxymoron."

He laughed. I didn't.

"I'll pick you up at five-thirty, and I'm sure whatever you wear will be fine. Oh, and you probably want to eat a little something before I get there. We'll grab dinner after the top secret activity portion of the evening, but you're going to be expending some energy, so fuel up."

"What? I'm expending energy in a dress and heels? C'mon, Dax. You gotta tell me what we're doing. What if this is not something I want to do?"

"Then I'll know not to ever plan it again. Trust me. I gotta run. I'll see you Thursday at five-thirty."

I spent the next few days waffling back and forth between being excited and feeling overwhelmed. All I knew was it would still be daylight out, we weren't eating until afterward, and it was going to require energy. A dress and heels would not have been my first choice for an outfit based on those facts alone.

When Tuesday arrived, I opted for my nude, T-strap platform sandals, knowing I could do a lot of walking or standing in those without the balls of my feet turning to pins and needles. I paired them with a navy blue sleeveless V-neck dress, fitted through the bodice with a flared skirt and scalloped hemline. The scalloped cut-out design lent it a fancy feel, but the cut of the dress could be casual as well.

My nerves were hyped with energy as I waited for him to arrive. It was the first time I'd seen him since our intimate encounter, so I was both excited and apprehensive.

I wasn't sure how we would react to each other after having been so physical and then spending over a week apart. Of course, the anxiety over the unknown activity and whether or not I would enjoy it didn't help calm my fears.

By the time Dax rang the doorbell, I was so keyed up to see him that nothing else mattered.

"Hello there," he said when I opened the door. That was all it took for everything to be all right.

We were in each other's arms almost immediately, and as he lifted me from the ground in a big, bear hug and pressed his lips to mine, I wondered why on earth I'd ever doubted that I wanted to spend time with the man.

He drove me to a small community center not far from my house. The parking lot was about half-full, and I couldn't see any signage or other clues to indicate what we were doing there.

"You ready?" he asked.

"How can I answer that when I have no idea what we're doing?"

Dax's laughter filled the truck. "You seem really perturbed by this. I had you pegged as the adventurous type."

"I'm all for an adventure, as long as I know what I'm doing and how to be prepared for it."

He took my hand in his and brought it to his lips. "Do you trust me?"

"In theory," I said.

"I have every confidence that you're going to be fine."

"Well, let's get it over with and we'll see."

The secret was out as soon as we entered the building's foyer and I saw the small sign with an arrow directing people to a classroom down the hall.

"Ballroom dancing lessons?" I asked, bursting into laughter. "Seriously?"

He darted his eyes away and back to me, a sheepish grin playing at the corners of his mouth. "We both enjoy dancing, and I've always wanted to learn more. I thought it might be fun."

I put my arms around his neck and stretched onto my toes to touch my lips to his. "You are amazing, you know that?"

"You probably already know how to do all this, but I just thought...it might be fun to do it together."

I was so accustomed to seeing him look confident in every situation that to see him somewhat uncertain made me giggle.

"What?" he asked.

"Nothing! I think it's a great idea, and I can't wait to dance with you."

Another couple entered and passed by with a glance in our direction.

"I guess we should get in there," Dax said, taking my hand as we walked down the hall.

The chairs and tables in the large rectangular room had been pushed to the sides to create an open area for dance. One wall was covered entirely in mirrors, and a large portable stereo was on the floor in the corner.

Three other couples were standing around talking, and a girl of maybe nineteen or twenty sat alone on a table by the window, swinging her feet back and forth. She wore a pair of traditional dance shoes with her yoga pants and a T-shirt, and I wondered if she was the instructor.

It had been so long since I'd been in any dance class that my body was a maelstrom of thoughts and emotions. Memories descended over me in the familiarity of the situation, taking me back to that other life so long ago.

The butterflies in my stomach fluttered in joy at the thought of dancing again, but I had my doubts about the caliber of instruction we'd receive from the girl sitting on the table. The bright pink gum bubbles she blew were huge, and each time she popped one loudly with her tongue, I worried it was going to be stuck all over her face.

Dax cleared his throat beside me, and I turned to look at him. His thumb was hooked into his front pocket, and he was strumming his fingers on his jeans while jingling his keys in his other hand. I watched his eyes move from person to person in the room, as though he were summing up their abilities.

"Are you okay?" I asked, looping my arm through his. "You look nervous."

"I am nervous. I've never done anything like this, and I don't much mind looking like a fool, but I don't want to feel like one."

I bent my arm around his and squeezed. "As someone just told me in the car, I have every confidence that you're going to be fine. You're a wonderful dancer."

"Thanks, but I've never had anybody teach me to dance or tell me what I'm doing wrong. I just go with what feels good."

Disaster struck bubble gum girl just as I had feared, and she frowned as she picked strands of pink from her false eyelashes and peeled it away from her nose.

"Something tells me this teacher is not going to be intimidating."

"Easy for you to say," Dax scoffed. "You'll probably be teaching the teacher a thing or two. Miss Professional Dancer."

"Ballet, maybe. Ballroom? No. I don't have any formal training in this, so we'll be looking like fools together."

He squeezed his hand over mine and smiled just as a tiny lady entered the room. She was petite in stature, only an inch or two over five feet, with brilliant white hair cut in a chin-length bob.

She wore a white fit-and-flare fifties-style dress covered in a royal blue floral pattern with a royal blue sweater tossed over her shoulders and buttoned at the neck. She wore thick, nude, traditional dance tights and a pair of red dancing shoes. When she squatted beside the portable stereo and put down a stack of CDs, I got a glimpse of a bright red crinoline peeking out from the hem of her dress.

"I take back everything I said about the teacher not being intimidating," I whispered to Dax.

He looked at me with his brows scrunched in confusion. "What do you mean?"

"I'm pretty sure that's our teacher," I nodded in her direction, "and I guarantee you she's going to be a stickler for perfection."

"Listen up, class," she called out in a gravelly voice that betrayed she'd spent at least part of her life as a smoker. "It is six o'clock, and we begin promptly at six. I will honor my commitment and start on time, and I expect you to honor your commitment and be on time. Now, let's get started. Gather round me so I don't have to yell."

I saw the bubble gum girl check her watch and frown before sliding off the table and walking toward the teacher.

A few other couples had straggled in, bringing the total couple count to seven, with a single girl in addition to bubble gum girl and one lone guy standing by himself on the outskirt.

"My name is Mrs. Betty," she said, as we all formed a semi-circle around her. "I will teach you the techniques you will need to master several styles of ballroom dancing, including a waltz, fox trot, cha cha, and samba, and then we will incorporate some swing if time allows over the course of this class."

A young guy hurried through the door, and the bubble gum girl ran over to greet him.

"Excuse me," Betty called out to him, her hand held high. "We start this class promptly at six, and if you intend to be late, you will disrupt every other person who has managed to be on time. So, you have a choice to make as to whether or not you're going to be able to honor this commitment."

He looked as though he might throw up, and I felt sorry for him. Perhaps it was due to the stares of everyone else in the room and the public admonishment from the instructor, but I got the feeling he was already questioning whether or not he was going to honor the commitment before he ever arrived.

"Now, as I was saying before someone was late, I can teach you the techniques, but it is up to you to practice, practice, practice. I can't make a dancer out of you, and some of you won't ever be dancers. But I can teach you what to do, and then you have to put in the time to master it to the best of your abilities. Now who's ready to have some fun?"

"Well, when you put it that way, who could refuse?" Dax whispered under his breath, and I covered my mouth to stifle a giggle.

"You two there," she said, pointing at the single attendees with an index finger from each hand. "You're by yourself?"

They both looked at each other and then at the rest of us, their expressions equally mortified.

"Are you by yourself?" Betty repeated, and they both nodded.

"The ad in the paper said you didn't need a partner," the young man said.

"You don't," Betty said. "The two of you will dance together. Now, where was I? Oh, to tell you a little about me. I've been teaching dance for sixty-one years, and yes, that makes me as old as dirt. But it also gives me wisdom and experience, and I promise you I will know whether or not you are practicing. Now, gentlemen, we'll start with you because you're going to be our leaders. Line up over here, and ladies, you get to watch. But pay attention, because you're going to need to know what they're doing."

"If she's been teaching for over sixty years, she has to be the oldest drill sergeant on the planet," Dax whispered.

"Excuse me," Betty waved her hand at Dax, "I need you over here with the gentleman. She'll be fine by herself, you'll see."

She turned to face the other gentlemen, and Dax smiled at me with wide eyes as he went to join them.

Betty carefully explained and demonstrated each step, then walked among them as they did as she instructed. Next, she turned the music on and did the demo again before standing in front of the group to critique their performance.

I felt a measure of pride that Dax picked up the steps right off the bat, and I could see the relief on his face when she corrected others around him but simply gave him a nod of approval.

I could feel his eyes upon me as she took the ladies through our moves, and I looked forward to the guys and girls being reunited to work together.

Betty was a tough instructor, and she expected unwavering focus and dedication to the task at hand. She called out any instances of goofing around immediately. But she knew her stuff, and the methods she used to teach were effective.

By the time we reached the stage of circling around the room in our waltz, Dax and I had hit a rhythm, counting together as we bobbed up and down with the tempo.

"Frame! Frame!" Betty said, tapping Dax on his arm. "Straighten your frame!"

"Oops," he whispered, lifting his arms and shoulders and straightening his back as I tried not to laugh.

We made two more rotations around the room without any admonishment.

"I think we've got this," Dax said. "I think with your professional background and my God-given talent, we're naturals."

He winked as he said it, and I smiled. "You think so, huh?"

"Yeah. She's probably going to ask us to demonstrate our technique for the—oh shit, she's coming."

He lifted his arms and straightened his back just as she got to us.

"Too much. You look stiff. Relax. Not that much. Frame! Frame! Pay attention to your frame."

His face was a blend of confusion, embarrassment, and determination, and he looked so adorable that I would have kissed him if I wasn't so scared of what Betty might say.

We'd made a few more trips around the room when she changed the song to one with a quicker tempo.

"I actually think it's easier to go faster," I said to Dax.

He nodded in agreement. "Yeah. I'm not focused so much on the counting when we go faster. The steps seem to fit better with the music."

Betty was fussing at the random pairing of the lone girl and lone guy.

"I realize you don't know each other, but you need to be closer. He's not going to bite you. See, look at the space between the two of them." Betty pointed at us, and we both instinctively straightened under her microscope. "See how they move? They're in sync with each other. They're moving as partners."

Dax's hand tightened on mine as we heard her words, and his gaze moved from my eyes to my lips and back up. I knew he wanted to kiss me as badly as I wanted to be kissed.

Betty clapped her hands together at exactly seven o'clock, shutting off the music and asking us all to gather around again.

"Now, tonight's class was for testing the waters. If you feel so inclined as to return, I will be here each week at this time for a duration of ten weeks. If you miss a class, you need to contact me to find out how to make it up. I can't teach you what you missed and teach the others what we're moving on to. If anyone has questions, please feel free to come ask me. Otherwise, good night, and thank you for coming."

# 34 PIZZA & BEER

Betty turned to me and smiled as the group disbursed. "You're a quick study, but those shoes won't cut it if you're coming back. You need dance shoes."

Her tone carried me back to being ten years old and being chastised for having worn the wrong tights to class. Despite being nearly fifty, I immediately stammered out an excuse in my defense. "I didn't know we were dancing. He surprised me."

Betty smiled, and her features softened. "Oh, a surprise! That's nice." She patted Dax's arm. "My Roger and I have been married for fifty-four years, and he still manages to surprise me now and then. How long have the two of you been married?"

Dax and I talked over each other as we both explained that we were not.

"Oh," Betty said. "Wouldn't have guessed it to see the love between the two of you."

She left us to go remove her CD from the stereo.

We stood silent for a second, and I wondered if Dax was as unsure of what to say next as I was. I avoided eye contact with him as I gathered my purse and sunglasses from the table where I'd left them.

"Thanks for throwing me under the bus," Dax said, grinning as he offered his hand to me once we'd left the dance room.

I took it, relieved that he wasn't going to address her comment. "What do you mean?"

"*He did it. He surprised me. I would have had my dance shoes if he'd only told me where we were going,*" he said in a voice I suppose he intended to sound like mine.

I laughed. "She liked that! That was a good thing!"

We had reached his truck, and he put his arms around my waist and

184

pulled me to him as we stood by the passenger door.

"Was it?" he asked, his tone a bit more serious. "Was it a good surprise? Did you enjoy it?"

"Very much so," I said, sliding my arms around his neck. "Thank you."

His gaze shifted to my lips again, and I trembled with the certainty that he was about to kiss me.

Our lips came together, gentle at first, but as he ran his hand up my back and cupped it around my neck, I pushed his mouth open with mine, and the kiss grew in intensity.

Another couple exited the building and walked past us in the parking lot, and Dax released my lips but still held me in his arms.

"I'm starving," he said.

"For food?" I asked, lifting an eyebrow as I grinned.

"All of the above," he growled with another quick kiss before opening the truck door and waiting for me to climb inside.

We drove to a nearby pizza place and settled into a booth in the back.

"I very much enjoyed dancing with you tonight," he said once the waitress had taken our order. "The way your face lit up. Your eyes so bright. You were grinning from ear to ear the whole time. Definitely in your element, that's for sure."

I shrugged. "It was fun. I enjoyed learning something new. Plus, it was hilarious to watch you and all the other men be scared witless by an almost ninety-year-old woman."

"It wasn't only the men," Dax said. "I felt you stiffen every time she came near us, trying not to provoke her wrath. Then you went and threw me under the bus to save face with her."

"I thought we already established that was a good thing! She might be tough, but she knows her stuff. I had a teacher like her once. An older lady who watched you like a hawk, ready to swoop down if you made a mistake. I was maybe ten at the time, and I was terrified of her. But I tell you what, she taught me technique and I firmly believe it was her teaching that allowed me to excel and achieve what I did at such a young age."

He tilted his head to the side, his eyes somber and questioning.

"So, why'd you quit?"

I swallowed hard and took a gulp of my beer, avoiding his inquisitive stare.

"You obviously loved it," he said. "Love it still. And from what you say, you were good. Damned good, it seems. I don't mean to pry, but I can't help but wonder why you left a successful career that meant so much to you."

I took a deep breath and released it in a slow exhale, unable to make eye contact with him.

"Life," I answered, looking across the crowded restaurant.

He was silent for a moment, and I got the distinct impression he was waiting for more, but I wasn't sure how much I wanted to give him.

"When I asked the other night how long you danced, you said not long enough," he said. "It must have been hard on you to give it up."

I met his eyes and the warmth I saw there made the lump in my throat grow larger.

"I was a single mother with two young kids, and I had to choose a job whose schedule and commitment would allow me to put them first."

"That's understandable."

My chest had tightened with the tension, and I sucked in another deep breath and squared my shoulders, trying to expand my rib cage and make my chest release.

"I taught dance for a while under one of my former teachers. I was able to bring Cabe with me, and he participated in the preschool programs they had at the center. But when Galen was born…"

Scenes from the past flashed in my mind in rapid succession, and my voice faltered.

"We don't have to talk about this," Dax said, reaching across the table to take my hand. "I didn't mean to upset you."

I forced a smile and shook my head. "You didn't. Just a lot of things to process tonight. It brought back memories, you know? It was odd being back in a studio of sorts. Learning new dance steps. All of it, really," I said, not daring to go into how my attraction to him and our budding relationship factored into those memories.

"I'm sorry. I thought it would be fun for you."

"It was fun." This time my smile was more genuine. "I had a great time dancing with you."

The waitress delivered our pizza, and we changed the subject. He told me about the week he'd had, and I learned more about branding calves and managing bulls in the spring mating season than I'd ever wanted to know. I also laughed harder than I had in quite some time.

It was so easy to enjoy being with Dax.

"Thanks again for taking me dancing," I said as we pulled into my driveway at the end of the evening. "I did enjoy it."

"Me, too. The next few weeks are still gonna be crazy at the ranch, but if you want to go back and do the other lessons, I can make it work."

A momentary thought of panic flashed in my mind when I considered being committed to a weekly date, but the thought of being in his arms and dancing by his side was enticing, and I nodded.

"Yeah. Let's do it," I said, surprised at my own willingness.

"Finding time to practice will be another story, though," Dax said as we walked to my door.

"Do the drills when you can; you know, what she showed you guys in the beginning."

"Oh, I will. I'll be out there in the pastures, counting off waltz steps. I just need to be careful that I don't catch the eye of an amorous bull while I'm dancing around out there."

I laughed at the mental image as I unlocked the door. He didn't move when I opened the door, and disappointment settled over me when I realized he wasn't going to follow me inside.

"You wanna come in?" I asked.

"I would love to, but something tells me that I wouldn't want to leave anytime soon, and I need to be back at the ranch for a four o'clock wake-up call."

I stood in the doorway, the height of the step almost putting me eye-to-eye with Dax.

He reached to cup my cheek in his hand, his thumb lightly stroking my skin and sending little vibrations all over my body.

"Can I have a rain check?" he asked.

"Maybe," I said, breathless as I watched him lean in to kiss me.

I clutched the front of his shirt as he moved his hand from my cheek to the back of my neck, tilting my head beneath his kiss while he pulled me closer with one arm around my waist.

"I'll try not to let you down," he whispered.

I pulled back and looked at him, my eyes searching his in the soft glow of the porch light. Did he somehow know what fears were in my heart?

"The dance steps," he said. "I'll do my best not to bring the wrath of Betty upon us."

I grinned as I straightened his collar and ran my finger along the edge of the shirt's neckline. "You do, and I'll have to throw you under the bus again."

"Again? So, you admit it," he said, squeezing his arms tightly around my waist.

I tossed my head back laughing, and he pressed his mouth against the exposed skin of my neck, gently biting down and sucking. It was like he'd sent a jolt of electricity straight to my loins, and I gasped as I grabbed onto his shoulders. His lips slowly made their way back to mine as I ran my fingers up the back of his neck and into his hair.

The kiss deepened quickly once our mouths connected, and when he pulled back, we were both breathing heavier.

"I gotta go, or there's no way in hell I'm gonna be able to leave you," he said, his voice thick with desire.

"Whether you drive tonight or in the morning, it's still the same distance," I said, twisting my fingers tighter into the hair at the nape of his neck.

"Oh, damn, you're not gonna show me any mercy, are you?"

I chuckled and took a step back, out of his embrace. "Okay, go. Get on the road. I won't keep you."

He caught my hand and turned it palm up to kiss my wrist. "What about that rain check? You never did answer me."

"I'm sure we can work something out. Maybe I'll drive to your place one night this week so we can practice our moves."

"Our moves?" His eyes were hopeful yet full of mischief.

"Our dance moves. Goodnight, cowboy." I pulled my hand from his grasp and blew him a kiss before I shut the door.

The scent of him lingered on my shirt long after he left, and I delayed taking it off as I got ready for bed just so I could breathe him in as long as possible.

# 35 SCATTERED BLUEBERRIES

We settled into an easy rhythm over the next few weeks. Though the ranch's demands on his time were extensive, we managed to make each dance lesson, and Betty seemed pleased with our progress. She even used us to demonstrate to the others a couple of times, which thrilled Dax to no end.

The magnitude of my emotions after each encounter would stir up panic within me, but because we didn't talk every day or see each other more than once or twice a week, I was able to keep it at bay. I missed him terribly between our visits, and my longing for him always ended up outweighing my fears.

I began to relax little by little. I began to believe that maybe it was possible to put my past behind me.

I'd purchased a new dress for dancing, and I was standing in front of the bathroom mirror twisting to and fro to watch it move when my phone rang. I worried it might be Dax saying he was going to be delayed picking me up, but I smiled when I saw Galen's name on the screen.

"Hi, sweetheart," I said, turning to see my profile in the mirror.

"Hey, Mom. You got a minute?"

I looked at my watch and considered what I still needed to do to be ready when Dax arrived. "I can talk for a few minutes. What's up?"

"Tate's mom wants to serve quail, elk, and buffalo at the rehearsal dinner."

"Wow, that's non-traditional."

"That's disgusting! Who's going to eat that, Mom? Why can't she do normal food?"

I put the phone on speaker so I could touch up my makeup as we talked. "Some people might like to try it. What else is she having?"

"That's it! I mean, she's having some sort of vegetable medley. God knows what that will be. Cactus? Beets? Something horrific, I'm sure."

"I'm sure there will be other options, sweetie."

"No. She sent me the menu. Quail, elk, and buffalo. Who does that? It's bizarre."

I sighed as I rubbed a bit of pomade into my palms and then smoothed it over my hair. "Maybe she's trying to create an adventure for your guests."

"You know as well as I do that she's just being difficult. She hates me, and I swear she's doing this on purpose to ruin my rehearsal dinner."

I tossed my head back to gargle the mouthwash, and Galen protested the sound.

"Ew. What are you doing?"

"I'm getting ready," I said once I'd spit in the sink.

"Where are you going?"

I paused, still not ready to tell my children that I was engaging in what appeared to be a full-fledged relationship.

"Out. Why don't you ask Tate to talk to his mom? See if he can get her to do a chicken option or perhaps a beef carving station."

"He says I'm overreacting. He said this is the only part of the wedding that she has a say-so in, and that I should let her do it the way she wants to."

"Hmm. Well, she is paying for the rehearsal dinner."

I flipped on the light in the closet and took out my dance shoes, which were still relatively new and barely broken in. The sight of them filled me with excitement for the night ahead, and I couldn't wait to be laughing in Dax's arms as we moved across the floor in unison. Well, mostly unison. We were still learning, after all.

"So, what if she's paying?" Galen said. "You're paying for the wedding, and you're not sitting here making demands and telling me you're going to do something ridiculous that no one will like."

"Did you talk to Tyler? Perhaps she could put in a word for you."

I strapped the shoes on and wiggled my toes in them, delighted with the way they felt.

"Tyler basically agrees with Tate. She said she'd talk to her, but she also said it's pretty typical for the groom's mom to plan the rehearsal dinner."

"Try not to get too worked up over it, sweetheart. I'm sure it's going to be a lovely event."

The smell of tangerine and peach blossom tinged with sandalwood filled the air around me as I sprayed perfume on the pulse points at my wrists, behind my ears, and above my ankles.

I closed my eyes to enjoy the scent as Galen groaned. "Oh, yeah. Because having people eat freaking elk will be lovely. Thanks, Mom."

As much as I loved my daughter, her list of complaints about the wedding were becoming a regular occurrence, and I was in too good of a mood to become embroiled in her drama.

"I'm not sure what you'd like me to say or do. I don't know Tate's mother. I've never met the woman, so I can't call her up and tell her she needs to change her menu. This is going to be your mother-in-law. I suggest you either let this go and allow her to plan her event, or you need to communicate with her yourself and tell her you're concerned about the menu. But politely. Don't go burning bridges over meat. I'm sorry, but I need to go."

"Wait, there's something else I needed to talk to you about."

I frowned with a sigh and turned off the lights in the bathroom, heading to the kitchen to make a protein smoothie before Dax arrived.

"Is it quick? I need to finish getting ready, and I have to run the blender. We can talk later if you need to."

Galen paused on the other end of the line, and I didn't know if she was upset that I didn't have time to talk or if she'd gotten distracted by something.

"You still there?"

"Yeah. I just really need to talk to you about this."

"So talk," I said, taking the ingredients for the smoothie out of the fridge.

"Okay."

I heard her take a deep breath, and a feeling of foreboding came over me.

"I was talking to Dad—um, Gerry—and he's offered to pay for my honeymoon."

The container of blueberries fell from my hand, scattering little purple orbs across the kitchen floor.

"Did you hear me? Mom?"

"Absolutely not," I said.

"Mom—"

"No. Absolutely not. He will not pay one cent for this event, do you hear me?"

"But Mom, that's ridiculous. There's no reason for you to pay for everything if he's willing to do something."

"No. I don't want him involved. Did you call him? Did you ask him for money?"

My entire body tensed with anger, and my hands began to shake.

"I was just talking to him about the wedding, and he asked where we were going. He said the two of you went to Aruba together. You never told me that. Was it beautiful?"

"Galen, he is using you to get at me. You have to tell him no. I don't want him involved in this wedding."

"That's so unfair. Why does everything he does have to be about you? Why can't it be that I'm his daughter and he wants to do something nice for me? Why do you always have to think the worst of him?"

"I think the worst of him because I know him better than you do."

"Twenty-six years ago, maybe. You don't know him now. He might have done some awful things to you, Mom, but he acknowledges he was wrong for that. Since he's been back in my life, he hasn't done any of the horrible things you warned me he would do. He hasn't lied to me. He hasn't broken promises. He hasn't tried to use me to get close to you. Maybe it's time you admit that he's changed."

I covered my eyes with my hand. "No. People like him don't change."

"How do you know? The only time you ever talk to him is when you're mad about something. He said you'd react this way. He even offered to just give me the money and have me tell you it came from somewhere else, just so you couldn't say no. Would he do that if he was trying to use me to get close to you? I don't think so."

I slapped the palm of my hand down on the tile in frustration, trying to keep my voice calm as I spoke.

"Galen, I do not want that man to be any part of this wedding. He did not raise you. He did not fulfill his duties as a father. He doesn't get to step in and write a check to play the role."

"But whose fault was that, really? He's told me how he tried to stay in our lives. That he wanted to give you money. To support us. He said he begged you to let him be involved with me and Cabe, and you said no. He wasn't a father because you wouldn't let him be. He would have been there for me, but you couldn't allow that, could you? So we had to go without a father all those years because of you. We had to believe our dad didn't care anything about us and didn't want to be with us when you knew all along that wasn't true."

Her words sliced open my heart, exposing my most vulnerable fears.

"I did what I thought was best for you and your brother. I kept you from him to protect you."

"Protect me from what? He's my father! I had a right to know him. I had a right to know my brother and sister. They are my family, and they love me. They're happy that we're finally united. I could have had a family all along if you hadn't been so blinded by anger at my dad."

"You did have a family!" I said through gritted teeth. "You had a family that loved you, nurtured you, and surrounded you with stability. Met your needs without fail. Your grandparents, Sandy, Alberto—how can you say you didn't have a family? So me, you, and Cabe weren't a family?" The emotion in my voice was raw, much harsher than I would have liked. "Do you think I wanted to raise the two of you alone? Do you think I wanted to watch my children deal with the hurt of not knowing their father? He had a

192

chance to do the right thing. To tell the truth. To step up to the plate. He chose to lie. He chose to have his cake and eat it, too. I will not sit here and let you rewrite the past for your own purposes. You had a family, and it's his own damned fault he wasn't part of it."

"He said you'd say that."

"You don't understand the magnitude of what he did," I said, as hot tears stung my eyes. "You have no idea how hard it was or what I went through."

"I'm sorry he hurt you, Mom, and so is he. But this is *my* life, and I choose to have my father and my other siblings be a part of it. I want to let him pay for my honeymoon, and I want Jeffrey and Julie at my wedding."

This was it. This was what I had dreaded since she first announced her engagement.

How could I be expected to sit at an event and see the product of his betrayal? The manifestation of his lies? The family he chose over me and my children?

Why should he be allowed to swoop in and play the part of the victim, the poor mistreated father, when the whole situation was his doing?

It was too much. I couldn't listen to her any longer. I wanted to scream and yell. I wanted someone to pay for my pain. But my daughter wasn't the person who deserved my wrath.

"I can't talk about this any longer. I have to go."

"Mom, I'm not doing this to upset you. I swear. I just want to—"

"Galen, I cannot talk about this any longer. Goodbye."

# 36 TWO SIDES OF A COIN

I paced the floor of the kitchen, my entire body trembling. My mind was at war as parental guilt and indignant rage battled for control of my emotions.

On some level, I understood where Galen was coming from. I knew how badly she wanted us all to be one big, happy family, but that was something I would never be able to do.

Whereas Cabe had internalized his father's absence and never mentioned him, Galen had begged and pleaded to meet her father once she became a teenager and developed a greater awareness that he was absent. I'd resisted until her behavior and her acting out became so extreme at age sixteen that it was evident that being around Gerry wouldn't be as detrimental as what she was doing to herself with alcohol and promiscuity.

I'd made the call I had sworn I would never make and asked him to meet her.

He flew into Orlando and spent the weekend in a nearby hotel, and they crammed years of childhood into one day at Walt Disney World while I sat at home and chewed my fingernails for the first time in my life.

Gerry played the part of the prodigal father after that, sending elaborate gifts for her birthday and Christmas and flying into town to surprise her with stays at the Ritz-Carlton or the Waldorf. She tried early on to play him against me, threatening to leave and go live with him until she realized that would never be an option.

Despite his flowery words of how much Galen meant to him, he refused to introduce her to his other children or to include her in any aspect of his life.

As she matured, she mentioned him less, and I assumed her contact with him had waned and the novelty had worn off. But then she'd reached out on social media to meet her half-siblings, and though I tried to think of her needs before mine and be supportive, I couldn't help feeling a little betrayed.

I felt even more betrayed to know she'd been talking to Gerry again, even going so far as to call him Dad. But to learn that Gerry had been telling Galen behind my back that his absence was my fault was too much.

I dialed his number with shaking hands, barely able to press the correct digits.

"How did I know I was going to be hearing from you?" he asked without even saying hello.

"How dare you! How dare you tell my daughter what a wonderful father you would have been if I hadn't stopped you?"

"She's my daughter, too, you know. Although, you've never wanted to acknowledge that other than when you threw your hands up in the air and called me begging for help."

"Damn you. I won't allow you to do this, Gerry. You can't sweep in and buy your way into her wedding. You haven't been a father. You weren't there for everything she's gone through. You don't get to play the part of generous daddy only when it suits you."

He sniggered, and the sound turned my stomach.

"Listen to you," he sneered. "Listen to the jealousy in your voice. You tried so hard to turn my own kids against me. To keep them for yourself and not let me know them. You may have succeeded with Cable, but Galen won't let you poison her mind about me any longer."

"Are you delusional? Do you even hear what you're saying? You're not the victim here, Gerry!" I yelled. "You did this! *You!* You created all this hurt, and I'll be damned if I'm going to take the blame."

"By all means, blame me. I've been your scapegoat for years, and you never let me try and correct my mistakes. You wouldn't let bygones be bygones so we could move past them. You've harbored this hatred for so long that it's made you bitter and nasty, Maggie, and our children have suffered for it."

"They're not *our* children!" I screamed, the words screeching out of me from somewhere deep in my gut. "They are *my* children. You don't deserve to have them in your life. You don't deserve to be their father."

"But I am their father, and that kills you, doesn't it? I wonder, Maggie, would you ever have told me that I was a father? If I hadn't ran into that gossipy girl from the ballet company, would I ever have even known about Cable?"

"Oh my God, you have some audacity. We both know why I didn't let you know I was pregnant. You want to talk about secrets, Gerry? How about not telling me you were married before you knocked me up? Huh, Gerry? And that wasn't enough, was it? You had to come back. You had to play out your elaborate charade and wear me down with your promises of how we'd be a family. Of how we'd make up for the time lost. And all the while…you know what? I'm not going down this path again. You don't get to pretend that it never happened."

He swore under his breath. "How many times have I said I'm sorry?"

"Not enough. It will never be enough. For what you did to me. To my son. To my daughter. Never. You know what? If you're truly sorry, if you mean those words, then let Galen have her wedding without your interference and without you bringing drama into it."

"I think you need to take a look in the mirror to see where the drama is coming from," he sneered. "I offered to pay for my daughter's honeymoon. That's a perfectly natural thing for a father to do. You'd think you might be grateful for that, but no. You have to twist it into something negative and ruin it for her."

"To Aruba? Is that your idea of a sick joke?"

"I happen to love Aruba. I have very fond memories there."

I stared at the ceiling in disbelief. "You're unbelievable. After everything you've done, you still refuse to take responsibility."

"Oh, please. I've taken responsibility. I offered you child support. I offered you whatever you needed for them. You refused any money from me. When you called and asked me to help with her at sixteen, I flew down there immediately. In fact, every time you've called and chewed my ass for something with these kids, I've done everything I could. Hell, I'm pretty sure most people would consider me paying for the honeymoon to be taking responsibility. But not you. Not Miss High and Mighty."

"Screw you, Gerry."

"Nice. But you're not as innocent in all this as you'd like to believe, Maggie. You know, Margot always said you got pregnant on purpose."

I hung up before he could finish.

# 37 SPECIAL DELIVERY

He was right in at least one regard. I never would have told him about Cabe.

I still don't know who told him.

I'd moved out of my parents' house soon after they found out I was pregnant. My mother begged me not to go, but I couldn't bear the disappointment on my father's face or the daily tears my mother shed.

Sandy, Alberto, and I moved into the little blue house, and I took the job teaching dance, working right up until the day my water broke nearly a full week after my due date.

It had spread like wildfire through the dancers that I was pregnant with Gerry Tucker's baby and that he had left town, so I don't know if the person who told him was being malicious or thought she was being helpful.

All I know is he showed up at the studio where I taught a few weeks before Cabe was born, demanding to talk to me. I refused to come out.

Alberto drove me to and from work every day after that, but Gerry didn't come back to the studio. I thought maybe he'd returned to New York, but I couldn't shake my fear of a confrontation at the hospital.

My father hired an attorney to decipher what rights Gerry had and what we could do if he showed up, and it nearly killed my dad to learn that it would be best in the long run to let Gerry see the baby.

Despite the flurry of emotions during the delivery and the pure joy of holding my son in my arms for the first time, my concern about Gerry was ever-present in my mind. I had no idea how I would react if he did come to the hospital. I hadn't seen him since the day we returned from Aruba, and my stomach was in knots that went far beyond the normal pains after giving birth.

He must have been watching for my parents to leave, because he showed up late in the evening, right after they went to the cafeteria to grab dinner and allow me a few minutes' rest. Dad had given strict instructions at the nurses' station that I was not to be disturbed by any visitors, and they'd been briefed that the baby's father may try to see him but was not welcome in my room.

A young nurse, not much older than I was at the time, must not have gotten the message. She had just come on her shift when she peeked in and told me there was a man asking to see me.

I don't know why I agreed he could come in. My emotions were all over the place with hormones, exhaustion, and the roller coaster that comes with delivering a child. It was surreal in many ways to think that the tiny baby I held was a result of Gerry and me, and my heart—which had been shattered and only barely glued back together enough to function—was feeling nostalgic for what might have been.

He had dark circles under his eyes, and he was thinner than I remembered as he walked to the bed and stared down at our son in my arms.

"Oh, God, Willow. He's beautiful."

My eyes filled with tears, as did his, and my heart hurt with the pain of it all.

"Why didn't you tell me?" he whispered.

My tears overflowed, and I struggled to wipe them before they fell on the sleeping baby in my arms.

"Can I hold him?" he asked, his own tears slowly rolling down his face.

I hesitated, unsure if I should let him.

My mind was filled with anger. At him, at the situation, and everything I'd gone through. But at the same time, the baby was his child.

*Our child.* A child we'd created together in what I had thought was love.

When I cut Gerry off the day my parents dropped the bombshell on me, it was like someone had died. One day he was there, and the next he was gone. As I'd experienced the pregnancy alone with all the complications of my career, my finances, and my living situation, there were so many nights that I'd wished for the way I thought things were. For his love. For his touch.

I dreamed of him. Dreamed of him coming back to tell me it was all a big mistake. In my dreams, he'd be ecstatic about the pregnancy, and he'd take me away from the crowded little house and help me make a proper nursery for our baby. Sometimes when I dreamed, we were married, and there was a young boy there, playing in a fenced-in yard. My heart would swell with happiness and contentment, and then I'd wake and remember that it had all been a lie.

So, when he stood by my hospital bed and tearfully asked to hold his son, I was torn between wanting to punish him and wanting to share with him what only the two of us could feel for that child.

He sat on the edge of my bed and when I placed my baby in his arms, he wept.

"This is my son, Willow. My firstborn son. I've missed it. I missed him kicking inside you. I missed seeing your belly filled with him. I missed it all. I've made such a huge mess of everything, and now it's all too late."

His words woke the baby, and as he stirred in his father's arms, Gerry smiled through his tears.

"Oh God, he's beautiful. He's the most incredible thing I've ever seen," he whispered as he gazed into the baby's eyes. He turned and looked at me, reaching to take my hand, but I curled it into a fist so he simply placed his hand over mine.

"I'm going to make this up to you, Willow. I swear on my life. I will fix this. I will make it up to you. And to him. This baby deserves to have a family. He deserves to have a mother and a father who love him. Who love each other. And I do love you, Willow. Oh, God, how I love you. I'm sorry. I know I didn't handle things well. I thought I could…fix it. I never meant to hurt you. I fell in love with you and I didn't know how to tell you the truth. I didn't know how to get out of it."

My tears poured in a steady stream as he said everything I'd wanted to hear for months, and yet, in the back of my mind, I knew none of it mattered. I knew I couldn't go back to the way I'd felt before.

The baby started to cry, and my body reacted immediately. I reached for him, and Gerry placed him back in my arms, his hand lingering on my elbow as he passed our child to me.

"Does he have a name?" he asked as he watched me nurse.

I shook my head, unwilling to share with him the ideas I'd come up with around the table with Sandy and Alberto.

"My brother's name was Cable," he said, wiping at his tears. "He was my hero. He died in Vietnam, and I always swore if I ever had a son, I'd name him after my brother. I know I don't have a right to ask anything of you, but this is my son. Would you consider giving him my brother's name?"

"I don't know, Gerry," I said, completely overwhelmed by the whole situation.

He paused, staring at the baby. "Will he have my last name at least?"

"I don't know that either. It's complicated."

He nodded. "I know. That's my fault. I swear to you I'm going to figure out how to fix this. Somehow. Some way. I'm going to make this right. I'm going to be the best damned father that you've ever seen. You just wait. I'll make it all up to you both."

A nurse came in to check my condition, and she asked Gerry to step out of the room for my examination.

When she left, my parents had returned, and I have no idea where Gerry went. I didn't tell my mom and dad he'd been there.

It messed with my head. My heart was conflicted. I knew I could never forgive Gerry. I knew I could never allow him back into my life, but the fact remained that he was the baby's father. Whether we were together or not—whether he was married or not—the baby was his son.

I didn't know what that would look like as it played out in reality, but I never dreamed as I signed the birth certificate that Gerry would end up playing no further role in his child's life.

Despite my father's insistence that it was insanity, I named him Cable Tucker Shaw. Cable to honor Gerry's request for his brother's memory. Tucker because it was Gerry's last name, and whether any of us liked it or not, the baby was his. But Shaw because I had carried him alone, and I had delivered him alone. His last name would be mine.

# 38 CLEAN-UP CREW

I had flung the phone across the counter when I hung up on Gerry, balling my fists at my sides. The rage inside me was too much to restrain. I screamed at the top of my lungs and swiped the smoothie ingredients off the counter onto the floor.

The almond milk carton exploded in a liquid eruption on impact, followed almost immediately by the splatter of the strawberries, carrots, and kale. The destructive release of energy gave me such satisfaction that I grabbed my mug tree and sent it crashing to the floor as well. The shattering sound of the ceramic splintering on the tile was exhilarating, but the feeling of triumph dissipated when I stared at my favorite mugs in jagged pieces amid the milky puddle of produce.

The dam inside me broke, and my tears flowed as I knelt to pick up the pieces.

The chime of the doorbell reminded me of what my night should have been, and my tears turned to anger. I clutched too tightly to the sharp edge in my hand, feeling the sting as my skin ripped and the nerve endings were exposed to air.

I stood and tossed the broken piece in the trash can, wrapping a paper towel around my hand as the blood oozed and dripped.

The doorbell rang again, and I had no choice but to answer it. I caught a glimpse of my appearance in the foyer mirror and stopped short. Black streams of mascara striped my face, and the front of my pretty new dress was wet with splatters of the wreckage as well as blueberry stains pressed into the skirt from where I'd knelt on the floor.

I took the paper towel from my hand and scrubbed at my cheeks, smearing the mascara and turning my face an ashy gray.

*Screw it,* I thought. There was no way I was going to be presentable, and

I couldn't leave Dax standing outside ringing the doorbell all night.

His face held a huge smile when I swung the door open, but as the word *hello* faded from his lips, the smile fell, and his brow creased with worry.

"Maggie, what happened? Are you okay?"

He rushed to put his arms around me, and I took a step back, holding up my hands for space.

"What happened? You're bleeding," he said as he reached to take my hand. I pulled it away and tucked the black-smeared paper towel against the cut.

"It's nothing. It's superficial. Look, I, uh, I'm not really up for dancing and dinner, okay? I'm sorry, but I can't do this tonight."

"That's okay." His voice was hesitant as he continued to take in my appearance. "We'll stay here. That's fine. Tell me what's wrong."

I shook my head and started closing the door, eager to get rid of him before I lost my tenuous grip on my emotions.

"I'm fine, really. It's family stuff. I want…I have to be alone."

He put his hand on the door. "Maggie, please. Tell me what happened. I can't leave you like this. Knowing you're not okay."

"Please, Dax. I don't want you to see me like this. I'm sorry I ruined our night and that you drove over here for nothing. Maybe if you go to the lesson, she'll let you follow along so you don't get behind. Hey, maybe you can dance with Betty." I attempted a smile, but it faltered, and the tears seeped past my defenses.

"Maggie—"

"Dax, please go. Please. I want you to go. I need to be by myself right now. I'll call you later."

I closed the door and leaned against it, sliding down to the floor and hugging my knees to my chest as the tears poured down my face.

There was nothing I wanted more than to fall into his arms. To pour my heart out and tell him everything. To feel like I had nothing to hide and nothing to be ashamed of.

But I didn't want to see disapproval in his eyes. I didn't want to see pity, either. I didn't want him to look at me with any less adoration or appreciation than he ever had.

No. I had to deal with my pain *alone*. It was my bad choices that had gotten me there, and it wasn't fair to Dax to include him in my sorrow.

The doorbell rang, and the door vibrated against my back with the force of him pounding on it.

"Maggie, open up. Open the door."

He rang the doorbell, and I scooted away from the door before he knocked again.

"C'mon, Maggie. Let me in. I'm not leaving, and your neighbors are going to stare if I stand out here yelling. Open up."

I hesitated, but when he rang the bell a third time, I stood and pulled the door open. He stepped inside before I could say a word.

"Hear me out," he said, his hands raised. "Let me say my piece and if you still want me to go, I'll respect your wishes."

I stood staring at him until I realized he was waiting for my acknowledgment, and I nodded for him to continue.

"I tried to do what you asked of me. I went and got in the truck, and I turned the key in the ignition, but I couldn't leave without saying this. I didn't drive all this way for dinner and dancing. I couldn't care less where we go and what we do. I want to spend time with you. And if that's a good time, and we're laughing, then great. But if that's a shitty time, and life's falling down around our ears, then that's okay, too. I still want to be with *you.*"

He took a step toward me and put his hands on my waist, his moves slow and tentative as he watched and waited for my reaction.

"Look, Maggie, I learned the hard way. You don't get a second chance to be there when someone needs you. It goes against everything in me to walk away when you're in pain. Now, if you tell me that's what you need, and you say you truly don't want me here, then I'll go. But I want to stay. I want to be here for you. I'll listen if you need to talk, and I'll hold you if you need to be held. And if you need to not talk and not be touched, well, then I can do that, too. *Maybe.* Maybe I can do that. I don't know."

He flashed me a half-grin, and my heart melted.

"I don't want you to go," I whispered.

His arms closed around me, and Dax pulled me to his chest, his fingers in my hair.

"Then don't send me away," he said. His voice rumbled against my ear as I pressed tight against him, wrapping my arms around his waist and holding on like my life depended on it.

It had been so long since I'd felt safe in someone's arms, and I clung to the feeling, even as my fears whispered that I could lose him if he knew the truth.

"I don't want you to think differently of me, Dax. I don't want you to see me as someone I'm not."

"What do you mean?" he asked, pulling back just enough to look down at me. "What are you talking about? I'm not going to see you differently just because something's wrong. We all have problems in our life."

I shook my head and released my grip on him, stepping back.

"I've done things, Dax. I made decisions in my past that I'm not proud of. Far-reaching decisions that I can't get away from."

He shrugged, his expression puzzled. "Okay, what is it? You were in prison? You killed someone? You were a spy? What?"

"No, nothing like that."

"Okay, well if you didn't kill anyone, it can't be that bad. You're dripping blood, by the way."

I looked down at the bloodied, mascara-smudged paper towel in my hand and walked toward the kitchen to rinse the wound, stopping when I saw the mess I'd forgotten.

"What the hell happened here?" he asked, his eyes wide as he took in the splattered and shattered chaos and then looked to me with a renewed concern.

"I was about to make a smoothie when all hell broke loose." I stepped carefully over the wreckage and went to the sink to run my hand under the faucet.

"How bad is it? Is it deep?" He leaned onto the counter and stared over my shoulder.

"Not bad. It's only a little cut but lots of blood. I just need to get a band-aid."

Dax was cleaning up the mess I'd made when I returned from the bathroom with my hand bandaged.

"You don't have to do that! I'll get it."

I rushed forward, but he held up his hand.

"I got it," he said. "Do you have a dustpan?"

Not even bothering to argue, I retrieved the dustpan from the laundry room and handed it to him.

He pulled the trash can closer so he could dump the ruined produce and smashed coffee cups.

"Any more paper towels?" he asked, throwing away the cardboard center of the empty roll.

I took the cleaner out from under the sink and grabbed a fresh roll of paper towels from the pantry before kneeling beside him on the floor. Once he'd removed all the ceramic pieces, Dax mopped up the last of the almond milk, and then I sprayed the floor and wiped it down. We crawled in opposite directions picking up blueberries and searching beneath the cabinets for any strays.

"Thank you," I said when the floor was done. I couldn't meet his eyes. It was bad enough that I had lost control of my emotions, and to have the results of that temper tantrum on display for Dax was embarrassing. But then to have him clean up after me without question or condemnation created an odd feeling, a mixture of gratitude and shame.

"No problem. You've got stuff on your dress. You want to change?"

I nodded, and he followed me down the hall to my room, leaning against the door frame and watching me with wary eyes. His expression was pensive, and I knew he had to be wondering what had transpired and what past deeds I'd referenced. He didn't push it, though.

When I came back out of my closet wearing a matching pair of velour pants and a short-sleeved hoodie, Dax was sitting in one of the plush chairs in the alcove of my bedroom that overlooked the pool. His gaze was intense as he stared out over the water, as I looked at him, my breath caught in my throat.

I don't know when I first realized that I'd fallen in love with Dax, and I still wasn't comfortable acknowledging it, even to myself.

In the three months since I'd met him, my life had taken on a renewed sense of wonder. While I was certainly content with my life before, I knew a happiness with him that I'd never had. I didn't want anything to come between us or to change that.

When he turned and looked at me, a faint smile played across his lips, though his eyes still looked apprehensive.

I wanted things to go back to normal. I wanted our casual, laidback vibe to return, but the dark cloud of the past filled the space between us, dampening the mood and charging the air with questions and uncertainty.

I went to the chair opposite of his and sat with my legs tucked underneath me.

"I'm sorry. About earlier. About all that," I said with a wave of my hand, trying to brush off the drama and minimize its effects.

Dax shook his head slightly. "Nothing to be sorry about. Are you all right?"

I lifted my hand and held out my bandaged palm. "I don't know how long this will stick on the inside of my hand, but it should be fine once the bleeding stops. It really wasn't that deep."

"I wasn't talking about your hand."

A shudder rippled my spine, and I wrapped my arms around myself, tucking my legs in tighter as I looked out toward the pool. Memories of my kids filled my head. We'd had many good times in that pool. My children had gone through their teenage years and early adulthood in the house, and its walls had witnessed so much love, yet so much turmoil. Had I done the wrong thing in keeping them from Gerry? Would it ever be possible for me to know for sure?

I exhaled and shut my eyes, laying back against the chair. We sat in silence for a few minutes, and finally, when I could wait no longer, I opened them again, ready to tell the awful, nasty truth and let the cards fall where they would.

# 39  PORTRAIT OF A GIRL

"You've asked me before about my past, and I haven't really told you much. That's because I made some choices that I'm not necessarily proud of, and those choices have caused a lot of pain. For me, my parents, my friends. My kids, most of all."

Dax nodded, leaning forward to put his elbows on his knees, clasping his hands together as he listened.

"It wasn't that I was trying to hide anything, but I didn't want you to look at me any differently. I didn't want you to see me as someone I'm not, based on decisions I made thirty years ago."

He tilted his head to one side, his brows coming together as he considered my words. "Obviously, I don't know what you're about to tell me, but I can't think of anything you could say that would change how I look at you today. The Maggie I know now wouldn't be here without the obstacles you've encountered, so I'd be hard-pressed to condemn whatever choices you've made."

I sat up in the chair, tugging a pillow from behind my back and hugging it to my chest as I brought one leg out from under me.

"When I met Gerry, the kids' dad, I had just been injured. Like, literally, the night I met him. Unfortunately, that meant that we had a lot of time to spend together. An amount of free time I'd never had before. I'd never dated anyone. I'd never been caught up in the partying scene of Miami. Suddenly, I was in this whole new world, and I didn't really take the time to heed all the warning flags."

"How old were you?"

"Nineteen. And never been kissed. Hard to believe, huh?" I smiled, and he smiled back. "It was a whirlwind romance. It took off and grew way too serious, way too fast. I didn't really know anything about him other than

206

how he made me feel. I'd never felt that way before, and I thought it was love. It seemed like love, and we both said it was love, but what did I know? I was naive, and I had a medical condition at the time due to my extreme workouts and my low body weight that prevented me from having regular periods. I foolishly thought I couldn't get pregnant if I wasn't having a period. Sex wasn't something my mother and I ever discussed. It wasn't something the doctor brought up with me while my mom was in the room. And since I'd never been sexually active, I didn't think to ask."

If Dax was uncomfortable with me discussing my sex life in my youth, he didn't show it. He sat and listened without any sign of judgment or surprise.

"Long story short, I found out I was pregnant with my son, Cabe, not long after I discovered that Gerry, Cabe's father, was still very much married to a woman in New York."

Dax's eyes widened and his eyebrows lifted slightly as he sat back in the chair. "Whoa."

"Yeah, a double-whammy."

"How'd you find out he was married?"

I took a deep breath and looked back toward the pool, squinting at the orange glow of the sun setting beyond the fence. "My parents told me."

"Really?" His eyes opened wider, and he gave a slight shake of his head. "That must have been an interesting conversation."

"You could say that. My parents were upset that I was seeing a man they knew nothing about—actually I went to Aruba with him against their wishes—and my dad hired a private investigator. They told me the day I got home from Aruba, and I broke all contact with him immediately. It wasn't until a couple of months and a whole lot of depression later that I realized I was pregnant."

"What did he say when you told him?"

"Gerry?"

Dax nodded.

I picked at a loose thread on the seam of my pants, avoiding his eyes.

"I didn't tell him. I had asked him not to call me again, and this was before the days of cell phones and social media and being able to see someone's life from afar. I disappeared from my apartment and my life, and I assumed he went back home to Margot, the wife." It was amazing how I still couldn't say her name without it tasting bitter in my mouth, even after all the years that had passed. "I mean, obviously if he had wanted to find me, he could have. It wouldn't have been hard to track down my parents, and he knew Sandy and Alberto, the best friends I lived with throughout my pregnancy."

Dax looked surprised. "You didn't live with your parents?"

"No. I hated the cloud of disappointment I'd cast over the house. Not only was I unwed and pregnant with a married man's child, but I'd lost my position at the ballet company. Their daughter was no longer the talented up and coming *ingenue* worthy of massive life-size portraits hanging over the grand staircase in the foyer."

His eyes darted to the bedroom door, outside which, said painting hung at the end of the hallway.

"Yeah. *That* painting," I said, standing and walking over to look at it. "I came home one weekend, and it had been removed. I was replaced by a beautiful watercolor swan in a pool surrounded by an English garden."

"Ouch," he said as he came and stood behind me.

"My mother said she did it so it wouldn't be a painful reminder for me, but I think it was more for them. They stood by me, though. Their love never wavered, but God, how it must have hurt them."

He put his hands on my shoulders and bent to press his lips to the top of my head.

"Sounds like they weren't the only ones who got hurt."

I leaned back against his chest, reaching up to intertwine my fingers with his on my shoulder.

"Why do you keep it?" he asked.

I'd never really thought about why, and I stared at the portrait, trying to determine what masochistic pleasure I derived from seeing it every day.

"It reminds me, I suppose. It was in the attic when they packed up to move to the house where they live now. I asked Mom if I could have it, and of course, she said yes. I see it when I come down the hallway, and it reminds me of who I was. Of what I lost. That girl in the painting had no idea a firestorm was about to consume her and destroy everything she believed in. I look at her, and she reminds me to stay guarded. To not allow myself to ever get that close to anyone again."

I'd been lost in the past as I spoke, but when I felt Dax stiffen, I realized who I was talking to and what my words would mean to him.

I turned in his arms.

"I'm sorry," I said. "I didn't mean…"

He shrugged. "You were being honest."

I stretched on my toes to reach his lips, and he returned my kiss, but his arms didn't tighten around me, and his back remained stiff.

"Are you hungry?" I asked. "I've been completely preoccupied, and I didn't even consider that you haven't eaten."

"I could eat," he said. "What did you have in mind?"

"I'm not really up for going out, nor am I dressed for it," I said, looking down at my lounge wear, "but we could order in. Chinese?"

"Sure. Whatever you want."

He followed me to the kitchen, and I couldn't help but notice his quiet demeanor, so out of character for him. I didn't know if it was my comments about the painting or the facts I'd revealed, but something had him deep in thought. His eyes held a sadness that hadn't been there before, and his gaze seemed to land anywhere but on me as he leaned back against the counter with his arms crossed.

I called the Chinese restaurant once we'd made our selections from the menu I kept in a drawer, and then I joined Dax at the kitchen table.

"Penny for your thoughts?" I asked.

He glanced in my direction and looked back down at his hands as he toyed with the napkin ring.

"Just processing."

His silence made me nervous, and I wished I could see inside his head.

"You said when you began that Gerry is the kids' dad. Your daughter and your son?"

I looked away from him and nodded. "Yes."

"So, I'm assuming at some point he found out you were pregnant?"

I nodded again. "Yeah. At the very end of my pregnancy, someone told him. I never found out who, and I don't know why he was in Miami at the time. But yeah. He knew about the baby, and he visited me in the hospital the day Cabe was born. In fact, Cabe is named after Gerry's brother. I know that probably sounds insane considering the circumstances, but it was his kid, so I felt like it was the right thing to do."

Confusion twisted Dax's features. "So, you guys got back together? He left his wife?"

I took a huge breath and rubbed my hands over my face, wishing I could fast-forward past the worst parts of my life story.

"He stuck around for the first six months of Cabe's life. No, we weren't together then, but my dad's attorney advised that Gerry had the right to see the baby, and if we wanted to avoid some kind of legal intervention with assigned visitation, I should let him come over. So I did. He brought diapers. He brought toys. He came every day for a while, and it was just too much. All the hurt, the anger. I was trying to adjust to a new life with a baby and the loss of the life I'd known. I couldn't deal with that and be around him, too. I couldn't get over what he'd done. So, we argued back and forth, and finally I asked him to leave town when Cabe was six months old. I told him it was too much of a reminder for him to be around, and that if he loved Cabe and wanted him to have any kind of stability, he should just go back to Margot and forget we existed."

"And he did?"

I nodded with a shrug. "Yeah, but not for the reason I thought."

Dax put up his hand. "Wait, okay, was he still with the wife that whole time then? Where was she? Where did she think he was for those six months?"

I shrugged again. "God only knows. I think she was home in New

York? I don't know, honestly. I didn't care at the time. I just wanted him gone. It was hell to have to share a child with someone who had ripped my heart from my chest, betrayed me in a huge way, and basically ruined my career."

"I bet," Dax said. He grew quiet again, and the unanswered question hung in the air between us.

"So, I guess you're wondering how I ended up with Galen if Gerry left so easily."

Dax looked at me, his expression unreadable. "The thought had crossed my mind."

I took a deep breath and closed my eyes. It was too late to turn back, and as embarrassing as it was, there was no way I could avoid telling Dax that getting pregnant with Cabe was not the biggest mistake I ever made. Getting pregnant with Galen was.

# 40 IN SEARCH OF HAPPILY EVER AFTER

Gerry may have gone back up north, but he didn't leave me alone. He called continuously until we changed our phone number and got one that was unlisted. He wrote me letters that I threw in the trash unopened.

Eventually, I settled into some semblance of normality. I taught dance during the week, taking Cabe to work with me, and we visited my parents most weekends. They adored Cabe, and despite the dark cloud that had hung over his birth, they couldn't get enough of him.

He was such an easy baby, and I didn't feel like a single parent since I had Sandy and Alberto to help me at home.

But despite being surrounded by people all the time, I couldn't shake the feeling of loneliness. My heart ached to love and be loved, and in the still of the night when everyone had gone to bed and the house was quiet, I cried myself to sleep more times than I cared to count.

That's not to say that I didn't have happiness in my life, or that I didn't have love. I was rich with love shared with my friends, my parents, and my beautiful son.

I felt like something was missing, though, and I never could find peace with the way things had turned out.

The week after Cabe's second birthday, I had taken him for a walk while Sandy and Alberto were performing in a Saturday matinee.

I noticed an unfamiliar car in our drive as we returned, and I slowed the stroller, uneasy about approaching without knowing who it was.

He had been sitting on the steps watching for me, and he stood and walked to the end of the drive as my hands tightened on the stroller and my stomach twisted in knots.

"Hello, Willow."

He smiled this huge, enthusiastic smile, like he thought I would be excited to see him. He was wrong.

"What are you doing here, Gerry?"

He ignored the question, squatting in front of the stroller to talk to Cabe. "Hey, buddy. Do you remember Daddy? Do you? Daddy remembers you! And I've got good news for you, Cable. Daddy is never going to leave you again, okay?"

Panic gripped me, and I turned the stroller so that he couldn't see Cabe. "What are you talking about? What's going on, Gerry?"

He stood and smiled again. "I told you I'd fix it. I told you I'd make it right. I filed for divorce, Willow. I'm back. I can't bear to live without you and Cable. I've rented a place here in Miami, and I'm going to prove to you that I deserve your love and your forgiveness. I'm going to be the father I always should have been."

I pushed the stroller around him and glared as I passed. "You're insane, and you're wasting your time. We're doing fine without you."

He followed me up the drive undeterred.

"I know you're angry. You have every right to be. But you'll see. I'm going to make it up to you."

I whirled around and got in his face. "You can't make it up to me. There is nothing you can do or say that would come close. The only thing I feel for you is contempt. You're not welcome here."

None of that seemed to matter to Gerry.

At first, he would come and visit Cabe, lying on the floor to play with him or spending time on the playground Alberto had set up in the back yard.

It killed me that I couldn't forbid him to be there without risking a court battle and losing all control over when he saw Cabe or how often.

After a while, he began to ask to take Cabe places, and I wasn't comfortable letting him go alone, so the three of us spent even more time together.

I don't know when the shift started. I don't remember a specific time when my anger began to diminish or when I started being able to laugh in his presence. There's no memory that stands out of things getting better or my stance against him softening.

It was gradual. It was the three of us always being together. It was seeing how much Cabe adored his father and how good Gerry was with him.

At some point, I stopped dreading his visits. I wouldn't say I was looking forward to them—yet—but the nausea that would set in when I knew he was coming ceased.

He didn't push the matter of a reconciliation. In fact, after that first day in the driveway, he never mentioned the possibility of there being an 'us' at all. He simply set about being the father I'd always dreamed of Cabe having, and I suppose in hindsight, that's how he wore me down. Maybe it was purposeful, and maybe it was genuine and happened to work in his favor, but I couldn't help wanting to see my child be happy.

My parents were unified with Sandy and Alberto in thinking that I spent way too much time with Gerry. They warned me not to fall for him again. Not to let myself be caught up in another web of deceit.

But for all appearances, he was telling the truth. He had an apartment that I was allowed to visit at any time without restriction. He was working out of an office in South Beach, and no matter when Cabe and I stopped by, he was there when he said he would be.

"Are you going to your parents' this weekend?" Sandy asked when she saw me packing my bag.

"No, Gerry booked a place in the Keys. He wants to take Cabe to see the dolphins."

"Do you think that's a good idea?" Sandy said. Her frown and her disapproval were both expected, but they still put me on the defensive.

"What do you want me to do, Sandy? Should I have him take my two-year-old to the Keys by himself?"

She bit her lip and looked away from me, and I went back to packing.

"I worry it's all getting a little too cozy. You guys are spending so much time together, and even when he's here, it's like the three of you are a family or something."

"Well, I suppose we are a family. A dysfunctional, untraditional family, but we are a family. A daddy and a mama and a baby."

"You used to think of it as a mama and a baby, and then a daddy and a baby. A daddy who had lied to the mommy and cheated on his wife to get the mommy pregnant."

Her words stung and knowing she spoke the truth only added salt to the wound.

"I'm doing the best I can, okay? This is certainly not the life I envisioned for myself, but it's the life I have now. Cabe is happy. He has two parents who love him very much, and he has stability and normalcy. That is more than I could have hoped for when he was born."

"But he can have those things without you and Gerry being together. People co-parent all the time."

"And what if he's telling the truth? What if we really were meant to be together, but he met and married the wrong person first? They got married young, and even he will tell you he was more in love with her money and her position in society than her. He gave all that up for us. He walked away from the money, the status, the power that the marriage brought him. He did that for me and Cabe. So, what if this is what's supposed to happen?"

Sandy shook her head. "I think you're reaching to try and make him fit into some princely mold so that you get the happily ever after in the end."

"But what if you're wrong and I'm right? What if all that pain—all that heartache—was just part of what we had to go through to get to here? Wouldn't everything I went through be worth it if it means we both know that we're truly committed to each other and committed to Cabe?"

"Oh, Mags. You're playing a dangerous game here. I don't think he is who you want him to be, and I'm scared you're setting yourself up to get hurt again. To be disappointed again. Then what happens to Cabe? When Gerry screws up and the two of you split again even more contentious than before, what happens to that precious boy then?"

I didn't want to listen to her. I didn't want her to be right. In fact, I wanted to prove them all wrong. I wanted to show them that I hadn't been the fool.

If Gerry really did love me, and if we ended up spending the rest of our lives together as a family, then I hadn't been a failure after all. Or at least that was my reasoning at the time.

"Look, I'm not saying that I'm going to move in with him next week or anything, okay? I'm taking it slow. Hell, he's been back almost a year, and it's not like I've jumped back in bed with him. I'm keeping my eyes open. I'm looking for any red flags. But is it so wrong for me to want Cabe to have his father in his life? And does it make me a terrible person if I want us to be a family? The way we should have been?"

"No, it doesn't make you a terrible person. I think it's natural and normal for you to want that. But this is not a natural and normal situation, Maggie. He failed to tell you he was married, and I'm pretty sure he failed to tell his wife he was screwing around with you."

"I haven't forgotten that. How could I? But she's no longer in the picture."

"Are you sure? Have you seen the divorce papers? Do you know for a fact that his marriage has ended?"

I zipped the duffel bag shut and dropped it on the floor. "It's not final yet. But I've seen the papers. He definitely filed for divorce. Their lawyers are just hammering out asset division, so it's taking a while."

Sandy's face registered her shock. "You told your parents it was final. You told me and Alberto it was final."

"Because I knew all of you would freak out, and I had enough pressure on me just trying to get through day-to-day with Gerry back in our lives. It's going to be final soon. The important thing is, he filed. He ended it. He moved back here, and he chose me and Cabe. That's what really matters."

"C'mon, Maggie. Don't be stupid."

"I've got to go get Cabe ready. How about you try to be supportive and want what's best for me and the baby? Okay?"

"At least tell me that you're using protection. The last thing you need is to get pregnant again."

"First of all, I've already told you it's not like that. We're both just focused on Cabe. And second of all, if somehow we did go down that path and end up there, the doctor put me on the pill to try and regulate my estrogen after Cabe was born, remember? I went from having virtually no periods my whole life to having them non-stop after the pregnancy wreaked havoc on my hormones. So rest your weary mind, Sandra. If abstinence fails me, the pill will be my back-up."

# 41 THAT RARE HALF-PERCENT

Key West marked a turning point in my relationship with Gerry. No one we encountered knew our past, so we were accepted at face value for being a family. We were simply two parents with an adorable son, without any baggage or disclaimers.

It felt good.

Away from the discerning opinions of my family and friends, I didn't need to be so stressed about every interaction or analyze every word and reaction.

I relaxed, and though it took a little bit of suspending reality to make it work, if I focused on the future and not the past, I could feel passion for Gerry again.

We began to walk closer, to sit closer, to lean toward each other when we spoke. Our hands lingered when we touched, and our constant proximity began to wear down my resolve.

Portraying a loving family was intoxicating, and I wanted it to be my reality. By the end of the trip, our budding closeness had turned intimate, and I'd allowed myself to hope that things could be different.

It was harder when we returned to everyone's scrutiny, and I began to look forward to times the three of us spent alone when I could push the past from my mind and enjoy the moment.

Cabe and I began staying over at Gerry's occasionally, much to the dismay of Alberto and Sandy. Sandy even threatened to tell my parents, but I pleaded with her to focus on how happy Cabe was and give us a chance to work things through without sounding the alarm.

Gerry remained steadfast in his commitment to us, and all the things I'd once loved about him were there again, but the reason we split wasn't.

So despite my reservations, I started falling for Gerry. All over again.

No one was more shocked than me when I returned to the doctor for a routine check-up and found out I was pregnant.

"But that's impossible! I'm on the pill."

The doctor smiled and spoke with a condescending tone. "You probably forgot to take one, or maybe you didn't take it at the same time every day. Some bodies are more sensitive to that than others."

"No. I was diligent about making sure I didn't miss one. I took it at nine o'clock every night, no matter what. I know I didn't miss one. This can't be right. Are you sure?"

She nodded, flipping through my chart. "It's possible that you had what we call a breakthrough ovulation or escape ovulation. It might be due to your history of estrogen issues, or it could be that you're one of the rare half percent or so that find the pill ineffective."

I drove to pick up Cabe from Gerry's in a daze, so completely stunned that I forgot to pick up the groceries for dinner.

But whereas my first pregnancy had been greeted with tears and hand wringing by everyone around me, Gerry was absolutely over the moon about having what he considered a second chance.

He picked me up and whirled me around his tiny living room. "This is fantastic! This is the greatest gift you could ever give me. Oh, Willow! This time we get to experience it together. We're having a baby!"

He spun me around again and repeated himself. "We're having a baby!"

Cabe clapped his hands with the enthusiasm of a two-year-old who has no idea why he's clapping but is deliriously happy to join in.

"We're having a baby!" he yelled in his little toddler voice, and Gerry laughed as he picked Cabe up and gathered him into our hug.

Somewhere in the black fog that had settled over me since the doctor gave me the news, a little ray of light began to shine.

Maybe it wasn't as bad as I had thought. Perhaps we could be a happy family after all.

# 42 COUNTDOWN

If my father had been disappointed the first time he found out I was pregnant, he was nothing less than devastated the second.

"How? How could you? Did you learn nothing at all from everything you went through?"

My mother sat in stunned silence, twisting her wedding band round and round her finger as Dad paced the floor and yelled.

"Mark my words, he's going to hurt you again. It's a matter of when, not if. The first time I blamed him, but this time, I'll blame you. And whatever happens to Cabe, I will hold you responsible for. This is your choice. You know who this man is and what he's capable of, and you're choosing to be blind to that. God help you, and God help that poor baby. Both of them!"

He'd stormed from the room, but he returned within minutes. Tears streamed down his face, and his voice was broken, cracking with pain.

"Is this my fault? Did I do something wrong? Was it the kind of father I was? Was I so horrible a father that this is what you would pick for my grandchildren?"

"No, it has nothing to do with you, Dad. You were a wonderful father," I cried, rising to go to him, unable to bear seeing the pain I had caused. "I didn't mean for this to happen. I'm sorry. I truly am. Cabe loves Gerry, and I'm sorry, but I love him, too. I can't help it. I want us to be a family."

He walked back out of the room with his hand over his mouth, and I turned to my mother but found no solace there.

"It's not love, Margaret," she said, never looking up from her hands. "You're trying to get back something you lost by clinging to something you never had. This won't end well."

I knelt in front of her, taking her hands in mine and willing her to look at me.

218

"What if it does? What if we get married and we raise our children and we're happy? Why does everyone assume that the worst is going to happen again? Why can't there be an option where I can be happy with my children and their father?"

She looked up, and when her eyes met mine, I wished she hadn't. I'd never seen such anger and disgust in my mother's face before.

"Because the type of man who stays home with his wife and children doesn't seduce young women while he already has a wife. I knew when he came back that something like this was bound to happen. For God's sake, if you were determined to be with him, why couldn't you at least wait until the two of you were married to get pregnant, Maggie?"

"We will be, Mom. Soon. Everything will be final by summer, so we can be married before the baby arrives."

Her eyes opened wide as my accidental admission registered. "Are you saying he's still married? You told me the divorce was already final."

"It's a technicality," I said, cursing myself for not being more careful with my words. "They only have to finalize the finances. It's okay. It will be final before the baby's here, and we'll be married. It's going to work out. Please, Mom. I need your support."

Her eyes had filled with tears again, and her chin trembled as she spoke. "You are the daughter that I prayed every night on my knees for God to send to me. Your father and I have done all we could to give you every opportunity, and I have stood by you since the day you were born, and I won't abandon you now. You have my love, and this baby will have my love. But I cannot support this decision. I never thought I could be so disappointed in you."

I sat back on my heels and stared at her, and when she stood and left the room without another word, I went home and begged Gerry to tell me everything would be okay.

We moved in together not too long after that, despite the angry protests from everyone in my life who cared about me or Cabe.

I was cautiously happy as we played house, feeling that at last my life might be back on track. I would get up early to cook breakfast for the two of them every morning, and I rushed home from teaching to make dinner each night. Cabe would squeal with delight when Gerry came home in the evening, running across the apartment with his arms outstretched to leap into his daddy's arms. They'd do bathtime antics after dinner, and then Gerry would tuck him in and read him a bedtime story, insisting that I take that time for myself.

"Why don't you read or take a bubble bath? Even if you only put your feet up. I can't help you carry the baby, but I can take over in the evenings with Cabe," he had said when I protested.

Seeing how much he and Cabe both enjoyed their bonding time made it easier for me to listen to him and use the time to rest.

It hurt that my parents and my best friends wanted nothing to do with my happiness, but I reasoned that the longer we were together and the better things got, eventually they'd have to forgive him (and me) and welcome us back into their lives.

Without their presence, it was like I'd traded one loneliness for another, but Cabe was happy having his daddy around, and I no longer cried myself to sleep.

Gerry tried to distract me with talk of wedding plans, but I couldn't get enthusiastic about planning when no one on my side was likely to show up.

Although I understood their reaction to the unexpected pregnancy, I honestly thought at some point the frost would thaw and I'd be back in good graces again.

Instead, my parents would come and take Cabe on outings, but they wouldn't get out of the car or come in for a visit. Even Sandy and Alberto gave me the cold shoulder, choosing to spend time with Cabe only when I had appointments or was teaching.

If anything, the isolation drove Gerry and me closer together in a sort of "me and him against the world" mentality. His excitement over my pregnancy was contagious, and we celebrated every little milestone, determined to make up for what we missed the first time.

I couldn't shake the ever-present feeling of impending doom, though. The divorce lingered over our heads and seemed to drag on endlessly. The hostility from my loved ones was a constant source of tension, and the increasing stress of finances and the constraints of a one-bedroom apartment increased in magnitude as my pregnancy progressed.

It often felt as though there were a timer counting down, but I wasn't certain what would happen when time ran out and whether or not it was something to look forward to.

# 43 KITCHEN CURTAINS

It was somewhere around my sixth month when Gerry came to the studio and told me he was taking me out for a surprise lunch. I thought him showing up was the surprise, so I was shocked when he held up a black silk scarf before I got in the car.

"Let's put this on."

"What? What are you doing?"

"If I told you, it wouldn't be a surprise," he said. He was grinning from ear to ear, his eyes sparkling as he laughed. "C'mon. I can't wait any longer. Hurry up. Turn around."

I turned, and he placed the folded cloth over my eyes and tied it behind my head.

"Is that too tight? Can you see anything?" He ran his finger beneath the scarf around my head, ensuring it didn't pinch anywhere.

"No, and no. I can't see a thing. Where are you taking me? Why do I need to be blindfolded?" The excitement of the unknown was thrilling, but the loss of my vision was unsettling. "Gerry? Where'd you go?"

I put my hands out to reach for him but came up empty.

"Gerry?"

"I'm right here," he said, sliding an arm around my waist. "I was getting something from the trunk. Here, let me help you in the car."

He eased me into the passenger seat, and I felt around the console to get my bearings. We drove about twenty minutes, but I had lost my sense of direction after the first couple of turns so I had no idea where we were when the car stopped.

"Don't take it off! I'll come around and get you," Gerry said, eagerness clear in his voice.

I laughed and placed my fingers on the blindfold, unsure of what to expect but anticipating something great based on his level of enthusiasm.

The car door opened, and Gerry took my hand in his and pulled me slowly from the car. "Watch your head," he cautioned as he placed his palm over the top of my head to help me duck under the car's roof.

He held both my hands as we walked.

"Are you walking backwards?" I asked.

"Yep."

"You need to watch where you're going. If you fall, I'm falling on top of you, baby belly first."

"I would never let that happen. There's three stairs, so be careful."

I counted three steps up, and then he stopped and let go of my hands.

"Don't move, and don't peek!"

"I'm not," I said, laughing aloud as the excitement and anticipation built to almost unbearable heights.

A lock clicked and a door opened, and immediately a rush of cold air blew across my skin. I lifted my face toward it, trying to sense anything I could about my whereabouts. I sniffed the air cautiously, but smelled nothing but Gerry's cologne. I strained to hear any identifying sounds, but other than a distant car engine, we were in peaceful surroundings.

Finally, Gerry took my hand and led me through a doorway.

"Okay, Willow, behold your surprise!"

Gerry untied the blindfold, and I blinked rapidly to adjust to the sudden change in light.

We stood inside a large living room with vaulted ceilings and a bank of floor to ceiling windows on the far side. Beyond the windows was a lush tropical oasis, and beyond that, I could see a canal with a small dock extending from the lawn.

"What is this?" I asked as my eyes adjusted and more of the room came into view.

On my left, there was a large alcove on the front of the house with an over-sized bay window. To the right of that was a wide hallway leading deeper into the house. In front of me were steps leading down to a recessed seating area facing the wall of windows on the rear of the house. To my right, a set of four stairs led up to a raised platform surrounded by a balcony railing, and to the left of that was a large, open kitchen with a huge island above which hung a wrought iron pot rack. Beyond the kitchen I could see a breakfast nook with another huge bay window.

I turned to face Gerry, still waiting for an answer to my question.

"Where are we?"

He tucked his fingers underneath my chin and leaned down to kiss my lips. "We're home, Willow. Our home. Welcome home, my love."

I took a step back and struggled to regain the air that had been swept from my lungs. "Wh-wh-what?"

Gerry laughed and came behind me to wrap both arms around my protruding belly, planting kisses on my neck that only added to my dizziness and lack of oxygen.

"Gerry! What's going on?"

My emotions were all over the place.

Hope was the first thing that surged up within me as I allowed myself to consider the possibility that what he said was true.

Our house? Our home? Could it be? Was there a way that this beautiful setting could be part of our story's happy ending? Would this be my living room where we would sit in the evenings and read books to Cabe? My kitchen where I would prepare meals for them and our nook where we would dine together each night? Was this the yard I had dreamed of for my son? For our son? And our future daughter?

But almost immediately, doubts set in. How could this be ours? How could we afford it? How could he buy a house in the midst of the legal proceedings when they were already fighting about dividing assets and ownership?

I pushed his hands from my stomach and pressed my hand to my forehead as though I could stop my head from spinning if I held it tightly enough.

"What's wrong?" Gerry asked. "You don't like it?" His eyes searched mine, the enthusiasm gone from his face and replaced by an uncertainty.

"What do you mean it's ours? What does that mean?"

He smiled then and took my hand to bring it to his lips. "I mean that I bought us a house. A home. A place for us to live together as a family."

"But how?"

"My lawyer says that she's ready to settle and I'll get a hefty sum. With that money, we'll easily be able to afford this place. I had to work the system a little to get it without it being tied up in court, but don't you worry about that. It's ours."

Tears sprang to my eyes, and my heart thumped hard and loud. I didn't dare allow myself to believe this could be happening, and yet it was. I tried to smile but couldn't. A tear rolled free and slowly blazed a path down my cheek. It tickled a bit as the wetness slid across my skin and hung on the side of my face before Gerry flicked it away with his finger.

"Why are you crying, Willow?" His voice was soft, husky, and filled with emotion.

"I can't believe this is happening," I whispered. "Pinch me and tell me I'm not dreaming."

He cupped my cheeks into his hands and put his mouth to mine, his tongue pressing gently to seek passage inside. I allowed him in, opening my heart further to the possibility of rewriting the end of our story.

"C'mon," he said as he released me and took my hand. "Let's see the rest of our house."

We went from room to room, and each time we crossed through a door, Gerry would launch into his ideas for what that room would become and how it would look. It didn't take long for his enthusiasm to wash away any nagging doubts I had. As he led me through his visions for our life, I could clearly see myself in the house and in the future he presented.

"This room will be perfect for Cable. We'll paint the walls blue like the sky, and maybe hire a mural artist to create a large tree with all sorts of creatures." He waved his arms toward the walls as he spoke, and I hugged myself to try and contain the joy bubbling inside as he drew pictures in my mind and on my heart. "Or maybe the high seas, with a large galleon for a bed and a pirate ship in the distance. Or we could drape the ceiling like a big top and have circus animals on the walls."

I giggled out loud and Gerry turned to me, his lips curled in a grin as he tilted his head to one side. "Whatever you want it to be, Willow. I'll make it happen. I'll do anything to see that look on your face. To see you this happy."

I crossed the floor to stand in front of him.

"Thank you, Gerry. The house is beautiful. I can't even...I don't even have the words."

"Well, you haven't even seen it all," he said as he gave me a quick kiss and then grabbed my hand. We passed two more bedrooms on the left, one of which was perfect for a nursery. Then he led me to the end of the hall and grinned at me, his hand on the knob. "Madame, your chamber awaits."

He swung open the door with great flourish and bowed. The large bedroom featured high ceilings with high rectangular windows along the long wall. A double set of French doors filled the opposite end of the room, leading out onto a beautiful patio where I could see a Jacuzzi tub under an arbor.

Gerry was already across the room and in the master bath, where he called for me to join him. Each side of the bathroom was lined with marble counters and a sink, and one side also featured a marble vanity and lighted mirror. The shower enclosure was nearly as big as my entire bathroom at the apartment, and along the back wall was a rectangular tub large enough to be a lap pool.

"What do you think?" Gerry asked as he spread his arms wide.

"It's beautiful."

He let his arms fall to his sides and frowned. "That's it? I just presented you with the single most romantic bathroom I've ever seen in my life, and all you can say is it's beautiful? Really?"

I laughed softly and shrugged. "What do you want me to say?"

He crossed the floor and wrapped me in his arms, walking me backward toward the bathroom counter. He lifted me to sit upon it as he planted his hips between my knees. His mouth hovered above mine as he slid his hands underneath my shirt and over my belly, lightly teasing his thumbs under the bottom of my bra. Ripples of sensation shot straight from his point of contact to deep within my abdomen, sparking desire that ebbed out into my limbs and made the world go hazy.

"I want you—" his lips nibbled at mine as he increased the pressure from his thumbs "—to tell me—" his tongue ran across my bottom lip and darted inside, drawing my own out in response "—that you can't wait—" he nudged my head to the side as he buried his mouth into my neck, suckling and biting his way from my ear down to my shoulder, which had been exposed as he shifted my shirt for better access "—to make love to me—" With one swift motion, he pulled the shirt over my head, running his tongue across my collarbone before exploring the deep crevice between my breasts. "—on this very counter."

Any ability to form words had gone with my shirt. My body cried out for him, yearned for him, ached for his touch and his taking. I wanted the happiness he offered. I wanted the home he offered. I wanted the life he offered. But in that moment, I mostly wanted the pleasure he offered—that he demanded and eagerly shared.

We christened the marble counter in our new home before moving to the floor, the cool tile hard and almost wet-feeling against the bare skin of my back. The ungiving surface ground against the bonier parts of my spine, and my hips grated against the floor as Gerry pushed into me with increasing fervor, but the pain was of no significance compared to the other sensations I felt.

I gave over to him. To a life with him. To my love for him. I broke the remaining mortar of the wall I'd built, and I allowed myself to fully embrace my dream of the future.

So much so that I busied myself for the next two months picking out curtains and furniture, incessantly flipping through paint decks in search of the perfect wall shades.

At the end of my seventh month, we only had about two weeks left on our apartment lease, so we took to spending each evening at the house getting it ready to move in.

I'd been having early contractions off and on, and though the doctor assured me they were no cause for alarm, I insisted that we go ahead and get a phone installed in case I had a problem while I was working at the house alone.

Cabe was playing with blocks in the living room, and I was measuring the kitchen windows for curtains when the ring of the phone startled me. I'd grown accustomed to the silence of the big empty house, and the bell sounded obnoxiously foreign as it echoed.

I figured it had to be Gerry saying he was on his way since no one else had the number yet.

"Hello, love," I said, cradling the receiver between my shoulder and my ear as I wound the measuring tape back into its case.

"Oh, my. He has you answering the phone. I should have known."

I don't know how I knew her voice, because I had certainly never heard it, but the chill that came over me and left me trembling could only have come from one person.

"Gerry's not here right now. Can I take a message?" I asked, resisting the urge to hang up.

"A message?" Margot said, her sarcasm as thick as her accent. "Yes, you can give my husband a message. You can tell him my water broke, and I'm in labor. You can tell him he needs to stop playing house with his floozie in Florida and come back home. Time's up. Our son needs his father, and our daughter will be here before morning. That's all."

The baby kicked hard inside me, and I gasped as I doubled over with my hand low on my belly.

"Oh, you didn't know? You're shacking up with *my* husband in *my* summer home and you didn't think to ask why he was decorating a nursery? Or was it you who picked that lovely shade of coral? I should have known when he sent the pictures. That man has always been damned near color blind. Do send him along home, will you?"

I'd read before that ballet dancers have a pain threshold three times higher than that of the average person. But even dancers have limits to how much pain they can endure.

# 44  UNTIL NOW

I'd been talking for nearly an hour, condensing the story for Dax as much as possible—skipping the sex parts, of course—and trying not to get emotional as I relived it.

"Holy shit," he said, his eyes wide as he sat back on the patio sofa where we'd moved after clearing away dinner. "What did you say to her?"

I shrugged. "I didn't say anything. I couldn't say anything. I had no voice. I let the phone fall to the floor. I picked up my son and walked to the car, and we drove around Miami for probably two hours. It wasn't like I had any place to go. I wasn't about to go to my parents'. I was too embarrassed to go to Alberto and Sandy's. And I couldn't bear to go back to the apartment. I had no home."

The desolation of the memory was too heavy to hide, and my eyes glassed over.

I pressed the paper towel from my hand against my eyes as Dax massaged the tightness in the muscles of my neck and shoulders.

"I got a hotel room the first night. Then when the situation didn't look any better in the light of day, I sucked up my pride and gathered my baby to show up on Alberto and Sandy's doorstep. Luckily, they took us in. I started having consistent contractions later that night, but the doctors were able to stop them. It happened three more times over the next month, and Galen Margaret was born with an emergency C-section one week before her due date. I think it was the only occasion she's ever been early for, and she's been giving me fits ever since."

"What happened with Gerry?"

"Nothing. He disappeared back up north without even trying to find us or to say goodbye to Cabe. Alberto and a couple of other friends went to the apartment with my key to get my stuff, and he was gone. My father's investigator did some digging, and it turns out that the delay in the divorce was him negotiating for more money to stay with her. For reasons I'm sure she needs therapy for, Margot wouldn't grant him a divorce, and he wouldn't stay without compensation. Evidently what that price would be took a while to decide upon. From what I understand, it included his name being added to several of her family's assets as well as the creation of some dummy corporation with Gerry named as CEO. The agreement was signed right before the two of them purchased the summer house in Miami. She agreed that he could stay and tie up loose ends while he got the house ready. But then she went into labor and called him home."

"Why would she want him if she had to pay him to be there? And why on earth would she want a house where she knew he had a mistress?"

I bristled at the word, and his hand stopped moving on my neck for a moment.

"Sorry. I didn't mean it like that."

"No. It's okay. It's the truth. It's what I was, unfortunately. I don't even get the luxury of saying I didn't know the second time since technically he was honest about that detail. He never said the divorce was final. I don't think she ever cared that there was someone else. I think it was something she was willing to overlook if she got to keep her husband, her children's father, and maintain appearances to her friends. Out of sight, out of mind."

"So why would he go to such elaborate lengths with you if he knew he was going back to her?"

I rubbed my hands over my face and ran my fingers through my hair. "Beats me! That's the million-dollar question I've asked myself over and over again for years. Why tell me it was our house? I don't know if he thought somehow once he got the money, he could back out of her deal, or if he was just mental enough to live out the lie as long as he could."

I stood and walked to the pool bar, unable to sit still with the demons of the past circling so close. I grabbed a water bottle from the fridge for each of us.

"You must have been devastated," Dax said as he took the water I offered.

"Yeah, but it wasn't just me. Why would he get so close to his son knowing he was going to leave? I've never understood what happened. I don't know if it was all a lie or if it was bits and pieces of truth. I mean, at some point, he wanted a divorce, and he chose to move to Miami, so I have to think he had some intent of finding Cabe and me. I saw the paperwork, so I know he filed. And I also saw the legal bills that came in every month and sucked every dollar we made. Maybe he was playing me all along as a back-up plan in case he didn't get what he wanted from her. He went back to New York one time while we were together to meet with the lawyers. I've always wondered if that's when the tide turned. Maybe they shared something that weekend that was enough to change his mind and get her pregnant. Other than that, I don't know when he would have found the time. He was home with me every night. Every weekend."

"She could have come to Miami at some point, no?"

"I suppose." I shrugged as I sat back down on the sofa and looked at Dax. "So, there you have it. I was dumb enough to not only fall for a man's lies and deception once, but to fall twice. Oh, and conceive and bear his children both times. Not that I'm saying I'd change that." I lifted my hand in protest. "I love my children. With every fiber of my being, I love them. But yeah, that's how stupid I was."

Dax put his arm around my shoulders and pulled me to him, burying his lips in my hair. "You weren't stupid, Maggie. You followed your heart, and you wanted your kid to have a family. Someone took advantage of that. He deceived you in the most heinous of ways. That says a lot more about him than it says about you."

I rested my hand on his thigh and squeezed, noting that the hard muscle was unyielding beneath the denim.

"I should have known, though. I should have listened to the people around me. I should have seen him for who he was. I screwed up. My children have paid the price for my mistakes, and I will never forgive myself for that."

"How has the relationship been since then? I mean, him and the kids? How did you and he interact as they grew up? I imagine it was difficult."

I ducked out from under Dax's arm and stood again, walking to the water's edge. "They had no relationship with him. I did everything I could to keep it that way. He would call occasionally to say he was coming to Florida, but I refused to let him see them. I left Miami when Galen was still a baby and resettled here in Orlando to get away from anything to do with him."

"And that was okay with him?"

I shrugged and turned to face him. "He didn't want my kids. He would call and ask to see them when it was convenient for him, but other than that it was like they didn't exist. He never put up much of a fight when I said no. I knew he wouldn't take me to court. He would never want to involve Margot with me or my kids. He offered to help financially several times over the years, but I didn't want his money. Not that it was even his, really. It was hers. But that money had meant more to him than my children, so I didn't want a penny of it."

"So, they've never known their father?"

"Cabe hasn't seen him since Gerry left for work the day of Margot's phone call. Galen acted out quite a bit as a teen, and I eventually caved and contacted Gerry so she could meet him. The two of them have kept in touch off and on."

"And the other kids? His kids with Margot?"

"Oh yeah, remember when I told you how easily he left me alone when Cabe was six months old and I asked him to go?"

Dax nodded.

"That was when Jeffrey was born, and that's why he went home. It had nothing to do with me or my request."

I sat down by the side of the pool and leaned back on my hands, straightening my legs out in front of me as I rolled my head back to look at the stars.

It was cleansing to get it all out and lay my secrets in front of him. It was like my insides had been purged, and I felt lighter. Less burdened.

"Do Galen and Cabe know about the other kids?"

"Yes. Galen reached out to them via social media a couple of years ago, and she and Julie, the girl born two months before her, have gotten quite close since they both live in Manhattan. I know Cabe has had some contact with the brother, but he doesn't mention it to me out of respect for my feelings."

"Wow. You couldn't make this stuff up. That's crazy."

I rolled my eyes and shook my head. "Crazy is an understatement."

"I can't for the life of me imagine why she'd want him back, knowing what she knew."

"She called me up, when Cabe was maybe seven and Galen was four. Blasted me up one side and down the other saying Gerry and I were back together. I let her know in no uncertain terms that nothing could be farther from the truth and that would never happen. It seems he had a new conquest, somewhere in Arizona, I think. Cabe said there's two more kids from that union, but Margot is still hanging in there as the dutiful wife as far as I know. I don't understand it."

"He's psycho," Dax said, his brow furrowed. "I'm telling you, you got the better end of the deal in getting rid of him, and your kids are lucky you were smart enough to protect them."

"I don't know that they'd agree with you. Not Galen, anyway. She's quite hostile with me for robbing her of having a father. She told me tonight how selfish I'd been, and Gerry's been only too willing to tell her it's my fault he was never around. She and I had a heated discussion tonight when she told me he wants to pay for the honeymoon, and then he and I had quite a row right after."

"So, were you picturing his head when you smashed the coffee mugs?"

I laughed, and it felt good to be able to.

"I don't know, Dax. I don't know who's right and who's wrong. I mean, obviously what he did was wrong, but I made the choices that put me there. That put the kids there. Maybe I should have let him be in their lives, you know? He's a lousy husband and a helluva lying ass for a boyfriend, but he was a good dad to Cabe when he was around."

Dax grunted. "Pardon me for saying so, but if he was a good dad, he wouldn't have fathered children with two different mothers at the same time. He knew he couldn't possibly be in their lives the way he'd need to be. And if he disrespected their mothers so much, there's no way he'd show the kids much respect in the long run. Besides, good dads don't go their children's entire lives without seeing them or being involved. I think you did the right thing. You may have caused them some heartache not knowing what they were missing, but it's likely he would have caused more damage if he'd had access to them. Not to mention the need to preserve your own sanity."

"Hmph. I don't know if that got preserved or not."

He stood and came over to extend his hand and pull me up to him. I sighed as he slid his arms around me, enclosing me in his strength and his warmth. I relaxed against him, feeling freer than I had in quite a while.

"It's a wonder you've ever been able to trust anyone again," he whispered against my hair as he stroked his hands up and down my back.

"I haven't," I mumbled into his shirt. Then I raised my head and looked up to see his green eyes looking down at me. "Until now."

Dax bent to place the most gentle of kisses on my lips, and then my nose, and my forehead.

"I am so sorry for what happened to you. I want to find him and tear him to pieces with my bare hands. I want to go back and scoop up young Maggie and protect her. I'm amazed that you're able to be the mother you are, and the woman you are, after all you've been through. But the fact that you would give me your trust—I'm blown away. I will treat it as the precious thing that it is and handle it with the greatest care."

He kissed me again, and I rose up onto my toes, wrapping my arms around his neck and pulling him down to me. The maelstrom of the night's emotions swirled into a passionate frenzy, and I wanted to claw at his skin and sink my teeth into him.

Our kiss turned more aggressive as I yanked his shirt from the waist of his jeans and walked backward toward the French doors leading to my bedroom, pulling him with me—though he came willingly enough.

Our mouths never parted as we made our way to my bed, tearing at each other's clothes until we could feel the heat of skin upon skin. He reached and swept the duvet aside with a grin before pushing me back onto the bed and pressing his weight on top of me.

I lifted my knee between his and pushed to roll him over on his back, sitting astride his hips as I eased myself down over him.

His sharp intake of breath matched my own, and I began to rock my hips back and forth. He lifted his hands to caress my nipples, and I tilted my head back and arched my spine, pushing my breasts into his grasp and pivoting my hips to bring him deeper inside me.

He gasped, and I moved faster, bracing one hand on his stomach as I slid the other hand down over my ribs, past my bellybutton, and into the warmth between us. I moaned at simultaneous stimulation from the pressure of him filling me, the friction of our frantic joining, and the circular motions of my own fingers.

It didn't take long for me to cry out in ecstasy, collapsing across his chest as he grabbed hold of my hips to thrust hard up against me until he reached his pinnacle of pleasure.

We lay sweating and panting, unwilling to move for quite a while after the passion subsided. I listened to his heartbeat as he stroked his fingers through my hair and down my back, tracing each vertebrae as my body continued to contract and release in response to his touch.

"Do you need to get on the road soon?" I whispered, dreading the answer.

"Do you want me to stay?"

I hesitated, wanting desperately to fall asleep in his arms, but knowing he had early morning obligations to meet at the ranch. "It's okay. I know you need to go take care of your animals."

He tucked his thumb under my chin and lifted my face to look at him. "Maggie, do you want me to stay? It's true that those animals never take a day off, and they don't work their schedule around mine. But there are some perks that come with being in charge, and if you tell me you need me to be here, then I'll do whatever it takes to make it happen. Now, do you want me to stay?"

"Yes," I said, lowering my lips to his as my hair draped over his face.

"Can you reach my phone in my jeans pocket?"

I was still sitting astride his hips, and he held his hands firmly on my thighs to keep me from falling as I leaned over the side of the bed to grab his jeans and hand him the phone. I sat back up and traced his abs with my fingernails as he texted someone at the ranch and waited for a reply.

When he got the confirmation he was waiting for, he set the phone on the nightstand and then put his hands under my rump, moving me to the side and rolling until I was beneath him. His touch was light, and his lips were like feathers on my skin as he made love to me so slowly and so gently that it was almost as if he feared I might break. By the time we lay spent again, the hour was late, and I curled up against him, my knee over his thigh and my arm around his waist. We drifted off to sleep and neither of us moved from that position until the alarm sounded in the morning.

# 45 A PARTY INVITATION

"Would you like an omelet?" I asked Dax with a yawn as he showered.

"I'd love one, but you don't have to be up for another hour, so I can grab something on the road."

"Nonsense. I'm awake, and you need something decent to eat. I already kept you up most of the night, so it's the least I can do."

He leaned around the tile enclosure and grinned, his wet hair dripping down his face. "Believe me, I didn't mind you keeping me up. Not at all."

He joined me in the kitchen when he was dressed, and I rubbed my hand across his facial stubble and grinned. "Have you ever had a beard?"

He nodded and scratched his chin. "Yeah. Most winters I let it grow out. Why? Do you like beards?"

"I've never had one personally, but I might like one on you."

I smiled as he put his arms around me, his lips touching mine before he took the china coffee cup I offered him.

"We're using the fancy cups this morning since I trashed all my favorites."

He leaned back against the kitchen counter and watched me flip his omelet onto a plate.

"So we got a little, um, sidetracked last night, and you didn't tell me how you ended things with your daughter. Did get it worked out?"

"As worked out as it's likely to get. She's going to invite Jeffrey and Julie to the wedding against my wishes, and her father is going to pay for her honeymoon. Also against my wishes."

"Is he coming to the wedding?"

I cut my eyes around to him with a death stare. "Over my dead body. She knows better. Or at least she should."

"Hmm. That's too bad. I'd like to meet Gerry and have a word with

233

him." He took a long sip of coffee, staring at me over the rim of his cup with no humor in his eyes. "You gonna be okay with his kids there?"

"I don't really have a choice. I have to put my own feelings aside and put my daughter first. It's her wedding. Her big day, not mine. They're important to her, and she wants them there."

He took the plate I handed him and followed me to the table to sit. "Yeah, it's her day, but if them being there is going to make other people miserable, how happy is she gonna be?"

"It's not going to bother anyone other than me and my parents, so we need to suck it up and deal with it for her benefit. It's not ideal, but I've been through worse. I want her to be happy."

"Why don't you want him to pay for the honeymoon? It seems to me he should be contributing something after all he's put y'all through."

I chewed my eggs and swallowed, wiping my mouth with a napkin. "I guess it goes back to the money thing. I look at it kind of like blood money. He sold us out to get that money, so I don't want any part of it, and I don't want her to feel comfortable taking it. I would like her to be more principled than that."

Dax shrugged and lifted an eyebrow. "Maybe she sees it differently. Maybe to her, he owes her something, and this is her way of getting it."

"Maybe."

We finished breakfast in silence, and then he helped me clear the dishes.

An idea had been flickering in the back of my head for some time, and after crossing such a big emotional hurdle to open up to Dax the night before, I felt empowered to take another step forward.

"So, I'm not sure what you're doing on Sunday," I said, looking down at the sink to hide my nervousness, "but Cabe and Tyler are coming over to celebrate my birthday. Nothing fancy. We'll probably cook something on the grill, and we'll watch a movie or get in the pool if it's hot out. But if you're not busy, maybe you could stop by."

Dax put his arms around my waist from behind and leaned forward to kiss my cheek. "I would love to. What time should I arrive, and what should I bring?"

"The kids will probably get here around one. Any time after that is fine."

He rested his chin on my shoulder and swayed his hips back and forth, pulling me from side to side with him. "You mentioned grilling. How about I bring steaks?"

"Oh, you don't have to do that. I'll pick something up."

He turned me in his arms to face him, grinning as he looked down at me. "Maggie, I run one of the biggest beef ranches in the country. You're not going to pick anything up that's better than what I could bring."

"True. Didn't think about that."

He kissed me as we said our goodbyes, his lips lingering on mine as I held my breath and tried to memorize every detail to hold with me when he was gone.

I called Cabe later that afternoon, anxious to gauge his reaction in case inviting Dax had been a mistake.

"Hey, Mom! What's up?"

"Hi, sweetheart. I wanted to talk to you about Sunday."

"Did you change your mind? You want to go out to eat instead of staying in?"

"No, you know I'd rather stay in and cook. But I invited someone, and I wanted to make sure you're okay with it."

Cabe chuckled. "It's about damned time. I was wondering if I was ever going to meet him."

"You're sure you don't mind if he comes? I don't want you to feel like it's an intrusion."

"Mom, don't be ridiculous. It's *your* birthday. You can invite whomever you want. To be honest, I was feeling a little left out since Tyler already got to meet him and I didn't. Bronwyn tells her you guys have been taking dance lessons?"

A warm blush colored my cheeks, and I smiled. "Yeah. We have. How did Bronwyn know?"

"I guess she says he practices in the barn. He's got the music cranked up and when she goes out there, he's doing waltz steps all by himself with the horses staring at him like he's nuts. At least that's what she told Tyler."

I laughed at the image of Dax dancing alone in the barn, and my heart warmed as I thought of him.

"He's a great guy, honey."

"He must be," Cabe said. "You've never invited anyone to dinner with us before. As long as he makes you happy and treats you right, I like him."

"You haven't even met him yet."

"Are you happy?"

I smiled and bit down on my lip as a rush of Dax memories flashed in my head. "Yes. I am. I truly am."

"Then I like him. I'll see you Sunday. Love you, Mom."

"I love you, babe."

# 46 MEETING OF THE MEN

Sunday took forever to arrive, but when it finally came, it was a gorgeous day. The sky was a brilliant blue without a cloud in sight, and although it was hot in the sun, a light breeze and the motion of the ceiling fans kept the shaded area of the patio pleasant.

Cabe and Tyler arrived a little before one with Deacon, and I swear I think Tyler was more excited for Cabe to meet Dax than I was.

"What time is Mr. Pearson arriving?" she asked as we cut up vegetables for the tossed salad.

"I told him any time after one, so he should be here soon."

"Are the steaks in the outside fridge?" Cabe asked, standing with the refrigerator door open as he searched. "I don't see them in here."

"Dax is bringing steaks," I said. "From the ranch."

Cabe looked up in appreciation and smiled. "Awesome. I'm liking this guy more and more. So, what's the protocol for interviewing your mom's boyfriend? Are there questions I'm supposed to ask? Do I need to see his credentials? His health records? His bank account?"

Tyler laughed as I tossed a carrot slice at his face.

"You don't need to ask him anything. Behave yourself. Please?"

"I'll be on my best behavior." He held his fingers up. "Scout's honor."

"What is up with you guys all taking a scout's honor when you weren't scouts? Oh, what movie did you bring?"

"*The Best Exotic Marigold Hotel*," Cabe said, grabbing a cherry tomato and popping it in his mouth. "It's about a bunch of old people who go stay in a resort in India to die."

"Sounds lovely. Exactly what I want to watch to celebrate turning fifty."

"Cabe!" Tyler rolled her eyes. "It's supposed to be really good, Maggie. It's got Dev Patel in it, and I know you like him. Dame Judi Dench is in it, and Dame Maggie Smith, and Bill Nighy."

"Like I said, a bunch of old people." Cabe laughed as Tyler pinched his arm.

The doorbell rang, and we all froze, staring at each other for a second before all three of us set into motion to be the first one to answer it.

Cabe reached it first, but by the time he turned the knob and pulled it open, I had gotten there to squeeze in and be the first to say hello.

Dax looked a bit startled to see so much commotion at the door, but then he laughed and I backed up to let him in.

He bent to plant a kiss on my lips, which felt natural and awkward at the same time. I'd seen Tyler and Cabe kiss plenty over the course of their relationship, but I'd never been on this end of it.

"Dax, you've met Tyler, and this is my son, Cabe."

The two men shook hands, standing almost eye to eye, although Dax was broader than Cabe, and substantially more muscular.

"Nice to meet you," Cabe said as they sized each other up in that way men do. "I've heard a lot about you."

"Likewise," Dax said, still gripping Cabe's hand. "I've been looking forward to meeting you."

They concluded their male greeting and dropped hands, and Dax picked up the cooler he had set on the floor as he entered.

"Steaks for the grill. Where do you want me to put them?"

"Right this way," Cabe said, leading Dax to the patio.

Tyler and I returned to the kitchen, and I couldn't help stealing glances out the window to see how things with the men were transpiring.

"They seem to be getting along well, huh?" Tyler asked, her eyes bright with excitement.

I nodded, staring at the two of them. I'd never dated anyone seriously enough to need Cabe's approval before, and I never realized how important it was to me.

"I love the way he looks at you," Tyler whispered over my shoulder as we watched them. "His eyes get all gooey, like you're the most beautiful thing he's ever seen."

"Are you saying I'm not?" I teased and turned to make a pitcher of tea.

The conversation never stalled during the meal, with topics ranging from sports to movies to ranching and the new technology Cabe was using in his job as a programmer.

When we'd eaten our fill, the three of them insisted that I stay on the patio as they cleared the dishes and cleaned up the kitchen.

"It's your birthday party," Tyler pleaded. "You don't clean up after your own party. Go put your feet up and enjoy the breeze. I'll get you another glass of wine, and you relax while we clean up."

I didn't argue any further. I propped the pillows on one end of the patio sofa and leaned back against them, bringing my feet up and laying my head back with eyes closed.

"We're just about done in here, Mom," Cabe said after a bit. "You ready for the movie, or you want to sit out here a while longer?"

"Come sit by me for a minute." I swung my feet around to put them on the floor, patting the sofa next to me as I waited for him to come sit. "I don't know if you've talked to her, but Galen and I had a bit of a tiff the other night. She said some things that have weighed on me, and I need to say something to you."

Worry clouded his clear, blue eyes, and he tilted his head. "What did she say to you? You know better than to let her get to you."

I shook my head. "It was fine. She was getting things off her chest. But I think there was some validity to them, and I want to address it." I took a deep breath and put my hand over his. "When your father left the second time, before Galen was born, I made a decision to cut all ties with him."

Cabe drew his eyebrows together at the mention of Gerry.

"I was hurt at the time. I'd been betrayed, as you know. I felt like the best thing for me, for us, was to have him out of our lives. I worried about what a relationship with him might do to you or Galen. I never wanted him to lie to either of you or betray you the way he did me. So, I kept him from you. I rebuffed any attempt on his part to be involved, and I forced the two of you to live without knowing your father."

"Mom,—"

I lifted my hand to stop him.

"Hear me out. I don't know if that was the right decision. I don't know if I did more damage by making you both feel like he didn't want you or he didn't care. I'm sure in his own way, he wanted you both. He cared for you deeply when the three of us lived together, Cabe, and as much as I was duped by his lies, I don't believe he was pretending to love you."

"You don't have to do this," Cabe said. "You don't have to make excuses for Gerry or justify his behavior."

"I know, but I do have to be responsible for mine. I don't know that I've ever apologized to you, Cabe. I want to say how sorry I am that I picked a father for you who turned out to be a lousy one, and how sorry I am that he was ripped from your life without any warning when you were young. Because of my decisions to keep him away, you grew up feeling like something was missing. I know how hard that was on you, and I'm sorry. I honestly thought I was doing the right thing, but now I'm not so sure." My voice cracked a little, and my son turned my hand in his and squeezed it as he smiled at me.

"Mom, I could not have wished for a better mother. Yeah, my father sucked. And yes, I missed out on having a dad and it pissed me off. A lot. I struggled with it for the longest time. I resented Jeffrey and Julie because I felt like they got the dad I never had. Like he picked them over me. But you know what I've found out since hanging out with Jeffrey?"

"What?"

"They didn't have him either. Yeah, he left us and went back up north to live with them, but he wasn't much more of a father to them than he was to me. He still didn't make baseball games or awards nights or teach them to catch a ball or ride a wave. Sure, he might have been there on Christmas morning or they could see him at the end of the dinner table now and then, but they had him just enough to want more. And I think in some ways, it was easier to have nothing at all, than to see it right in front of you—close enough to touch it—but still not be able to have it."

"You guys coming?" Tyler called out the door.

"Be right there, babe," Cabe answered. "Look, Mom. All of us can make ourselves crazy asking *what if.* But there's no way to know the answer. We do the best we can do with the information we have at the time, and if we get more information, we do better. I don't hold it against you at all that my father wasn't around. That's on him. He chose to be somewhere else, and you just held him to that choice. Galen's a drama queen. You know that. If it wasn't this tragedy, she'd be harping on another one. Don't let her get to you. You have nothing to apologize for. You were a great mom, and you still are."

"She wants Jeffrey and Julie to come to her wedding."

He sighed and nodded. "I know, and I know that must bother you, but look. I wanted to hate them. I really did. But if you take a little time to get to know them, you can't hate them. They've survived the same crazy as us. We gotta stick together. As hard as it may be, try not to look at them as Gerry's kids. Try to just look at them as someone important to me and Galen."

I put my arms around his shoulders and kissed the cheek above his beard. "How'd you get to be so smart?"

"My mom's like this fifty-year-old sage, full of wisdom."

"Ha!" I playfully slapped his arm. "I'll have you know I am forty-nine. I don't turn fifty until Thursday."

"Whatever. Let's go eat cheesecake and watch an old people movie so you know how you're supposed to act."

# 47 NO ROOM SERVICE

I didn't have time on my actual birthday to be depressed about turning fifty. The day was a flurry of good wishes and celebrations from people in my office to calls from friends and enough floral deliveries to fill my world with color.

Betty had the entire dancing class sing *Happy Birthday* to me, and she assured me that fifty was just a number. Having watched her spry moves for the weeks leading up to the big milestone, I was inclined to heed her advice.

Dax took me out for an amazing dinner after class ended, and we'd settled on the patio sofa with my feet in his lap for a sensual foot rub when he brought up my present.

"So, I have an idea of what I'd like to do for your birthday."

"What do you mean?" I asked, cocking my head in confusion. "We celebrated Sunday with the kids, and we had dinner tonight."

"Well, yeah, but I wanted to do something special."

"You already have. You don't have to do anything else," I said.

"I know I don't *have* to, but I want to. I'd like to take you somewhere."

My back stiffened slightly at the idea of going away together. Despite our intimacy and our near daily conversations on the phone, I was still enjoying the fact that we hadn't grown too serious for comfort. Our customary pace of seeing each other once or twice a week was enough to keep me wanting more, but not enough to make me feel pressured.

"Have you ever been camping?" he asked, and I cracked up laughing, immediately relaxing because there was no threat this was actually going to happen.

"Um, that would be a big no. Unless I get to count any hotel without room service as camping."

Dax smiled and continued to work his magic on the soles of my feet. "I want to show you my favorite place on the ranch, but it's too far to be experienced in a day's horseback ride."

He moved his hands along my ankles and then up to softly knead my calf muscles, sending a warm rush of blood farther up.

The idea of being alone with Dax amid the beauty of the ranch was certainly enticing, but the idea of camping was not.

"You mentioned that you have a helicopter. Can't you fly us there?"

He laughed and took one hand slowly above my knee. My pulse quickened in response.

"No place to land. Besides, I want you to see how beautiful it is at night, and how peaceful it is at sunrise."

His hand was quite a few inches above my knee, and he had shifted his weight to move closer to me.

I separated my legs slightly, allowing his hand to roam between my thighs, grabbing onto the sofa as the delightful ache inside me morphed into a burning need.

"So whaddya say?" he whispered, his eyes intent upon mine as his fingers made me quiver. "Will you go camping with me this weekend?"

I had no desire to go camping, but he was driving me wild with other desires, and I probably would have agreed to most anything to get him to take me to bed and finish what he'd started.

Besides, I reasoned in my highly distracted mind, how bad could camping be in an air-conditioned camper with a full kitchen, bathroom, and king-size bed?

It wasn't until I saw the bed rolls on the back of the horses as I drove up to the barn Saturday morning that it registered that he'd mentioned a horseback ride. I still wasn't too alarmed, because I assumed that the horses would somehow follow along behind us as we drove the truck and camper.

"Why are there three horses?" I asked, wondering who was joining us and feeling a moment of disappointment that we wouldn't be alone.

"To carry supplies," he answered.

"Why can't we just carry the supplies in the back of the truck?"

He looked at me in confusion for a moment and then he grinned. "We're not taking the truck. It's a remote area. We have to get there on horseback."

My brain slowed as it tried to process what this meant.

"But, how will we take the camper without the truck?"

His grin turned to laughter, and he wrapped both arms around me. "Maggie Mae, we're not taking the camper. We're sleeping in a tent."

My mouth dropped open, and I leaned far back in his arms, pushing against his chest. "What? A tent? Oh, hell no."

I broke free of his grasp and stared at him in shock.

His laughter grew louder and he reached for me again, but I took a step back.

"I don't do tents," I stated without the slightest hint of a smile.

"How do you know? Have you ever slept in a tent?"

"No, but I've never slept in the middle of the road either, and I can safely say I don't do that."

"I thought you enjoyed adventure."

"I do. Within reason. That's not adventure. That's barbaric."

"How will you ever know whether or not you like it if you're not willing to try it?"

His smile was beyond charming, and the hope in his eyes was hard to look away from.

"Dax, I'm not earthy. Not at all. Have you seen anything in my life that gave you the impression that I was?"

"No, I haven't, and I must say, staying at your house has given me a new appreciation for higher thread counts and gourmet coffees. But there's something about sleeping under the stars with a chorus of crickets in the background."

I looked at him with skepticism clearly etched across my face.

The mere thought of sleeping out in the middle of nowhere with nothing between me and nature but a thin layer of nylon made my skin crawl.

"I don't know, Dax. I'm kind of partial to my bed. And showering. Indoor plumbing is high on my list of required amenities."

He cupped my face in his hands and smiled. "Sleeping outdoors is something everyone should do at least once. You'll be able to mark it off your bucket list."

"I can assure you that sleeping in a tent is nowhere on my bucket list. Like, you can scroll all the way to the bottom, and it's not there."

His lips touched mine and then he pulled back to look into my eyes. "Okay, so maybe sleeping in a tent with you is on *my* bucket list."

"Then why aren't you planning this for *your* birthday?"

His laughter rang out as he pulled me into a hug and squeezed me against him.

"Point taken. If you really don't want to go, we don't have to. I think you would enjoy it, but it is your birthday, and we can find something else to get into this weekend."

Despite my initial reservations, a twinge of curiosity had taken root.

I'd never been one to back away from a challenge, and though camping wasn't something I'd actively choose to do, I liked the idea of having Dax all to myself for the weekend. What I'd seen of the ranch on horseback had been beautiful, and I knew the place he'd chosen would be no less spectacular.

My mind waffled back and forth between wanting to know what he had planned and wanting to sleep in a comfy bed.

Dax nodded toward the horses. "Say the word and I'll unpack them. It's up to you."

I happened to be on the 'Go for it!' side of indecision at that moment, and I spoke quickly before I could change my mind again.

"No. Let's go. Let's do it."

His face lit up with excitement. "Are you sure? We don't have to."

"I may regret it later, but what the hell? Let's go camping, cowboy."

His smile was huge as his lips covered mine, and by the time he released me, I was lightheaded and ready to sleep anywhere he wanted if it meant I could be in his arms.

# 48 NATURAL BEAUTY

We rode for several hours, stopping occasionally for Dax to show me something of interest and taking a longer break to eat the sandwiches he'd packed.

I had been a bit nervous about riding Fallon again after our last painful parting, but Dax had borrowed Dixie from his mother for me.

"She's less skittish than Fallon," Dax said. "But just in case, I took Cody over to the big barn and made sure he was safely contained."

"Are you sure about that? He is Houdini, you know."

Dax smiled. "True. I think we're safe, though."

"Be sure and tell your mom thanks for letting me borrow her horse."

"She wasn't going to be riding her. She has plenty of others if she wants to ride. She did make me promise to bring you to dinner in exchange for Dixie, though."

I looked away from him and chose not to respond, uncertain of how I felt about meeting the parents.

It had taken me a while to be okay with the fact that Dax and I were in a relationship, and I didn't want to rush into any new levels. We were in a good place, and though I'd introduced him to Cabe and Tyler, I still wasn't ready to play the part of the girlfriend for a formal family introduction.

We'd crossed over acre after acre of flat pasture land, and I was thankful for the shade of the forest when we finally reached the tree line.

"Need some water?" Dax said, offering me a canteen when he saw the water bottle attached to my waistband was empty.

I looked at the narrow mouth of the container, and peered into the darkness it held.

"How do you make sure the inside of this gets clean?"

Dax laughed. "I clean it? With soap and water?"

The parched dryness of my mouth outweighed my germ aversion, and I shrugged and turned the canteen up to let the cool, refreshing liquid quench my thirst.

"So, have you always enjoyed being outdoors?" I asked as I handed it back to him.

"Yep. From the time I could walk. They had to put the locks higher on the doors to keep me in. Then when I got older, my brother and I would leave the house early in the morning on Saturdays and not come home until dinner. We'd explored nearly every acre of this property by the time we graduated from high school."

I scrunched my nose and swatted at a bug that was flying near my face.

"Not me. I have always been an A/C baby. I appreciate nature. I enjoy it. Going for a hike, taking a walk, visiting the mountains or the beach. But I enjoy being inside more. Especially when it's hot out. Give me a museum, a theater, or a show anytime."

"I'm the exact opposite. I can appreciate the museum, the theater, and maybe the show. But I'd rather be outdoors."

By the time we neared our destination, my hips and buttocks were aching, unaccustomed to the constant friction of the saddle from Dixie's steady gait.

I'd spent the first part of the ride holding tight to the reins, determined not to drop them like I had with Fallon, and my shoulders and neck were tense until I forced myself to loosen up.

There had been an opening in the trees ahead of us for a while, and I gasped as we got close enough for me to see what was in the clearing. A crystal clear pool of water, a bit larger than a pond, sat inside a circle of trees. The depths of the water appeared almost turquoise blue, and it was so clear I could see the large rocks on the bottom as I squinted against the reflection of the sun on the water's surface.

"Oh! Beautiful. Gorgeous. Wish you were here!" I waved my arm at the splendor in front of us.

"What?" Dax asked.

"*French Kiss*. Meg Ryan. Don't tell me you haven't seen it!"

"I'll add it to my list."

"This is breathtaking," I said.

Dax smiled and winked at me. "I told you."

"This is it? This is your favorite place?"

He nodded. "Yeah. My brother and I found this spring years ago, and we used to come out here and camp all the time when we were younger. After...well, after my wife died, I spent a lot of time out here. It's quiet. Peaceful. So far removed from the world that it's easy to forget it exists."

We went around the right side of the pool, and he stopped near a flattened area with evidence of past campfires. Just past that were two posts in the ground with a cross-beam between them, and Dax led us there to tie up the horses as we dismounted.

My butt and inner thighs protested with fire as I got off Dixie.

"Holy cow, how do you ride a horse every day?" I asked, rubbing the inside of my thighs and stretching my legs to try and ease the cramping of my butt muscles.

Dax's grin held mischief. "I've built up callouses on my ass over the years."

"Not true," I said, returning his mischievous grin with my own. "I've seen and touched that ass, and there's not a callous to be found."

He laughed and took me in his arms, giving me a light kiss before releasing me with a smile.

"I'm gonna set up camp and feed and water the horses. Take a look around, but be sure to watch for snakes if you go close to the water."

My eyes and mouth both popped open. "Snakes?"

He laughed and took off his hat to scratch his head. "You've lived in Florida your whole life. Surely, you're aware that any time you're near water, there's a good chance there might be snakes."

"Yeah, I'm aware of it, but it's not ever been something that was a concern in regards to my sleeping arrangements. Can snakes get into tents?"

"Well, yeah, they can, if you leave the tent open, which we won't. Don't worry your pretty red head. I won't let anything hurt you."

"Famous last words of the hero just before the heroine hits a stroke of bad luck."

He proceeded with taking the supplies off the horses, glancing over his shoulder at me and shaking his head with his ever-present grin.

"Are you sure I can't do anything to help?" I asked.

"No. It's a pretty simple set-up, and I've got it down to a science."

I sat on a huge rock near the water's edge, carefully inspecting the surrounding area for any sign of slithering creatures.

Dax whistled a tune as he set up the tent and worked to organize the campsite. His T-shirt was a snug fit, and the contours of his back and shoulders were clearly visible beneath the thin cotton as he tugged and lifted. I watched him move and marveled at the immediate reaction of my body. Despite the throbbing burn from the horseback ride, a much more pleasant fire ignited between my legs and began to spread as I pictured the night ahead.

Once he'd pitched the tent and gotten his supplies squared away, he turned and grinned at me, tossing his hat inside the doorway before zipping it shut. He grabbed the hem of his shirt and pulled it over his head and then pulled off his boots.

"What are you doing?" I asked as he started to unbuckle his jeans. I glanced at the woods in all directions, though I knew there was no one around for miles. When I turned back, he stood before me in all his naked glory, taking my breath away yet again.

"C'mon, Maggie Mae. Let's go swimming."

His words didn't register as he walked toward me with my brain so distracted by his physique.

But when he took my hand and pulled me from the rock to take my shirt over my head, my thoughts snapped back into focus, and I grabbed my shirt and yanked it back down.

"Swimming? Are you nuts? You just told me there's snakes."

He reached behind me to pull my shirt up from the back. "I said there might be snakes. There might not be. If we splash and make lots of noise, they'll stay away from us."

I pushed his hands away and peered at the water, straining to see any serpentine movement beneath the transparent surface.

"How deep is it?" I asked, staring at the huge rocks on the bottom of the pool and noticing the dark shadows beneath them and openings into the earth that looked like portals to hell.

"Several hundred feet in the center."

I swung my head back to look at him, surprised at his words. "Several hundred?"

He nodded. "It's a natural spring. I don't know for sure how deep it is at its origin, but we've been diving down there for years and we've never found the bottom."

I looked back at the water, wary of what might be lurking in those dark depths.

"Are you sure this is safe?" I asked. "We're a long way from help, and I'm willing to bet the cell service out here is the pits."

Dax laughed. "It wouldn't be much of an escape if we were still connected. Now, are you gonna leave me standing here with my privates getting tickled by the breeze, or are you gonna get undressed and join me for a swim?"

"You go ahead," I said, tucking my shirt back in. "I think I'll just watch from this rock."

"Suit yourself, but you don't know what you're missing."

He stepped up onto the rock and dove into the water, his muscular frame cutting a vee through the water as he broke the surface and swam underneath before coming up for a breath.

"Woo hoo!" he yelled, his voice amplified by the silence of our surroundings. "There's nothing like spring water to wake you up and make you feel alive."

I envied his complete abandon as I watched him swim, the sun beating down on me as its heat also rose up from the surface of the rock beneath me.

After a few minutes of Dax cavorting underwater and coming up grinning like he was at an amusement park, the sweat rolling down my back had become more unpleasant than the thought of what might be in the pool.

I stood and pulled my shirt over my head, folding it carefully and laying it on the rock where I'd been sitting.

Dax came up for air just as I slid my khaki pants down my legs, and he let out a whoop of excitement. "You're coming in?"

"I suppose."

When I had folded my bra and panties and set them on top of my pants and shirt, I climbed onto the rock next to them and stared out across the water.

It was strangely liberating to be standing in the middle of the woods completely nude. The light breeze coming off the water cooled the sheen of sweat that lay upon my skin, and I closed my eyes and spread my arms to embrace the feeling.

"Not that I'm complaining about the view, but are you gonna jump or just stand there all day?" Dax asked.

I held my nose and plunged feet first into the water, unprepared for the frigid temperature awaiting me. All the air was knocked from my lungs as I sunk beneath the surface, and I kicked furiously to come back up and gulp a breath.

"Lord have mercy, this is cold! Why didn't you tell me it was below freezing?"

"Because you wouldn't have come in," Dax said, swimming over to wrap his powerful arms around me. His skin was cold, even colder than the water, and I pulled back a little and kicked away from him.

"You're freezing," I said, pumping my feet and legs to stay afloat and try and get warm.

"It's invigorating. You'll get used to it. C'mere." He extended his arms to welcome me, and it only took a few minutes of our bodies intertwined and our mouths crushed together to make the water temperature more bearable.

The pool was much deeper than it had looked from above, and I went under a couple of times to try to touch the bottom with my feet, but I couldn't.

"So, you and your brother just stumbled on this place?" I asked, leaning back to look at the circle of trees surrounding us and the brilliant blue of the sky above us.

"There's several springs on the property. Some of them we actually use with our trench system to keep water flowing for the cattle. But this one is the most isolated. It was our go-to hangout in high school, and all our friends knew about it, but it was too far for our parents to check in on us."

"Naughty boys. So, are you sure none of your friends are going to show up this weekend?" I asked, looking down at my nakedness distorted by the ripples of the water as we moved.

"Nah. No one comes out here anymore. Except me."

I wondered if he'd brought his wife to his special place, but it seemed pretty obvious that he would have if it meant so much to him. I didn't want to ask, because I didn't want to know, but I did ask the other question that had been burning at the back of my mind.

"Did you and your wife go out dancing often?"

"No. Deanna wasn't a dancer. At all. Now, her sister—Revae—that girl could dance. She wouldn't leave the dance floor until the lights came up and the music turned off. The four of us would go out, and Revae and I would hit the dance floor while William and Deanna sat and cheered us on from the sidelines."

"You still keep in touch with them? With William and Revae?"

His smile faltered, but his eyes were warm with feeling. "Revae passed away a little over a year ago after a long illness. But yeah, William and I keep in touch. We were friends before we met the girls, and we'll always be family. Their daughter, Piper, was just here two weeks ago, in fact. She brought a horse down for one of our ranch hands."

He lay back and floated on the water, his arms and legs outstretched.

I lifted my legs and spread my arms to join him. The green of the trees against the blue of the sky was breathtaking, and the uninhibited freedom of nudity was almost as exhilarating as the water.

We floated for a while, occasionally bumping into each other.

I heard him splash and go under near me, but I was still surprised when he surfaced right beside me, closing the warmth of his mouth over my breast as it protruded from the water's surface.

He slid his hand between my legs from underneath, and it was all I could do to remain afloat as he explored with his icy fingers.

"Unless you want me to drown," I whispered, "we might want to take this activity out of the water."

He laughed and kissed me before swimming toward the shore.

The water had been so relaxing that I'd forgotten to be on the lookout for snakes, but as we approached the bank, I became hyper-vigilant again. Long grass hung over the edge of the embankment, and the dark stalks growing beneath the water hid the sides of the natural pool.

Dax led me directly to a pile of rocks stacked beneath the surface, and I realized it was an established point of entry and exit. He climbed out of the pool with ease and turned back to offer me his hand, pulling me up and out of the water and into his arms.

My body shook with cold as the sun hit my dripping skin, hugging myself as I pressed against Dax, even though his own body was pretty much the same temperature as mine.

"Let's get you dry," he said, leading me over to the tent and unzipping the entry flap.

He reached in and got a towel, kneeling before me to dry my legs and then making his way up my body with it, leaving kisses on my skin as he went.

"As delightful as this is, I need to get a comb through my hair before we get sidetracked, or I'll never get the tangles out."

He pulled back the flap of the tent, and I bent to crawl inside, amazed at how spacious it looked within.

"It's roomy," I said as he joined me in the tent, zipping the flap closed behind him.

He had laid out the bed rolls on one side of the tent, using blankets as makeshift pillows. On the other side of the tent he'd neatly arranged his bag and mine along with the camp supplies. I knelt to dig through my bag and pulled out my conditioner, squirting it into my hands and then working it through my hair with a widetooth comb.

When I turned to face him, he was laid on his side on the bedroll, and I grinned as I crawled across the tent to join him.

We took our time pleasuring each other—exploring, touching, and caressing until the chill of the water on our skin had been replaced by a passion-driven heat.

I tossed aside my worries about woodland creatures and forgot any reservations I might have had about intimacy in the outdoors.

By the time we lay basking in the aftermath, the interior of the tent looked as though wild animals had attacked it, and any semblance of order was gone.

# 49 THE EARTH MOVED

The day's ride combined with the swim and amorous activity had sapped all our energy, and we fell asleep in the delightful cross breeze coming through the mesh side panels of the tent.

It was nearly dark outside when I woke to the sound of Dax unzipping the doorway.

I sat up, a bit disoriented, and he turned with a smile, leaning over to give me a kiss.

"I need to gather some firewood before it gets too dark."

I stretched my arms high above me and arched my back, already feeling the effects of the hard ground. "Well, don't get lost. I have no idea how to find my way out of the woods and to the barn if you don't come back."

"I won't get out of sight of the camp. Don't worry."

I lay back down as he exited the tent, pulling the thin blanket over me as I stared at the mesh skylight in the ceiling.

A state of contentment settled over me, and I closed my eyes and considered how much my life had changed since we met.

He'd brought me out of a shell I wasn't aware I'd been confined in, and the wonder of it all was both exciting and frightening.

The more time we spent together, the more I wanted to see him. When we were apart, I mentally cataloged topics of interest or things that happened throughout my day, eager for our next conversation.

He was my first thought when I woke each morning, and I drifted to sleep with him foremost in my mind each night.

My carefully tended wall had begun to tumble, and though I was still terrified of what that would mean for my heart, I had no desire to stop that wall from falling.

I rose and left the tent, a bit more self-conscious about my state of undress without Dax by my side. I grabbed my clothes, which were still warm from sitting in the sun, and quickly dressed.

Dax came back to camp right as I finished tucking my shirt into my khakis, and as always, my heart leapt at the sight of him.

He had put on his jeans, his boots, and his hat, but he wore no shirt, and the image of my rugged cowboy strolling out of the woods half-dressed was immediately committed to memory for use the next time I had to go to bed alone.

"Are you hungry?" he asked with a smile. "Because I'm starving."

My stomach grumbled at the thought of food. "I could definitely eat. Is there something I could do to help you?"

"Sure," he said, setting down the sticks and branches he'd gathered. "If you'll look in the tent, there's a cooler bag. In it are the steaks for dinner and then there's a leather pack that has two potatoes, already wrapped in foil. Can you bring me those?"

I tried to restore some semblance of order to the tent as I dug through the bags to find the pack with the potatoes. When I opened the cooler to get the steaks, I saw a Ziploc bag with several mini Snickers bars, and I smiled.

"You brought Snickers?" I asked as I handed him the steaks and potatoes.

"You have them in a glass canister on your counter, and it's the only candy I've ever seen you eat."

I smiled and stretched up to plant a kiss on his cheek. "Thank you."

"No problem. I couldn't figure out how to get a birthday cake in a saddle bag, but I figured I could manage chocolate. How about you bring me a couple to hold me over until dinner's done?"

We munched on Snickers as he cooked the steaks in an iron skillet over the campfire, occasionally turning the potatoes he had skewered with sticks and propped over the heat.

The sky was dark by the time we finished eating, and I helped Dax wash our dishes with water he'd scooped in a bucket from the spring.

The woods surrounding us were black without the light of the sun, but the glow of the campfire illuminated our immediate area.

We had placed a blanket on the ground in front of a log when we sat to eat, and I settled cross-legged on the blanket with my back against the log while Dax checked on the horses.

It was a beautiful night, and I wanted to imprint it on my mind so I could remember every detail.

The fire popped and crackled as heat radiated out across the campsite.

The trees danced in the breeze and their leaves rustled to the tune of the crickets and frogs.

I shifted my weight onto one hip, leaning to the side with my palm flat on the ground so I could tilt my head back and watch the clouds pass across the deep blue-black sky, occasionally parting to reveal the twinkling of a star.

A splash of wet cold hit my hand, and I looked down to see a long black ribbon curling across the blanket, pausing in its crawl about halfway across the back of my hand.

It seemed that I levitated, lifting off the blanket and hovering in mid-air for a moment as I screamed and struggled to get my feet out from underneath me so I could run.

I bolted toward the tree line, stopping when I realized I had outrun the ability of the light to show me where I was stepping.

I turned and ran back toward the fire, still screaming, hopping up and down as I ran, trying not to let my feet touch the ground any longer than necessary. My whole body itched with the sensation of things crawling on my skin, and I beat at my clothes to vanquish the imaginary invaders.

"It's okay. It's only a black racer. He's harmless," Dax said, walking toward me.

"Harmless? Tell that to my heart, because it's about to beat out of my chest and give me a heart attack."

I knew Dax was struggling not to laugh, and I wanted to punch him for even considering the situation humorous.

"I meant it's not venomous," he said. "You probably scared him more than he scared you."

"Not likely."

"Well, you damned sure scared the hell outta me and the horses. I didn't know what was happening until I saw the little fellow scampering off the blanket."

"Little? He was huge."

Dax shrugged. "About two feet."

"He was longer than that."

The memory of seeing the snake crawling across my hand replayed in my head, and I shuddered.

The infuriating man in front of me couldn't hold it in any longer and he burst out laughing. It took all I had not to kick him in the shin.

"I'm sorry," he said, putting his hands up as he looked at my thunderous expression, "but I've never seen anyone move that fast or get started that slow. You were like a cartoon character who was winding up in one spot and then you took off in a blur."

He bent over laughing, and I put my hands on his shoulders and shoved him backward.

"I don't find this funny in the slightest. If you think I'm going to sleep in a tent where snakes can crawl all over me," I shuddered again, "then you're crazy. We need to go back to the barn. Now."

I crossed my arms over my chest and glared at him as he struggled to get his laughter under control.

"C'mon, Maggie Mae, we've had the tent sealed tight all evening. I'll get in with the flashlight before we go to bed to make sure there's nothing moving in there other than you and me."

"What if they get in while we're sleeping?"

I could see mirth playing at the corners of his mouth and my eyes narrowed.

"They won't," he said. "He's probably told all his friends about the crazy redhead by now, and they'll steer clear of the campsite."

"Don't patronize me, Dax. Can a snake get in there?"

"No. We'll have the tent zipped up tight. Nothing will get in. I promise."

I bit my lip and wished that I could click my heels together and be back home.

He stepped forward and put his arms around me, but I kept mine crossed.

"I'm sorry I laughed at you," he said. "I know that had to be pretty scary, and I'm sorry. But if you had only seen it from my point of view…."

I could feel his body tremble as he fought not to laugh again, and I glared up at him.

"Not laughing. Not funny."

"I know. You're right. It's not." He tried to kiss me, and I tried to resist, but mine was a half-hearted effort, and it didn't take long for me to relax against him and open up to his apology.

"I have a surprise for you," he said, leading me back to the tent as my eyes scanned the ground for any sign of movement.

He unzipped the entrance and went in, reemerging with a small Bluetooth speaker.

"I downloaded the music for our lessons onto my phone so I could practice anywhere. We can do that, or I downloaded a few other songs that make me want to dance with you when I hear them."

I was curious what songs he meant, and while I certainly didn't forget about the incident with the snake, by the time we'd gone through a few numbers on his playlist, I'd been able to push it to the back of my mind and relax again.

A few of his choices had been upbeat tempos that had us working up a sweat near the fire, so at first, I was happy when the breeze picked up. But then the temperature began to drop, and the tops of the trees started to sway as the wind intensified.

"Uh-oh. That's not good," Dax said, looking up at the swirling clouds overhead as he held me in his arms.

"Rain?" I lifted my face to smell the air and feel the moisture in the wind.

Dax nodded and released me to fold the blanket. "I need to get the horses hobbled so I can move them out from under the trees in case of lightning. Can you put that stuff inside the tent?"

"Is the tent waterproof?" I asked as I gathered the few items we'd left near the fire, keeping a close eye on the ground for any signs of my slithery friend.

"Yeah, I need to zip the skylight and pull the rain guards down over the side windows."

He walked the horses over to the more open area of the clearing while I put away anything that wasn't already in the tent. Then he came back to weatherproof the tent's openings.

While he set about doing that, I spread my arms wide and let the wind blow against me. There was something almost electric in the air, and the energy of the pending storm flowed through me and charged me with excitement.

I could see Dax out of the corner of my eye, standing near the tent watching me.

"What? Why are you looking at me?"

"Because you're so damned beautiful," he whispered. He walked toward me with a hunger in his eyes that only fueled the adrenaline pumping through my veins.

I flung my arms around his neck, and he twisted his hands in my hair to pull it back from my face, taking my mouth in his as the wind raged around us.

There were no warning sprinkles or intermittent drops. One minute we were dry, and the next minute the skies opened up and a deluge of water poured down upon us.

Dax grabbed my hand, and we sprinted for the tent, getting soaked as he struggled with the zipper.

The campfire hissed in the background in protest to being extinguished by the rain, and a clap of thunder shook the trees around us.

We fell into the tent laughing once he got it open, me scanning the darkness as Dax pulled the zipper shut on both the nylon outer layer and the mesh inner layer of the door.

He turned on the battery-operated lantern and did a quick inspection for my benefit before setting the lantern in the corner and returning to my arms.

"You're soaked," he said between kisses.

"So are you."

He peeled the wet shirt over my head and reached behind me to deftly unsnap my bra with a flick of his thumb.

His skin was slick with rain, and I shivered as he took me in his arms, pressing his bare chest against mine.

Heavy raindrops battered the tent, and another boom of thunder crashed around us.

"Sounds like it's gonna be a doozy," he said, looking up at the ceiling of the tent.

"Will we be okay in here?"

He looked back down at me and nodded. "Yeah. We'll be fine."

"I normally love watching a storm roll in from my patio, but there, I can always get up and go inside the house if it gets too bad."

He cupped my cheek in his hand, and I turned to kiss his palm.

"I'm not going to let anything happen to you, Maggie." His voice was barely above a whisper, and it held a husky quality that intensified my desire.

"As romantic as that sounds, I don't think you can save me from Mother Nature."

"I'll die trying," he said, his mouth already on mine as the words left his lips. He trailed his hands down my back and then spanned them over my ribs, his thumbs grazing over my nipples, stiff from wet cold and begging for his touch.

He unfastened my pants, and we both laughed as he struggled to push the wet material down with it plastered to my skin.

I wrestled them off and knelt on the floor of the tent as I waited for him to remove his jeans. He stood before me, and I took him in my hands and in my mouth, my own body's erotic response rising as he moaned and buried his hands in my hair. I grabbed the backs of his sculpted thighs and pulled him deeper, turned on by the power of being able to make him react the way he was.

He moved his hands to my shoulders and pulled me up to standing, scooping me up to wrap my legs around his hips and parting my thighs to ease me over the length of him.

I threw my arms around his neck and clung to him as he moved my body up and down in rhythm with his thrusts, my own pleasure building as his groans rose in intensity to match that of the storm outside. With one swift motion, he bent to lay me on the floor of the tent, plunging into me as the thunder shook the ground and the tent swayed with the pounding of the wind.

He cried out my name, and I joined him in climax as a huge bolt of lightning lit up the night sky.

"Wow," I whispered as he lay on top of me, his breathing heavy and his body trembling. "I've read about people seeing stars when they orgasm, but I just saw lightning. We must have some pretty intense lovemaking skills."

He chuckled, and I smoothed his hair away from his face as he nestled his head on my breasts.

"I think I felt the earth move," he said.

"Me, too."

A big gust of wind slammed into the tent, and I flinched beneath Dax's weight.

"I hope the wind doesn't pick this tent up and deposit us in the middle of the spring."

He lifted his head and looked around, and then laid it back on my chest. "It's tied down pretty well. I think it will hold."

His arms were snuggled along my sides, and he squeezed me as he shifted to take most of his weight to the floor, leaving his head on the pillow my body provided and his thigh tossed across mine.

He kissed the rise of my breast beneath his face, and hugged me tighter.

The air felt ripe for an exchange of love, and I braced, wanting him to say it, but willing him not to. Not yet.

The wind died down and the moment passed, but I'd already said it in my heart.

# 50 A ROCK & A HARD PLACE

"Did my mom tell you she went camping last weekend? In a tent?" Cabe asked as he finished drying the dishes after dinner. "She must really like this guy."

"Mmm-huh," Tyler mumbled.

"What's up with you?" Cabe asked as he watched Tyler cross the living room floor for the fourth time.

"What do you mean?"

He smiled. "Well, I just mentioned my mom's love life, which is one of your favorite topics lately, and you barely gave me a response. You're pacing. You've cracked your knuckles twice even though you know it drives me insane, and you barely touched your dinner. Considering that chicken piccata is one of my best meals, that's odd in and of itself. What's going on?"

She flopped down in the large chair in the corner and laid her head back, closing her eyes and releasing a huge sigh.

"That bad, huh?" Cabe said. "Should I be worried?"

Deacon stood and left his chew toy to run his head underneath Tyler's hand, nudging her softly at first, and then more forcefully when she didn't respond.

"Even the dog's worried, Buttercup. 'Fess up and tell us how bad it is."

Tyler scratched behind Deacon's ears as she opened her eyes and turned her head to face Cabe.

"I don't know what to do," she said, her voice quiet.

"About what? What's wrong, babe?"

Cabe folded the dish towel and laid it on the cabinet before walking over to sit on the couch, taking Tyler's hand in his. Deacon nudged at both their hands and whined when neither responded with more petting.

"I'm having an issue with a bride," she said.

Cabe exhaled loudly. "Whew! A bride we can handle. I thought you were giving me some kind of bad news, and I wasn't sure what it was gonna be. I thought maybe your mother was coming to visit or something."

Tyler shuddered and rolled her eyes. "Oh, Lord, please. Don't even say that. That's the last thing I need right now."

"So what wedding crisis has befallen this bride? What's got you so worked up?"

She opened her mouth to speak, but then met his eyes and stopped as her own filled with tears.

"Babe, are you crying? What the hell? Come over here." Cabe sat back against the couch, pulling her up out of the chair and onto his lap. "You know you can't let these bridezillas get to you. How many times have we been through this? If the bride is a miserable person, nothing you can do will make her happy, and that's not on you. You just do the best job you can and keep telling yourself she's just another bride. There'll be a different one next week."

Tyler's voice cracked a bit when she spoke. "But this isn't just another bride. It's your sister."

Cabe stiffened and stopped stroking Tyler's hair. He moved her to sit up so he could face her.

"What did she do? What did she say? If she upset you—"

Tyler shook her head. "It's not that."

"She's lucky you agreed to do this wedding after what she did to us."

"Cabe, your sister was looking out for you. She thought I wasn't the right person to make you happy. We've moved past that, remember?"

He slid Tyler from his lap and stood, taking his own turn at pacing the living room.

"I knew this was a bad idea. I knew you shouldn't have agreed to do this."

"Would you stop? She didn't do or say anything to me. She's been really nice, actually."

He stopped pacing and turned to face Tyler. "Galen? Nice? That's unlikely."

Tyler sighed and rubbed her eyes. "No, she has been. Really. I think she genuinely appreciates my help with everything. She's just put me in an awkward position, and I don't know what to do."

"What do you mean? Awkward, how?"

She ran her hand along Deacon's back and sank her fingers into his fur. "Normally, I'm the bride's advocate. I'm the person who makes sure the wedding turns out the way she wants it to. Sometimes that means I'm running interference between her and the family, or between her and the groom, and or sometimes between her and the vendors. But I'm the neutral party who gets to step in and say that what the bride wants is what we're doing."

"Okay. So what does Galen want to do that's causing you so much stress?"

Tyler leaned forward and cupped Deacon's face in her hands, ignoring the tear that rolled down her cheek. Deacon leapt toward her, putting his front paws in her lap and licking the tear from her face.

"It's okay, buddy," she cooed to the dog. "I'm fine." She wiped away his slobber and the remnants of her tear with the back of her hand and looked up at her husband, whose wary expression barely concealed the anger she knew was simmering beneath the surface any time his sister was involved.

"Before I tell you," she stood and went to Cabe, placing her hands on his chest, "you have to promise me you're not going to get upset."

"I can't do that. You know I can't do that."

"It's her wedding, babe. It's her special day, and you have to allow her to have her own feelings about how it happens."

His eyes narrowed, and he took a step back. "Tell me this has nothing to do with Gerry Tucker."

Tyler's eyes glassed over and another tear escaped. "Cabe, it's her wedding and—"

"Absolutely not. No way in hell, Ty. She's got Jeffrey and Julie coming, and that's hard enough for my mom. No way is that man coming anywhere near this wedding."

Tyler reached for Cabe, and he took another step back. "I understand, Cabe, I really do. But I'm torn as to what's the right thing."

"I'm not. Gerry Tucker has not done one damned thing to be her father other than providing his DNA and sending some gifts. He doesn't get to be part of this."

"But it's not your decision, babe. It's hers."

Cabe shook his head.

"Listen, Cabe, I understand why you don't want him there. Why Maggie wouldn't want him there. But this is Galen's big day. It has to matter that she wants him there."

"Why? Why on earth would she want him there? This is ridiculous."

He picked up his phone from the table.

"Stop, Cabe." Tyler grabbed his arm as she pleaded. "Don't call her. Please. Technically, she's my client, and I shouldn't have even discussed this with you, but—"

"Oh, there's no way I'm not calling her. What? Were you going to wait until the day of and spring this on my mother?"

"No, I told her she needs to tell Maggie, but she hasn't yet, and I don't know what to do."

"Well, I'm telling you what we're doing. I'm calling her and putting a stop to this."

"No. Cabe, I'm begging you not to do that."

His finger hovered above the screen, and he glared at Tyler, his jaw clenched tight.

"Please? Cabe? I had to tell you because we need to discuss this. But I didn't tell you so that you'll call my bride and destroy her faith in me."

"Her faith in you?" he scoffed, the phone still in his hand though he hadn't yet dialed his sister. "What about my mom's faith in you? She's already agreed to have his other children in the wedding because it was important to my sister. Do you have any idea how difficult that must be for her? It may be Galen's wedding, but it's important to my mom, too. And let's not forget she's paying for the whole damned thing."

Tyler exhaled and scrunched her nose against further tears. "I know. Believe me, I know. I've tried to talk your sister out of this. But Gerry *is* her father. It's not unusual for a bride to want her father to walk her down the aisle."

"*To what?*" Cabe took another step back and immediately dialed his sister's phone. "She's out of her mind."

Tyler held her breath as she heard the phone ringing even though Cabe had it held to his ear. She prayed Galen wouldn't answer, and whether it was an answer to prayer or a lucky coincidence, she was relieved to hear the voice mail recording on the other end of the line.

"Call me. Now," Cabe growled into the phone before ending the call. He sat on the couch and tossed the phone on the table. "Unbelievable."

"Please just try to see it from her point of view," Tyler said, sitting cross-legged on the couch beside him and closing her hand over his. "You yourself said she's always wanted to be 'Daddy's little girl'. This is important to her, Cabe. She's not trying to hurt Maggie or you or anyone. She's just a bride who wants her dad to walk her down the aisle. Can't you see that?"

Cabe raised his eyes to meet Tyler's, and her heart flinched at the pain she saw in the clear blue depths.

"This will ruin the whole event for my mom. There's no way she will be comfortable with him there. No way she can enjoy herself. My grandparents will freak the hell out." He exhaled and pulled his hand from Tyler's to run it through his hair. "Leave it to Galen to cause everyone drama, and at the same time, make it feel like we're all doing the wrong thing if it's not about her."

"Maybe Maggie will understand. I mean, she seemed okay with Jeffrey and Julie."

Cabe laid his head back against the couch. "Mom is always going to do what she thinks is the right thing for us. No matter how much it hurts her."

"But what if this *is* the right thing for Galen? What if having her dad there is what she needs?"

He closed his eyes and rubbed them with his thumbs. "Having her dad years ago was what she needed. But he wasn't there. He shouldn't get to show up and parade down the aisle like a damned peacock."

"Maybe he won't even come. It's gotta be uncomfortable for him, too, right? He knows how your mom feels about him. He's got to know your grandparents hate him. He's very well aware you don't want anything to do with him. Maybe he'll do the right thing and not come." She paused for a moment. "Of course, if he does that, then he breaks Galen's heart all over again and lets her down."

Cabe picked up Tyler's hand and stroked the back of it with his thumb. "He's going to let her down. Whether it's the wedding day or some day after, there's no doubt he'll let her down. That may be what it takes for her to see him for who he is. And who he's not."

He pulled Tyler into his arms as she uncrossed her legs to snuggle up to his chest.

"I'm sorry I got upset, Buttercup." He kissed the top of her head and squeezed her against him. "I know you're trying to keep the peace with everyone, and I really appreciate all you're doing. To help Mom. To help Galen. I love you."

She tilted her head back to look up at him, closing her eyes as his lips touched hers.

"I love you, too. But I still don't know what to do."

"I'll talk to Galen. Calmly," he said as Tyler opened her mouth to protest. "I want to make sure she's thought this through before Mom gets wind of it. She hasn't told her yet, has she?"

Tyler shook her head.

"Okay, good. When she calls me back, I'll talk to her. I'll take care of it."

The beat of his heart thumped against Tyler's ear as she laid her head back on his chest, both of them silent as they tried to think of a solution that would keep the people they loved from getting hurt.

# 51 AND THE AWARD GOES TO...

Betty threw a party at the community center to celebrate the end of our weekly dance lessons, and I was torn between sadness that they were over and relief at no longer having a weekly commitment.

I loved the time spent with Dax on the dance floor, and I truly enjoyed Betty's instruction and learning new dance techniques. But with our busy schedules, the Thursday night lesson was often the only time we saw each other during the week, and I looked forward to being able to do other things with him during that time.

She presented awards to each couple, and as we applauded the recipients of *Most Improved*, *Best Enthusiasm*, and *Most Likely to Come Back for More*, I wondered what title Dax and I would be given.

She called us up to the microphone and handed Dax the certificate as she proclaimed us the *Most Inspiring Couple* for our excellence in technique and our obvious affection for one another. We smiled and thanked her, and judging by Dax's excitement level, you would have thought she'd given us a Tony award.

"You know, Maggie, I've told you before, but you have such a skill for picking up steps," Betty said as she joined me near the punch bowl after handing out all her awards. "Have you ever considered teaching?"

"She used to be a dance teacher," Dax said before I could answer. "She taught ballet. In fact, she was an amazing dancer in her own right. She danced with the Miami Ballet."

I stared at him, uncomfortable with having my past revealed and put on display.

"I thought you had the lines for ballet," Betty said. "That's wonderful. This must be child's play for you, then. Ballet is much more strenuous than ballroom."

"Well, I, uh, I haven't danced in a while, so this was plenty strenuous enough," I said, my face warm and my pulse pounding.

"How long ago were you with Miami Ballet?" Betty asked.

"A lifetime. I was much younger then."

The room had grown hot, and I tried to think of a way to change the subject without seeming rude. I couldn't remember the last time I'd been questioned about my previous career. It wasn't something I ever discussed with anyone.

Betty smiled, and her eyes grew bright as she held up her finger. "I have several classes I run all over Central Florida, and I have quite a few teachers underneath my umbrella. I'd love to talk to you about teaching for me if you'd be interested."

I downed the remainder of my punch and forced a smile. "I don't know. My job keeps me very busy, and I don't know how I'd feel about teaching again."

"Well, let me know if you change your mind," Betty said, patting my arm.

Dax seemed oblivious to my discomfort as he turned to talk to another dancer who had called to him. He laughed and interacted with the others throughout the celebration, but despite my efforts to enjoy the party, I couldn't shake my feeling of irritation.

"Maggie? Dax?" Betty called out as everyone was headed to their cars at the end of the party. "Can I have a moment?"

I stifled a sigh, hoping she wasn't going to pry further into my past and ask questions I had no desire to answer.

"I've been so impressed with the two of you, as you know, and that was even before I knew you had a professional background." She smiled, and I tried to return the gesture. "I host a recital in November for various students of mine. I would love to have the two of you be part of it."

"Oh, wow," Dax said. "A recital? How cool is that? Like, to dance in front of people?"

Betty grinned at him. "Well, yes. Recitals usually have an audience. You'd need costumes, of course, but I could help with that. And we'd need to choose music and do some choreography, which I would help with as well. Although, I'd love your input, Maggie, as a professional."

"I'm not a professional." My answer was curt, which wasn't my intention, but I felt like I was on a runaway train that was taking me places I didn't want to go.

"Oh, I only meant from an artistic standpoint. You don't have to let me know right away. We've got time. Think about it. Talk it over, and get back with me. I'd love to have you there."

She walked away, and Dax looked at me with the goofiest grin I'd ever seen.

"Well, hot damn! A recital. You and me. How about that? The *Most Inspiring Couple* were asked to inspire at a recital," he said, holding up the certificate next to his enormous grin.

"I'm not feeling well," I said, turning to walk toward the car. "Can we go?"

His face fell as I turned away, and guilt twisted my insides for robbing him of his enthusiasm. I couldn't help it, though. I felt turned inside out. Like something I'd kept carefully hidden had been exposed to the world.

Not to mention that even the thought of performing again made me nauseous. Obviously, an amateur ballroom dance recital was nothing like being center stage for the ballet, but I hadn't performed in any capacity since that fateful night when my toe broke and my life careened off track. I couldn't imagine willingly revisiting the vulnerability of memories and the reminder of things lost.

I made my way to my car and got in, slamming the door behind me.

"Are you okay?" Dax asked as he got in on the passenger's side. "What's wrong? I didn't see you eat anything. Is it your stomach? Do you need something to eat?"

"No, I don't need anything to eat. I need you to not take something that I confided in a dark moment and blast it out to the world."

Shock registered on his face and his mouth fell open. "Wait? What? What did I do?"

"We've been dancing here for over two months, and have you ever once heard me mention that I was a ballet dancer or that I taught dance?"

He closed his mouth and drew his brows together. "No, but I figured it just never came up."

I exhaled sharply and turned the key in the ignition. "It never came up because I didn't want it to come up. I don't talk about my past, Dax. I don't tell people about it, I don't bring it up, and I don't care to discuss it with anyone. I told you because I trusted you, and I never expected you to tell anyone else."

"Whoa, whoa, whoa. I would never betray what you've told me in confidence, but I had no idea your being a dancer and teaching dance was top secret. It's not like it's something to be ashamed of."

I whirled to face him. "Are you saying the rest of what I shared with you is something I should be ashamed of?"

His mouth dropped open again. "What? No! Not at all. What happened? I don't understand."

"I turned my back on being a dancer. It was one of the most painful decisions I've ever made, but I gave it up because I had to. I don't want to be reminded of that time, and I definitely don't want to answer questions from Betty on why I left or what happened to my career."

"But she didn't ask you those questions. She was impressed with you.

She was complimenting you."

"You don't understand."

He threw his hands up and shook his head. "You're right. I don't. You obviously love to dance, and you are so damned good at it that everyone in the room can't take their eyes off you when you're on the floor, including the teacher. I know you think you had to give it up, but don't you think you've punished yourself enough? Isn't it time you let yourself enjoy dancing again? You can't tell me you haven't had fun these past ten weeks."

"I didn't give up dance to punish myself. I gave up dance because I had two kids to feed."

"I don't think so. I think you could have kept teaching and still fed your kids. You could have kept dancing, but you were embarrassed. You were angry with yourself, so you gave up the one thing you loved the most as penance for what you saw as your crimes. But you're the only person demanding a punishment. You can dance. You can enjoy dancing again. You're the only one stopping you."

"Well, thank you for the psychoanalysis, Dr. Pearson. I wasn't aware you had a degree in the field."

I backed out of the parking space and roared out of the parking lot, slinging gravel behind my tires.

We rode in silence for a few blocks before Dax cleared his throat.

"Look, Maggie, I'm sorry that I upset you. I was just proud of you, and I wanted Betty to know what you had accomplished. I didn't know—"

"No, you didn't know. You assumed. You assumed I wanted to dance, so you took me to dance lessons. Now you assume I want to be in a recital and be up there performing on some rinky-dink stage in some community center with a bunch of parents and spouses watching half-ass dance routines choreographed by someone who learned to dance when the Charleston was invented. Well, you're wrong."

The silence returned and remained for the rest of the ride home.

My face flushed hot, and my hands trembled on the wheel. The sane, rational part of me was horrified by the way I'd spoken to Dax. I'd been so harsh with him, even though I knew he hadn't meant any harm and that it was my own issues causing me to overreact. I couldn't deny the truth in his words, but the putrid old wounds had been torn open, and their vile nastiness was seeping into my system and clouding my judgment.

"Can we talk about this?" Dax asked, exiting the car after I slammed the car door and walked up the driveway to my front entrance.

I didn't answer him. I didn't want to talk about it any further. I didn't want to delve any deeper or tear off any more scabs. I also didn't want to have to back down and apologize or admit I was wrong.

But I didn't want him to leave, either. I didn't want him to walk away and leave me seething in the stew of my own making.

So, I said nothing.

I opened the door and tossed my keys on the foyer table, heading to the bar to pour a glass of wine.

Dax came in a few steps behind me and slowly closed the door, standing next to it as he stared at me.

I turned my back so I didn't have to see him, and I was relieved when I heard his footsteps cross the tile and then the door to the hall bathroom closed.

I went out on the patio and plopped down on the sofa, unsure of how to back down from the ledge I'd climbed out on.

My pulse rate had started to calm, and the calmer I got, the more I realized how out of line I'd been with Dax. I'd let old fears and old embarrassments rise to the surface and take control.

My phone beeped on the table, and I looked down to see an email notification from Galen. I should have waited until everything had calmed down. I should have let Dax come out of the bathroom, and I should have apologized for overreacting and tried to explain the jumble of feelings that were at war inside me.

But I didn't. I slid my finger across the notification and opened my daughter's email, not knowing my night was about to get much worse.

# 52 YOU'VE GOT MAIL

*Dear Mom,*

*I realize an email is probably not the way to address this, but I don't know what else to do. I know you're going to be upset, and then we'll both get emotional, and I feel like you won't be able to hear what I really need to say.*

*So, I'm going to type it out here, and then you can read it and get however emotional you'd like. Then, maybe when the dust settles, we can talk.*

*First and foremost, I want to say how much I appreciate all you've done for me. The sacrifices you've made, the love you've shown, and the support you've given have not gone unnoticed, and though I don't always tell you like I should, I can't thank you enough for everything.*

*I know we haven't always had the easiest relationship, and sometimes I think it's because we're too much alike, and sometimes I think we're too different. But you're my mom, and I love you. I don't know where I'd be without you.*

*As I've been preparing for my wedding to Tate, I'm very aware that you never got a wedding, and that I'm experiencing something you were robbed of. I can't imagine what pain you went through with Gerry. I think my relationship with Tate makes me see it differently than I did when I was younger. I don't know what I'd do if I found out Tate was lying to me or if something happened to us like what you experienced.*

*I'm truly sorry for the pain me and Cabe being born caused you, and I have wished a million times that you could have had a different life. One you got to choose.*

*I know you'll just say what you always do—that you love us and you wouldn't change a thing if it meant you couldn't have had us.*

*That's great of you to say, but seriously. Your life would have turned out so much differently if you hadn't met my dad and had us. And I have to think in a lot of ways, it would have been a better life.*

*So please know that when I made this decision, it wasn't because I didn't think of your feelings or because I don't understand why it will upset you. I get it. I really do.*

*But all that being said, I didn't choose for Gerry Tucker to be my father. I had no choice in that matter at all. Whether either of us likes it or not, he's my dad. I've wrestled with that and struggled with that in different ways for my whole entire life, and I want to come to peace with it.*

*I want my father to be part of my wedding. I want him to walk me down the aisle like any other girl would want her father to do. I want to have something that is a normal dad and daughter thing because up until this point in my life, that's something I've never had.*

*I can picture your face right now as you read this. It hurts my heart to even think of how you might be reacting. I'm sorry. I never meant to hurt you.*

*I hope this is the only wedding I ever have. I want to grow old with Tate and have his babies and hold his hand when it's bent and wrinkled.*

*So, I don't think I'll get another chance to have this moment. I know that if you had been able to have a wedding, you would have wanted Papa to walk you down the aisle. And yes, your relationship with him was much different than mine with Gerry, but still. I want what everyone else wants for their wedding day.*

*Maybe, just maybe, this can be a new beginning. Maybe this is the turning point, and Gerry walking me down the aisle will be the start of a new relationship with him. Maybe he'll want to be more involved and maybe me making this gesture will help him see what he's missing out on.*

*Jeffrey, Julie, and Cabe all tell me I'm nuts for ever thinking he will change, but I have to try. He's the only dad I have, and I want to know I did everything I could to have a relationship with him.*

*Can you please forgive me? And can you please do this for me? Can you allow him to be there…for me?*

*I love you, Mom. I won't do this against your wishes, but I am asking you to consider what it means to me.*

*Galen*

# 53 OVERFLOW

Dax had come out to the patio at some point while I was reading, and he sat on the side of the sofa watching me read as the tears streamed down my face.

I dropped the phone to my lap when I was done and buried my face in my hands, trying to escape the complete insanity of the whole situation.

I couldn't win. I would never be free of Gerry Tucker and the pain he'd caused. Everything in my life since him had been colored in some way by the choices I'd made, and even tonight with my outburst after dance, I was still allowing the past to dictate my present.

My daughter's pain stabbed my heart, and I knew I couldn't deny her what was rightfully hers, yet I couldn't bear to watch him walk my baby down the aisle in a role he'd never deserved to play.

Dax put his hand on my back and I jerked free, standing to walk away. "I need to be alone, Dax."

"Maggie, we need to talk."

"No. No, we don't. I can't talk right now." The barrage of feelings assaulting me was overwhelming, and I didn't want to completely lose control in front of him.

He came and stood behind me, and I wiped at my tears, trying to pull it together long enough to see him out.

"Maggie, I'm sorry. I was out of line in telling you how to feel and—"

"Dax, I can't deal with this right now. I need to call my daughter."

"Is everything okay? Did something happen with Galen?"

I walked past him and into the kitchen to refill my glass of wine. "Galen's fine. It's me who's screwed up. As you well know."

He followed me inside. "Is everything okay with the wedding?"

"The wedding is great. The father of the bride is getting a red carpet rolled out for him, and if I protest, I'm the one with issues. Why is that? Why is it that no matter how hard I try to do the right thing, it's somehow never enough? I always have to give more."

"If it bothers you for him to be there, tell her it's not going to work. Surely, she can understand why you feel the way you do."

I turned up the wine glass to drink but saw a piece of cork floating in it, so I went to the sink and poured it out in frustration. "Oh, she understands. But she's right. It's her wedding, and it's not her fault that he's her father. That's on me. That's all my fault. So, I have to be the one to make it right."

"Okay, so then you let him come and walk her down the aisle."

"I don't want him to walk her down the aisle," I yelled. "I don't want him anywhere near her. Or me. Or anyone in my family. He did this to us. Why doesn't he have to have consequences, too? Why does it all fall on me?"

"I don't know, but if you want to put her feelings first, and she wants to have him there, then you gotta figure out a way to be okay with it."

"Thank you once again, Dr. Pearson, for another riveting analysis. I had no idea a solution was so easy to find. Thank God you were here to help."

Dax frowned and ran his fingers through his hair. "I'm starting to feel like no matter what I say tonight, it's not going to be the right thing. I'm not the enemy here, Maggie. I'm trying to help."

"Well, you're not, okay? You're only adding more pressure. There's no winning solution here. I can either break my daughter's heart or piss off my son and my parents, and either way, I'm going to be miserable. And that sucks. I can't win. I made one damned mistake which led to a whole bunch of other mistakes, and I will never be free of it. Never! It doesn't matter how hard I try to move past it. It keeps coming back."

I slammed my hands on the kitchen counter and turned my back to him.

He stood where he was, and I prayed he would just leave before I said more things I would regret. My pulse was pounding so hard that my head hurt, and an angry panic was boiling up inside me as I struggled to maintain control.

"Look at it this way," Dax said. "After the wedding, there's pretty much not any reason for you to deal with him again. The kids are both adults. They'll both be married. You won't have to see him again. So, let him walk her down the aisle. I'll make sure he doesn't come anywhere near you that day."

"What?" I turned to face him as my mind projected scenes of Dax and Gerry fighting at the wedding, my parents asking me who Dax was, and all our family and friends jumping to conclusions about our relationship. The pressure intensified. "You're planning on being there?"

Hurt flashed across his face, and he frowned. "Yeah, I'm planning on being there. It's my house, and if I think there's going to be a confrontation, I'm damned well going to be there. But I guess I thought I'd be invited. Maybe that's just another one of my incorrect assumptions, huh?"

His words added more guilt, which was the one thing I couldn't possibly take more of in that moment. My frustration with the world exploded in a nasty way.

"Maybe we've both made some incorrect assumptions," I snarled. "Like assuming this was going anywhere. We couldn't be more complete opposites if we tried. I'm not ever moving out to live in a camper on a cow ranch, and I'm pretty sure you're not going to hang up your boots and move to the city with me. So, what are we doing? We're just going to drag this out until one of us decides it's not working and walks away. Then whoever's left gets to pick up the pieces and deal with the heartbreak. No, thank you. Let's just call this what it is. We've both had a good time, but I don't need to meet your parents and you don't need to meet mine. There's no future here."

I turned so I couldn't see the pain in his eyes. A little voice in the back of my head was screaming at me to stop, but I was too far gone.

"I need to call my daughter, so if we're done here…. "

He walked around the island and stood in front of me, making it harder to avoid eye contact. He opened his mouth to speak, and I put up my hand.

"Don't. Don't say anything, Dax. It will just make it harder. Just go. It was never going to work anyway."

He walked away, pulling my heart with him as he went, and I closed my eyes and bit down hard on my lip to keep from crying out in pain.

"You know," he said from behind me, "at some point, you're going to have to forgive yourself and let it go. You won't be free until you can do that."

"You don't understand," I said without looking back. "You don't know what it's like to hurt the people you love and not be able to fix it. I'm better off alone."

## 54  BESTIE WISDOM

I called Sandy as soon as his truck left the driveway.

"I've screwed up. Oh, Sandy. I messed everything up. I can't fix it. I can't make it right. It's all screwed up."

"Slow down, slow down. What exactly is it you're so sure you screwed up?"

"Everything. All of it."

"Okay, well, I'm pretty sure it's impossible for one person to single-handedly screw up *everything*. You're not *that* powerful. So, let's narrow it down and take it one issue at a time. Is this offspring-related, parent-related, job-related, or love life-related?"

"Pretty much all of the above."

"Can you give me something to go on? What happened?"

"Galen wants Gerry to walk her down the aisle."

"Ah. I can't say I didn't see that one coming. Hold on, and let me tell Hannah to pause the movie. This isn't going to be a short one."

"I'm sorry," I said when Sandy returned. "Here I am, yet again, coming to you about Gerry Freaking Tucker."

"Oh, please. Don't piss me off by saying stupid stuff. You know we don't apologize for needing each other. Now, what happened? Did you talk to Galen?"

"No. She wrote an email because she doesn't feel like she can talk to me. My daughter can't talk to me. That's not the kind of mother I wanted to be. You know how my parents will react if Gerry shows up, and I can't begin to imagine what Cabe will do. Not to mention that I don't want Gerry there. Galen had some good points, though, and it means a lot to her for him to walk her down the aisle. I don't know what to do."

"Well, it is her wedding. And as much as I'd like to see the S.O.B.

dropped off somewhere in Siberia without a coat, he is her father. Why don't you compromise? She wants him to walk her down the aisle? Let him. But then he leaves after the ceremony and you get to enjoy the reception in peace."

My mind automatically rejected any option that included Gerry, but I had to admit that her idea had merit.

"I don't know. Maybe that could work."

"As far as Bill and Peggy, you have to talk to your mom and let her know this is what Galen wants," Sandy said. "Your mother is a freaking rock, and she'll do anything for those kids. You know that. Talk to her and let her deal with Bill. She's the best at managing him anyway."

Sandy's calm demeanor was bringing my blood pressure back down, but I still felt a measure of panic when I considered everything I needed to deal with.

"Everyone's been so excited about the wedding, and I feel like this is going to ruin it."

But it's not," she said. "At the end of the day, if Tate and Galen are married, and they're happy, that's all that matters. I can tell you from all the weddings I've done flowers for, any number of things can happen, but it's not usually as bad as it seems."

"I don't know. This all seems pretty bad right now. How's Cabe going to react? He had planned on walking his sister down the aisle. To be replaced by Gerry is not going to go over well."

"Cabe's got a good head on his shoulders. He cares a lot about his family. He's gonna do the right thing. You just tell him what you need from him."

"But that's just it, Sandy. Why do we all have to do the right thing, and Gerry doesn't? Why am I still jumping through hoops to make this okay?"

She sighed. "Maybe him walking her down the aisle is the right thing. I don't know. I know you've had to make up for a lot to those kids. But this is kind of the last hurrah. Once Galen's married, you're done with Gerry. She can deal with him if she chooses to. Cabe can do what he wants. But you're done when the wedding is over."

"That's what Dax said." My heart clenched like it was in a vise grip when I said his name.

"Is he there? Is he with you?"

"No. He left. I think I broke up with him."

"What the hell? What do you mean you *think* you broke up with him?"

I closed my eyes and took a deep breath. "I sort of told him we had no future and he needed to go."

"Why would you do that?"

"Because we're complete opposites, Sandy! He's all cowboy, outdoors, sleep in the woods, ride in a truck. And I'm...not."

"From what you told me about your trip to the woods, you adjusted pretty well, Ms. Skinny Dipper. What about all the things the two of you have in common? Are you just scratching those off the list so you can get rid of him?"

"It's not going to work, Sandy. I'm not moving out to that ranch, and he's not moving here."

"I didn't realize the two of you were discussing moving in. When did this happen?"

I groaned and walked out onto the patio to breathe in fresh air. "We haven't discussed it, but I need to be realistic. There's no future with Dax."

"C'mon, Maggie. I know things feel out of control right now, and you're overwhelmed, so you're going to push away the one person you can get rid of. The only problem I see with that strategy is that you're in love with him."

I sat on the sofa and propped my head in my hand.

"I'll take your silence as confirmation that you know I'm right," she said. "Look, Mags. I've been begging you to put yourself out there for years. I know you're scared, and I know this wedding is bringing a lot of things to a head. But you seem to have something pretty special with this guy. Don't let any bullshit with Gerry take that away from you. God knows, he's taken enough already."

"Dax and I were asked by our ballroom dance teacher to perform in a dance recital."

"That's awesome! You two must have some pretty good rhythm. Is this a recital I can attend?"

"I'm not doing it!"

"Why not?" Sandy asked.

I exhaled and rubbed my temples to try and ease the pain. "I can't. I can't get up there and dance after all this time. I can't go from being the principal dancer of Miami City Ballet to doing the cha cha at the community center."

"Mags, nothing you do now will change the fact that you were the principal dancer. That accomplishment stands no matter how your tenure ended. And nothing you do now will change the fact that you haven't been that for thirty years. Let it go. We all can look back at our glory days and wonder where they went. Do you enjoy dancing?"

"Yes."

"Do you enjoy dancing with Dax?"

"God, yes," I said, my voice cracking.

"Then what the hell are you thinking? Dance with the man. It doesn't matter who you were then. It only matters who you are now. If you're going to dance the cha cha at a community center, then be the best damned cha cha dancer there. You've got a cowboy hunk who gives you multiple orgasms in one night, sings to you, watches chick flicks, and wants to dance on a stage with you? Do you realize how ridiculous you sound right now?"

"I was horrible to him, Sandy. I said such nasty things. I really screwed up."

"Then you're telling the wrong person. Hang up and call him. Or better yet, drive to the ranch and show him. Don't let that man wake up tomorrow morning not knowing he's loved."

"But I don't know how this can work. Our lives are so different."

"Give me a break, Mags. No one ever knows how it will work out. We go into it. We give it our all. We do our best. And life throws stuff at us and tries to break us. Sometimes people who seem perfect for each other fail, and sometimes those who seem destined to fail defy all odds and stay together. If you love him, you gotta try."

"What if I get hurt?" I whispered.

"Well, honey, then you retreat, and you lick your wounds and eat a gallon of ice cream, and you put yourself back out there. It's past time to take a risk. You have someone worth taking the risk for."

"Easier said than done. Thanks, Sandy. You're awesome."

She sighed. "Yeah, I am, aren't I? I can dispense all this advice because I lucked up and got the best partner anyone could ever have. Speaking of whom, she's waiting on me to restart the movie. You okay? You off the ledge?"

"Yeah. Give Hannah a hug for me. Tell her I love her. Love you both."

"We love you, too. Now go rope that cowboy."

## 55 NIGHT DRIVE

I feared that if I called and told Dax I was coming, he either wouldn't answer the phone or he'd tell me not to come, so I didn't call.

The first half of the drive, I replayed our conversation in my head, cringing at some of the things I'd said. The second half, I developed a script of what I wanted to say, mentally revising and deleting until the moment I parked by his truck at the barn.

Cody greeted me as soon as I got out of the car, but then he took off and left me behind. There were no lights to guide me as I made my way through the barn, and I nearly broke into a run when the neigh of one of the horses startled me.

The sliding metal door leading out to the camper was open, but the camper was dark. I wondered if it was possible that he'd already gone to bed. I'd changed my clothes and gotten on the road soon after I hung up with Sandy, so he couldn't have been home very long before I arrived. I knocked tentatively just in case he was sleeping, though. I didn't think waking him up would be a good start to my apology.

I waited a few seconds with my head tilted toward the door listening for any sound inside, and then I knocked again, a little bolder than before.

"I'm not sure who you're looking for, but he's not home," came a voice from the darkness, making me nearly jump out of my skin as I yelped in fear.

I turned to see Dax in the large hammock strung from the camper to the tree, his face barely visible in the dark.

"Oh, that's too bad," I said. "I had a message for him." My voice trembled, and I hugged my jacket tighter around me.

"I can give him a message," he said, swaying slightly back and forth in the hammock, bringing his profile in and out of the moonlight.

"I don't know," I said. "When I planned it out in my head, he was supposed to open the door, and then I had this line from a movie I was going to deliver, and he wouldn't have been able to resist."

"Must have been a pretty clever line. Why don't you try it out on me, and I'll let you know if I think it would work."

I walked toward the hammock, my heart in my throat as I considered the very real possibility that I had tossed away the best thing to happen to me in years.

"Well, I would have started by saying hello. And then I would have explained to him that I was overwhelmed earlier. That I felt pressured by Betty, and by dancing, and by my daughter, my family, the wedding, and well, even by him, even though he wasn't directly applying the pressure. I would have told him that I was sorry that I lashed out at him, that I was sorry for the terrible things I said. And then I would have told him that I loved him, and I would have ended by saying that I was just a girl, standing in front of a boy, asking him to love her."

"I don't know about that first part, but the last part was pretty clever."

"It's from *Notting Hill*," I said, wishing he would sit up so I could see his face.

"Yeah, I know."

"So, what do you think he would have said? I mean, if he had opened the door, and I had said all that?"

He put his boot on the ground and stopped the hammock from swinging. Then he sat up and stood, turning up the beer can he held in his hand and draining it.

"Would you like a beer?" he asked, holding one out to me.

"That's what he would have said?" I was fighting to keep my voice light. "That's an odd response."

"I find it interesting that you chose *Notting Hill*. If memory serves me correctly, his argument was that they were too opposite, and it would end up tearing them apart in the long run."

"I didn't…." My voice faltered, and I had no words. I had spoken the truth about our differences, and I couldn't pretend they didn't exist.

He tossed the can in the recycle bin by the barn and popped open another beer, the hiss of the foam loud in the silence of the night. "You were right, you know? We do have several things in common, but we're pretty much opposites. We have a lot we could learn from each other and a lot we could share. I think one of our biggest differences is the way we view love. For you, falling in love seems to be a negative. It hurt you, and it got twisted and warped somehow into something to be avoided at all costs."

He stood up straight and stretched his back before walking to the fence behind the camper.

"See, I was lucky. My experience of love was much different from yours.

I had a love that most people only dream of. The kind that songs are written about. But then I lost it, and I didn't have any hope of ever feeling love again."

He took a swig of beer, his face lit up in the moonlight as he gazed out across the field.

"You were wrong about me not understanding, Maggie. I know all too well about hurting the people you love and not being able to fix it. You're not the only one who's haunted by the past."

I moved toward him, but his stance wasn't welcoming, and I stopped short of going to his side.

"Deanna had gone to her sister's that Sunday. It was the middle of the busy fall season, and we agreed that she would drive up to Revae's that morning and come back that night. I was working around the clock separating calves from the herd and going through all the steps to prepare them to ship out, and I needed her to deal with the thoroughbreds in the barn here so my focus could be there. She called and said Revae wanted her to spend the night, and she didn't feel like driving back so late."

He sighed, and I took another step closer to him.

"I was irritated. I was tired. Exhausted, really. I made some asinine comment about them being her horses and her responsibility, and the conversation grew heated. She insisted it was best for her to spend the night and get up early the next morning to come home. I hung up on her, and I think it was the only time I'd ever done that."

He paused, and I took another step to stand beside him at the fence, though I didn't dare touch him or look at his face. It seemed an intrusion.

"An hour went by and then she called," he said. "But I was mad, so I didn't answer. Then about forty-five minutes later, my phone rang again, and it was a state trooper telling me Deanna's car had left the road. She'd headed home pretty soon after I hung up on her, and she hit a bad storm. A truck pulling a trailer hydroplaned, hitting her car and sending her flying. She flipped multiple times as she left the road, and her car landed upside down a little ways into the woods."

My hand went to my mouth, and I realized I'd been holding my breath as he talked.

"She wasn't conscious when the paramedics reached her, and she never regained consciousness. She stayed in a coma for six weeks. But she had been conscious after the crash. It was her that called for the ambulance, telling them where she was and that she was pinned in the car with no feeling in her legs. According to her phone log, after calling 911, she called me. But I didn't answer. And when I finally listened to her message after the trooper called, there was nothing there. Only silence on the line."

He turned and left the fence, and I didn't know if I should follow him or leave him alone. I heard the door to the camper, and I made my way toward it. He'd left it open, so I assumed he wanted me to come inside.

I didn't see him, and I closed the door behind me and stood waiting, unsure of what to do or say in the light of such heartbreak.

He emerged from the bedroom a moment later, handing me an ultrasound with a grainy picture of a tiny fetus.

"I had no idea she was pregnant. We'd tried for years, and we'd pretty much given up on it ever happening. The doctor told me at the hospital that she was about twelve weeks along. I found a card much later, when I finally had the guts to go through her things. She had planned to tell me over a romantic dinner with that picture of the baby inside the card. She wrote that she waited to tell me until she'd heard the heartbeat and seen the baby move because she wanted to know it was really happening. I'd been too busy to realize why the dinner was important, and I'd put her off when she tried to plan it."

The paper shook in my hand, and I handed it back to him carefully, treating it like the fragile memento it was.

"Deanna hung in there for six weeks defying the doctors who said there was no way she should be alive. I believe she was fighting for that baby. But then on a Thursday morning, she died. And our baby died with her."

His donation to the trauma unit suddenly made sense, and I felt sick as all the dots connected.

"So, I do understand, Maggie, about hurting the people we love and not being able to fix it. And I had resigned myself to never feeling love again. I thought that any happiness I could ever have had died with her. It was my punishment, and I was all too happy to suffer it."

He looked at me then, making eye contact with me for the first time since I'd arrived.

"But then you came along. I looked up and saw you that day when Kratos had tossed me in the water, and it was like something came to life inside my chest. My heart started beating with a purpose it hadn't had in years, and it was like I could finally breathe again for the first time in forever."

He placed the picture on the end table, turning to take my hand and lead me to sit next to him on the couch.

"You see, you run from love because of the pain it caused you. But I'm in awe of love. I can't believe I've been given the opportunity to feel it again. It was my fault Deanna died. She should have been safe at her sister's. She never should have been on the road that night. She should have been able to carry that baby to term and be the mama I always knew she would be. If I had been a better husband, a better man...but I wasn't."

I opened my mouth to say something, but he shook his head and continued.

"I don't know why I got a second chance, Maggie. I don't know why the universe sent you across my path. But I know I was certain my fate meant I would never love again, and then you came. So, I don't intend to pressure you, or push you, but I'll tell you this. I'm not giving up on us without a fight. By God's grace, I've been allowed to fall in love with you, and I'll do everything in my power to protect this and nurture it, to never take it for granted."

I pulled my hands from his and placed them on each side of his face, gazing into eyes haunted but hopeful.

"I don't want you to give up on us. I do love you, Dax, and I'd be lying if I said I wasn't terrified by it, but I can't imagine my life without you in it."

I pressed my lips softly against his, and then his arms were around me, crushing me in an embrace as our passion built and our kiss conveyed the depth of emotions we felt.

Our lovemaking that night was frantic and frenzied, each of us aware of how close we'd come to losing it all. We whispered *I love yous* as we joined our bodies together, clinging to each other long after the desperate need inside us had been satiated, and holding tight to what was precious even in our sleep.

# 56 STAND UP

In the weeks that followed, Dax and I grew closer, and if anything, the things we'd revealed that night only made us appreciate each other more. We didn't specifically address our looming differences or the decisions we'd need to one day make, but we committed to each other that we would work it out when the time came.

It felt as though a huge weight had been lifted from my shoulders, and I relaxed into our relationship with a fresh perspective of enjoying it more and worrying about it less.

Although I still wasn't comfortable with the fact that Gerry was attending the wedding, Sandy's suggestion had lifted another weight from me. Galen was grateful to have Gerry walking her down the aisle, but she agreed it would be better for everyone if he would leave after the ceremony. Part of me had held out hope he might refuse to come, but I didn't want her devastated, so I was relieved for her when she told me he said yes.

In what I am sure was a difficult conversation, Cabe and Galen somehow worked out their views on the subject without me getting in the middle of it, and though I knew it stung Cabe that he wouldn't be walking her down the aisle, he agreed that his sister was entitled to have a different relationship with their father than the one Cabe wanted.

I probably should have told my parents right away about Gerry coming, but I'd avoided it, wanting to put off the inevitable as long as possible.

My father called as I was carrying groceries in from the car. It wasn't unusual for Dad to call me a few times a week, so I didn't think anything of answering.

"Hi, Dad. What's up?" I asked as I set the produce in the sink to be washed.

"Is this true? Is Gerry Tucker coming to Galen's wedding?"

No matter how old I get, the tone of my father's voice can still make my palms damp and twist my stomach in a bundle of nerves. It's like a time travel machine taking me back to being a teenager. A pregnant teenager who had disappointed him and ripped his heart out with her actions.

"I'm fine. Thanks for asking," I said, ignoring his question for the moment as I adjusted the phone on my shoulder.

"Why aren't you doing something about this? This is ridiculous. You can't allow it."

I had dreaded the conversation from the moment the decision was made, and I couldn't help but wonder who had done me the unfortunate favor of telling him before I could.

"It's her wedding, Dad. She's an adult. She's able to invite whomever she chooses."

"No. Absolutely not. You have to put your foot down. He cannot be any part of this wedding."

I stopped myself from sighing, knowing it would only infuriate him more. "Gerry is her father. He has every right to be there."

"No, he doesn't. Creating a child doesn't make you a father."

"Look, Galen wants him there. It's important to her, and it's *her* wedding. We're going to honor her wishes."

"Who's paying for this shindig?"

The sigh escaped me despite my best efforts. "I am, with Galen and Tate's help. Gerry has offered to pay a portion, and I've told him it's not necessary."

"So, you've been in communication with him? Why didn't you tell him he's not welcome?"

I walked to the window and pressed my forehead against it as I gazed out at the pool, drawing strength from the cool glass and the solid surface holding me up.

"Galen wants him there. I'm going to honor her wishes, and I'm going to ask you to put her needs first and do the same."

"Put her needs first? I am putting her needs first. She needs to stay away from him. Evidently, she doesn't understand what kind of monster that man is! What have you told her? Have you told her he ruined your career? That he ruined your life? Have you told her what a lying, no-good, cheating crook he is? Does she know?"

"Dad, c'mon. Let's not do this again."

"You need to remind her of who he is. Of where he was when she was born and why he wasn't there. Have you told her? Does she know?"

I softly banged my forehead against the glass a couple of times and moved to sit in a dining chair.

"She knows plenty, Dad. This is not about me and Gerry. It's about Gerry and Galen. She deserves—"

His voice cut me off in a rage. "She deserves to know what kind of lying scumbag Gerry Tucker is. If you won't tell her, I will."

"Dad, stop! Just stop. Whether you like it or not, that's her father. She's come to some sort of peace with him, and she needs that. This means a lot to her to have her father walk her down the aisle."

"Walk her down the aisle? You've got to be kidding me. Have you lost your mind? I never thought I'd hear you defending Gerry Tucker. Have you forgotten who you're dealing with?"

I closed my eyes and sat back against the chair. "No, Dad. I haven't forgotten at all. And if I ever had forgotten, you would have been all too happy to remind me."

"What's that supposed to mean?"

"It means that I can't ever move past this with you. I will never live down disappointing you. For the rest of your life or for the rest of mine, you're going to keep reminding me how bad I screwed up with Gerry Tucker. No matter what I accomplish in my life, no matter how well those kids are doing as adults, you are still going to hold that against me and not let me forget it."

"You shouldn't forget it. You shouldn't forget what he's capable of. And if anything, you should be protecting her from him."

I raised my hands and looked at the ceiling in exasperation. "I've spent her whole life protecting her! What did that get me? Part of her hates me for not allowing her to know her father. For not allowing him to be part of her life growing up. Maybe I should have. Maybe I should have let them see on their own who he was and what injuries he could cause. But I tried to keep them from that because it was my job to protect them. That's what you said, right? Do you remember what you said to me? What you told me when you found out I was pregnant with Galen? And what you said when you found out that Gerry had gone? Because I sure remember."

He was uncharacteristically silent, and I paused, giving him time to answer and giving me time to calm my voice. When I spoke again, my voice was measured and under control.

"You told me you were ashamed of me. You told me it was an insult to who you were as a father that I would have chosen that man to father my children. You said that if I couldn't pick them any better than that, then I should live my life alone because my kids would be better off with no dad at all than subjected to my poor choices."

The weight of his words thrown back at him hung heavy in the air, and the silence from the other end of the phone was deafening.

"I did what you asked, Dad. I stayed alone. I shunned any attention from any suitor at all to ensure that I wouldn't make the wrong choice again. I gave my life to those kids to make up for the dad I gave them, and I don't regret that. But what did it get us? Galen spent half her life mad as hell at the world and latched onto every man who would pay her the least bit of attention. Cabe damned near destroyed his relationship with Tyler running from the pain of what he saw as his father's rejection. And me? I hit the ripe old age of fifty having long ago closed off my heart to ever loving again. I almost lost the most wonderful, passionate man who somehow sees the moon and stars in me, because you told me I didn't deserve to be loved again."

"I never—"

"Oh, but you did. In so many ways. You might not have said it in words, but your actions and your attitude told me I wasn't worthy of forgiveness. That I wasn't worthy of second chances. That I wasn't capable of picking someone to love. And I believed you."

His voice was quiet, rough with emotion. "That's not fair, Mags. I said those words in anger. In hurt. I was hurt for you. For those kids. I wanted to protect you—and them—and I couldn't. I never meant to make you feel that way. I never wanted you to live your life alone."

A huge lump constricted my throat, and I refused to cry on the phone with him. "Look, Dad, I'm sorry this got heated. The bottom line is this is Galen's wedding. Her life."

"But surely if she knew—"

"Dad, enough. She knows, and she still chooses to have her father in her life. I did as you asked all these years. Now I'm asking that you do as I ask. Honor my wishes, and hers, and stay out of this. I'll talk to you later."

I ended the call without waiting for his answer, and by the time I'd finished making dinner, I felt lighter and stronger. Like I'd faced a dragon and stood my ground.

# 57 CUSTOMIZED BUBBLES

Galen arrived late-July, and as happy as I was to have her home, I missed my privacy. It seemed every spare minute was spent shopping for the wedding, planning for the wedding, discussing the wedding, or crying over the wedding. After a couple of weeks of nonstop drama, I was more than ready for the wedding to be done.

I longed to get back to lazy evenings on the patio with my feet in Dax's lap, or time spent watching movies in bed in the cozy comfort of the camper, and nights spent exploring passion to the point of exhaustion.

Our roles as mother and daughter had somehow reversed. I was the lovesick teenager pining for her beau and counting down the hours to see him again, and Galen was perfectly content to sit home with me while Tate spent the weeks leading up to the wedding with his parents and with friends.

"One more week," I said to Dax as we shared a kiss by his truck after meeting for lunch.

"You sound more excited for this wedding than the bride."

"I'm excited for it to be over and the bride to be out of my house. I love her, but Lord, that girl is high maintenance. I'd forgotten what it was like to live with her."

Dax chuckled and pulled me closer to him. "When do I get to see you again? For an extended period of time longer than lunch?"

"I don't know. What did you have in mind?"

He kissed me, parting my lips with his tongue and giving me a tantalizing reminder of how long it had been since we'd been intimate.

"That's a hint of what I have in mind," he whispered, pulling my hips against his so I could get a better idea of what he was thinking.

"Galen goes to bed pretty late," I toyed with a button on his shirt, "but I could leave the back gate open. You could sneak into my room if you want."

Dax looked up at the sky and grinned. "How old are we again?"

"C'mon. I don't want to get grilled by my daughter for having a man sleep over. Where's your sense of adventure?"

"You're gonna get me shot."

I tossed my head back and laughed. "I guess we can wait another week."

"I didn't say no," he said, taking my chin in his hand and continuing his oral explorations.

We agreed that he'd be at my house at ten-thirty, and I spent the entire night in restless anticipation of his visit.

"Mom, do you think that we should get the place cards printed?" Galen asked as she walked into my room. "Sherry said she'd do them by hand, but I'm thinking they might look better printed. Or we could hire a calligrapher. What's with the candles?"

"Oh, it was smelling stuffy in here, so I lit a couple of candles."

"A couple? It looks like you're getting ready to have a séance. And did you spray perfume?" She scrunched her nose and sniffed the air.

"Yeah. I spritzed on some perfume."

Galen shrugged. "Okay, because that's not weird at all. So, what do you think we should do about the place cards? I need to make a decision if we're going to hire someone."

"I think you already told Sherry she could do them. You don't want to call her this close in and tell her you changed your mind. It will be fine."

I glanced at the clock again. It was a few minutes after ten. I faked a huge yawn and stretched. "I'm gonna hit the hay. I've got a long day tomorrow. You sleep well, honey."

Her expression was puzzled as I hugged her.

"Are you okay? You're being really weird."

"I'm fine. I'm ready to go to bed. That's all."

"All right. Well, I'm going to go online and see if it's too late to order bubbles."

"I thought you weren't going to do bubbles."

She frowned. "I wasn't. I wanted to do birdseed, but I guess Bronwyn said they don't do that for some reason. Then I wanted to do butterflies, but Tyler said that's a disaster since some of the butterflies don't wake up or thaw out in time and then you have some that arrive dead. I definitely don't want dead butterflies. That's not romantic. Tate wants to do sparklers, but I told him no way. I'm not risking my dress getting burned. So, I guess I'm going to order bubbles if I can get the customized ones shipped. If not, I'll have to get some generic ones at the craft store."

I couldn't stop glancing at the clock as she talked, and I thought she was never going to finish.

"Bubbles are a great idea. Good night, honey."

"Hey, did you ever hear back from Dax about the arbor? Is he definitely able to do that? Because if not, Tate's dad said he might could build something. But to be honest, I think this Dax guy would probably be a bit more skilled with a hammer than Tate's dad. Dax is more rugged, you know? Who would have ever thought you would date somebody rugged?"

I kept an eye on the French doors in case he arrived early. "Indeed. Who would have thought? Good night, sweetheart."

"Okay. Good night. Boy, you really must be tired. I can't even talk to you about the wedding," she said as I put my hand on her lower back and gently nudged her toward the door.

"Honey, I love talking about your wedding. But we've talked about the wedding pretty much nonstop since you came home. And we'll talk about the wedding again tomorrow. I'm sure of it. But right now, I'm ready to go to bed."

"Well, good night," she said as she stood in the hallway and stared at me.

"Good night. I love you." I closed the bedroom door and ran to the French doors leading out to the patio, swinging them open so Dax could come right in when he arrived. I had already folded back the duvet and put the pillows away, and my entire body pulsated in anticipation of his touch.

I was listening hard for his arrival, and the gate creaked at exactly ten-thirty. I went to the open doors and looked across the patio to the rest of the house. The kitchen light was on, but I could hear the television in the living room, so I was relatively certain Galen wasn't in the kitchen. If she was on the couch where I guessed she would be, there was no way she'd be able to see Dax enter.

I covered my mouth with my hand to suppress the laughter when I saw him tiptoe around the side of the house and scurry across my end of the patio to duck inside my room.

"Hello there, Maggie Mae," he whispered, picking me up in a big bear hug and spinning me around as we kissed.

I slid down the front of his body and pushed away from him long enough to close the French doors.

"Did you have any problems getting in?" I said as I returned to his arms.

"No. I parked down the street, just in case, and I came in between your house and your neighbor's, praying they didn't have any motion lights or sensors on the side of their house."

I chuckled at the mental image of Dax caught in floodlights, and then I took his hand and led him to the bed.

"God, I've missed you in my arms," he said, kicking off his boots and climbing into bed to face me as we lay on our sides.

"It's funny, because we don't normally see each other more than two or three times a week, but feeling like I *can't* see you is torture."

"You're telling me. Are you sure you don't want to just explain to your daughter that you're an adult?"

"Another time. She's under so much stress right now with the wedding, and I didn't even tell her we were dating until she got here. I don't want to push her over the edge. No one wants to think of their mother having sex, you know?"

"I certainly don't," Dax scoffed with a bit of a shudder. "But don't you think she may assume?"

"Maybe. But it's different when it's in your face, and you can't deny it. She's only met you the one time at lunch, so I don't know how she'd feel about knowing you were spending the night. I just want to give her more time."

"Speaking of time, when do I have to sneak back out and leave?"

"Oh, she's never up early. You can leave when I do."

"So, I get to sleep with you in my arms? How heavenly!"

He untied the sash on my robe and tucked his hands inside it, running his hands over my gown and caressing me through the layer of silk that separated us.

"Is this new?" he asked, burying his face in my neck. "I like it. It's soft."

I nodded as I lifted my hands to sink my fingers into his hair, pulling him closer to me as his lips nibbled along my neck and the sensitive area behind my ear.

He shifted his weight to put me onto my back, his leg over mine as he pushed the robe out of his way and skimmed his hand over my body and down to the edge of the gown. He continued to explore my neck and shoulder with his tongue as he slid his hand underneath the bottom of the gown, slowly pushing the silk upward as his fingers spread across my inner thigh. A delightful, ticklish tremor ran over me, and I giggled as I shuddered.

My body yearned for him, and I lifted my hips toward his hand as he pushed the silk above my thighs and slid his fingers into the wetness between them.

"You're not wearing any panties," he whispered as his mouth left my collarbone for his teeth to pull at my nipple through the silk gown.

"That's very perceptive of you," I said, gasping as his fingers found their rhythm and his tongue flicked across the sensitive peak of my breast.

"Mom?" Galen's voice came through the door, and I shoved Dax to the side, pulling my gown over my legs and clutching the robe around me.

"Yes, dear?"

She tried the knob, and I was grateful that I had flipped the lock when I closed it.

I jumped from the bed and hastily tied the robe sash, motioning to Dax to get in the bathroom and flinging open the door once he was safely out of sight.

"Why is your door locked?" Galen said, her face scrunched together in confusion. "You never lock your door."

"Oh, must have been an accident," I said, stretching my arm up and along the edge of the door, effectively blocking her from entering.

"I found these bubbles, but I'm not sure which font I should use and whether or not I should do our names or our initials. I'm just thinking the names are going to be so tiny that no one will see them, you know? But if I get the initials, do I get my initials and his initials or since we'll be married by the time they do bubbles, do I get our first initials together with the same initial for the last name? I have to order them by midnight tonight to get the customized version in time, and then we'll have to pay expedited shipping."

"Do first initials and same last one. Good night, honey."

Her eyes suddenly opened wider as she looked past me into my room, and I turned to follow her gaze. Dax's boots were laying on the floor at the foot of my bed with his belt tossed across them.

"Mom," she whispered, her eyes and mouth both open wide. "Do you have a man in your bedroom? Ha! Oh my God. You do! You snuck your boyfriend in your bedroom! This is awesome. This is classic. What are you, trying to be Galen now? I thought I was the only one to sneak guys in the house." She burst out laughing as hot blood rushed to my face and a flush of sweat covered me.

"Hey, you were sixteen at the time. I'm fifty. There's a big difference."

"Go, Mom!" She lifted her hand for a high-five, and I reluctantly gave her one. "I didn't know old people still did stuff like this. That's awesome!"

"Old people? Really?"

"You know what I mean. I'm not saying you're old or anything, but this kind of gives me hope for the future. Wow."

I put my hands on my hips and stuck my tongue out at her. "Well, now that I've assured you that sex doesn't end at thirty, can I please close my door?"

She shook her head rapidly and put her hand over her eyes. "Oh, God. I'm gonna be sitting in the living room knowing that the two of you are having sex right down the hall. That's gross. Sorry," she said, spreading her fingers to look at me, "but that's disgusting."

"We'll try not to be loud. Good night, Galen," I said, closing the door and flipping the lock.

"I hope you're using protection," she shouted as she went down the hall. "I don't need any younger siblings running around."

"Mother Nature already took care of that!" I shouted back as I turned to watch Dax come out of the bathroom.

"So, the cat's out of the bag?" he asked.

"I suppose."

"You want me to go?"

"Hell, no!" I said, dropping my robe and pulling the gown over my head as I crossed the floor to put my arms around him. "She already knows you're here now." I tugged at his shirt until he lifted his arms for me to pull it over his head. "How about you finish what you started, cowboy?"

# 58 POOL PARTY

"Are you sure you want to do this?" I asked Dax as we stood outside my front door. Laughter and conversation from the back patio and pool was loud enough that we could hear it in front of the house.

"I already said I did," he replied with a grin.

"I know, but it's gonna be loud. And wild. You'll probably get asked a million questions, and they'll probably try to embarrass me or something. I thought it would be easier for you to meet everybody here, you know? At the rehearsal tomorrow and the wedding Saturday, there will be so much going on and so many people. Not that there's not a lot of people here, but there will be more there. The most important people are here. The ones I want you to meet. To spend time with."

"Maggie, I already agreed to do this. I want to do it. So, are you going to try to talk me out of it, or are you going to open the door so we can go inside?"

"Thank you. Really. I mean, you've already met Cabe and Tyler, and you've already met Galen. But my parents are here. Sandy and Hannah. Alberto. Some of my cousins. It's a lot."

"Maggie? It's fine."

"I'm sorry. I've never done this before. I've never introduced a boyfriend to everyone. I never knew it would be so nerve-wracking. Okay, I'm opening the door now."

"That's good. I brought ice cream, as you requested, and if you wait any longer, it's going to be dripping all over us."

I swung open the door and entered the chaos, hoping my family and friends would go easy on him. Not that I didn't think Dax could handle it, but it was an odd feeling to love someone so much and want them to be accepted by the others you loved. Unfortunately, given my background, that wasn't something I'd ever experienced.

"I thought you guys were never gonna come inside, Mom," Galen said. "Were you making out on the porch or something?"

I ignored her dig, one of several she'd made since discovering I was a red-blooded human being who actually still had sex at the ripe old age of fifty. It was a mind-boggling concept for her.

"Here," I said, taking the bag from Dax and giving it to Galen. "Put this ice cream in the freezer."

Dax and I held hands as we passed through the French doors and onto the patio. Cabe and my father were at the grill cooking hot dogs and hamburgers. Tyler, Sandy, and Hannah were discussing Rome with Alberto. My mother was sitting on the side of the pool with her feet in the water, talking to my cousin Bree, who was holding her grandson Daniel as he splashed in her arms. Daniel's dad, my cousin Danny, was playing Frisbee with Tate.

"Hey everybody! Listen up. Mom's boyfriend is here!" Galen shouted from behind us as she came out onto the patio. I glared at her, but before I could say anything, we were surrounded by smiling faces.

I introduced him to everyone, and to his credit, he never let on if he was overwhelmed. His smile came easy, and his laugh was hearty, and before too long, he was in the yard tossing the Frisbee like he'd been part of the family all along.

"He's a hottie," Sandy said as we made margaritas at the pool bar. "Damn, girl. I had a mental image from all these stories you've been telling me, but I underestimated your descriptions."

"He *is* fine," Hannah said, gazing across the pool to the yard where Dax was jumping to catch the Frisbee. "You did good, Mags."

"Thanks. If my lesbian friends are impressed with my boyfriend's looks, then he must be pretty hot, huh?"

We laughed as I poured the margaritas into glasses.

Everyone seemed to snag a moment alone with Dax at some point in the evening. I'd look up to see him deep in conversation, and if he happened to catch me staring, he'd smile and give me a wink guaranteed to turn me on no matter who I was talking to.

"I must say, I'm impressed to see the two of you still together," Alberto said as he watched me flambé Galen's special request of Bananas Foster. "You seem very happy, Mags. Content. Peaceful."

"I am. I don't even know how to describe it, because it's not something I ever felt before. I was happy before. But this is different. It's like I didn't know anything was missing, and now that he's here, I can't imagine how I would ever be without him."

Alberto leaned on the counter and watched me spoon the hot caramel mixture into bowls.

"So, should I be looking for a new pool house to rent when I visit Orlando, or is there room for me out at the ranch?"

I shot him a look. "Don't get ahead of yourself. I don't think either of us will be giving up our houses any time soon. We have talked about it—briefly, not in any depth, mind you—but we're both happy the way things are. I have my independence. My house. My schedule. He has his. We're together any time we can be or want to be. It's working for us. And as long as it is, we won't make any changes."

"Hear, hear to the modern romance," Alberto said, raising his wine glass to me.

"You need any help, Maggie?" Tyler asked, peeking around the French door leading to the patio.

"Yes, sweetie. As a matter of fact, if you can carry these bowls out as I get them filled, that would be great. If not, the ice cream may all be melted by the time it's served. Alberto, grab the spoons? The dessert spoons. Third drawer down over by the desk. Ty, ask Dax if he'd rather have chocolate cake or Bananas Foster."

Tyler took the bowls outside, and within a couple of minutes, Dax came in.

"Can I have both?" he asked, coming behind me at the counter and placing his hands on my waist.

"You certainly can. But not on the same plate. Those two flavors shouldn't marry."

"Ha! Mom, you said marry! And I'm getting married!" Galen shouted as she came in the house and headed down the hall to the restroom.

"Someone's had too much wine," Alberto said with a chuckle.

"Mr. Bill said he wants chocolate cake," Tyler said, loading her arms with another round of bowls.

"Like I don't know that, Dad. I made the chocolate cake specifically for him because he hates Bananas Foster." I shook my head as I put a slice of chocolate cake on a plate with a scoop of ice cream over it.

"You need any help?" Dax asked.

"No, I'm good." I turned in his arms and gave him a quick kiss, holding my hands out away from him so I didn't get smudges of chocolate, ice cream, or caramel sauce on his shirt. "You having a good time?"

"I'm having a great time," he said. "I'm gonna get in the pool after we have dessert. You want to join me?"

"She can't. Her mad drawing skills are needed for Pictionary," Sandy said as she came inside and grabbed a roll of paper towels. "And if anyone asks, you want to be on Maggie's team."

"Pictionary, huh?" Dax said as I turned back to serving dessert. "You never told me about these mad drawing skills of yours."

"She's amazing," Alberto said. "She can guess from little more than a straight line with uncanny accuracy."

Four rounds of Pictionary later, I had retained my family title of champion, and Dax proclaimed that I did indeed have mad skills.

Eventually, the party began to wind down. Bree and Danny left with Daniel. My mother helped clean the kitchen and then announced she was retiring to the pool house for a shower and bed. Cabe and Tyler left to go let Deacon out since they'd left him at home, unsure of how the crazy dog would react with so many people.

My dad moved to the living room to watch sports updates, and Galen and Tate were in the shallow end of the pool, wrapped in each other's arms and whispering to one another.

"We're going to head out," Sandy said. "I'll see you tomorrow at the rehearsal, Dax. Mags, I'll see you in the morning for brunch."

I hugged her and Hannah and thanked them both for coming, then turned to Alberto.

"It's so odd for you to be in town and not be staying with me. I'm sorry I had to boot you."

He smiled, and his blue eyes were warm as he took my hand. "Honey, your parents and your daughter take precedent for sleeping space. I get it. The hotel you put me in has room service and a fabulous spa, so I'm happy."

"All right. I'll call you if we're able to do lunch tomorrow, but more than likely I'll have to wait and see you at the rehearsal."

"No worries. I'll book a massage and relax by the hotel pool if you girls are busy. Dax, nice meeting you," Alberto said, releasing my hand to shake Dax's.

"Likewise," Dax said. "Look forward to talking more this weekend."

"Bye, Mags. Love you." Alberto hugged me and followed Sandy and Hannah out the door.

"I better get going, too," Dax said when we were alone. "Although I wish I didn't have to. I loved watching you tonight. You looked so happy. So loved. You have this beautiful light that shines through you, Maggie Mae. I'm a very lucky man."

I stood on tiptoes to kiss him, and he wrapped his arms around me, deepening the kiss beyond what I was comfortable with when my father or daughter might walk through the room at any time.

"Behave," I whispered. "You're going to get me in trouble."

"I want you," he said with his lips against my ear, his voice so low that I could barely hear him. "When can I have you again?"

"Two more days, love, and the wedding will be over."

"Until then." He smiled and released me, but took my hand and brought it to his lips. "You know I love you."

I nodded, my heart swelling with happiness. "You know you're loved."

"Yes, I do," he said, smiling as he let go of my hand. I watched him walk to the truck and drive away before going back inside.

My father was in the kitchen, helping himself to the chocolate cake.

"Another piece?" I asked, arching an eyebrow.

"Don't tell your mother. You know I can't resist your chocolate cake. You make the best there is."

"Thanks, Dad." I took the cake server and washed it, then I replaced the lid on the cake plate.

"He's nice," Dad said. "I like him."

"He is nice, isn't he? I like him, too." My smile beamed as I wiped down the counter.

"I never wanted you to be unhappy, Margaret. You deserve all the happiness in the world. And all the love, too."

I turned my back to rinse my hands in the sink, fighting to swallow the emotion that had risen in my throat at his words.

"I didn't realize I'd never told you," he said, pausing to take a breath, "but I am incredibly proud of you. I'm proud of the mother you are, the woman you are, the way you've lived your life. I couldn't be more proud. In fact, you are what I am most proud of in my life. I'm sorry you didn't know that. You are the best thing that ever happened to your mother and me, Maggie."

The lump wouldn't go down, and I blinked back tears as I turned to throw my arms around his neck. He hugged me tight and patted my back.

"Thanks, Dad."

He pulled back and looked at me, his own eyes misty. "If you love this fellow, then you have my full support. Be happy, Maggie."

I nodded. "I will, Dad. I love you."

I hugged him again, and he squeezed his arms around me. "I love you, too, baby girl."

# 59 WE ARE FAMILY

Galen and Tyler had both told me the resemblance between Jeffrey and Cabe was startling, but when I saw him at the wedding rehearsal, I couldn't believe my eyes. It was like my son had a twin I'd never known. They shared the same facial structure, the same eyes, nose, and mouth. Jeffrey didn't have a beard, and his hair was darker, but they were of equal height and the overall similarities were downright eerie.

I couldn't stop staring at him, and when he'd noticed for the fourth time, I smiled and apologized.

"I'm sorry," I said. "I know I keep staring at you, but I can't get over how much the two of you look alike."

He smiled. "I think it catches everyone off guard. We've gotten used to being asked if we're twins when we go places together."

I nodded, wondering how often the two of them had been doing things together. I made a mental note to ask Cabe once the wedding weekend was over.

Julie was delightful, but it was bizarre to see her and Galen share such closeness. In fact, the four of them—Cabe, Jeffrey, Julie, and Galen—all interacted with such ease and camaraderie that I felt like I was the outsider with my own children at times.

It was surreal.

When I had first learned of Jeffrey and Julie's existence, they were daggers who pierced my heart and rendered it unable to keep beating at any regular pace. Knowing there were children in his marriage was the final painful nail that sealed the coffin on anything Gerry could have said to me, and it had set in motion the path that would leave my children without a father.

But these two adults who stood before me and laughed in unison with my own children were blameless in my painful journey. It was impossible to hold the past against them in any way, no matter how awkward it was to accept their presence as normal.

The day had been splendid so far. We'd enjoyed a ladies brunch with Galen and her bridesmaids as well as Tyler, Sandy, Hannah, Julie, and my mom, after which we all went for manicures.

The rest of the afternoon had been a blur of last-minute preparations with my house filled with female chatter.

The fact that Gerry would be at the rehearsal had been in my thoughts the entire day, and though I dreaded seeing him, I was anxious to get the whole event underway.

"Any sign of Galen's father?" Dax asked as we stood on the back porch of the house at Silver Creek and watched Bronwyn line up the wedding party under the oak tree.

"No. Evidently, he texted Galen that he was running late. It looks like they're almost done here, so with any luck, he won't make it before it's over."

"Hmm. Did you find out if he's planning on being at the rehearsal dinner?"

I turned to look up at Dax. "Galen said no. Do you want to go ahead and head over there? Bronwyn already told me where I sit and when I walk down the aisle, so I don't need to be here."

"Sure. Whatever you want to do," Dax said.

I walked over to the ceremony site and told Galen we would see her at the rehearsal dinner at Tate's parents' house.

"Okay, Mom. We're almost finished. Can you take my bag from the car and leave it in the bridal suite?"

"Sure, sweetheart."

Dax and I walked to my car and retrieved her suitcase for the honeymoon, carrying it up to the bridal suite so she wouldn't have to worry with it on the wedding day.

I looked at the upstairs room through a different lens knowing that it had been meant for Dax and Deanna, and as I watched him put the suitcase by the fireplace, my heart hurt to think of how painful the room must be for him.

He had turned to go back downstairs when I noticed I could see the ceremony site through the sliding glass doors. I went and looked down at the group, surprised to see that Gerry had arrived while Dax and I were in the house.

His hair was nearly all gray, with only a tinge of its original color left. I couldn't see his face clearly, but even from the second-floor window, I could tell he'd aged considerably in the years since I'd seen him. I watched Galen hug him, but my eyes were on Cabe as Gerry shook Tate's hand. My son's back was ramrod straight and stiff, and I noticed Tyler immediately went to Cabe's side.

Gerry shook Jeffrey's hand and gave Julie a kiss on the cheek, and I was struck by how cold their interactions appeared. He nodded to Cabe, who nodded back, and then Gerry turned his focus to Galen.

It was the first time their father had been in the same place with the four children, and I wondered if it was lost on him how wrong that was.

"So that's Gerry?" Dax asked behind me as he looked out the window.

"That's Gerry."

"I don't like him," Dax said with a shrug.

I smiled. "Me, either. Something else we have in common."

"You want to go out there?"

"Not at all."

"You ready to go then?"

"Yeah," I said, sliding my arm around his waist as we descended the stairs, both of us leaving our past behind as we exited the house.

# 60 HEAD HELD HIGH

Galen and I had stayed up late watching movies and talking after the rehearsal dinner, enjoying the bittersweet moments of bonding on the last night she'd be in my home as a single woman.

The morning of the wedding dawned bright and beautiful, but already hot as blazes before the sun was very high in the sky.

The day was a whirlwind of hair and makeup appointments and fielding phone calls from various family members and friends. I didn't envy Tyler her job as a wedding planner after seeing the chaos first-hand, and I knew it was even harder on her to play the double role of sister-in-law and planner, though I'm sure Bronwyn's presence was a big help.

Dax was on a ladder assisting Sandy with the floral decorations on the arbor he'd built for Galen's ceremony, and I was enjoying the shade of the back porch while the photographer conducted pre-ceremony photos on the lawn. At Tyler's suggestion, Tate and Galen had opted to do all their pictures ahead of time, forgoing the tradition of the bride avoiding the groom so they could get outside shots without worrying about the impending darkness after the sunset ceremony.

"She's beautiful, isn't she?"

I stiffened at the sound of Gerry's voice so close behind me as I watched Galen and Cabe laugh and pose for a photo. I thought I'd been prepared for the inevitable moment that we'd be thrown together in the same space, but as the anger twisted my stomach in knots, I realized I'd never be ready to exchange pleasantries with him. Especially not about my daughter.

"She looks so much like you," he said. "Like you did then. Of course, you haven't aged a bit. Still beautiful as ever."

"Don't," I said, forcing my voice to show no emotion.

He moved to stand shoulder to shoulder with me, and I stood my ground, resisting the urge to sidestep away from him.

"Will we ever be able to look at our daughter, at our children, and have a civil conversation? Without you sounding like you'd rather stab my eyes out than look at me?"

My stomach revolted at him calling them 'our' children, and I moved my hand over my abdomen to calm the storm inside.

"I've apologized so many times over the years that I have no more words left to say I'm sorry," he said, his voice no louder than a whisper. "Can you not find it in your heart to forgive me? Even now? When they both clearly want you to?"

I turned to face him, my hands clenched in fists by my side. "You have no idea what they want. You may be able to manipulate her, for now, but don't think I don't see it. You'll never play Cabe. He'll never be putty in your hands."

He flashed a faint smile as he looked away from me, toward Cabe and Galen as they laughed in an embrace with Tyler and Tate, smiling for the camera and oblivious to our exchange.

"Is that what you think you were? Putty in my hands?"

I scoffed and turned back to watch the kids, crossing my arms and tucking my hands in so he wouldn't see them shaking.

"Do you want to know my biggest regret, Maggie?"

The silence I offered in answer didn't faze him.

"I know I've made mistakes—big ones, to be sure. I've hurt people. I've nearly destroyed my family. I've done things I can't take back."

"I'm glad you can acknowledge all that," I ground out through gritted teeth. "It's nice to know you have regrets. You should regret not being there for your kids. Any of them. From any of the women you sired them with."

"So much anger still. You know they say there's a fine line between love and hate. Have you ever considered that maybe the reason you're still so upset is because you know what we had was real?"

I wanted to hit him. I wanted to claw at his face with my nails until his flesh was shredded and torn. I wanted to kick him in the crotch and stand over him while he writhed in pain.

Cabe's eyes met mine as they posed for one last shot, and the concern and anger that flashed across his expression darkened his features.

I smiled and shook my head, trying to convey that I was all right and willing him not to make a scene and draw attention to Gerry and me. I would allow nothing that Gerry Tucker did to mar Galen's special day.

"It's you," Gerry said, his voice so close and low that my skin crawled. "I loved you, Willow. I know you will never believe me, but I will swear on my deathbed that it's true. I knew it the first time I laid eyes on you, and I should have handled the whole thing differently. The biggest regret of my life is screwing that up. I should have ended things with Margot before I ever let things start with us. I should have stayed away from you until I was a free man, and I shouldn't have taken what you freely gave until I was able to return the gift. I just loved you too much to let go."

"I believe if memory serves me correctly, it was the money you loved too much to let go."

He shrugged.

"I can admit that. I was scared to give up the money. I didn't know how to exist without it. I didn't know who I was without it. But I did love you. You were the love of my life. You're not the only one who was in pain. I had to live without the one person I most wanted to be with."

A guttural laugh escaped me. "Just stop. You made that choice. You had all the information. I didn't. You made choices for both of us. For all of us. Don't pretend now that it meant something it didn't."

"It was our child who carried my brother's name. It was you who has haunted my dreams every night since we parted. Losing you was the one mistake I could never escape. I wanted that life with you so badly."

Cabe was walking toward us, and I could see Galen behind him, still standing with Tate though her eyes were on Gerry and me, her face filled with concern.

"That life was a lie," I said, stepping off the porch to walk toward my son and head off any confrontation.

"I wanted it to be true," Gerry said.

I looked back over my shoulder at him but never stopped walking away. "Wanting something to be true doesn't make it true."

I closed the distance quickly to meet Cabe, looping my arm through his as he glared past me at Gerry.

"C'mon," I said. "Let's go back over here with your sister."

"You okay?"

I nodded, patting his arm and intertwining our fingers. "I'm fine, handsome. As long as you and Galen are happy, I'm fine. Blessed beyond measure."

He stole a glance back toward Gerry, and when the tension released from Cabe's body, I knew he wasn't following us. My own shoulders relaxed and though the knot in my stomach was still tight, I no longer felt like its contents might be thrown all over the lawn.

"Everything okay?" Galen asked, leaving Tate's side to come and place her hand on my arm.

"Yes. Everything's fine. Don't you worry. This is your day, sweetheart, and you have nothing to worry about."

She smiled, and seeing her happy strengthened me.

"I wanted to get a pic with Da—with Gerry. Is that okay with you? I won't do it if it upsets you."

A tiny knife pierced the knot in my stomach and twisted it tighter.

"Of course. Yes. You need a picture with him." My voice sounded high-strung, and I swallowed hard against the bile that rose in my throat. I turned and saw that Gerry was still standing on the porch where I'd left him, his eyes fixed on Galen and me.

"Gerry?" I called out in the friendliest voice I could muster. "Galen would like a photo with you."

Surprise registered on his face, and he looked uncertain. It was not a look I'd seen on him very often, and more than ever in that moment, I saw his age. The lines on his face. The gray in his hair. The weight of a lifetime of selfish lies pulling his shoulders down.

Cabe squeezed my hand as Gerry joined Galen in front of the camera, and Tyler slid her arm around my waist as she squeezed from the other side. I could tell they thought they were holding me up, bolstering me against watching Gerry and Galen together, something I'd fought against for her entire life.

While I appreciated the support, both physically and emotionally, my head was held high of its own accord. I may have made mistakes in choosing their father, but I'd done my best by my kids to protect them from him. As adults, they needed to make their own choices regarding him, and I needed to support them. Even if that meant allowing them to get hurt.

I watched Galen as she looked up at him, her hands in his. Her face was a mixture of adoration and apprehension, and I knew she was more worried that he would hurt her than she had let on.

She was strong, though. She was a fighter. And I knew she would be okay in the end.

She was her mother's daughter, after all.

He may have broken the girl I was, but the woman I became had come out on top in every way.

I let go of Cabe's hand and stepped out of Tyler's embrace. "I'm gonna go check and see how Dax and Sandy are doing with the arbor."

# 61 A UNIFIED FRONT

Everyone sought the comfort of air conditioning as soon as the ceremony ended, filing inside the main house to enjoy passed hors d'oeuvres and hit the bar for refreshments as they sighed in relief to be out of the heat.

Cabe had not acknowledged his father's presence other than a brief nod the two exchanged when Gerry arrived. He had focused on his sister's smile to avoid watching their father escort her down the aisle in a show of pomp and circumstance that the man should never have had a part of.

He'd promised Galen he would keep quiet and not make a scene, but when Cabe saw Gerry go out on the back porch of the house as everyone else was enjoying the cocktail reception, he excused himself from conversation and followed his father outside.

"Isn't it time for you to be leaving?" Cabe asked as he walked up to Gerry with his arms crossed. "You agreed to go after the ceremony."

"Ah, Cable. You decided you'd speak to the old man after all."

"You've done your part. Now go."

"You know," Gerry said, lighting a cigarillo and turning it between his fingers, "at some point, you're going to fall off that high horse you ride on. You look down at me, but you're going to make your mistakes in life, son, and you'll see that none of us are perfect."

"Say your goodbyes to Galen and leave."

"I'm enjoying time with my daughter. In fact, I'm enjoying having all my children together for the first time. I don't think I'm ready to leave yet."

"All your children? Aren't you forgetting about the two daughters in Arizona? Or do you not acknowledge them?"

Gerry raised his eyebrows and took a long drag on the cigarillo. "You think you know so much, Cable. Maybe you need to ask your sister if she wants me to go. It's her wedding, after all. I'm here at her invitation, not

304

yours. I've walked her down the aisle, at her request. And now I intend to stay and have a father/daughter dance. Also at her request."

"That wasn't the agreement," Cabe said, his jaw tight and his voice barely concealing his anger.

"Well, the agreement changed. Talk to the bride."

Gerry exhaled smoke in Cabe's direction and turned to face the lake in a dismissive gesture.

"The agreement stands. You're not welcome here, and you're not staying for the reception. My mother and my family will enjoy this celebration without you here putting a damper on everyone's spirits. You're leaving now." Cabe's voice didn't waver, and his stance didn't change.

"Again, you need to take this up with the bride. I've already promised my daughter a dance."

"I'm not taking anything up with the bride. She knows what the agreement was. You're going to go in and tell her that something came up and you need to go."

Gerry blew smoke up at the sky and laughed, though his laughter held no humor. "Why would I do that? Why would I break my daughter's heart on her wedding day when I've just promised her a dance?"

"Because that's what you do," Cabe said. "You break promises. You break hearts. She's going to learn that eventually anyway, and it might as well be now. You're not robbing my mother of the opportunity of enjoying this night. She has given her entire adult life to us. She picked up the pieces after you left and made sure we had everything we needed to thrive despite you. Tonight, she gets to reap her rewards and enjoy this special occasion for our family. *You* are not part of our family."

"And what are you going to do if I say no, Cable?" Gerry dropped the cigarillo and ground it out with the toe of his shoe, sticking his hands in pockets.

"I'll remove you myself."

"And I'll help him," said Jeffrey, behind Cabe.

If Cabe was surprised that his brother had walked up behind him, he didn't show it. He didn't react at all.

Gerry, on the other hand, looked up with eyes wide and eyebrows raised as he stared at his sons. "Really, Jeffrey? Choosing sides?"

"And I don't think they need my help," Dax said, stepping out on the porch from where he'd stood listening just inside the door, "but if they do, they have it."

"And who are you?" Gerry asked, his eyebrows pulled together as he lifted his head to look at the taller man.

"I'm the one with the legal recourse to kick you off my property, but I'm also the one you'll have to come through if I think you're going to cause Maggie or her family any unhappiness at all."

The three men stood side by side facing Gerry, unified with crossed arms and wide stances.

"Ah, looks like Maggie has herself a lovesick suitor. Great. Look, you can't possibly expect me to go in there and tell Galen that I'm leaving. You're all railing at me not to make people unhappy, and yet you're asking me to do just that."

"She'll be fine," Cabe said.

"So, then you go tell her you're asking me to leave."

Cabe shook his head. "No. For once, you're going to take responsibility and suffer the consequences. You're going to hold up your end of the agreement, and it's going to be on you."

Gerry sighed and looked back toward the lake, rubbing his hand over his chin.

"It wasn't that great of a party anyway," he said, glaring at Dax. "The food sucks."

He moved to go past the three men, but when none of them stepped aside, Gerry was forced to go off the porch to get around them.

"You forgot your butt," Dax said, pointing to the remnants of the cigarillo on the ground. "There's a trash receptacle right over there."

Gerry met Dax's eyes with a forced grin, and then he turned to pick up the cigarillo butt, tossing it in the can as he went back inside.

Cabe watched through the window as Gerry went to Galen, pulling her aside as they talked with bent heads, and then making his way toward the front door.

"Thank you," Cabe said with a nod to Jeffrey and Dax.

"Any time, brother," Jeffrey said, clapping his hand on Cabe's shoulder as they entered the party together.

Cabe went to Galen immediately. "You okay?" he asked.

Her smile was genuine, and her eyes were bright as she hugged him. "Yeah, I'm great. I just got married!"

"I saw Gerry talking to you. Everything all right?"

"Yeah. He had wanted to stay and do some kind of dance, but I had told him I didn't think it was a good idea. He insisted at first, but then he said he'd thought about it more and decided to just go. That's best, don't you think?"

Cabe nodded. "Yeah, I think that's best."

"You're going to dance with me, right?"

"Hell, yeah!" Cabe put his arms around his little sister, holding her tight as he met his wife's gaze from across the room and winked at her.

# 62 FULL MOON

"Do I want to know what that was about?" I asked as Dax joined me by the bar.

"What?"

I rolled my eyes and cocked my head to the side to stare at him. "You, my son, and his brother on the back porch with Gerry? And then Gerry coming in to talk to Galen privately and leaving?"

"It was a matter regarding taking out the trash."

I nodded slowly, willing to let it go for the moment since he didn't seem to want to say more. "Should I be concerned?"

Dax shook his head. "Not at all."

"If you say so."

Someone tapped my arm, and the rest of the night flew by in a blur of conversations, dances, and laughter.

Dax coaxed my mother onto the dance floor more than once, and I couldn't remember the last time I'd seen her laugh so much.

At one point, we were all out there dancing—Cabe with Tyler, Galen with Tate, Mom with Dad, and Dax with me. It was one of those freeze moments, the kind of experience that makes you wish time would stop so you could soak up all the enjoyment possible from the happiness you're feeling.

"He's quite a dancer, your Dax," Mom said as we blotted our makeup with towels in the restroom.

"Yes, he is."

"A man that can dance like that has to be pretty skilled in other areas as well."

My mouth dropped open, and I stared at her reflection in the mirror. "Mom!"

"What? You think just because I'm seventy-five, I don't think about that sort of thing? Your father has always been a wonderful dancer, you know."

"Mom, stop. That's disgusting."

The irony wasn't lost on me that it really didn't matter how old you were. No one wanted to think of their mother and sex.

"He's got a good heart, that one," she said, meeting my eyes in the mirror. "He loves you, Margaret. You can see it written all over his face every time he looks at you. The way he speaks of you! Oh. It makes my heart happy, dear. You've endured enough loneliness for a lifetime. Be happy. Enjoy this man's love. And enjoy his skills!" She laughed and patted my arm as she turned to go, and I looked at my reflection in the mirror with a smile.

My hair was still as vividly red and full as it had ever been. There were lines at the corners of my eyes, and lasting evidence of my smile around my mouth. But I could honestly say I'd never felt more beautiful or more content with who I was.

Dax was talking to Cabe and Jeffrey when I came back into the room, and he held his arm out as soon as he saw me, curling it around me as I joined them, squeezing me to him and planting a kiss on the top of my head.

I listened to the three of them talk sports for a bit, and then I crossed the room to find my daughter.

"Hello, there. How's married life so far?" I asked as Galen reached up to fumble with her veil.

"It's wonderful, Mom. I can't thank you enough for this amazing wedding. It's everything I dreamed it would be."

"That was the goal."

"Could we take my veil off now? It keeps getting snagged when people hug me and it's pulling at my hair."

"Sure, turn around."

I dug through her thick, red locks, the same color as my own, and found each of the bobby pins holding the tulle in place. When I'd freed it, she gave her head a shake and touched her fingers to her hair.

"Does it look okay?"

"It looks beautiful," I said, smoothing back a few pieces that had been pulled when I removed the pins. "You look beautiful, baby. I love you so."

"I love you, too, Mom." She hugged me and though I'd thought my heart couldn't contain any more happiness in one evening, it swelled to hold more.

It had all turned out okay. My children were happy. Their lives were good. My parents were laughing, and they beamed with joy and pride. Dax fit in seamlessly with my family, his eyes often on me when I scanned the room to find him.

I folded Galen's veil carefully and climbed the stairs to the bridal suite to leave it with her things.

I stood in the center of the room and considered once again that this was to have been Deanna and Dax's sanctuary from the world. I walked to the spacious master closet and flipped on the light, venturing inside to run my hands along the shelves. Her shelves. This woman I never knew whose tragic fate had given me so much.

"I'm sorry," I whispered to her as I stared up at the beautiful crystal chandelier in the center of the closet's ceiling. "I'm so sorry that happened to you. I'm so sorry for all you lost and all you never got to experience." My eyes filled with tears, and I closed them, wrapping my arms around myself as I tried to send love and kindness to her.

"I'll treat him well. I promise. I'll love him and be good to him. I'll try and make up for everything he's been through. I'll honor your memory with my love."

I heard a movement, and my eyes popped open, startled to think that I wasn't alone.

"Maggie?" Tyler's voice called out from the stairs. "You up here? They're getting ready to do the bubble exit."

"I'm coming," I said, brushing a tear from my cheek. I flipped the light off and said a silent goodbye as I rushed to meet Tyler on the stairs. "You've done such an incredible job, Tyler. Everything has been perfect. I can't thank you enough."

We embraced, and she snickered. "Not exactly perfect, but close enough."

"What went wrong?"

She shook her head. "I never divulge that information to a mother of a bride unless I have to. C'mon, let's go see your daughter off into her happily ever after."

"Ty?"

She paused a couple of steps beneath me and looked back up. "Yeah?"

"I'm so happy you're a part of our family. I love you."

"I love you, too, Maggie."

Dax and Cabe were waiting for us outside, but I paused to hug Galen one more time before we joined the guests lined up on the front walk. Tyler had arranged for the limo to drive away with Galen and Tate for the bubble exit, and then the car would circle back to drop them off after the guests had gone.

It took some time to gather all the gifts and decorations after the party ended, and it was well after midnight by the time my parents left along with Sandy, Hannah, and Alberto. Galen and Tate had retired upstairs, and Tyler and Cabe were the last to leave once the catering truck was gone.

"Well, it's over," Dax said as we stood on the front porch watching

Tyler and Cabe's taillights departing down the drive.

"It's over," I groaned. "My feet are killing me."

I kicked off the Jimmy Choo sandals and ran my fingers through the straps to pick them up as my toes wiggled in freedom.

"I know the tub in the camper isn't very big, but I could run it for you if you want," Dax said.

I smiled up at him and moved a step closer, standing on my toes to press my chest against his as I wrapped my arms around his neck, dangling the sandals behind him.

"Too bad there's not a spring close by with no snakes in it. I could use some of that cold, refreshing water right about now."

His eyes widened and then that mischievous grin that I loved appeared. "Are you serious? You want to go for a swim?"

"Where?" I asked, knowing there was no way he was planning an all-night trek to get to the spring.

"C'mon." He took my hand and led me toward the barn. "Do you have any pants with you?"

"No. Why? Where are we going?"

"It's okay. You can ride side-saddle in your dress sitting in front of me."

"Dexter Pearson, where are we going?"

"Trust me."

I smiled as I stood and watched him put a saddle on Dallas. "You know I do, but I'd love some idea of where we're going."

"My lady said she wanted to go swimming."

He got on the horse and reached down to pull me up, settling me sideways on the saddle in front of him.

The moon was full and bright above us as he headed across the fields, and I rather enjoyed the intimate closeness of sharing a saddle with him.

I'd never gone in the direction he took us, and after he'd gotten off to open and close at least three gates, I saw a fenced-in area ahead of us with two diving boards clearly visible in the moonlight.

"A pool?" I asked. "An actual swimming pool? With diving boards?"

He laughed as he dismounted and reached up to grab me by the waist and pull me down to him.

"Yeah. It's part of the recreation area for the families of the ranch hands. But no one would come out here this late."

"Are you sure?" I asked, looking around me at the playground equipment and a large area of dirt marked off with bases.

"I'm positive. There's no teens in the families right now, and I feel safe saying none of the parents are going to be out here after midnight taking a swim."

I kept searching the surrounding area for any sign of movement as we undressed, but the night was still, and with the humidity hanging thick in the air, not even the wind was moving.

Dax shone a flashlight on the pool and checked the skimmer basket to dispel my serpentine fears, and then he jumped in with a loud splash.

He came up right away, swinging his wet hair out of his face and looking up at me with a grin that made my insides melt.

"It feels great. What are you waiting for?"

I held my nose and jumped feet first, spreading my limbs as I sank into the cool water, allowing it to wash the sweat of the day from my skin.

Dax swam to me, and I wrapped my arms and legs around him as he carried me to the slope in the pool and stood just deep enough for the water to cover his shoulders, his hands beneath my rump though the water's buoyancy held most of my weight.

"Who knew turning fifty would bring out the exhibitionist in me? This is the second time I've been nude out in the open since I hit the big five-o."

"Well, damn. I hate to think what I'm going to be guilty of when I hit fifty. Especially with such a hot cougar being a bad influence on me."

"Cougar?" I splashed his face with water, and he pulled me under, rolling our bodies together in a twist of entangled limbs.

We came back up with mouths and tongues together, his arousal rising against me beneath the water's surface.

"Are you going to pull those pistols or whistle Dixie?" I whispered.

He leaned back and looked at me in confusion. "Is that a movie quote?"

"*The Outlaw Josey Wales.* C'mon. You have to have seen that. It's a Western. You're a cowboy. It's one of my dad's favorite all-time films, and he's not even a cowboy."

"I may have seen it when I was a kid."

"This can't be. We have to watch this movie."

He moved a bit deeper in the water, and adjusted his hands beneath me. "Right now?"

"No. But soon. Right now, I have other plans for you, cowboy."

"Oh, really?" he asked as I took his face in my hands and kissed him. "What plans?" he mumbled as I flicked my tongue across his lips and inside his mouth.

"I've never made love in a pool," I whispered between kisses. "I've decided it's the next write-in item on my bucket list."

By the time we headed back to the camper, skin damp beneath our clothes and hair dripping, I'd crossed the new item off the list and was already thinking of others I could add.

"What about horseback?" I said. "I'd have to be facing you, of course."

Dax laughed. "You're quite the insatiable minx."

"Are you complaining?"

"Hell, no. Just doing my best to keep up."

I stared at the moon above us, and then looked out across the land as

Dax's arm tightened around my waist.

"Dax, if anyone had told me a year ago I'd be riding on horseback in the middle of the night after skinny dipping and pool sex, I would have said they were nuts."

"And now?" Dax asked, nuzzling his face into my neck as I wrapped my arms around his shoulders.

"My life has changed. Now, I would rather share one lifetime with you than face all the ages of this world alone."

"Now, that one I know. Arwen said that to Aragorn in *The Lord of the Rings.*"

"Theirs is one of my favorite love stories," I whispered, laying my head on his shoulder.

"Ours is mine."

# EPILOGUE

I gazed out at the audience, finding Sandy and Hannah immediately among those standing and applauding, and then making eye contact with my parents and my children as Dax raised my hand for us to take another bow.

"Great job, lovebirds!" Betty said as we exited the stage, and Dax picked me up in his arms and spun me.

"Oh my God! I can't believe we did that. That was incredible. I want to do it again!" he said.

I laughed at his enthusiasm and tossed my head back as he spun me again.

My family and friends crowded around us when we came out of the community center after the show, all of them talking over each other to congratulate us.

"Great job."

"You two were amazing."

"Mom, you were beautiful."

"It was splendid, dear," my mother said. "The two of you move together in such unison. It's pure joy to watch."

"She makes it easy, that's for sure," Dax said, pulling my hand to his lips and kissing it.

Sandy's smile beamed as she threw her arms around me. "I can't believe how happy you looked. I've never, seriously, *never* seen you that happy when you dance."

"I may have to sign us up to take your class," Tyler said, casting a hopeful glance toward Cabe. "What do you say, honey? You want your mom and Dax to teach us a few moves?"

"Sure. I'm up for it." Cabe kissed my cheek and handed me a bouquet of flowers.

"How are the classes going?" my mom asked.

"Great. We've had good attendance so far. Dax even got a few couples from the ranch to come out, but I think that's mostly because they wanted to see the boss man dance."

Everyone laughed as Dax shrugged.

"What can I say? I'll take any opportunity to dance with this lovely lady."

"Are you still only teaching once a week?" Sandy asked.

"Yeah. Betty and I talked about adding another class, somewhere more on this side of town by my house, but it's easier for Dax if we stick with the one we started closer to the ranch. I think one's enough for now. I have my riding lessons on Saturday mornings, and we're getting ready to move into the holiday season at work."

"Well, now that we're settled in Orlando and Hannah's job has calmed down, I'm seriously thinking we're going to sign up if you start a class near us," Sandy said as Hannah nodded. "I haven't danced in years, but that looked like too much fun to miss out on. You think you could teach me a thing or two?"

"I'll try," I said. "If I could learn it, you know you can!"

We all went to our separate cars and met at the restaurant for dinner, and then Tyler and Cabe went home along with Hannah and Sandy while my parents returned to my pool house for the night.

"Thank you for tonight," Dax said as we sat alone on my patio, my feet in his lap as he massaged my aching soles. "It really meant a lot to me, and I had a blast."

"Me, too. I'm sorry I was such a jerk about it at first. It was great, and I'm kind of sad it's done."

"There's always next year."

"Yes, that's true. And we'll have students of our own to invite next time."

"I love seeing you happy, Maggie Mae."

"I love being happy. I love that we're happy together."

He slid closer to me on the sofa and leaned in for a kiss.

"You have bewitched me body and soul, and I love, I love, I love you," he said, looking into my eyes.

I smiled and hoped I could remember the rest of the *Pride and Prejudice* quote. "And wish from this day forth never to be parted from you."

"I am yours, Maggie Mae, now and forevermore. That's not a quote. That's just my heart talking."

His lips brushed mine, and I decided that love is the best dance of all.

# Want to read more about Tyler & Cabe?

Go back to the beginning of their love story and follow Tyler's funny and poignant diary entries as she encounters crazy bridezillas and outlandish blind dates in her journey to find her own modern-day Prince Charming. Along the way, Tyler discovers that real-life love is often more complicated than the fairy tales she grew up believing. A lot happens between Once Upon a Time and Happily Ever After.

Check out the Tales Behind the Veils series on www.violethowe.com.

## Love Romantic Suspense?

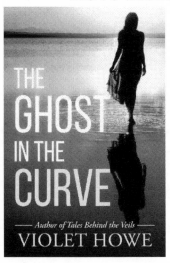

This lighthearted romantic suspense has a charming paranormal twist! Sloane Reid never believed in ghosts before she met Chelsea. Now she's trying to solve the mystery the young girl has struggled with since her death. But Sloane can't solve it alone, and before local deputy Tristan Rogers will help her, she'll have to convince him she's not crazy. Or a criminal. As they work together to unlock the secrets of the past, Sloane soon discovers it may be her own life that needs saving.

To purchase, visit www.books2read.com/GhostintheCurve or www.violethowe.com.

# ABOUT THE AUTHOR

Violet Howe enjoys writing romance and mystery with humor. She lives in Florida with her husband—her knight in shining armor—and their two handsome sons. They share their home with three adorable but spoiled dogs. When she's not writing, Violet is usually watching movies, reading, or planning her next travel adventure. You can follow Violet's ramblings on her blog,
The Goddess Howe.

www.violethowe.com
Facebook.com/VioletHoweAuthor
@Violet_Howe
Instagram.com/VioletHowe

## Newsletter

Sign up at www.violethowe.com to receive Violet's monthly newsletter with updates on new releases, appearances, prize drawings, and info on joining Violet's Facebook Reader Group, the Ultra Violets.

# THANK YOU

Thank you for taking the time to read this book.
I sincerely hope you enjoyed it! If you did, then please tell somebody! Tell
your friends. Tell your family. Tell a co-worker. Tell the person next to you
in line at the grocery store.

One of the best compliments you can give an author is to leave a review on
Amazon, Goodreads, or any other social media site you frequent.

Made in the USA
Middletown, DE
20 February 2020